"YOUR FATHER'S PROBABLY RIGHT, SAMANTHA,"

Blake said, removing his wool jacket. "You'd be a lot safer back East. I love you enough to know what's best for you."

"No! You don't want me to go. I know you don't."

"Of course I don't." He turned to face her. "But I also don't want anything to happen to you."

"It won't as long as I'm with you." She knew deep inside there was only one way to keep him here. Once she belonged to him . . .

Samantha had no idea how the thought had come to her so suddenly, or where she got her courage. Perhaps it was love that did this. A tear slipped down her face as she untied and removed her fur cape. She threw it into a chair, then unpinned her hat and took two combs from her hair. "I might have to go away, Blake." She began unbuttoning the front of her dress. "But whether I stay or I go, we might never get another chance," she told him boldly. "This might be the worst sin I ever commit, but I love you . . . and if something happens to you, I want you to have been my first man. I want you to stay here . . . with me."

DISCOVER DEANA JAMES!

CAPTIVE ANGEL (2524, $4.50/$5.50)
Abandoned, penniless, and suddenly responsible for the biggest tobacco plantation in Colleton County, distraught Caroline Gillard had no time to dissolve into tears. By day the willowy red-head labored to exhaustion beside her slaves . . . but each night left her restless with longing for her wayward husband. She'd make the sea captain regret his betrayal until he begged her to take him back!

MASQUE OF SAPPHIRE (2885, $4.50/$5.50)
Judith Talbot-Harrow left England with a heavy heart. She was going to America to join a father she despised and a sister she distrusted. She was certainly in no mood to put up with the insulting actions of the arrogant Yankee privateer who boarded her ship, ransacked her things, then "apologized" with an indecent, brazen kiss! She vowed that someday he'd pay dearly for the liberties he had taken and the desires he had awakened.

SPEAK ONLY LOVE (3439, $4.95/$5.95)
Long ago, the shock of her mother's death had robbed Vivian Marleigh of the power of speech. Now she was being forced to marry a bitter man with brandy on his breath. But she could not say what was in her heart. It was up to the viscount to spark the fires that would melt her icy reserve.

WILD TEXAS HEART (3205, $4.95/$5.95)
Fan Breckenridge was terrified when the stranger found her near-naked and shivering beneath the Texas stars. Unable to remember who she was or what had happened, all she had in the world was the deed to a patch of land that might yield oil . . . and the fierce loving of this wildcatter who called himself Irons.

Available wherever paperbacks are sold, or order direct from the Publisher. Send cover price plus 50¢ per copy for mailing and handling to Zebra Books, Dept. 3791, 475 Park Avenue South, New York, N.Y. 10016. Residents of New York and Tennessee must include sales tax. DO NOT SEND CASH. For a free Zebra/Pinnacle catalog please write to the above address.

ROSANNE BITTNER

CARESS

ZEBRA BOOKS
KENSINGTON PUBLISHING CORP.

ZEBRA BOOKS

are published by

Kensington Publishing Corp.
475 Park Avenue South
New York, NY 10016

Copyright © 1992 by Rosanne Bittner

First printing: July, 1992

Printed in the United States of America

INTRODUCTION

CARESS is set in the turbulent times before the Civil War, when people began to turn on each other over the issues of slavery, a time when no one could be trusted. Border wars and illegal elections caused so much fighting in Kansas that it earned the dubious nickname of "Bleeding Kansas."

The characters in this novel and their personal stories are entirely fictitious. Any resemblance to persons who actually lived during the years of this novel, and in its setting, is purely coincidental; although I am sure my story comes painfully close to the stories of real people who experienced this historic era.

Rosanne Bittner

Whenever I hear anyone arguing for slavery, I feel a strong impulse to see it tried on him personally.

—Abraham Lincoln

One

1854

Samantha Walters set her pamphlets on a bench so that she could retie her cape. She shivered against the cold, damp weather. October had brought rain nearly every day, and her shoes and the hem of her dress were splattered with mud. Still, she thought, at least she didn't have to dread the coming winter. Kansas winters were much milder than in Vermont, where she had lived most of her eighteen years. Last winter, her first in Kansas, had not brought anywhere near the snow to which she and her family had become accustomed in New England.

She took a deep breath, studying the passing shoppers and businessmen in the street, thinking with some anger how Lawrence's population had suddenly burgeoned, now that the citizens of Kansas Territory could vote on whether or not they wanted slavery. The sudden growth in Kansas's population could be directly attributed to people filtering in from Missouri, claiming Kansas citizenship so that they could stuff the ballot boxes with proslavery votes. Her dedication to helping her father, the Reverend

Howard Walters, convince people to vote for a free territory, was becoming more challenging every day. Her strength and determination came from firmly believing that slavery was wrong in every respect.

She heard a thump behind her then, and some of her pamphlets went flying across the wet, muddy boardwalk. Samantha turned to see a group of young men close to her age standing behind her, grinning. "Sorry about that, honey," one of them spoke up. "You want some help picking them up?"

"No, thank you, Fred Brewster," she fumed, her face flushing with anger. She glared at the town bully, a tall, well-built young man who might be handsome if not for a face pitted from smallpox at a young age, made worse by a bad case of acne. Brewster had taken to following her around deliberately trying to aggravate her when she was shopping or passing out antislavery pamphlets for her father.

Samantha stooped to pick up the pamphlets Fred had knocked askew. Several of them were ruined, and Brewster and his friends laughed.

"Suit yourself," Fred teased, his dark eyes drinking in the pretty shape of the preacher's daughter. "I offered to help." He studied Samantha's dark, wavy hair, which had a hint of red to it in the sunlight. He had often imagined getting the pristine but fiery Samantha Walters off alone somewhere and teaching her about men, with or without her consent.

"Don't you know it's dangerous for a young girl to be handing out abolitionist propoganda in these times," one of the others spoke up. "A girl could get in all kinds of trouble."

Samantha gathered the pamphlets and rose, facing all of them squarely. "I'm not the one making the trouble," she answered, meeting Fred's eyes then. "At

10

least I'm making good use of my time, doing something *constructive*. I'm not walking the streets like a bum, with no purpose to my life. If you ever decide to do something with *your* life, Fred Brewster, and become a useful citizen, my father will be happy to welcome you into his church and help you find a job." She took a pamphlet and shoved it into his hand. "This explains all about the Kansas-Nebraska Act and also tells about some of the horrors of slavery and why it's so wrong and un-Christian. You're old enough to vote, so do something right for once and vote against *slavery!*"

Fred's eyes narrowed. He tore up the pamphlet and threw the pieces at her face. "I don't want your damn pamphlet, bitch! I can't even *read!* And what makes you think I'd vote *against* slavery?" He looked at his snickering friends. "We're not nigger lovers like you and your Bible-preaching pa! You better be careful, Miss Walters. Pretty white girls who go around speaking up for those Negro men sometimes get a bad reputation, if you know what I mean."

Samantha's fury knew no bounds. Her mother had scolded her more times than she could count for being unable to control her temper, but she knew she was losing it again. Hurt and anger culminated in a swift, hard kick to Fred's shinbone. He cried out, reaching down and grabbing his leg. As Samantha shoved her way past him and his friends, Fred cursed at her while onlookers laughed.

Samantha hurriedly walked across the street. She knew she would have to ask forgiveness for her physical attack on Fred Brewster, but part of her was convinced God wouldn't really mind. She was relieved Fred did not follow her and taunt her more, and she breathed a little easier when she noticed a family from her father's church. She smiled and

11

approached them, handing them one of the pamphlets.

"Be sure to vote next spring," she told them in greeting. "We've got to keep Kansas a free territory, Mrs. Mills."

The woman and her husband each took a pamphlet. "Isn't it a little early to be doing this?" Jack Mills asked. "Quite a while before we vote."

"Yes, it is. But Father says it's none too soon to start spreading the word and making sure everyone votes, Mr. Mills. We have to be strong on this, or the people sneaking into Kansas from Missouri will outvote us and we'll be a slave territory. We just can't let that happen. Father is hoping these pamphlets will make people understand the new act and will help us rally more supporters by explaining some of the terrible acts slave-owners commit against the poor Negroes. We've got to make sure people understand how wrong slavery is."

The farmer frowned, the lines in his aging face growing deeper. "Miss Walters, you and your folks, you're still fairly new to this part of the country. Now, we're against slavery, too, but I don't think you understand how deep the hatred goes around here. You've got to be more careful. Haven't you heard about all the raids along the Kansas-Missouri border? Jayhawkers are fighting bushwhackers and . . . well, your pa shouldn't let you walk the streets alone passing these things out. I know Lawrence is pretty much the center for Free Staters, but more and more proslavery men have been filtering in. Why, the town is full of spies, ma'am. A person doesn't know *who* to trust."

"I trust in the Lord, Mr. Mills. That's all I need to know. I'm doing His work, and He'll watch over me."

12

Mills grinned slightly. "He the one who told you to kick Fred Brewster?" he asked.

Samantha reddened as the man laughed lightly. "Don't tell my folks, will you?" she asked in return.

Mills shook his head. "I won't tell. Besides, that troublemaker deserved it. I was only watching because I saw him knock your pamphlets off the bench and I was worried you'd find trouble. I guess maybe you *aren't* in so much danger after all."

Samantha smiled. "Thank you for keeping an eye out for me. Be sure to tell all your friends, and even strangers, about their right to vote. I'll give you a few more pamphlets so you can give them to others."

Mills nodded, taking the extra pamphlets and leaving with his family. Samantha turned and rounded a corner, heading down another street and praying that her courage would hold. Her parents had forbidden her to include this street in her campaign, since it was dotted with several saloons. This was an area seldom frequented by respectable women; and since most of the infiltrating bush-whackers from Missouri were men, Samantha's father was convinced most of the "spies" could be hanging around this part of town.

Still, she reasoned, raising her chin boldly, these were the kind of people who needed to be converted to the antislavery position, not families like the Millses. If she was truly going to do any good in this issue, she had to approach the hard-hearted and make them see the light. Maybe if a few of them read her pamphlets and truly understood how wrong slavery was, they would change their minds.

She pressed on, pretending to have no fear as she smiled and handed out pamphlets to men who cast her glances that held a mixture of distrust and humor. Some sneered, some just nodded respectfully

13

and took a pamphlet. Most just stuffed them in their pockets, but some actually tossed them aside. One man pressed his pamphlet into the mud with a heavy boot and looked her over as though she were a piece of chocolate cake and he was hungry. One man offered a rude remark about what she was "selling," but Samantha refused to be swayed.

Piano music and loud voices poured from the saloons. She started to hand a pamphlet to another man, then gasped when he suddenly grabbed hold of her wrist. He was a big man, perhaps in his forties, a man who was not ugly but had no outstanding features other than his size. He wore a well-tailored suit and sported a graying mustache that matched the gray at his temples, and his dark eyes drilled into her with deliberate threat.

"You'd be best to get off this street, little lady. Preaching belongs in the church. If we want to hear or read about the terrible sin of slavery, we'll come to *church* to hear it!" He gave her a light shove.

Instinct told Samantha this man was a more serious threat than Fred Brewster. Kicking him would not be a wise choice. Besides, she was in enemy territory now. She backed away, the man's sudden grasp leaving her so startled that she did not think to look before turning and stepping off the boardwalk.

"Watch it!" someone shouted from the seat of a supply wagon just then clattering by. The front wheel splashed through a huge puddle as did the rear wheel, before Samantha could get out of the way. Mud splattered her from her face to the hem of her dress, and the man who had just threatened her burst into loud laughter, joined by several of his friends who stood nearby.

The wagon came to a halt as its driver yanked on the reins to stop the four mules that pulled it. The driver jumped down. "You all right, ma'am?"

"*No!*" Samantha shouted in reply, her temper exploding again. "*Look* at me!" She realized it was an accident, but having it happen in front of the man who had just threatened her made it more humiliating. She vented her frustration on the driver of the wagon, needing an outlet for her anger at the man who had grabbed her and who still stood on the boardwalk laughing at her.

"What kind of a gentleman are you?" she shouted at the wagon driver, "Nearly running down a woman!" She did not notice that a Negro man sat in the wagon seat.

The driver bent over to pick up her ruined pamphlets. "Ma'am, I'm sorry," he was saying, "but you *did* almost walk right into my wagon. I couldn't help what happened."

Samantha looked up into the face of a broad-shouldered, handsome man who had probably not yet seen thirty. Her embarrassment and frustration began to overwhelm her so that her eyes filled with tears. She took the pamphlets from him. "Oh, they're ruined now! Father will be furious," she fumed.

The driver pushed back his hat slightly. "Is there anything I can do, ma'am? Anyplace I can take you so you can get out of those muddy clothes?"

"Yes, Hastings," the man in front of the saloon answered for her. "Take her and her whole damn family back to New England and tell them to leave Kansas alone. Now she knows what Kansas thinks of abolitionists. I imagine there's some horse shit mixed in with the mud. That should tell her something."

Samantha felt the driver of the wagon moving slightly away from her as she shook her dress to get some of the mud off it. She turned to answer the driver, only to realize he seemed to be facing off the man on the boardwalk.

"Well, if it isn't Nick West," he was saying. "What the hell are you doing in Lawrence, West?"

The man who had grabbed Samantha's wrist straightened, stepping away from the saloon door and closer to the wagon driver. "I could ask you the same thing, Hastings. I figured once your daddy died that you ran off to parts unknown with your tail between your legs."

Samantha realized the two men knew each other. More than that, the look in their eyes told her they were bitter enemies. She knew now that the driver's last name was Hastings, and as she gathered her thoughts, she realized, too that she had no right being angry with him. She stepped back a little, already angry with herself for coming here in the first place. If there was going to be trouble, she had started the whole thing. She glanced up at the wagon, just then noticing the young Negro man, and her heart pounded harder. She prayed everyone would calm down, but the man called Nick West took a threatening pose in front of Hastings.

"I didn't run anywhere," Hastings was telling West. "I've been biding my time—looking for you."

The one called Nick West glanced at the Negro man on the wagon seat as his friends from the saloon gathered closer. "Here in Lawrence?"

"I'm as surprised to see you as you are to see me," Hastings answered. "I'm here on business. I work for Hale Freighting now."

"That a fact?" West puffed on a thin cigar, then tossed it out into the muddy street. "Kind of dangerous, working for that abolitionist, isn't it?"

"The way I look at it," Hastings answered the

16

man, "in Lawrence, it's more dangerous to be a proslaver."

West's eyebrows arched. "Not if we get enough people into Kansas to back us up."

"I suppose you're one of those *new* citizens from Missouri who's all of a sudden interested in settling in Kansas."

"A man's got a right to settle wherever he wants," West replied.

"Not when he's just fixing to stuff a ballot box with his vote and then leave."

West shoved his thumbs into his vest pockets. "It's no different from abolitionists bringing in people from northern states."

"The friends we convince to move here from New England intend to settle for good," Samantha spoke up, her anger rising again. "They're honest, hard-working people who want to see Kansas grow, and they want to see this territory free of slavery. They haven't just snuck across the border to get in a vote with the intention of leaving again."

West's eyes moved to Samantha, but Hastings did not take his eyes off West. "You've got a cocky mouth for such a small piece of woman," West told her. "We've got a name for nigger-loving white girls, honey, and it's not pretty."

"Shut your mouth, West," Hastings told the man. "I think you owe the lady an apology."

West moved his eyes back to Hastings. "I owe her nothing."

Samantha watched Hastings's hands move into fists, and she stepped farther back. "You owe *plenty* of people, West," he growled. "And if we're going to bring up labels, how about the one that fits you? *Murderer!*"

17

West seemed to pale slightly. "That's a pretty strong word to toss around in front of all these people," he answered.

"And I wouldn't speak it if I didn't think it was true!"

"What happened to your pa was done by border raiders, Hastings. I had nothing to do with it. It's about time you understood that for once and for all."

"You had *everything* to do with it! I don't need physical proof. I know it—in my *gut!*"

West snickered. "Why don't you take your nigger and that little slut out of here before—"

He was unable to finish. Hastings landed into him, slamming him with a mighty force against the outside wall of the saloon. "My friend's name is George!" he growled. "And that young lady looks too proper to be around filth like you!"

Samantha watched in shock as a vicious fight ensued, Nick West's friends gathering around to cheer the man on. Samantha winced at each sickening blow. Faces bloody, both men fell together and rolled off the boardwalk and into the cold mud, half boxing and half wrestling, their muddy clothes becoming heavy and slowing their movements.

Samantha's eyes teared, and she was filled with guilt. The man called Hastings seemed adept at fighting, and he landed several hard punches to West's middle and jaw, obviously gaining the upper hand until two of West's friends grabbed Hastings from behind and pulled him off their friend. Two more joined in keeping a firm hold on a snarling, struggling Hastings then, as West got to his feet, wiping at a bloody face with the sleeve of his suit.

"You've got to learn not to go accusing an innocent man in front of a whole town," West sputtered. He walked up to Hastings, and Samantha groaned with pity as West landed two vicious blows to Hastings's middle while he stood helplessly pinned by the other four men.

Samantha moved toward them, unsure what she could do to help but feeling obligated to do something. Another man moved in front of her then, blocking her way. "Ain't your affair, missy," the man told her with a sneer. He grasped her shoulder and gave her a shove.

"Leave the lady alone," the Negro man called George shouted down from the wagon.

The man turned to look at him, while West landed three more punches into Hastings, then told the others to let go of him. They threw him facedown into the mud.

"What did you say, nigger?" The man near Samantha spoke up, walking threateningly toward George.

Samantha watched in terror, realizing the kind of danger poor George was in for speaking up in her behalf.

"I said to leave her alone," George answered defiantly. "You're quite a bunch. Real brave, aren't you? Takes a lot of guts to fight a man five to one and shove around one small woman."

"George, stay . . . out of it," Hastings panted, getting to his knees. Blood poured from his mouth and nose, as he grasped at his belly.

West and his men, and those who had gathered to watch the fight, suddenly quieted. Samantha could feel the tension in the air as Free Staters and proslavery men began to gather. The fight that had begun between Hastings and West appeared to be about ready to break into something much bigger.

"Your master there just gave you some good advice, nigger," the man near Samantha told George.

"He's not my master. Blake is my friend." George rose in his seat, and a few people quietly gasped at his size. Samantha guessed he stood a good six and a half feet tall, with broad shoulders and a powerful build. "Gang up on him again, and he won't be fighting alone," he told the others.

"Why don't you get down off that wagon, nigger, and we'll teach you a good lesson about smart-mouthed blackies," the white man beckoned.

Samantha felt desperate. In spite of his size, she knew what would happen to George if he climbed down, and he looked ready to answer the challenge. She lunged past the white man toward the front of the wagon. "Stop this," she called to all of them. "Stop it now! The fight was between Mr. West and Mr. Hastings! Now it's over!"

Hastings got to his feet. "Stay out of the way, ma'am," he gasped, his breath still short from the blows to his middle.

"No nigger talks to me like that," the white man bellowed. He headed toward Samantha. "Get out of the way, slut!"

Giving little thought to what she was doing, Samantha grabbed a whip from the side of the wagon and lashed out with it. She had no idea how to use one, and pure luck alone brought its stinging tip across the side of the man's face. Everyone, including Blake Hastings, stared at her in surprise; Samantha, afraid and desperate, knew it was a bold move, but at the moment she didn't care whether it was right or wrong.

"Why, you little bitch," the man uttered, putting a hand to his bleeding cheek. "I'll teach you and the nigger both!" He headed toward her again, and again Samantha lashed out with the whip. The man caught it in his hand and yanked, causing her to fall facedown into the mud. Before the man could get to her, Hastings landed into him, and another fight was on. This time twenty to thirty men joined in, Free Staters against proslavery men. A few painted women who had been looking on backed away, screaming and running inside buildings.

Samantha struggled to her feet, her dress and cape soaked with brown water. "Get in the wagon," someone shouted. "Get in!" A hand grabbed at her and she looked up at George. She grasped his hand and he hoisted her up as though she weighed nothing. "Get down," he told her, pushing her over the seat and into the wagon bed. "Blake, come on!" he shouted as Samantha landed amid an array of flour sacks and hay bales. She peeked over the side of the big wagon to see Hastings land several hard blows into the man who had threatened her and George. Their attacker finally landed in a watering trough, out cold.

Hastings turned as George snapped the reins and urged the mules into motion. He ran to grab the side of the wagon, jumping on as the Negro headed the wagon away from the melée that continued. Samantha watched out the back of the wagon as the whole street seemed to break into battle. The local sheriff was heading in that direction, and Samantha's heart filled with mixed emotions. She was sorry any of it had started at all, and though she felt a little guilty, she also harbored a secret satisfaction at having stood up to the man who had threatened her and George.

Hastings flung a leg over the side of the wagon and landed hard beside her then, panting, bleeding, his clothes and sheepskin jacket caked with mud. "Oh, Mr. Hastings," Samantha fretted, leaning over him. "I'm so sorry! This is all my fault!"

"Not at all," he answered, managing to sit up. "It's really mine. I'm the one who lit into West."

The wagon bounced hard, and Samantha landed against him. As he grasped her arms and held on to her, their eyes met. Blake was startled by how blue her eyes were, and he felt an instant liking for this young woman who had so bravely stood up for his friend. "What were you doing walking around alone in that area?" he asked her.

Samantha held her chin proudly. "I was handing out anti-slavery pamphlets."

The wagon lurched and leaned as George hurriedly turned a corner. Hastings had to hang on to Samantha to keep her from being tossed around in the bed. "Take it easy, George!" he shouted. "We ought to be out of danger now."

The wagon slowed as George guided the horses into the courtyard of a school, then finally stopped. "How you doing, Blake?" he asked.

Blake touched a still-bleeding lip. "I've been better." His eyes moved to Samantha again, sweeping over her in a way that made her blush, although the color was hardly noticeable under all the mud. He broke into a handsome grin, then winced with the pain of it. "Aren't we a pretty-looking pair? We look like a couple of sewer rats."

Samantha smiled shyly, suddenly embarrassed. "I just realized how I must look." She sobered. "I'm so sorry, Mr. Hastings. I shouldn't have yelled at you and caused all that commotion. I was just angry with Mr. West. He grabbed me and threatened me."

A look of renewed anger and hatred filled Blake's dark eyes. "Yeah. The man is good at that."

"You apparently know him then."

Blake wiped at more blood. "Very well. I never

thought I'd see him here in Lawrence. It's obvious why he's here."

"You don't seem too fond of him."

"I hate his guts. He's a murderer." He rubbed at his ribs. "I'm sorry for the hard words, ma'am." He met her eyes again. "Hell, I don't even know your name."

She ignored the cuss word, realizing he was in pain at the moment, and a very angry man. "Samantha Walters. Most just call me Sam."

He nodded. "Well, I'm Blake Hastings." He looked up at George. "That man up there is my best friend—George Freedom. How's that for a last name? He gave it to himself after my father signed papers making him a free man."

Samantha looked at George. "I'm glad to meet you. Thank you for sticking up for me back there. It was a very dangerous thing for you to do."

George grinned. "I'm used to trouble, ma'am. And I can take care of myself."

Blake laughed lightly. "George can clean the clock of ten men at once."

"You do pretty good yourself," George answered.

Blake snickered, leaning his head back against a flour sack. "Yes, well, I got my dues today."

Samantha watched him with pity. "You must be in a lot of pain. Please come to my house, Mr. Hastings. My mother will help clean you up and fix your wounds."

"Not necessary—we'll take you home where you'll be safe. Tell George where to go; and please, call me Blake."

Samantha turned her attention again to George and gave him directions. When she glanced back at Blake, she realized he looked as if he might pass out. She quickly moved to grasp his shoulders and let him lie back into her lap. She stroked his forehead, feeling a terrible guilt mixed with a strange new emotion she had never felt before, a strong attraction to this man who had dived into a life-threatening fight in her defense. He roused slightly, opening his eyes to look up at her, and she grasped his hand.

"You'll be all right," she assured him. "My mother will help you."

"I'd rather have you do it," he told her, his words slightly slurred. "Something tells me under all that mud there lurks . . . a very pretty woman." His eyes closed again and he thought with a strange relief that this Samantha Walters must not be married if she still lived with her parents. Besides, what husband would let such a pretty young thing walk the streets alone? He suspected her own parents had no idea she was traipsing through such dangerous territory.

"Please don't pass out on me, Mr. Hastings. We'll be at my house any minute now. You'll be all right."

He rolled over and coughed, wiping blood from his mouth again on his jacket sleeve. "Some day I'll get that son of a bitch," he mumbled. "He'll die the way all murderers ought to die." He leaned back into her lap.

"Did he really kill your father?"

Blake caught her eyes and held them for a long, silent moment as the wagon pulled into the driveway of the Walters parsonage. "Yes," he answered, "but I can't prove it. It's just something I know." He closed his eyes again, putting a hand to his jaw. "It's a long story . . . not worth telling to someone I hardly know, especially not to a delicate, innocent little lady like you."

"Delicate! Do I *look* delicate?"

He opened his eyes and stared at her muddy face and clothes, remembering how she had wielded the whip. He managed a grin. "No, you sure as hell don't. Remind me never to go up against you. I think I'd rather face West and his men again."

Samantha studied his gentle brown eyes, feeling strangely moved, but the spell was quickly broken when she heard her mother's voice from the front porch. "Yes?" the woman called out to George. "Can I help you?"

"Got your daughter in the back of the wagon, ma'am. A friend of mine, too. He's been hurt. Hope you can help him."

"What! What has happened to Sam?" the woman exclaimed, heading for the wagon.

"I'm in trouble now," Samantha said, rolling her eyes.

Blake squeezed her hand gently. "I'll do what I can to take most of the blame."

Samantha's apprehension at facing her mother suddenly left her. The woman came to the back of the wagon, sputtering and gasping as she helped her filthy, wet daughter out of the wagon. George came around to help Blake. "We haven't even found a place to stay the night yet," he told Sam's mother, "so our things are still in the wagon. I'll get some clean clothes out for Blake once we get him into the house."

George explained what had happened, and Mrs. Walters went into a fit of scolding when she heard where Samantha had gone, carrying on that she knew better. She looked ready to faint when George told about the incident with the whip. "You actually used violence!" the woman exclaimed.

"Mother, I had no choice. The man was coming after me—and George, too. You know what they would have done to George if they had got him down off the wagon."

"You shouldn't have been there in the first place.

Then you wouldn't have nearly got yourself killed, and none of this would have happened! You have got to learn to control your daring impulses, Samantha Walters, as well as your temper. Now get upstairs and clean yourself up. I'll see what I can do for Mr. Hastings."

"It was mostly my fault," Blake added in Samantha's defense. "I'm the one who started the fight, ma'am."

"Well, I know my daughter. She has a way of getting herself into this kind of trouble."

Blake watched Samantha as she headed for the stairs. She looked back at him and noticed a sly grin on his face. She suddenly didn't care how angry her mother might be. All that mattered was that Blake Hastings was in her house, that he was not angry with her.

She hurried upstairs to her room to change clothes and wash. She couldn't wash her hair properly until she went down to the kitchen to use the hand pump, but she rinsed the front of it as best she could, deciding she would be more thorough after Blake left. She wanted to hurry, afraid he would be gone before she had a chance to see him again.

She liked Blake Hastings. She hardly knew him, but just the fact that he had a Negro for a best friend said something about the man's sentiments. He was brave and daring, and she liked that. She guessed he was probably a good ten years older than she, and he was so much more masculine than any of the young men who had expressed an interest in wooing her.

She pulled on a yellow gingham dress and brushed her damp hair, then pinched her cheeks for color and hurried back downstairs. Her heart fell when she noticed Blake no longer sat in the kitchen chair where she had left him. George was standing nearby.

"He's in your folks' bedroom putting on some clean clothes," he said to her. He turned to Samantha's mother, an uncomfortable look in his eyes. "You sure it's all right for me to be in your house, ma'am?" he asked. "I can wait outside."

"Nonsense. We aren't like the others, George. You defended our daughter knowing it meant danger to your person. Besides, we're here to work for the end of slavery. Up in Vermont we helped many of your people flee to safety in Canada." She looked at Samantha. "I have invited George and Mr. Hastings to supper tonight," she told her. "It's the least we can do for the trouble you caused, young lady. And don't you ever go into that saloon area again!"

"I won't, Mother," Samantha answered quietly, secretly overjoyed that this would not be the last time she saw Blake Hastings, who appeared at the bedroom door then, wearing denim pants and a blue calico shirt, which he was still buttoning.

Both stared in pleased surprise. Now that the mud and blood were washed away, each realized the other was more appealing to the eyes than either had realized at first. Samantha reddened at the realization that Blake seemed to be reading her thoughts.

"Well, now I'll be able to recognize you when I see you again," he told her, coming closer. Samantha guessed him to be nearly six feet tall, since that was the height of her father and this man seemed about the same. But Blake Hastings was much brawnier, with broad shoulders and a square jawline. His face was tanned dark, and his thick, dark hair hung in neatly cut layers about his ears and neck.

"Yes," she answered, feeling suddenly as delicate and small as he had teased she was earlier. She studied the cuts and bruises on his face. In spite of the

27

slight swelling of one lip, his handsomeness could not be hidden. "I want to apologize again for yelling at you that way and walking into the street without looking."

"No apology necessary. Actually, I'm glad to know where Nick West is. Helps me keep track of him and know what he's up to."

"What happened, Blake," she asked, absentmindedly using his first name as though she had always known him, "with you and that Mr. West?"

He sighed, running a hand through his hair. "Like I said, it's a long story, and I'd rather not talk about it now. Maybe this evening when we come back for supper." He looked at her mother. "You sure you want us?" he asked. "It really isn't necessary."

"It most certainly *is* necessary," the woman answered. "I won't take no for an answer. Besides, Samantha's father will be here then and he'll have a lot of questions. It will be easier on Samantha if you're here to help explain." The woman moved her eyes to her daughter in consternation. "Not that my daughter deserves to get out of this lightly."

Blake grinned. "If it will help Samantha, I'll come for supper. And I appreciate your inviting George. I can see where Samantha gets her courage and daring. From what I've seen and heard so far, I have a feeling her whole family is the same way."

Mrs. Walters stood a little straighter, feeling complimented. Samantha felt a secret relief, realizing the remark had instantly put her mother in a better mood. She wondered if Blake Hastings really meant it, or if it was a ploy to help ease her mother's anger with her. He turned to Samantha.

"I'll be seeing you this evening then?" he told her.

She wanted to reach out and touch him. "Yes. I'm glad you're coming."

"So am I," he answered. He turned and picked up his muddy boots, wincing with pain as he did so. "Soon as we find a room, you'd better wrap these ribs, George."

"I'll get the rest of your clothes," George answered, going into the bedroom to pick them up. He carried them outside, and Blake cast one more look at Samantha, nodding before he left. "Bye, Sam." He followed George to the wagon.

"You got an ache for that pretty little spitfire?" George asked, keeping his voice low.

"You're damn right. I'm going to have to find a reason to hang around Lawrence more," Blake answered, throwing his boots into the back of the wagon.

"Nick West wouldn't have anything to do with your staying around, would he?" George said then, climbing up into the wagon and picking up the reins.

Blake grimaced as he climbed into the seat. "He might," he answered. "Let's get these goods delivered and find a room for the night."

"You anxious to get back here and see Miss Walters again?"

Blake grinned. "What do you think?"

George just laughed and kicked off the brake. The wagon lurched and pulled away, and deep inside, George's heart was heavy with a feeling of loss. Blake's attraction to Samantha Walters brought back memories of Jesse March, the young woman George loved. He awakened one day to discover Jesse had been quietly sold to a Missouri farmer, but he was not told the man's name. He had never seen her again.

Two

George and Blake unloaded their supplies at Barnard's General Store, Blake moving with less agility than normal because of his injuries.

"You shouldn't be doing anything at all," George told him, taking a sack of feed from his friend's arms. "You want to be in good shape for that supper tonight, don't you? You about passed out this morning, and you don't want to miss your chance at seeing that pretty little filly again."

Blake grinned, feeling light-headed. "You're probably right," he answered. "But you shouldn't have to do it all."

George shook his head, turning to hoist the sack onto a growing pile in a back room of the store. "I've worked a lot harder, and you know it. If it wasn't for your pa, I'd likely be dead right now. You sit down and take it easy. I'll finish unloading."

Blake turned away, sitting down in a wooden chair just outside the door. He watched George quietly for a few minutes, thinking how many other "Georges" there were in the South—men of both brains and brawn, forced to live subservient lives, men whose pride was beaten out of them with whips or clubs,

31

whose wives and children were torn from them. Since Blake's father had managed to purchase George and set him free, something the man had been devoted to doing for as many slaves as he could afford, George had quickly mastered reading and writing, and he had worked hard at learning to speak well. He was a good man, and Blake felt sorry that the woman he loved had been sold just before Blake's father bought George. He hoped that someday, by some miracle, they would find her and would be able to buy her back.

"What are you going to do, now that you know Nick West is in town?" George asked, interrupting Blake's thoughts.

Blake touched a sore lip. "I don't know yet. I only know that between him and Samantha Walters, I intend to make a lot more trips into Lawrence."

"It's getting more dangerous for us all the time, moving back and forth across the border. There's bushwhackers crawling around the back woods like ants."

"I know, but John Hale is a good man—and so brave to be such a strong abolitionist in Missouri, where he's surrounded by proslavery men. I owe him; we both owe him, since he's the one who lent my father the money to buy you away from that bastard who owned you. Dad died before he could pay Hale off, so I'm determined to do it."

George sighed, sitting down for a moment on the steps behind the store. "I'm sorry about that, Blake."

"Sorry? Hell, it wasn't your fault. When Dad and I came along and saw you hanging from that whipping post . . ." Blake paused, still getting a sick feeling at the memory of the sight of George's back. The remaining scars were close to hideous, and to this day, no matter how hot the weather, George would not remove his shirt in front of anyone. "We both would have sold our souls to get you out of there."

"Turns out your pa gave up more than that."

Blake sighed, grief returning to his heart. "I just wish I could prove it was Nick West and his men. Somehow, someday, I'll make him pay with his life."

"You'll end up at the end of a rope, just like your pa."

Blake's eyes teared at the memory of the horrible sight. He took a cigarette from his pocket and studied it in his hand for a moment. "At least I'll have done something to deserve it; not that I see anything wrong with killing Nick West but the law would. Dad . . ." He put the cigarette to his mouth. "He didn't do anything to earn that." He lit the cigarette and took a deep drag. "Let's get this stuff unloaded and find a room. I've got to lie down a while before we go to the Walters's house tonight."

They finished unloading, George insisting on doing most of the work, then collected the shipping fee from the store's owner and drove the freight wagon to the nearest hotel. "You're going to get the same argument from this hotel as all the others," George told Blake, putting on the brake and climbing down to tie the mules.

"This is Lawrence—the gathering point for abolitionists and Free Staters. You'll get a room here, George," Blake answered, putting a hand on the man's shoulder. They walked inside, and George hung back while Blake talked to the clerk, a tall, dark woman who stiffened at the sight of George. Blake asked for a choice of two rooms or one room with two beds.

"One room—one bed," the woman told him.

"Fine," Blake answered. "One of us can sleep in a

bedroll on the floor."

The woman's eyes hardened. "I'm sorry, but we . . . we don't allow his kind," she added, indicating George.

Blake gave her a look of disdain. "His kind? What kind is that, ma'am?"

She reddened slightly. "You know. Negroes."

Blake pushed back his hat, his anger obvious. "Where I go—he goes. He's just a man, like any other. I thought Lawrence was a town of mostly Free Staters."

The woman folded her arms defensively. "We are. I am as much against slavery as the strongest abolitionist, but that doesn't mean I have to let a Negro man sleep in my beds or even on my carpets. It's wrong to abuse them the way slave owners do, but there is still something about them that just doesn't seem . . . well . . . clean."

"He's as clean as you or me," Blake answered, his voice rising.

"Maybe so. But if I let him sleep here, I'll lose some of my other business. Besides, such things bring trouble. From the look of your face, sir, you have already found some. I will not have my other guests upset, and if you continue to argue the point, *you* will not get a room!"

"Let it be, Blake," George spoke up.

"He can sleep out back," the woman said coolly. "There's a nice clean loft above the stables. If you have horses, you can bed them there."

"It's going to be cold tonight," Blake argued.

"I'll be all right," George assured him. "I'm used to it. You know that. I've got plenty of blankets. You take the room, Blake. You've got to have a decent place to lay down and rest. I'll take the mules around back and unhitch them and get set up in the loft."

Blake held the woman's eyes, thinking of several labels he'd like to pin on her. He turned the guest book and signed his name, throwing down the pen and taking some money from his pocket. "How much?"

"Two dollars for the room—fifty cents a day for each animal you put up in the stall. There is feed for them."

"How about the charge for George staying in the loft?" Blake asked sarcastically.

The woman stiffened. "He can stay for free."

"How generous of you," Blake answered. He slammed the money on the desk. "For two dollars I'd better get some hot water when I ask for it, and a damn comfortable bed."

"You'll find our accommodations are quite nice, I'm sure," the woman said.

"I'm sure George will, too," Blake sneered. He turned to go out and get his personal supplies.

"There's some things you've got to learn to accept, my friend," George told him, walking out with him. "If I can accept it, you should be able to."

Blake picked up his bag, facing the man. "Why in hell is it harder for me than for you?"

George grinned. "Probably because it's your kind of people who are doing it, and that makes you feel a little guilty."

Blake grinned. "You're right." He sighed, shaking his head. "You're pretty good at figuring people, George." He walked toward the steps. "Get your dirty clothes together. After I've slept a while I'll get those muddy clothes of mine and find a laundry. I'll put yours in with mine, so they'll never know the difference. We can at least get your clothes washed."

George untied the mules. "I'll have them ready." He met Blake's eyes, and he felt the deep, sincere friendship. Ever since Blake's father had purchased him, he and Blake had struck up an easy friendship. Now Blake's father, and the farm they all had worked on together, were gone. There was only Blake, and George was not quite sure just how he would get along without the man. Freedom was still new to him. He still had a lot to learn about his new world. "Thanks for trying," he said to Blake.

"Someday it's going to change, George. You'll see."

George grinned, but the hurt was obvious. "We'll both be old, old men when that happens—if it ever does. I have a feeling this whole country is headed for big trouble, Blake. What happened today with West and his men, what happened just now in that hotel— it's going to come to all-out war before it's over, and it won't be a pretty sight."

"I hope you're wrong, George, but I have a feeling you're right. See you later." Blake walked inside the hotel, casting another derisive look at the woman behind the desk before climbing the stairs to his room. He went inside and locked the door, his injuries overwhelming him again so that he was forced to drop his bag and sprawl across the bed without even taking off his boots. His last thoughts were of Sam. He would see her again tonight. That made him feel better about everything, brought a pleasant, peaceful feeling to his tortured soul.

George ate quietly, feeling somewhat awkward at the Walters dining table, in spite of their genuine desire to have him join them.

"I admire my daughter's devotion to our cause, Blake," the Reverend Howard Walters was saying, "but after what happened today, it's obviously too dangerous for her. I've given her strict instructions not to go anywhere near town for a while, not even to shop."

"Father, that's silly. I would be perfectly fine," Samantha answered. "I'm not afraid at all."

The reverend, who sat straight and tall in his high-backed chair, cast her a scolding look, his face flushing as it always did when he repressed his anger. "That's part of your problem. You have no fear, Samantha Walters. Now I'm not saying anyone should be afraid of anything, but sometimes a little bit of fear can bring on much-needed wisdom in moments of peril. You've got to learn when to forge ahead, Samantha, and when to step back."

Samantha met Blake's eyes, feeling pleasant urges at the sight of him. He wore neat cotton pants and a ruffled shirt, with a jacket and string tie. He had bathed and shaved, and his dark hair was full and shiny. His face was still bruised and cut, but the marks could not hide his handsome lines. "Blake knows we don't have to be afraid to fight for what we know is right," she said, looking at her father.

Blake reddened a little. "Well, I have to agree with your father, Sam. You'd better lay low for a while." He looked at the reverend. "As for me, I'm afraid I have the same temper problem your daughter has, especially when it comes to Nick West."

Walters frowned. "Yes, what is this—something about the man killing your *father?*"

Blake swallowed a piece of ham and wiped at his mouth with a napkin. He glanced at Clyde Beecher, a lay leader in the Methodist Church where Reverend Walters preached. Beecher was a native of Kansas and a devout Christian who had become a close friend of the family since the Walters had come to Kansas. Since first arriving and being introduced to Beecher,

Blake had felt uneasy. There was something about him Blake did not trust. It was nothing he could put his finger on, just something in the man's eyes. He wanted to warn the reverend that he had to be careful of his friends, considering the work he was doing against slavery; but he hardly knew this family and felt he had no right interfering. Beecher was friendly enough, and the reverend had explained that Beecher helped in the print shop whenever they prepared more pamphlets to be handed out to the public. Sometimes, when the reverend was ill or had to be with a dying parishioner, Beecher even delivered the sermon.

"Happened about a year and a half ago," he explained aloud then, noticing Beecher was paying very close attention. "My father was an abolitionist. We had a farm a few miles east of Independence. Whenever Dad could afford it, he'd buy a slave from a neighboring plantation owner—usually one who was ailing in some way and about to be sold someplace where he or she would be treated badly. He'd buy them and then set them free. That's how we got George here. We were making a delivery of grain to this one farm where we'd never seen before. I guess George had a habit of being a little belligerent, something no slave can afford to be. He was being punished for it, but since we're sitting at the table eating, I won't go into details about the condition he was in when we found him."

George sat staring at his plate while Blake spoke.

"At any rate, the owner was just angry enough at the time to let us buy George. Said he was a troublemaker. Considering George's size and strength, if the man would have had time to think about it, he probably never would have sold him for what he did, but then again, George was also half dead, so maybe he figured he wouldn't live anyway. My father gave him the grain for nothing, plus the horses and wagon we'd hauled it with, *plus* an IOU. He had to borrow the rest of the money from Mr. Hale—the man I work for now. I'm still working to pay off the debt."

"So, this Hale fellow is also an abolitionist?" Beecher asked.

Blake glanced at the man. Beecher reminded him of a dark cloud, the kind you see just before a storm. His skin was darker than that of most white men. His hair and eyes were dark, his clothes were all black. To Blake the question seemed more than casual curiosity, but most people in Independence knew John Hale was an abolitionist, so Blake saw no harm in answering the question honestly. "Yes," he replied. "He's a brave, dedicated man."

The reverend leaned back in his chair. "What's all this got to do with Nick West?"

Blake glanced at Samantha before continuing, unable to get enough of the sight of her. She was beautiful tonight in a blue gingham dress that matched her blue eyes, her dark hair drawn back at the sides with blue bows. He had caught Beecher staring at her more than once, and although he still hardly knew her, Beecher's looks brought a frustrated jealousy to his heart, as well as a surge of protective feelings.

He picked up a hot roll and toyed with it in his hand. "West had a farm a few miles west of us, a big farm—lots of slaves. He'd given my father trouble before, calling him the usual names proslavery men have for abolitionists. When the Kansas-Nebraska Act went through, things got worse. Then my father bought this young Negro woman off another plantation owner—just a couple days before we

39

found and bought George. That's why we had to borrow money to buy him."

He broke open the roll, while everyone sat listening intently, including Clyde Beecher. "At any rate, he gave the girl her freedom papers and made arrangements with an underground network to get her to the North where she'd be safer. Nick West came by a couple of days later, furious. He had planned on buying the pretty young girl himself, and I don't need to explain how he intended to use her."

Samantha reddened, and no one but Blake noticed the look of hunger in Beecher's eyes. Blake looked at the reverend. "West told my father that someone ought to put him out of business and stop him from buying and freeing Negroes. It wasn't more than four or five days later that I found my father dead. He had gone out to the north pasture to check on some missing cattle. When he didn't come back I went looking for him—and found him hanging by the neck in an old shed. It was obvious there had been a struggle."

Samantha's mother let out a gasp of horror and pity, and Samantha's heart swelled with sorrow for Blake Hastings.

"I don't need any witnesses to know who did it, but under the law I can't prove it," Blake went on. "My father had a lot of debts, so I sold the farm to pay them off. Like I said, I'm still working to pay off John Hale, which I should be able to do in another week or two. Even so, I'll probably keep working for him." He put his hand on George's arm. "At least he's given work to George. Eventually George and I plan to get away from all the hatred and bloodshed—maybe head west."

Samantha's heart fell at the words. Surely he wouldn't go soon! And surely supper tonight

40

wouldn't be the last she would see of Blake Hastings!

"Well, I'm terribly sorry about your father, Blake," the reverend spoke up.

"We all are," Beecher said then, showing a look of deep concern. "It's terrible how this whole issue has caused so much hatred and bloodshed."

"My family and I are doing what we can to stop any expansion of slavery," the reverend added. "We came out here to do what we can to ensure Kansas and Nebraska will vote to be free territories. We have even convinced many of our friends in Vermont to move to Kansas, to settle here and be a part of the vote when it comes up in a few months."

"Bushwhackers say it's no different from bringing in people from Missouri," Milicent Walters put in. "But we and the people who have followed us are sincere in settling here and being solid citizens of Kansas. Most of those sneaking across the border from Missouri are simply intending to stuff the ballot boxes with their proslavery votes and then run right back to Missouri. Missouri doesn't want to be surrounded by free territory."

"Well, I have a feeling that's what Nick West is doing here," Blake told her. "I tried to find him several times at his place back in Missouri after my father was hanged, but he wasn't there. I checked at a land office today before coming here, and I discovered he bought a good piece of land north of here—just to be able to say he's a Kansas citizen, I'm sure."

"Well, now that we know the kind of man he is, we'll have to watch out for him," Beecher spoke up, his voice almost too low and quiet for his stocky size.

Blake moved to meet his eyes. "Yes, we will, won't we?" Their eyes held, and again Blake felt uneasy.

41

What was the man doing here? Didn't he have a place of his own?

"No brothers and sisters?" the reverend was asking Blake. "No wife?"

Samantha was secretly glad her father had asked the question that had been on her own mind. Was Blake Hastings an unattached man?

"I had two brothers, but they both died at a young age," Blake answered. "Both would have been older than I. My mother died in childbirth when she had me. As far as a wife . . ." He felt Samantha's eyes on him. "There was a woman once, a few years ago. I intended to marry her, but she got thrown by a horse one day when we were out riding. Broke her neck."

The sorrow in his eyes was heart-rending, and Samantha felt a mixture of pity and jealousy. It seemed silly to be jealous of someone who was dead, even sillier to be jealous at all, considering the fact that she had just met Blake Hastings and might never see him again.

"You've had a lot of tragedy in your life, Mr. Hastings," Samantha's mother offered. "How sad. If there is anything we can do, any way we can help—"

"Yes, you rescued our daughter this morning from certain peril, diving into that man who threatened her after already fighting with that West fellow," the reverend added. "I feel we owe you something."

Blake smiled almost bashfully. "You've already repaid me with a very fine meal and your wonderful hospitality—and most of all by inviting George to your table. Not many whites would do that, even the ones who call themselves abolitionists. The woman at the hotel wouldn't let him stay there. He's sleeping in the stable loft out back."

"Why, that's shameful," Milicent Walters protested.

"He can stay right here," the reverend put in.

"No, sir," George told them. "I'm just fine where I am. Besides, we'll be leaving in the morning."

Again Samantha's heart fell. Leaving? For good?

"There is much work to be done, that is obvious," the reverend said. "If and when we are able to completely abolish slavery in this country, the Negroes will still have a lot of troubles. We'll have thousands of freed slaves who have never known any other way of life. They'll have to make it on their own, and they'll need help. God knows, not many whites will be ready or willing to help them."

"I have a feeling that before that happens, this country is going to split apart," Blake replied. "George feels it, too. Ending slavery isn't going to come easily—or peacefully. What's happening right here in Lawrence, and what happened to my father, are both proof of that."

Milicent sighed. "Well, let's not end this conversation on such a dire note. I have apple pie in the kitchen. Surely you and George would enjoy some pie and coffee? And perhaps Samantha will play the piano for us afterward."

"That would be fine," Blake answered, rising respectfully when the woman got up to go to the kitchen. He guessed Milicent Walters to be about fifty years old. She was a short, small woman who still held a lingering beauty. It was obvious Samantha inherited her beauty, and her blue eyes, from her mother.

Samantha's father was rather heavyset, a tall, balding man with heavy white sideburns and a ruddy complexion. The man was obviously dedicated to his preaching and to his belief in the freeing of all slaves. The whole family had left the only place they had ever called home to come to a new, untamed territory where there were few of the luxuries they had known back East—just to help the cause of freedom. Blake had learned through conversation that Samantha had an older brother, Drew, who attended Harvard College studying to be a lawyer.

Blake met Samantha's eyes again, seeing there the same feelings he was himself experiencing. She did not want this to be the last time she saw him, and neither did he. He was even more determined to come back to Lawrence after this next freighting job and get permission from Reverend Walters to see more of his daughter. Besides, he realized now that Samantha was in a position of peril, and he did not like the thought of it. He knew firsthand what could happen to people who fought for the freedom of slaves; and he could not quell his feelings of uneasiness over the presence of Clyde Beecher.

Reverend Walters was a good, brave man, but Blake felt the man's Christian beliefs made him too trusting of anyone who claimed to be joining his cause. Kansas and Missouri both were filled now with spies, people who spoke out of both sides of their mouths. He suspected Clyde Beecher was just such a person. He hoped he was wrong, but if he wasn't, Samantha and her whole family could be in more danger than they knew.

The evening passed on a lighter note. Samantha played several tunes on the piano, feeling Blake's eyes on her as she drummed out several hymns and a few patriotic songs. Blake managed to talk George into singing a couple of songs unique to his own people, sad, intriguing songs of slavery and longing for home. George's voice was low and full, and he captured everyone's attention with his soulful rendition of songs his people often sang in rhythmic harmony while working. Samantha thought

44

George a very handsome man and she wondered if he had ever been in love. Had he perhaps had a wife once who was sold away from him? Most of his people led such sad lives.

"Sometimes music is the only thing that would get us through a day," George was telling the reverend.

"Do you have family, George?" Milicent asked.

"None that I know of. It's a common practice to take a healthy, strong baby from its mother soon as it's weaned and sell it off to somebody else, so no Negro child gets too attached to its mother. That way there's no fuss made by the child when it's sold. That's what was done with me. I never knew my mother or my father—or whether I have any brothers and sisters."

"That's awful," Samantha said quietly. "I can't imagine not knowing my parents or my brother."

"They do the same with husbands and wives," George added. "Sometimes they pick a woman's mate so she'll have good, strong babies. They don't care about feelings, just producing healthy offspring for future workers—kind of like breeding the best cattle or horses."

Samantha reddened, unable to look at Blake.

"I guess I spoke out of turn there," George added.

"No," the reverend told him. "My wife and Samantha have heard most of the horrors of slavery. The more they learn, the more they understand how important our cause is. What about you, George? Did you ever have a wife?"

A strange look of sorrow came into George's eyes. "No, sir." He gave no further explanation, but it was obvious to Samantha he had loved someone once.

"You should be careful," Beecher spoke up. He sat off by himself in a corner, and his words were directed to George. "You'd better stick close by your friend there, and keep your freedom papers on hand. A

45

strapping Negro like yourself is worth a lot of money to some men. Without the proper identification, you could be mistaken for a runaway and resold."

George and Blake both stared at the man, then looked at each other. Blake knew right away that George held the same distrust of Beecher that he did. "Yes, sir, I'm right careful," George answered.

Beecher rose. "I think I'll be going, Howard," he told Samantha's father. "Thank you for the fine meal and equally fine entertainment. It's always a pleasure to listen to Sam play and sing." He walked up to Blake and put out his hand. "Nice meeting you, Hastings. Will we see you again?"

Blake reached out and took his hand, squeezing lightly, feeling a squeeze in return—not the kind of squeeze a man gives in friendly gesture, but more of a threat, as far as he was concerned. He rose, holding Beecher's eyes steadily, squeezing a little harder. "I imagine I'll be this way again," he answered. "You live close by?"

Beecher, a well-built man who stood nearly as tall as Blake, released his hold. Blake guessed him to be perhaps the same age as Nick West, beginning to age but still plenty strong. "Not far," Beecher answered. "Just a few houses down. My place is quite small, just two rooms. I'm a widower, with not much money to my name . . ." He looked at the reverend. "My fortune is my faith. And good friends like Reverend Walters," he added with a smile. He looked back at Blake. "Put your faith in God, Mr. Hastings, not in your fists and your temper. God can get us through whatever lies ahead for us all. Heaven knows there are many trials awaiting us."

He turned and shook Walters's hand, and the reverend walked him to the door out in the hall, both men talking about the church service coming the day after tomorrow. Blake watched until they disappeared around the corner, then looked at George, who had a look of disgust on his face. "Me, too," Blake said under his breath. He looked at Milicent, who had risen and was looking through some sheet music for Samantha. "Mrs. Walters, would it be possible to have a couple of minutes alone with your daughter?" he asked.

Samantha's heart raced at the words. He wanted to see her alone! Did he have something special to say to her? She prayed her mother would agree. Milicent looked somewhat flustered and unsure, then smiled. "Yes, I suppose that would be all right."

"I'll go on outside and wait for you," George told him.

"Well, you be *sure* to wait. Don't go walking back to the hotel alone."

George bowed. "Yes, master."

Blake gave him a scowl, as Milicent and Samantha laughed lightly. George nodded to Milicent. "Thank you, ma'am, for a wonderful meal and such nice hospitality. I won't forget you people."

"Well, we won't forget you, either, George. And when you're back in Lawrence, you come see us again. You'll always be welcome. Let me walk you out." The woman moved with George to the door, turning before leaving and giving Blake the look of a concerned mother. She went out and closed the parlor doors. Blake turned to Samantha, who still sat on the piano bench. Their eyes held as he moved closer and sat down beside her, pecking at a couple of ivory keys.

"You play really well," he told her, turning slightly to face her and resting one arm on the top of the piano.

47

Samantha felt an unnerving warmth pulse through her veins at his closeness. Power and strength seemed to surround her, yet she sensed a gentleness about him, knew from his friendship with George that even though he might not sit in church every Sunday, he was a man capable of love and compassion. "Thank you," she answered. "I . . . I'm sorry . . . about all the losses you've suffered."

He shrugged. "Then again, I'm better off than some others. Life is all a matter of perspective."

She wondered about the woman he had loved. Could he love again? "You *will* come back to Lawrence, won't you?"

He grinned softly. "I have to. The new route we're on runs between Independence and Lawrence."

She frowned. "Isn't that awfully dangerous? The border is filled with jayhawkers and bushwhackers. Those who know Mr. Hale is an abolitionist might bring you harm, let alone the fact that your best friend is a freed Negro."

He sighed. "In these times it doesn't matter which side you're on. You're still in danger." He reached over to take her hand, enveloping it in his own strong hand. "I want you to be careful, Sam. Do like your father says and stay off the streets for a while, and especially the area where you were this morning."

He was so close she thought for a minute he might try to kiss her. "I will. Not for father, but for you."

Blake nodded. "Good. And be careful what you say around Clyde Beecher."

"Mr. Beecher?" Her eyebrows arched in surprise. "He's a devoted lay leader, one of my father's best friends ever since we came here. He eats supper with us two or three times a week, and he even—"

He squeezed her hand. "I know he's a good friend

48

of the family. I know your parents trust him, but I don't.''

"But you don't even know him!"

"Some men you don't *need* to know well to have a pretty good idea of their makeup. I've spent all of two hours in his company and I don't like him. Don't say anything to your parents—not yet. Just promise me you'll be careful what you say around him. These are bad times, Sam.''

"What about you? I hardly know you, but you expect me to trust you and not trust a man my family has known well for months.''

He grinned again. "I think you already know you can trust me. But I guess I'm stepping out of bounds. It's just that I happen to have taken a liking to you, Sam, so I'm going to worry about you while I'm gone.''

She could not hide her pleasure at the remark. "You will?" She smiled. "I'll worry about you, too. How long will you be gone?''

"I'm not sure. Hale has some other runs for us to make before coming back to Lawrence. It could be a month.''

She searched his gentle brown eyes, studied the fine lines of his handsome face, the square jaw, the way his dark brows perfectly framed his wide-set, dark eyes, his straight nose and the way it seemed the perfect size for his solid face. His smile was captivating, and for the first time ever her young body was filled with a desire to be with a man in every womanly sense.

"That sounds like such a long time," she answered. She blushed and looked at her lap. "And that remark sounded very forward.''

"No, it didn't. I was afraid it wouldn't matter to

you. In fact, all evening I've been getting up the courage to ask if you minded if I came visiting again when I come back. Just to see you, I mean. Maybe you think I'm too old—"

"Oh, no!" She met his eyes again. "After all, I'm eighteen. I'm not a child. I don't know how old you are, but it doesn't matter. I'd like very much . . ." She hesitated, dropping her eyes again. "I'd like it very much if you came visiting again, Blake."

He rubbed a thumb over the back of her hand. "To answer your question, I'm twenty-nine. Maybe you think that's not too old, but your parents might."

"They only care how good a man is." She met his eyes again. "And I know in my heart you're a good man, Blake Hastings. I do want you to come back. And I'm going to worry about you. How will I know if you're all right?"

He gave her a wink. "I'll try to drop you a letter or two. Just don't talk about them in front of Beecher. I have a feeling I don't want him knowing my every movement."

She frowned. "Are you mixed up with the underground railroad?"

"You're better off not knowing everything I do. Just be careful. Promise?"

She nodded. "Promise."

He studied her blue eyes, longing to touch her hair, to taste her virgin mouth. "Fight or no fight, I'm glad for what happened this morning. Otherwise we might never have met, Samantha Walters."

He raised her hand and kissed the back of it. Samantha felt fire tear through her veins, and her lips trembled at the thought of his mouth covering her own. "I'm glad, too," she answered. "I'm just sorry you got hurt. I hope . . . I hope nothing bad happens between you and that Nick West."

She saw the sudden hatred in his eyes and wished she had not mentioned the name. "Something bad *will* happen someday, but it will be to him, not me." He rose from the bench, keeping hold of her hand and leading her to the parlor doors. "Remember, be careful. And I *will* be back."

She wondered if he could hear her heart beating. "And I'll be waiting right here."

He sighed, reluctantly opening the doors and going out into the hallway. He took his hat and jacket from the rack near the door and gave her one last look, his eyes moving over her in a way that let her know he wanted her. In that one moment she felt more of a woman than she ever had before, felt the girl inside her fading away and the woman emerging. "Good-bye, Blake."

"Good-bye, Sam." He nodded, then stepped outside to join her parents, who were on the porch talking to George. Samantha stood at the screen door and watched as he gave them a final thank-you for the meal and hospitality. He walked off into the night then with George, and Samantha felt like dancing. Blake Hastings was attracted to her! He was coming back just to see her! She had never had any feelings for any man her own age like the feelings she had for Blake. She had always wondered what it would feel like to be in love, and now she suspected the way she felt about Blake must be close. Was it foolish to think such a thing so soon? Maybe she was being a child after all. Maybe he was leading her on. Maybe he wouldn't come back at all.

Of course he would! She knew instinctively he would not lie to her. What an eventful day it had been. She felt so alive, ready to meet the challenge of her father's cause head-on; she felt braver, proud of herself for standing up to the men who had threatened her. The day had been frightening but exciting, and she smiled at the thought that her parents didn't know about her kicking Fred Brewster. If her father knew that he would surely confine her to her room for a good long time.

She rushed up the stairs to lie back on her bed and think about Blake Hastings, her heart aching at the thought of his being gone a whole month.

Outside, Blake and George headed back to the hotel. "You got the same feeling about that Clyde Beecher as I do?" George asked his friend.

"That he's a spy?"

"You see the look in his eyes when he mentioned how valuable I'd be to some men?"

"I saw it. He's one to keep an eye on. Soon as we finish this next job, I'm thinking of coming back to Lawrence and finding work right here. I'll have my debt paid to John, and I imagine you could find work here, too."

"Miss Samantha Walters wouldn't have anything to do with that decision, would she?"

Blake laughed lightly. "She has a lot to do with it. I've got to see her again, George."

"I don't blame you. I just wish . . ."

They walked on in silence a moment. "I know," Blake told him. "I'm sorry about Jesse, George. Maybe it's time you tried to get over her and find yourself someone else."

"Maybe. Maybe if you end up settling here, I'll just go on west myself."

"Let's just see what happens. No sense making any decisions right now. Besides, for now you're safer sticking with me."

"I imagine so." George stopped walking. "They're good people, Blake. I hope that Beecher isn't up to something."

Blake sighed. "So do I. I'm just anxious to get this next run over with and get back here."

George snickered. "That girl got under your skin right fast, didn't she?"

Blake grinned. "She's beautiful, but it isn't just that. Watching her today . . . She's strong and brave and determined. She's got spirit. There's quite a woman inside that pretty body, and I suddenly can't stand the thought of some other man discovering that woman. I don't know exactly how I feel about her yet. I only know I have to see her again."

"Then let's get some sleep and get an early start. Sooner we get back to Independence and make our other deliveries, the sooner you get back here."

"Right." The two men left each other, Blake going to his room, George heading for the stables to take his place in the loft, neither of them aware that Clyde Beecher was taking advantage of the darkness to make his way unseen to the back door of the saloon where he knew Nick West was spending the night with his favorite whore.

Three

"So, he's working for John Hale, is he?" Nick West rubbed at tired eyes, his whole body wracked with pain from the fight with Blake. He realized that if the other men had not got Blake off him, he might not even be alive tonight. Blake had a good fifteen years of youth on him, and he had been out to kill.

"I think they're doing more than hauling freight," Clyde Beecher answered. "I could tell by watching his eyes. I wouldn't be surprised if they sometimes hide runaway slaves in that wagon, or maybe haul illegal guns for jawhawkers."

"Wouldn't surprise me, either, considering that nigger is his best friend." West reached over to a nightstand for a cigar. He sat naked, with a sheet over himself, on the edge of a bed, a prostitute sprawled naked beside him, sleeping hard from too much drink. "What a waste, that big black running around free. I'd like to show him what I do to niggers with smart mouths."

"Maybe someday you'll get your chance," Beecher answered. "Blake Hastings has a yearning for Samantha Walters. He watched her this evening like a stud horse itching to get over the fence. He's coming back. We'll be able to keep a good eye on him if he starts hanging around Lawrence more."

"I'm not sure I *want* him to come back, after the trouble he gave me today. I'll round up some men to follow him when he leaves in the morning. Soon as he and that black are out in border country, I want them shot. With all the raiding that's going on, people won't know who to blame. If he comes back here and adds himself to the abolitionist strength already settling in this town, it will make our job that much harder. I don't intend to lose that vote, Beecher. Kansas is going to be a slave territory, and we're going to help that happen. You got any more names for me?"

"Reverend Walters expects a lot more people to show up at Sunday services. There will be plenty of distant farmers and border settlers attending. I'll have some names for you then."

"Just be sure you get them right—locations and all. I don't want my bushwhackers attacking pro-slavery families. Maybe more raiding and killing will convince the rest of the abolitionists to change their tune—or face the possibility of being dragged from their homes in the middle of the night to be shot."

Beecher grinned. "I'll give you the right ones. They all trust me as much as the preacher himself. Maybe we should arrange for him to be shot. Then I could take over."

"No, not yet. That would make Walters too much of a martyr and rally the abolitionists more. Eventually we'll get rid of him, but not yet. Work from the outside. Keep them scared and running, afraid to go to meetings. Between killing them off and scaring the rest of them away from meetings, the vote is sure to go our way. By then Kansas will be overrun with proslavery people from Missouri anyway. You just keeping doing what you're doing and provide me with names. In the meantime, I'll take care of Blake Hastings and his nigger."

Beecher nodded, rising. He glanced at the prostitute. "You, uh, you through with her?"

West looked over at her with disdain. "I'm through. You can have her if you want. I wasn't much use tonight anyway, with this sore body. I'm going downstairs to get a drink." The man rose, pulling on a pair of long johns, while Beecher removed his coat and hat, then sat down to remove his boots. "The best ones are the young Negro girls," West added, pulling on his pants. "I've got one back at my place in Missouri who's a lot better than that slut there. Maybe it seems better because she always fights me. I bought her about a year and a half ago. Name's Jesse. Took me a long time to get her to submit without a battle. Once they feel the whip and the fist enough, they understand their place."

Beecher removed his shirt. "That's a fact. I wouldn't mind putting Samantha Walters in her place, but I have to look the part of the devoted Christian friend."

"You stay away from her. Don't make any wrong moves, especially not now. We've accomplished too much. I'm paying you well to stay close to that family and give me the names of Walters's followers. Keep your hands clean."

Beecher turned the prostitute over, running his hands over her breasts. "I'll keep them clean, but not tonight."

Both men laughed, and West pulled on a shirt and went out, closing the door. He thought about Jesse March, deciding perhaps he should go back to his farm sometime soon and spend a couple of nights

57

with his young, shapely little Negro girl. She was past the tears now. She knew her place. It had taken several days to make her understand, but now she did, and he enjoyed the fact that she still hated him but submitted to him at his beck and call.

First things first. There was the little matter of Blake Hastings to take care of. Once it was finished, he would have a fine, strong male Negro to add to his collection. He headed down the stairs and called out to one of his men. "I've got a job for you," he told him quietly.

Samantha watched her father with pride as he captured the full attention of his congregation, reminding them again of the horrors of slavery, and how important their vote would be in the coming months. He talked about equality and how all men of every color were loved by God, how no man could set himself up to own another.

Today, for the first time, Samantha had trouble giving her father her full attention. Blake Hastings was on his way to Independence, out there in the terribly dangerous border country. If it was true about Nick West killing his father, after the trouble Blake had given the man two days ago, wasn't it possible West would go after Blake? The thought of something happening to Blake, of never seeing him again, brought literal pain to her chest. How strange that she could feel this way after knowing him only a few hours.

". . . all be threatened by bushwhackers, but we must stand strong," the reverend was saying. Samantha hated how feelings over slavery and states' rights was turning into something so dangerous and ugly. Why couldn't people just talk things out, come to some kind of compromise? It seemed the bitterness and hatred was building. One family had come in this morning with the sad news that they would have to give up their farm because bushwhackers had too often trampled and burned their crops and stolen cattle and horses. They could not afford to keep going, and they talked about heading back East.

"You mustn't go," Reverend Walters had urged them. "We need your vote. Stay here in Lawrence. We'll help you find work, put you up in our own home temporarily if necessary."

It was the first time Samantha had begun to wonder about Blake's distrust of Clyde Beecher, who approached the family after her father left them and told them that if they were too shattered emotionally, perhaps they *should* go back East. "One or two votes aren't going to make a lot of difference," she heard Beecher tell them. "I know you want to support the reverend, and I most certainly do, too, but I understand that sometimes a man can meet his limit, and you have to think about what is best for your children. Stay for the reverend's sake, if you feel you should. But he will understand if you leave."

Samantha pretended to thumb through a hymnal as she kept her ears open. Beecher began asking the family about their neighbors. "Could any of them have been in on what happened?"

"Oh, no, they're all abolitionists just like us," the man had answered.

Beecher went on to ask just where their farm was located—how many abolitionist families lived nearby—what were their names? "We have to keep track of friends and enemies," he explained. "The reverend needs to know how many families are out there who will support us. I'll pay all of them a visit and urge them to be strong and faithful in their support of a free territory."

"Oh, yes, a visit from you or the reverend would surely boost their morale," the woman answered him.

The family left, and Samantha noticed an odd smirk on Beecher's face. Was it her imagination? Was she being leery of him just because Blake had planted the suspicion in her mind? He frowned then and shook his head, turning to look at her. "It's a shame, isn't it? So much hatred and prejudice. Maybe someday we can all live in peace."

Their eyes held, and Samantha tried to read Beecher's, but she could not. She reasoned that he was her father's friend. Surely her father, who had known the man much longer than Blake, was right in his opinion of Beecher. "I hope so," she answered.

She wached Beecher now, sitting up front with two other deacons while her father preached. She wanted her father to be right about the man, but it made sense to her that Blake might surely have a better understanding of who could and could not be trusted. After all, he was much more a man of the world than her father; he was a man who had lived "out there" among the riffraff. Perhaps Blake was not a churchgoer, and he was apparently a man who had known and participated in violence, who sometimes cussed and probably drank, but he was experienced with a side of life her father did not understand.

She folded her hands and prayed for wisdom, feeling guilty that she would put more faith in the opinion of a man she hardly knew over her own father. She told herself she was being foolish, reminded herself that Clyde Beecher had never been anything but respectful and supportive.

They all rose to sing a hymn, and Beecher joined

with as much gusto as the others, his face and eyes showing so much faith and devotion.

George stirred the beans in a black fry pan that sat on a flat rock in the middle of the campfire. "You got that feeling we're being followed?" he asked Blake.

Blake took a deep drag on a cigarette, his eyes moving around the dark outer circle beyond the light of the flames. "You, too?"

"Felt it all day. Maybe because after that fight with Nick West, I figured the man might not care to have you come back to Lawrence. If you're right about him killing your pa, he'd just as soon get rid of you, too."

"I already considered that. That's why you and I are going to sleep down inside the wagon tonight. We're going to build up our bed rolls to make it look like we're sleeping by the fire."

George nodded. "A good idea." He shivered. "It will be cold in the wagon."

"Better cold and alive than cold and dead. Let's eat and get settled in before someone catches up and sees what we're doing." Blake tossed aside his cigarette and picked up a tin plate, reaching over and scooping some beans into it. He took a towel-wrapped loaf of bread from a supply sack and broke off a piece, handing it to George. "Nice of Mrs. Walters to give us this," he commented, thinking again about Samantha and hoping she was safe. "We might as well eat up before it's too stale."

George nodded, taking the bread. "You suppose that Beecher knows we suspect him of something?"

"Hard to say. I'd rather he didn't. He'll be less careful." Blake ate a spoonful of beans, then broke off some bread for himself. He wore a handgun at his side now, as he always did as soon as he was away from town and civilization. His rifle lay beside him, and another lay beside George. Both men wore sheepskin jackets against the cold night air. Blake swallowed a piece of bread. "Sure will be nice when we can live in peace someday and not have to worry about who to trust, won't it?"

"Sure will. You think that day is coming?"

"Sure it is."

"I just hope we're both alive to enjoy it."

Blake made no reply, wondering if hoping for peace was just a foolish dream. They finished their meal in near silence, then cleaned up the dishes and repacked them. They stuffed their bedrolls with rocks and sod and spare blankets, rolling a blanket at the end of each one as though to use as a pillow and perching their hats against the pillows to look as though they were drawn over their eyes. They climbed into the freight wagon then, both thinking how cold they would be with only a couple of blankets left to cover themselves inside the wagon, and nothing to use for a pillow but a few rolled-up flour sacks.

"Damn," Blake muttered as he settled in. "Right now a warm bed with Samantha Walters lying beside me sounds like utter paradise."

George laughed lightly. "You'd better get your mind off such thoughts or you'll drive yourself crazy, especially laying in this cold, hard wagon. Do we have to do this the next three nights till we reach Independence?"

"I'm afraid so, unless whoever is out there makes their move soon. Make sure your rifle is in easy reach."

"Laying right here beside me. For now our rifles

will have to take the place of a woman."

Blake grinned as he closed his eyes. He realized that for the first time he had no interest in looking up the prostitutes when he got back to Independence. Suddenly not just any woman would do. It was Samantha Walters he wanted, and he wanted more than sex. He wanted the whole woman. It was a little frightening to realize he had actually found someone he just might be able to love. He had vowed once he would never love again . . . not the way he had loved Susan.

It had taken a long time to get over her. Perhaps it was because of the way she had died—so abruptly, so shockingly sudden. One moment they were riding and laughing, planning their wedding, the next moment her horse had reared when a snake slithered nearby. Susan fell and was silent—just like that. In an instant her neck was broken and she was dead. Only time had helped heal the hurt and the shock of it.

He was still young enough to start a family, realized he couldn't wander the rest of his life with no purpose, no family. He wanted that more than anything—family; for he had lost all of his at such a young age. He had enjoyed supper with the Walterses, enjoyed the family atmosphere, Sam's piano playing and singing. It was obvious she would be a good wife and mother, a good homemaker. She was beautiful and healthy and brave . . . and she wanted him. He could see it in her eyes. If he treated her right, was careful and patient with her, he could mold her into a woman who knew how to enjoy her man, who would welcome him in her bed. The thought of it brought an ache to his insides that made it all the more difficult to get to sleep, not to mention the hard wagon bed and the cold night air.

He was not sure how long he lay thinking about Sam, or how much time had passed in fits of sleep and wakefulness before he heard a muffled voice. Immediately all his senses were alert. He reached across to George, who grasped his arm. "I hear it," he whispered.

Blake moved closer to him, careful not to make the wagon move. "Stay low," he whispered. "Let them get into the firelight. If they start shooting, let them use up their bullets before we start firing back."

Both men remained rigid and ready, stiffening when there came a sudden burst of gunfire, the sound of several men all firing their guns at the same time. Obviously they were unloading their weapons into the bedrolls, and in his heart, Blake's hatred for Nick West only deepened at the thought of being brutally ambushed in his sleep. So, this was the way West operated. But again, he would be able to prove nothing.

"Now!" he growled to George.

Both men rose, cocking their rifles and standing up to aim them over the side of the freight wagon. Their startled attackers looked up at them in surprise as both men began firing. The bushwhackers returned fire with what bullets they had left, and pieces of wood splintered off the top of the wagon bed. George and Blake both ignored the stinging wood, firing back and taking down four men in only seconds. Horses whinnied and mules brayed amid the sounds of men crying out in pain.

In moments the air hung silent. Blake leaped out of the wagon, hurrying to inspect the bodies of the men who had been shot. Only one was still barely alive. He leaned over the man, grasping him by the shirtfront. "Who sent you?" he growled.

The man just moaned. His eyes rolled back and he

was dead. Blake dropped his body. "Damn! We should have left one of them alive! I need proof that *West* ordered this!"

"Let's search them. Maybe they've got something on them," George suggested.

Both men rummaged through the bodies, finding identification, but nothing in the way of evidence that would link them to Nick West. "All for nothing," Blake muttered throwing down a wallet.

"Should we report this in Independence?" George asked.

Blake sighed, studying the bodies. "No. Too many proslavery factions in that town. They might turn it on us. We'll bury them right here. Keep their identification and we'll report it back in Lawrence when we return. We'll have a lot more support there. Keep the shot up blankets and gear for proof. They're probably all proslavery men snuck in from Missouri, living in Lawrence now—Nick West's men. Maybe we'll hand the identification over to West himself and watch the look on his face when he sees we're still alive. We'll know then and there if he was behind this." He let out a light groan then, grasping at the top of his left shoulder.

"Blake! You hurt?"

"Not bad. Just up here in the top of my shoulder. The bullet must have gone clean through."

"Let me fix it up for you. Come over by the fire and take off your jacket and shirt." George hurried to get a canteen and some whiskey to wash and cleanse the wound, while Blake sat down near the fire and added some wood to it. George came back to inspect the wound. "A few inches the wrong way and it would have been your neck or your face," he said with concern.

"At least the wound gives me more proof that they

were shooting at us," Blake answered. "Not that anyone will call it murder either way. He shook his head. "This isn't just a small, illegal fight here and there, George. This is war. You said it was coming. I think it's already here. It might take Congress a while to face what's happening, and in the meantime a lot of innocent people are going to get hurt."

George poured whiskey on the wound and Blake winced. "You're right. This is war, all right," he answered. "You think it's right, not reporting this till we get back to Lawrence? That will be three of four weeks."

"In these times, what does it matter? There are killings along the border every day. If whoever did this wants to know what happened, they'll come looking and find the graves. Maybe they'll think you and I are in two of them. Who knows?"

George pressed a piece of cloth against Blake's wound. "All *I* know is, I've killed a couple of white men. My kind doesn't need reason. He hangs anyway."

"You aren't going to hang. You won't be with me when I report it, and I'll swear you didn't do any of the killing. Lawrence is becoming the center for abolitionists. Men like West can't last there much longer. We were attacked, and that gave us the right. It's no different from settlers shooting back at bushwhackers."

"I didn't think things would get this bad."

"Neither did I. That's why we've got to stop the supply runs. It's less safe for you than for me. If bushwhackers manage to shoot me down, they'll take you off into slavery again. Or they might accuse you of murder and get you hanged. This gives us all the more reason to finish up with Hale and get back to Lawrence and stay there."

"It won't ever be settled as long as that Nick West is alive."

Blake gritted his teeth as George wrapped gauze around his shoulder and under his arm. "That's the biggest problem. Maybe I'll find a way to take care of it. I just wish the bastard didn't work behind other men, always looking so innocent. Someday he's going to slip up, and I'm going to be there when it happens."

George tied the gauze, then inspected his work. "I'm not sure how good a job I did. There's not enough light."

"It's good enough. Thanks. In the morning we'll bury the bodies and run off their horses. I don't want to be caught in Independence with a bunch of horses that don't belong to us."

George turned and picked up a blanket, holding it up to look at the holes in it. "Damn," he muttered. "Good thing you thought to sleep in the wagon or we'd have a lot of air going through us right now."

Blake stared at the holes, feeling a shiver move down his spine. "I wish the President could see this," he answered. "He'd see this country is already at war."

Samantha sorted and stacked signs and pamphlets at the printer's office, glad to be out of the house again. It had been three weeks since Blake and George left, and she had spent most of that time in the house. Missing Blake—and worrying about him—had made the time pass much too slowly. She had spent that time embroidering, reading, playing the piano, and sometimes helping her father prepare his sermons.

Now that she could help in the printing office

again, the time would go faster. Surely Blake would come any day now. Her heart raced at the thought, and every morning she bathed and primped herself in anticipation of seeing him again. Would he forget her while he was gone, maybe change his mind? How did she know he didn't have another woman in whom he was interested, maybe back in Independence? She had not thought of that until now. Surely such a handsome man attracted women easily— women who knew much more about men than she did, women more clever at snaring a man.

"I'm taking these up the street to pass them out," her father told her then, interrupting her thoughts. "You stay right here until I get back."

"Father, I'm perfectly capable of helping—"

"No. I want no more incidents like the one you had a few weeks ago. You stay right here with Mr. Stetson." He took an armful of pamphlets and a stack of the abolitionist newspaper he and Joseph Stetson, the owner of the print shop, had begun publishing, and headed outside. Samantha sat down in the back room, picking up the newspaper to read through it. It contained articles about government decisions on states' rights and slavery, a full explanation of the Kansas-Nebraska Act, and stories of atrocities told firsthand by freed and runaway slaves.

Samantha scanned the articles she herself had helped Mr. Stetson lay out, checking to be sure they had come out with no printing mistakes. She heard a commotion in the front office then, and she tossed the newspaper aside, jumping up from her chair to go and see what was wrong.

"Get out of here, you troublemaking hoodlums," she heard Stetson ordering someone. There came a thud and a grunt, and Samantha hurried into the front office to see Stetson lying on the floor next to the press, his head bleeding badly. Fred Brewster stood over him, holding a piece of steel pipe.

"You're the troublemaker," he sneered. "Printing that abolitionist newspaper." He looked up then to see Samantha staring wide-eyed at him, and Brewster broke into a grin. "Destroy everything you see," he told the men who were with him. "I'll take care of Miss Walters."

Samantha turned, heading for the back door, hearing the awful sounds of equipment being smashed and overturned. Strong hands grabbed her before she could open the door, and an arm came around her neck, nearly choking her. She felt Fred Brewster's big hand grasping at her breasts, while he slobbered at her cheek.

"You've got to learn what happens to people who make their beds with niggers," he sneered. "We know what you are now, don't we, honey?"

Samantha began kicking backward at his shins, and he let go just enough that she could scream. She grabbed his arm and bit hard, making him cry out. He jerked her around and she felt a hard blow to the side of her face. "Once I'm through, we'll be sweethearts," he told her, hitting her again and knocking her to the floor. "Nobody is going to see us back here. You'll come looking for me after this, honey. You'll belong to Fred Brewster, and you'll be obligated to be just mine. Once a man claims his woman, she's got to *stay* with him."

Everything was black before her eyes, and she could taste blood. She wanted to fight him, but her body would not respond. She felt nauseated at his ugly words, felt him ripping at the bodice of her dress, felt his hands on her breasts, while in the background there continued the awful sounds of destruction. Fred tried to kiss her, while his big hands fumbled under her dress, ripping at her bloomers.

"We want a turn when you're through." She heard another voice. Someone else was in the room, watching! Her fury knew no bounds. Not only was the thought of Fred Brewster and his friends touching her revolting, but she suddenly thought of Blake. Somehow she felt she belonged to him, wondered what he would think if someone else claimed her first. She could not let it be this way! From somewhere deep inside she managed another scream. She reached out with her hand, feeling for anything she could use for a weapon. She felt something heavy, not even knowing it was a steel weight Stetson had resting on a stack of loose paper to keep it from blowing around when he opened the back door. She swung the weight and hit a solid object. Brewster grunted and rolled off her.

"The little bitch," someone growled. "We'll teach her, Fred."

"Jeez, look at her," someone else said. "Get the rest of her clothes off."

She felt more hands then, felt more clothes being ripped away. There came another blow to her face when she again tried to scream. Through a haze she thought she heard more voices then, shouts of anger. Samantha felt all holds released on her, and she crawled away amid the sounds of men scuffling and fighting.

"You'll all hang for this!" someone yelled.

"Get that one who ran out" came another voice. "Bastards!"

"How's Stetson? He gonna live?"

"I don't know. Get him to a doctor, and tell the doc to get back to my place as soon as he can."

Someone put something around her, and Samantha realized her dress had been torn nearly completely off her. Her humiliation knew no bounds. "It's all right, honey." She heard her father's voice then, felt him pick her up in his arms. "This is the end of it. There aren't many proslavery men left in Lawrence. Once we put away Brewster and his friends, there will be a lot less danger."

"We've got to start patrolling the streets," someone else said as Samantha felt herself being carried outside. She kept her father's jacket pulled close around her, heard people mumbling, men cursing.

"Lawrence will not stand for this," someone spoke up. "From here on, we fight even harder for a free territory!"

People cheered. "If Stetson and the preacher's daughter can risk their lives, so can we" came another voice.

Samantha remained huddled against her father. Had she been raped? Everything was such a blur she wasn't even sure. She could only remember the ugly words, the prying hands, the horror of Fred Brewster and his friends mauling her. What would Blake think of her now? Was she somehow soiled? How could she bear the shame of it? How could she ever tell Blake?

"What happened?" She recognized Clyde Beecher's voice and wondered how Beecher always managed to suddenly appear when her father had a particular need.

"Fred Brewster and his hoodlums," her father replied. "They attacked the printing office. Stetson is in a bad way."

"Good God. You take Samantha home. I'll send for Dr. Beckett."

Beecher watched the reverend hurry away with Samantha, the scowl on his face having nothing to do with concern over what had just happened. He

71

was upset that Brewster and his thugs had attacked Samantha. One of Nick West's men had been paid by West to casually comment to the boys that the abolitionist cause would suffer a severe setback if Stetson's print shop was destroyed and Stetson himself got a good thrashing. West knew the suggestion was all the young bullies needed to spur them on.

Still, Beecher was sure West wanted the boys to simply rough up Stetson, not to nearly kill the man. And attacking Samantha was certainly not part of the plan. The entire incident had only spurred the town abolitionists into more action, something West did not want. Now more drastic measures would have to be taken.

Beecher headed for the doctor's office. As soon as he told him to tend to Samantha Walters, he would report what had happened to Nick West. West was going to be angry that Brewster and his hoodlums had carried the attack further than intended. People would be outraged by an attack on the preacher's daughter, but maybe after things quieted down, they would all think twice about standing up against slavery. The violence was no longer confined to the border areas, but now had come to Lawrence.

He wondered what had happened to Blake Hastings and his Negro. The men sent to kill Blake and capture George Freedom had never returned. But neither had Samantha heard anything from Blake, he was sure. Beecher had dined at the Walters home often enough to know Sam's moods, and he knew by the despondent way she replied to his questions that there had been no word from Blake.

Where were Blake and his nigger? And what had happened to Nick's men? Who was dead and who was alive? He entered Dr. Beckett's office, where the man was already working on Joseph Stetson's badly bleeding head. Stetson looked dead. "When you're through here, the Walters will be needing you," Beecher told the doctor. "Those thugs attacked Samantha Walters in the back room of the printing office."

Beckett looked up at him in alarm. "What did they do to her?"

"Don't know for sure, except she got beat up pretty bad, and her clothes were half torn off. It's pretty obvious what happened."

The doctor and the man helping him looked at each other in anger and concern. "I'll get over there soon as I can," Dr. Beckett answered.

Beecher left, heading for his own house to saddle a horse and go to Nick West's place north of town. He grinned. In spite of Brewster's stupid mistake, he enjoyed planting the thought in people's minds that Samantha Walters had been raped. It served her right to have to carry the shame of it, even if it interfered with West's plans. She was such a cocky little spitfire. Maybe this would take some of the air out of her and make her stay home where she belonged.

Four

Nick West looked up from the table, his face paling slightly at the sight of Blake Hastings walking toward him. West was about to put a bite of steak into his mouth, but set the fork back onto his plate. He dabbed at his mouth with a napkin, trying to appear casual toward a business associate with whom he was dining at one of Lawrence's better restaurants.

Blake came closer, and people stared as he tossed several money wallets onto the table, knocking over a small glass of wine. "I'll let you contact whatever relatives these bushwhackers might have," Blake said, loudly enough for others to hear. The merchant with West reddened, picking up his napkin and glancing at Blake, who was wearing a gun! He immediately scooted back his chair to get out of the way.

West cleared his throat, glancing from the wallets to Blake. "What are you talking about?"

"You know damn *well* what I'm talking about! The next time you want somebody killed, West, do the job *yourself!* You hired men to kill my father and you hired men to kill *me!*"

The color rose in West's face, glowing a dark red

against the starched white collar of his shirt. His blue eyes turned icy. "I'm getting damn tired of you accusing me of murder in front of other people," the man answered in a gruff voice.

"I don't make such accusations unless I'm sure of them. I've already reported this to the sheriff, who I might remind you is an abolitionist. He and a lot of other people in Lawrence will be watching you closely from here on, West. You proslavery men are getting less popular all the time."

The startled merchant who had scooted away slowly rose, deciding he wanted nothing to do with another man's argument. He hurried out, worried that if others in the popular restaurant connected him with a proslavery man, they might boycott his establishment.

"All the identification and money is there," Blake told West. "Horses and gear were turned loose. If you want to find them, send some men to see me and I can tell you where these men are buried and where I left their horses." He picked up the expensive bottle of wine West had ordered and poured some into an empty glass, taking a swallow. "You live pretty high, don't you, West?"

"Get the hell out! You have no right coming in here and embarrassing me this way!"

"What's wrong? You disappointed to see me, sorry I'm not in a grave out there on the trail to Independence? You didn't really think I wasn't ready for an ambush, did you?" Blake slammed the bottle down. Some patrons jumped in their seats at the sound; several looked away, embarrassed for Nick West but wondering if the stranger was telling the truth. Blake was so intent on getting at West that he didn't even notice Clyde Beecher sitting several tables away, watching the entire incident with keen interest. "I can't prove you hired those men or I'd have the sheriff here with me," Blake continued, his dark eyes blazing. "But you and I both know who was behind this. Your days are numbered, West. They were numbered the day your men hanged my father. It's *your* turn to start looking over your shoulder!"

In an instant Blake had his gun out of its holster, and people gasped when he rammed the barrel under West's chin. West's eyes widened with both rage and fear, and he stiffened, afraid to move a muscle. Beecher sat still, wondering if Blake would be crazy enough to shoot West right here in cold blood.

"Someday it will be just you and me, West," Blake sneered. "I'll get my revenge. Not in public like this—not in any way that will get me hanged. But I'll get it! You think about that!"

Blake lowered the gun, then suddenly shot it into West's steak, the loud explosion making women scream and causing several people to duck under their tables. West jerked back at the shot, and his dinner plate lay shattered, glass mixed in with meat, some of both on the floor and in West's lap.

"Enjoy your meal," Blake told West. When he turned and walked out, people slowly climbed back into their seats. A few got up and left immediately, and West sat clutching his napkin, staring at the ruined steak. With a shaking hand he reached out and picked up one of the wallets, opening it to see which one of his men it belonged to. If all four of the men he had sent after Blake were dead, he had lost a lot of good help, but he reasoned that at least none of them had lived long enough to name West as the one who had sent them. If one was still alive, Blake would have used him as a witness and would have had him arrested. "Bastard," he muttered under his breath.

A waitress came from the kitchen, looking frightened to death as she approached West. "Is there . . . something I can do, Mr. West?"

West forced back his anger. He needed to put on a good show for the others present. Most knew he was against abolition, but he didn't want any of them thinking he had anything to do with bushwhackers. That was no way to win people to his side. "Yes," he answered, loud enough for the others to hear. "You can clean up this mess for me and get me another steak. I'll not let that lying idiot ruin my meal. The man is crazy!"

He stood up, brushing pieces of meat and glass from his neatly pressed pants. "Mr. Hastings apparently had a run-in with bushwhackers, but I wouldn't have the slightest idea why. Perhaps he's running guns to abolitionists along the border, helping keep the bloody border wars going. *He's* the violent one, not me." West looked around at the others. "We all have our beliefs, but most of us do not believe in bloodshed," he spoke up louder. "That man who just left is the kind who keeps the violence alive. I have no idea why he suspects me of having anything to do with what might have happened to *him*. I only know we have to settle our differences *peacefully*, not the way Blake Hastings just tried to settle them!"

"That's right," one of the others chimed in. "We don't agree with your beliefs about slavery, Mr. West, but we do agree that the bloodshed along the border has to stop."

"It's a disgrace." Beecher picked up on West's cue. "The Reverend Walters, a confirmed abolitionist, would not agree with such behavior. It's men like Blake Hastings who keep the hatred fed, who cause some of the bloodshed. No matter how right or wrong the belief, we can't keep killing people over it."

West glanced at Beecher, pretending to hardly know him. "Thank you. I completely agree," he told the man. He looked away, picking up the wallets and nodding to a waiter passing by. "Do me a favor and run these back to the sheriff. You tell him I have no idea who these men are or why Blake Hastings dumped these on my table and accosted me in public. Tell the sheriff to find the families of these men himself."

"Yes, sir," the waiter answered, taking the wallets.

Beecher rose from his table, fully understanding what West would want him to do. He walked past West, paying his bill and leaving to head for the Walters home. The last thing West wanted was for Blake Hastings to become too familiar and friendly with the family and with Samantha Walters. Their combined force in the cause of freedom could be too damaging. Now that Beecher and West knew Blake was definitely still alive, it was time to discourage the man from staying in Lawrence. The best way to do that was to work on Reverend Walters, find a way to stop any relationship between Blake and Samantha before it had a chance to grow.

Blake smoothed his brown cotton broadcloth jacket, wondering if the silk waistcoat he wore beneath it made it look as though he was trying too hard to make an impression. His entire suit of clothes, from his wide-brimmed hat of the latest fashion to his brown, high-topped shoes, was new. He had gone to the bath house and soaked himself for a good hour, helping soothe his anger and putting

79

him in a better mood to call on Samantha. With a clean-shaven face and leaving behind his six-gun, he felt he couldn't strike a more acceptable pose than he did at this moment.

It had been nearly a month since he had seen Samantha. Would the same desire still be there in her eyes? He studied the lovely frosted design on the window of the front door of the Walters home before knocking, thinking how he would like to have a home like this some day, with shutters decorating the windows, lace curtains, and a broad porch where he and Samantha could sit in the evenings and talk about their day. If things worked out with Samantha the way he hoped, he would work hard to give her a nice home.

He knocked at the door, then looked back to make sure the sleek black mare he had purchased in Independence was well tied. The door opened, and he turned to meet the eyes of Reverend Walters, quickly removing his hat. "Hello, Reverend Walters. It's good to see you again."

Though Walters nodded and offered his hand, there was a strangely apprehensive look in his eyes. "Hello, Blake. Come right in. Is George with you?"

"He decided not to come with me this visit. I told him this time, it's rather personal."

An almost sad look came into Walters's eyes. "I had a feeling it was. Come into the parlor."

Blake followed the man inside the house, hanging his hat on the hat rack near the door, thinking what a fine housekeeper Milicent Walters was. The hardwood floor was polished to a shine. He walked behind the reverend through the sliding wooden doors to the left and into the parlor. Walters closed the doors and offered Blake a seat. Blake began to feel apprehensive. Something was wrong. He had half expected Samantha to see him coming, to hurry down the stairs to greet him.

"Milicent just took some tea up to Samantha," the reverend told him, taking a chair across from Blake. "She'll tell Sam you're here. It's up to my daughter whether or not she wants to see you, but I am not certain it would be good for either of you."

Blake frowned. "I don't understand, Reverend. Why wouldn't she want to see me? I mean, she knew I'd be coming back, *wanted* me to come. I might as well say it out. I came here to ask your permission to call on Sam. I've come to Lawrence to stay, Reverend Walters. I quit my freighting job."

Walters's eyebrows arched. "Well, that's good. Perhaps staying right here in Lawrence will mean you won't get involved in any more dangerous doings and violent encounters."

"Violent encounters? I'm afraid you have me a little confused, Reverend."

"I'm talking about what happened earlier today in a restaurant." Reverend Walters watched a touch of anger move into Blake's eyes. "Blake, I'm as incensed over the proslavery faction as you, but I don't preach violence, and I don't like my Samantha being directly involved. Trouble seems to follow you, and she's been through enough—"

"What do you mean—been through enough? What is it you aren't telling me? Why do you have to ask Samantha if she wants to see me? I figured she'd be down here in a second."

The reverend sighed, leaning forward and resting his elbows on his knees. "There was a ruckus at the print shop a few days ago. Fred Brewster, one of the town bullies, and a young man who's fallen in with the proslavery men, attacked Joe Stetson and wrecked the print shop. Stetson is in a bad way, still unconscious, not expected to live. They're waiting trial until they know if he lives or dies."

"What does that have to do with Samantha?"

Reverend Walters frowned, the sadness coming into his eyes. "She . . . uh . . . she was in the back room of the printer's at the time. She'd been helping me do some collating. I had just left before Brewster and his thugs arrived. They attacked Samantha—beat her—" The man's voice choked and he stopped for a moment, while Blake sat listening with growing rage. "By the time help arrived, her . . . clothes were badly torn and she had been terribly humiliated. She's been very despondent ever since. Thinks she's somehow soiled."

"My God," Blake muttered, rising to pace. "Did those bastards rape her?"

"No. Her mother and I keep telling her she shouldn't feel so ashamed. The doctor examined her, which only added to her humiliation. He said the only damage is the bruises and scratches—and of course the emotional damage—but she wasn't . . . they didn't have time to do what they intended to do. In fact, Brewster himself was hurt pretty bad when Samantha hit him in the head with a steel paperweight."

Blake could not help a small inner smile at the remark. He could just picture the fight Sam would have put up. He stared out the window at a carriage passing by. "I hope Brewster hangs. If he doesn't, I'll find a way to take care of him myself," he said, his voice gruff with anger.

Walters sighed, rising from his chair. "That is part of the reason I'm not sure you should allow yourself to be too interested in Samantha," he told Blake. "Your temper—"

"Who told you about the incident at the restaurant?" Blake interrupted, turning to face the reverend.

Walters straightened defensively. "Why, Clyde Beecher did. He was here just an hour or so ago."

Blake's dark eyes blazed. "I'm not surprised. I don't trust the man, Reverend, and you shouldn't, either!"

Walters's eyes widened. "Clyde Beecher is a devout Christian, a good friend of the family."

"Reverend, he just wants to keep me away from you and Samantha because he knows that together we can fight even harder for the free vote."

The reverend waved him off. "I find that hard to believe."

"I know you do, but I think Beecher is up to no good. Just like with Nick West, I have no proof, but I know it inside. Don't you even want to know *why* I confronted West today? For God's sake, Reverend, I'm on *your* side! You must know that."

"Of course I do. I admire your courage in befriending George Freedom and in helping that Mr. Hale in his abolitionist movement. But I don't preach violence, Blake."

"Sometimes violence is the only way. I told you about my father, Reverend. I have every right to believe Nick West was responsible! Don't you think it's more than a coincidence after I had that run-in with West here a month ago that just two nights later my camp was attacked? Four men came after us, Reverend—*four!* If George and I hadn't made up fake bedrolls, we'd each have a good twenty bullet holes in us and we'd be six feet under—*if* those men would even have bothered to *bury* us! I still have a sore shoulder from taking one of those bullets! I know exactly who was responsible, and embarrassing Nick West at that restaurant is a far cry from what the man *really* deserves! I'm not a violent man by nature. I want peace as much as the next man. But contrary to your teachings, I'm not one to turn the other cheek, Reverend. I'm sorry, but I don't really think God meant for us to take that teaching so literally. I think that when what we believe in is right, sometimes He expects us to be more aggressive. Why else would He have drowned the Egyptians in the Red Sea or a world full of sinners in the Great Flood? Why else—"

Blake stopped talking when the parlor doors opened. Samantha stood in the entrance, wearing a plain, soft gray dress. Her long dark hair was pulled back into a bun, and Blake thought her face looked thinner, paler. His heart ached at the lingering bruises on her face. She blushed when their eyes met, and he saw the mixture of joy and shame in her eyes.

She looked at her father. "I'd like to talk to Blake alone, Father. It's all right. Mother is bringing both of us some tea."

Walters scowled, walking up to her. "Are you sure, Samantha?"

Samantha lifted her chin slightly, and Blake saw a stubborn pride taking over. "Yes. And please don't judge Blake by the trouble he's had in Lawrence. We know firsthand how easily violence can come to us without the asking, Father. Sometimes we have to fight back. Have you forgotten what might have happened to me the last time Blake was here if he had not been there to defend me?"

"I haven't forgotten. I also have not forgotten that it was because of his fight with Nick West that it all came about."

"He was fighting for his honor, for his dead father. And he was protecting George Freedom. Isn't that what *we're* trying to do? Protect men like George?"

"My first duty is to protect my family."

"Then keep Clyde Beecher out of your house,"

Blake told the man.

Walters looked at him. "If you want to continue to see my daughter, Blake, I am asking you to say no more against my good friend. I won't listen to it, and I won't allow any more visits from you if you continue to insinuate Mr. Beecher is some kind of spy. I like you very much, Blake. I'm very sorry about your past tragedies, and I understand why it is difficult for you to trust some people, but I know in my heart you're wrong about Clyde Beecher. As far as the trouble you've had, that didn't bother me the last time you were here. But I have lately seen for myself the ugliness of violence . . . ." Samantha turned away and walked to the piano at her father's words. "And you have to understand why I want to protect Samantha from any more such incidents—why I worry that letting you see her could bring her more harm."

"I understand completely," Blake answered. "I have no idea if Sam even wants to keep seeing me. We still hardly know each other. But I can assure you that if I *do* keep seeing her, I'll make damn sure no trouble comes her way. I would protect her with my life."

Their eyes held as Milicent Walters brought in a tray of tea. "Yes, I suppose you would," the reverend said to Blake. "I can't help realizing what happened a few days ago was no one's fault but my own. I shouldn't have taken her there in the first place. I guess even I am responsible for some of the things that have happened and I have no right putting it all on you."

"Stop blaming yourself, Father," Samantha told him, turning to face both men. "And stop talking as though I'm a child who isn't even listening. Please just leave us alone."

Milicent set the tray of tea on a table, turning to her husband. "Let them talk, Howard. What harm is there in it right here in our own house? Just remember that Blake feels just as strongly as we do about slavery. At least his presence has gotten Samantha out of bed and downstairs."

Walters sighed, his eyes showing the deep grief he still felt over what had happened to his daughter. He left the room, and Blake turned to Samantha, stepping closer.

"I apologize for Father's behavior," Samantha told him. "He's been different since it happened— angrier, more defensive."

"That isn't difficult to understand." Blake ached to hold her. "I'm the one who's sorry, Sam."

"For what?"

"For not being here at the time."

She turned away. "It wouldn't have mattered. Even if you had been there at that particular time and place, you would have ended up being attacked by all five of them and getting hurt."

"I think *they* are the ones who would be hurting. I believe I'll pay Fred Brewster a little visit in jail!"

She turned quickly to face him again. "Please don't! You've gotten yourself into enough trouble."

"Don't worry about me."

"I can't help it." Her eyes teared. "You . . . didn't write. I thought all kinds of terrible things." She looked him over. "Are you all right now? I heard you tell Father you were ambushed and shot."

"I'm all right." He reached out hesitantly to take her arm. He felt her stiffen as he led her to a love-seat, and he imagined the fear and revulsion Brewster and his thugs had planted in her mind against men. He knew it would take him a while to bring back that eager desire he had seen in her eyes when he first met her. "Sam, I didn't write like I promised because I didn't want Beecher to find out I was all right. I have a feeling he would have run right to Nick West with the news, and I wanted to keep West wondering until I got back here myself where I could keep an eye on him."

She looked at her lap. "You're wrong about Beecher, I'm sure. But be that as it may, you told me not to mention your letters in front of him, and I wouldn't have."

"I was afraid you'd let something slip. It wouldn't have been so important under normal circumstances, but after we were ambushed, I had to be even more careful. I'm sorry."

"Is George all right?"

"He's fine. I got a room at a boardinghouse across town, and George is staying in a small shack the blacksmith agreed to rent to him. We're going to look for work tomorrow."

She met his eyes again. Oh, how handsome he looked, and how good he smelled! If only she wasn't filled now with this ugly dread. He seemed so good and so gentle when he was around her. But what if she was his wife and he had husbandly rights? Would he force himself on her? Would he make it ugly like Fred Brewster had? Surely not Blake! And he must truly care for her. He had come back to Lawrence to stay. "You aren't going away again?" she asked.

He shook his head. "I left the freighting job. I'm staying right here in Lawrence."

"Because of Nick West?"

A smile drifted across his full lips as he searched her lovely eyes. "No. Because of you. That is, if you'll let me come visiting."

Her eyes teared more. How she hated the fact that she cried so easily now. It wasn't like her. She turned away again. "Are you sure you want to?"

He put an arm on the back of the loveseat and reached over with his other hand to take her own hand gently. "Why shouldn't I want to? Thoughts of you have been driving me crazy ever since I first left, Sam. You're beautiful and daring and brave and—"

"Stop it," she interrupted, sniffing. "I'm . . . it's different now."

"No, it isn't," he said, his voice firmer. "Damn it, Sam, look at me. Stop hanging your head like that. Where's the proud, feisty Samantha Walters I left a few weeks ago?"

Samantha swallowed, wiping at a tear with her free hand. "She got the pride beat out of her," she answered. "A roomful of men saw—"

"Samantha, nothing could change my feelings for you. Good God, it wasn't *your* fault! You were there for the right reasons, being the brave and determined woman you are. Your father says you even clobbered Fred Brewster a pretty good one with a paperweight. You gave them what for, just like the man who grabbed the whip from you that day I met you. What in God's name makes you think you have to be ashamed of anything?"

She shrugged. "Some people in town probably think the worst. And . . . if Fred Brewster goes to trial, I'll have to testify . . . what he did to me."

"And you'll *do* it. You'll tell that jury in a loud, strong voice that that bastard attacked you for no good reason. You'll tell them with the pride of a woman who is brave and strong and was totally in the right."

"Fred might say bad things about me."

"People in this town know you, Samantha. They know your reputation. They won't believe a word of it."

She sniffed and wiped at a tear. "I was . . . mostly afraid of what *you* would think."

He touched her chin, gently making her look at him. "I'll tell you what I think." He lightly touched her bruises with the back of his hand. "I think I'll have a hard time holding back when I see Fred Brewster. I think it will be very difficult for me not to kill him. And I think you're just as beautiful and brave as ever. The shame will be in hanging your head, Samantha. The shame will come only if you refuse to testify at that trial as to *exactly* what happened! Don't let Fred Brewster get away with this."

The touch of his fingers sent a surprising warmth through her body. She wondered how one man's touch could be so revolting and another's so beautiful. "Will you be there?"

"You know I will."

Their eyes held, and again he was close enough to kiss her; but he knew this was not the time. He struggled to keep his rage bottled up while he was with her, not wanting to upset her any further. He kept a hand at the side of her face and leaned forward, gently kissing only her forehead. "You'll never be hurt again, not while I'm here. That's a promise."

"I'm afraid the way things are getting, you would have to be with me practically twenty-four hours a day to keep a promise like that," she answered. She met his eyes, and she knew he was thinking he'd like to do just that. She blushed at the remark, pulling slightly away. "Father says things are getting worse, that the border wars aren't just on the border anymore."

Blake sighed, leaning forward to rest his elbows on his knees. Samantha noticed how strong his hands looked, shivered at the memory of the feel of big hands slamming into her face. She wanted to cry at imagining Blake could do such a thing. She knew instinctively that he never would, and she chastised herself for letting Fred Brewster destroy her good thoughts.

"I'm afraid your father is probably right," he answered. "George and I both feel the trouble won't stop at places like Lawrence. It's going to eventually involve the whole country. Some southern states are already threatening to secede from the Union. It's like a big rock rolling downhill—nothing can stop it."

"It makes a person afraid to . . . to care too much. We don't know what's going to happen to us or to our loved ones."

He wondered if she considered him a loved one. "We can't let it stop us from living and loving, Sam. Life has to go on. We can only take a day at a time."

She nodded. "I'm glad you're all right. Four men! You could have been—" She looked away. "If you had never come back, I'm not sure what I would have done. It would have been like everything that mattered was finished, especially after my attack. In one sense I wanted so much for you to come back, and in another sense I dreaded it—wanting to know you were all right but afraid of what you would think."

He touched her shoulder. "Well, now you know I'm all right and that I'm here to stay. And you know what I think." He sighed, squeezing her shoulder. "It must have been terrible for you. It makes me sick that I wasn't here."

He felt her begin to tremble. "It's not that I'm the kind who is easily horrified. I've seen violent things—like that fight you were in that day, and I usually fight back when I'm threatened. It wouldn't have been so bad if they had just hit me. But . . . the

90

other—" She stifled a sob, throwing her head back and breathing deeply.

"Sam, why don't you just let it out? Go ahead and cry."

"No! I won't let him make me cry!"

"Then do it for yourself. It's God's way of helping us get rid of the pain inside. Do you think I've never cried, just because I'm a man? I learned at an early age that crying can help in the healing."

Her body jerked in another sob, and she covered her eyes. "I don't want to cry in front of you."

He pulled her against his shoulder. "Damn it, Sam, it's all right." She let the tears come, and Blake held her, relishing the smell of her hair, the feel of her in his arms. Rage tore through him at the picture of Fred Brewster and his thugs hurting her, trying to rape her. Thank God they had not taken what he was beginning to believe more and more belonged to him. After several minutes her tears abated. Blake dug a clean handkerchief from his back pocket and handed it to her. "Feels better, doesn't it?"

She nodded, sniffing and blowing her nose. "I'm sorry. What a terrible welcome."

"Let's make one rule right now. You quit apologizing—for what happened, for your condition, for everything. Nothing was your fault. You make your mind up right now that you're going to get Fred Brewster for this. You're going to walk the streets with your head held high and never show an ounce of shame for anything. Agreed?"

She managed a slight smile. "Agreed."

"And you won't let what happened make you distrust all men—especially not me. I would never hurt you, Samantha. Surely you know that."

She met his eyes again, feeling suddenly stronger. "I know," she answered. "Will you stay for supper?

You can bring George."

He smiled at her. "I'd rather take you out to supper, if your father doesn't mind."

She touched her face. "But . . . my bruises still show."

"So? You aren't going to be ashamed, remember? Besides, a little powder and leaving your hair down loose will help." He touched her hair. "I like it that way. Don't wear it all scraped into a bun again. You have such beautiful hair, Sam."

She felt suddenly lost in him, surprised at her feelings after what had happened. "Then I'll wear it loose," she answered. She drew back then, almost afraid of the intense feelings he managed to arouse in her. Bad memories kept interfering with these new, wonderful emotions. "You aren't in any trouble over the ambush?" she asked, suddenly wanting to change the subject.

"No. It was bushwhackers. The sheriff understands. I did what I had to do."

"You . . . killed all of them?"

"They would have killed me, Sam. It was dark, hard to aim just to injure. I just kept shooting until none of them shot back."

"It doesn't bother you . . . killing men?"

His eyes showed his sorrow. "It always bothers a man, at least one who's got a conscience. But I can't fully regret killing men who meant to kill me, Sam. As soon as they kicked at those bedrolls and discovered no one was in them, they would have discovered us in the wagon. We made up fake bedrolls, letting them empty their guns into them."

"What about George? Surely you didn't kill all of them alone. George must have done some shooting."

He put a finger to her lips. "Don't you know what that would mean for him? No, ma'am. *I* did all the shooting. That's how it got told, and that's how it will stay told. Don't ever bring it up, especially in front of Beecher."

"You still don't trust him."

"No. I won't bother your father with the subject again, but I still want you to be careful."

She wondered how she could be sitting here letting him touch her, this man who had killed other men. Still, what he had done had been part of something close to war. If there *was* a war, men would join armies and march on each other and kill each other, and no one would think anything of it. Somehow war was supposed to make it all right.

"I'll pray for you," she told him. "Surely God understands why you did what you did."

"I hope so," He rose, taking her hand, and she stood up with him. "I want to be with you as much as I can, Sam. I'll even come to your father's church on Sundays."

She smiled. "It's not so terrible."

He laughed lightly, and she realized she loved his laugh. "Heaven knows I probably need it." He grasped her arms, sobering. "You all right now?"

She smiled. "Much better. Thank you for listening, for putting up with the tears."

"If you can't cry in front of someone, they aren't much of a friend. I like to think we're at least that— friends."

"Yes. I'm glad to call you and George both my friends."

Their eyes held, and he could almost taste her lips. He reminded himself he had to be very careful now. She was still full of ugly memories. "Thank you for that much. I'll rent a buggy and be by around seven to pick you up."

"I'll be ready." They both felt the unspoken

emotions, each afraid for their own personal reasons to say too much too soon, both wondering if it was really possible to be thinking of love when they knew each other such a short time. Samantha pulled away from him then, going to the doors and opening them. She called to her parents and told them Blake had asked her to supper. The reverend came inside and faced Blake with a mixture of doubt and relief in his eyes.

"I suppose it's all right, as long as you promise us, Blake, that there will be no trouble. You won't wear a gun."

Blake stepped closer. "I won't wear a gun. But you know as well as I that the way things are in this town right now I can't promise there won't be trouble. I certainly don't intend to start any myself, if that's what you mean. I just want to take Sam to supper, get her out of the house. It will do her good."

The reverend sighed. "Yes, I suppose it will." He brightened a little when he studied his daughter. "You already look better, Sam. I guess if Blake can do that for you, I can let him take you to supper."

Blake did not want any hard feelings between himself and Samantha's father. "I want to keep seeing your daughter, Reverend. If that means saying no more about Beecher, then I'll keep my opinion to myself. I apologize for suggesting your friend might be up to no good. And I'd like to come to Sunday services if I may."

Walters glowed at that remark. "Of course! Maybe a little religion will help tame your temper."

Blake scowled, telling himself to remember Walters's background and beliefs. "I'm afraid I still feel there are times when violence is necessary, Reverend. It's a subject we'll have to discuss more."

They were interrupted then when a neighbor came

running up onto the Walters porch and pounded on the door. "Reverend," he called out. Walters opened the door. "Just thought you should know, Reverend. Joe Stetson died. I reckon that Brewster kid will be tried for murder now."

Blake looked at Samantha, and a shiver ran through her. Fred Brewster would surely be hanged now. He would not bother her again. Still, a dark cloud of hatred now hung over the whole town.

Five

Samantha clung to Blake's hand as they walked together into the courtroom ahead of Samantha's parents and Clyde Beecher. Blake glanced across the room to see Nick West seated in a small section with what Blake suspected were other proslavery people.

West turned at the sound of whispered conversation and met Blake's eyes, realizing that if looks could kill he would most certainly be a dead man. He wanted nothing more than for Blake Hastings to be the one who died, but he realized he had to be clever about it, now that Blake had threatened him twice in public. After those confrontations, and the incident when Blake was ambushed, to just have him shot down in the street would be too obvious. He would have to find a better way, and he was willing to bide his time to be sure he didn't get blamed.

Besides, he reasoned, the longer he waited, the less suspicious people would be of him. At least with Blake right here in Lawrence, he could keep an eye on him, but he did not like the idea that Blake was having the same thoughts—that he was biding his own time. And while he was at it, he was getting closer to the Walters family, something West had hoped could be stopped. Clyde Beecher had tried, working through Samantha's father, constantly reminding the preacher that Blake Hastings was a man with a volatile temper, who thought the answer to everything was using his fists. Blake had still managed to overcome the doubts Beecher kept trying to instill in Walters, and West guessed that the stubborn Samantha would probably see Blake whether her father liked it or not. Everyone in town knew Blake and Sam had been together nearly every evening since Blake returned from Independence.

West turned away as Blake and Sam walked to the front of the courtroom, Samantha sensing the whispers and stares were for her. She and Blake sat down on a long bench, and Sam stared straight ahead, anxious for this day to be over with. She could not bring herself to look over at Fred Brewster and his friends, who all sat to the left in front of the judge. Her stomach ached at the realization that probably all of them had seen her breasts and bare shoulders and her legs. Had they joked about it among themselves? Was Fred Brewster thinking about what he had seen, what he had touched?

A strong, warm hand came around her own, and she knew Blake could read her thoughts, knew her agony. In the past three weeks she had come to know the man more intimately. He had come to see her nearly every night after working at his new job at the sawmill, sometimes bringing George, often coming alone so they could take long walks and talk. Blake had a way of making her tell him everything she was feeling, and they had explored each other's childhood feelings and dreams.

Blake's own childhood had been tragic, and their

98

background and upbringing had been very different. But those differences seemed less important as they got to know each other better. They seemed to fit together perfectly, both never losing that powerful attraction they had felt at first meeting. Blake had not kissed her or made any disrespectful moves; he had only held her at times, giving her reassuring hugs or squeezing her hand in a supportive gesture, as he was doing now.

Samantha had grown to trust Blake implicitly, and she had no doubt she was in love. Neither of them had expressed it in that term, but she knew he was feeling the same way; and she felt more and more relaxed with him. Her experience with Brewster had made it all so ugly, but Blake had managed to erase the horror and replace it with an awakened desire to be a woman again.

Samantha's parents sat down beside Blake, and Clyde Beecher sat on the other side of them. Blake had not brought up the subject of Beecher since that first day he came to see her, but Samantha knew how he felt about the man, and she could sense his tension whenever Beecher joined them at the supper table. The evenings Beecher was going to be present, Blake often took Samantha out to eat instead.

Judge William Bale pounded his gavel, and the proceedings began. The jury was seated, and the judge explained the case, which everyone in the courtroom, including the jury, already knew well. Various men were called to the witness stand to testify that when they heard the commotion inside the print shop, they had entered to find Brewster and all four of his friends in the back room of the shop, standing over a nearly unconscious Samantha Walters.

All of the witnesses, including Samantha's father,

were forced to explain the condition in which they had found Samantha. Samantha just stared at the bench in front of her, her cheeks feeling hot. At one point Brewster himself snickered, and Samantha felt Blake's hand tighten over her own nearly to the point of pain. She knew it was taking all his strength to keep from charging over to Brewster and landing into him.

"The point is, Your Honor," Brewster's defense attorney said after telling Reverend Walters to be seated, "all these witnesses can testify to seeing those boys assault Miss Walters. But none of them can testify as to which boy, if any of them, actually killed Joe Stetson. My clients claim a piece of equipment fell on the man when they began raiding the shop, that his death was an accident. Now considering their age and highly emotional state, it is understandable that they might have been a little overzealous when they spotted Miss Walters. She is, after all, a beautiful young woman, and prone to place herself in dangerous situations. In these times, a young woman should stay out of such danger."

Blake's hand tightened around Samantha's again, and she knew his anger was building.

The defense attorney, Robert Knowles, continued his arguments. "Battles over the issue of slavery and states' rights go on every day, Your Honor. I contend that these boys just got carried away—that they did not intend to kill Joe Stetson, and that they should be charged only with destruction of property and assault against Miss Walters. Those charges alone will put them away long enough for them to learn a good lesson. We have no witnesses to the actual alleged assault on Mr. Stetson. Even Miss Walters, who was obviously in the back room at the time, cannot verify that these young men actually beat Mr.

100

Stetson. And considering her delicate situation, I hope this court does not intend to call on the poor woman to testify in front of this courtroom to things we already know happened to her."

"I most certainly *do* want to testify," Samantha said, rising. "I am not so delicate, Your Honor, that I can't tell the truth here and make sure Fred Brewster and his friends never walk the streets freely again!"

The courtroom burst into a low roar of murmurs, and Judge Bale pounded his gavel. The prosecutor rose, and Blake began to get the feeling the man was against a free territory, perhaps one of Nick West's paid supporters. The man could and should have called Samantha to the stand to testify against Brewster, but he had not done so. Blake wondered if both the defense attorney and the prosecutor were being paid under the table by Nick West.

"Your Honor, we already know what happened to Miss Walters," the prosecutor spoke up then. "I did not call her because I wanted to spare her the embarrassment."

"Your job is to get to the truth, Mr. Collings," the judge scolded. "How do we know Miss Walters cannot shed some new light on this if she isn't called to testify? I order her to testify myself, and if you won't question her, I will."

Blake watched Collings glance at Nick West with a helpless look on his face. Apparently West was doing what he could to keep Fred Brewster from suffering the punishment for murder. Blake rose to let Samantha by, putting a hand to her waist in a reassuring gesture as she made her way on shaking legs past him and her parents and out into the aisle. She prayed for courage as she felt a thousand eyes on her. She walked to the witness stand and took an oath to tell the truth, after which the prosecutor rather reluctantly asked her to tell the jury what had happened the day of her attack.

"We won't ask you for details of your personal attack," Mr. Collings told her. "The defense has already admitted to it. The primary concern here, Miss Walters, is whether or not Fred Brewster and his friends actually attacked Joseph Stetson with the intent to kill him."

Samantha moved her eyes to Brewster. She knew that if he somehow got out of this, she had not seen the last of him. The memory of what he had done burned inside her, and a new strength and determination welled up in her. Perhaps he had been physically stronger that day, but at this moment she was the one who could destroy him. She refused to let his hate-filled eyes deter her as she turned her attention to the jury.

"Before I testify to Mr. Stetson's attack, I would like to say that what Fred Brewster did to me should not be taken lightly, or be made out to be the act of a young man's overexcitement." She looked at the defense attorney. "Nor should it be blamed on me for being in the wrong place at the wrong time. I had every right to be at the print shop that day, and I was bothering no one. Fred Brewster had accosted me and harassed me several other times before that day. Everyone knows he's the town bully and a trouble-maker."

Defense attorney Knowles objected to the statement, but Judge Bale overruled him. Samantha glanced at Blake, who gave her a look of support. She addressed the jury again. "Fred Brewster chased me down as I tried to flee out the back door. He called me names and told me in no uncertain terms what he intended to do with me. He viciously beat me and tried to rape me," she said boldly, "but I hit him with a paperweight. Then his friends tried to do the same to me, but help came before they . . ." She hesitated, swallowing, feeling the stares. "The point is, what they did was more than boyish playfulness. They meant me extreme harm and humiliation, and might have even killed me like they killed Mr. Stetson."

Again Attorney Knowles objected to her remarks, and the judge sustained the objection. He told Samantha to state only the facts, not personal judgment.

"That *is* a fact, Your Honor," she told him. She looked at Knowles. "Fred Brewster and his friends say that what happened to Mr. Stetson was an accident—that Mr. Stetson was accidentally hurt when they began wrecking the print shop. But that is not true."

"You were in the back room," Knowles reminded her.

Samantha saw Brewster beginning to stiffen. "That's right," she answered. "But I know what I heard and saw. It's true there were a couple of crashing sounds as soon as Brewster and his friends came inside. That's what made me get up and go see what was happening. At that time Mr. Stetson was just fine, because I heard him talking. He yelled at someone. He said, 'Get out, you troublemaking hoodlums.' It was then I heard the sound of a hard blow to something, and I heard a man grunt with pain. There is no mistaking it was the sound of Mr. Stetson being hit. When I reached the doorway, Mr. Stetson was lying on the floor, his head bleeding, Fred Brewster standing over him with a steel pipe in his hand. He looked at Mr. Stetson and said, '*You're* the troublemaker, printing that abolitionist newspaper." It was *then* that Brewster noticed me standing in the doorway. And it was *then* that he ordered his friends to destroy everything in sight. 'I'll take care of Miss Walters,' he told them. That's when I headed for the back door, because I knew Brewster meant me great harm. He caught me before I reached the door. You know the rest."

"You lying bitch," Fred Brewster blurted out, rising from his chair.

The sheriff moved to shove him back in the chair, and the courtroom again burst into gasps and murmuring. Samantha saw Blake half rise, and her heart pounded with dread. Her father grabbed Blake's arm and urged him to sit back down. Attorney Knowles paled slightly, and again the judge pounded his gavel and asked for quiet. He ordered Brewster to restrain himself or be taken from the courtroom. Beecher glanced at Nick West, who had a disgusted look on his face.

"Isn't it possible you're twisting your story deliberately to set Fred Brewster up for murder, Miss Walters?" Knowles asked Samantha once the courtroom quieted. "Isn't it possible you're just doing this to get back at him for his attack on you?"

Samantha held her chin proudly. "No. You are accusing me of perjury, Mr. Knowles. I have never told a lie in my life. I was brought up in a strict Christian family, and I would rather see Fred Brewster go free than to lie in order to put a man in prison or get him hanged, no matter how much he might deserve it."

"Your Honor—"

"Pay no heed to the last statement," Judge Bale told the jury.

"I have told the truth," Samantha spoke up. "I heard what I heard. Mr. Stetson was struck down *before* Brewster's friends started wrecking the shop. And it was Fred Brewster himself who stood over the man with a weapon in his hand."

"Slut! Liar!" Brewster yelled.

"Get that man out of the courtroom," the judge ordered the sheriff.

Samantha's eyes teared with embarrassment as the sheriff and a deputy grabbed hold of Brewster by each arm and led him away. The big, strong Brewster suddenly elbowed both men and made a dash for the door, but in an instant Blake was out of his seat and literally leaping over Samantha's parents. He dived into Brewster, both men landing into the opposite benches. People screamed and one man grunted as Brewster's body landed on him. Blake jerked the young man up, holding him by the shirtfront while he brought a booted foot into Brewster's groin in two hard kicks. Brewster cried out with excruciating pain, folding down to his knees, while Blake stood over him threateningly, the sheepskin jacket he had left on making him seem even bigger than he already was.

"I want that man out of my courtroom also," the judge yelled, indicating Blake. He pounded his gavel several times while the courtroom echoed with loud voices. Blake shook off the two men who started to grab him and glanced apologetically at Samantha before walking out on his own.

Samantha covered her eyes, realizing Blake was just reacting to the pain and frustration of the testimony that came out during the trial. Brewster was dragged from the courtroom, and it took several minutes for things to quiet down. Both prosecutor Collings and Attorney Knowles said they were through questioning Samantha. She left the witness chair, walking to her parents and grabbing up her fur-lined velvet cape. She headed out the door, wanting only to find Blake. To her relief he was close by, pacing on the steps of the courthouse and smoking a cigarette. Their eyes held as Samantha came closer.

"I'm sorry," he told her. "I couldn't help it."

"It's all right."

He turned away. "Bastard!" he muttered, making a fist. He literally trembled with rage.

"Let's take a walk, Blake. There's nothing more either one of us can do here." She walked up and took his arm, leading him away from the building. They walked around behind it, their shoes crunching against the hardened snow that was several days old. Samantha breathed deeply of the crisp December air. "I'm just glad it's over, whether they believe me or not."

"They'll believe you." Blake stopped walking, throwing down the cigarette. He grasped her arm. "You did well, Samantha. I was real proud of you standing up to them like that."

The air was so cold she could see his breath, but Samantha was barely aware of the chill. She smiled lightly. "I didn't want to testify at all. I could easily have gotten out of it. Even the prosecutor didn't call me. But when they talked about my 'delicate' condition, that really made me mad."

Blake finally smiled. "I could tell it did. I knew you'd come through. You're going to be all right, Samantha Walters."

Their eyes held. Samantha stood rigid as he came closer then, part of her wanting to turn away, another part of her wanting to know at last what it was like to be kissed by this man. He met her lips lightly at first, gently parting them, delicately flicking at her mouth with his tongue. He wanted so badly to claim her, to somehow make up for what she had been through. In spite of the cold, his lips were soft and warm.

Samantha sensed that seeing Fred Brewster had aroused a sense of possessiveness in Blake's soul. Never had she known such a kiss, or felt such fire. She found herself returning the kiss, moved her arms around his neck. She groaned lightly as the kiss deepened and he drew her into his powerful arms, crushing her against himself.

He finally released her mouth, leaving her breathless as she rested her head against his chest, nestling her face against his heavy jacket. He kept her close. "I love you, Sam," he told her softly. "No one will ever hurt you like that again, I promise. I love you, and I want to be with you all the time. I want to live with you, sleep with you, build a house for you, have a family. Your father isn't firmly convinced we're right for each other, but *I* am. We'll work on him. Just tell me you love me, too, that you'll think about marrying me."

She felt weak, happy, on fire. "Surely you know I've loved you almost from the beginning," she told him. "I was just afraid to say it. Yes, I want very much to be your wife. Just promise you'll be patient with me."

"You must know I'd never rush you or hurt you. I just want to be with you, Sam, to make sure you're mine and that no one can take you away from me."

"I want the same." She loved the comfort and safety of resting her head against his chest. She loved his gentle hold, the smell of him. "When you went back to Independence, I was afraid there was a woman there that maybe you went to see—maybe someone you cared about."

"There hasn't been anyone who really meant anything to me since Susan died—not until I met you." He drew back slightly, meeting her eyes. "I'll talk to your father."

"You'd better wait a few more weeks. He'll think it's too soon."

"I don't care. The way things are now, time is important. We never know how long we'll have each other."

"Don't say that! We're going to grow old together, Blake."

He touched her face. "I want to believe that." To her surprise, his eyes filled with tears. "It's just that . . . after Susan . . . I mean, one minute we were making wedding plans and the next she was gone. Talking about marriage brings it all back."

She took his hand, kissing the palm. "Nothing is going to happen to me," she told him. "It will be different this time." Her heart rushed with love and excitement. Blake Hastings had actually asked her to marry him!

He moved an arm around her and led her farther away. "I'll work as hard as I can, Sam, work two jobs if necessary, in order to save the money to build a house of our own, maybe buy some land and have my own farm again. In the meantime, I guess we'll have to live at the boardinghouse. Would you mind that?"

Samantha felt a warm tingle at the thought of actually living with him, being with him day and night, sleeping in his bed. Again the ugly memories tried to move in on her and destroy the joy of the thought. She shook them away. "As long as we're together, it doesn't matter."

"Samantha." They both turned at the sound of Reverend Walters calling her name. He came walking toward them. "We wondered where you had gone off to," he said as he came closer, short of breath from hurrying. "The jury is off making their decision. The judge said he would send for Fred Brewster again when they made up their minds." He took his daughter's hand. "You did a fine, brave thing today, Sam. We're proud of you." He looked at Blake. "I have to admit it seemed to help her a lot when you came back," he told him. "But, Blake—" He shook his head. "You let that temper get the best of you again in there."

"After what Brewster did to her, I'd have gone crazy without the chance to vent some of my anger," Blake answered. "I hope they have to *carry* him back here, and I hope they vote to *hang* him! I'll personally attend the hanging and enjoy every minute of it. So should you, Reverend."

The man sighed. "I try not to let myself feel such emotions, but in this case I am inclined to agree. Why don't we all go back to the house. Someone will let us know how it turns out." The man put an arm around Samantha. "Your mother is waiting for us at the front of the courthouse. We're having a meeting tonight at the house with several church members about visiting some of the outlying farms and seeing what they need. Your mother will need your help, Samantha, in serving refreshments."

"Will Clyde Beecher be there?" Blake asked.

The reverend stopped and turned. "Yes. Of course."

Blake sighed. "Why don't you take my advice, sir, and try having a few meetings without his knowledge? You told me just a couple of days ago that three more abolitionist families who live outside of Lawrence and who attend your church were raided. What will it take to make you understand it could be Beecher who is setting them up? Do you intend to wait until someone dies?"

The reverend's face darkened, and Samantha's heart fell at Blake's words. She knew they would only open an old wound and make it less likely her father would consent to marriage. "I thought we had finished our discussion on that subject, Blake. You've been seeing Samantha for over three weeks now, and you haven't brought it up."

"I intended to let it be, until you told me about those families."

"Blake, you're a good man. But I'm afraid certain things that have happened to you have made you too afraid to trust people. There comes a time when a man *has* to take a chance and *begin* to trust, or he spends his whole life being cynical and unhappy. I know how Samantha feels about you, but that doesn't mean I have to allow you to insult my friends."

Blake shook his head. "I wish you would just try to see it my way, Reverend. Watch the man, listen to the questions he asks at the supper table, the questions he asks me—"

"Perhaps you shouldn't be at the meeting tonight, Blake," the reverend interrupted. "If you let this out and start making accusations toward Mr. Beecher in front of the others, you'll stir up a whole beehive of distrust, and the people who do come from the outlying areas will think maybe even *I* am a traitor! I could lose my following over your suspicions, and I won't have it. These people need me, need a place to come where they can get hope and support. I thought we had this settled, Blake!"

Blake held the man's eyes. "It was *never* settled! I've just been keeping my mouth shut, but after sitting in there today and listening again to the horror Samantha suffered, I can't stand the thought of her being in even worse danger from the very fact that Clyde Beecher had made himself a part of the family—that he could be telling enemy factions every move you make, giving out names of every—"

110

"No more!" the reverend interrupted, putting up his hand. "I am taking Samantha home, and I think you should stay away for a day or two and think about what is more important to you—trying vainly to prove you're right about a Christian man like Clyde Beecher or seeing Samantha."

"Father! You *know* how I feel about Blake!"

Reverend Walters's mouth was set in a hard line, and he kept his eyes on Blake. "Yes, I do. But I am still not convinced it is for the best. You're a good man in many ways, Blake—hardworking, conscientious, compassionate—but also passionate, in a way that gets you in trouble."

"I told you before, I'm not the one who goes looking for that trouble, no more than Samantha was looking for it the day she was attacked. Don't ask me to stay away from her, Reverend. I happen to love her and I want to *marry* her. I just haven't had the chance to talk to you about it. It's been a long time since I felt this way, Reverend. I want a wife and family, and I'm willing to work an extra job to save up to buy some land for a farm. Please don't make this more difficult for us."

Samantha turned away from both of them, feeling tears wanting to come. Blake held the reverend's eyes, showing his own sincerity. Walters sighed. "I have no doubt you would be a devoted husband, Blake. But these are very troubled times—not conducive to be marrying and risking having children. After all, this country could break into war, and no one needs to tell me you'd go marching off to fight for abolition and the Union the minute the first shot was fired. Where would that leave Samantha? Not only that, but what about your problem with Nick West? Do you intend to marry Samantha and then murder West and go off to prison or hang? Let alone the fact that it could be the other way around. Nick West might finally get to you, and leave my daughter a widow. Maybe even *she* would be in more danger! No, Blake. I don't think you've thought this through. You're still too full of anger and revenge to be taking a wife."

Samantha whirled. "Father, I *want* to marry Blake! I *love* him! I don't care about the danger. I've never known you to be so stubborn!"

"It's all right, Sam," Blake put in, his eyes on her father. "I can see Beecher has been doing some clever talking, making sure your father won't listen to anything I have to say about him—making sure he believes I'm no good for you."

"That isn't so," the reverend argued. "But aside from all that, Blake, the fact remains you have unfinished business with Nick West. I just don't think this is a good time to be getting married, nor do I think you and Samantha have known each other long enough to make such a decision. I think that right now Samantha is just a little bit mixed up in her feelings."

"I'm *not* mixed up," Samantha put in, facing the man squarely. "I know exactly how I feel. I love Blake and I want to marry him."

Blake put his hands on her shoulders. "Let it be for now, Sam. George is waiting for me at the sawmill. It could be hours before the jury members make up their minds. I might as well get back to work. I'll see you tomorrow."

"But what about tonight?" She turned to face him, seeing the anger in his eyes.

"Your father has made it clear that I am not welcome tonight."

"I never said you weren't welcome, Blake," Walters told him. "I said it might be wise to stay away. You'll be welcome again tomorrow, you and

George both. I am not refusing to let you see Sam. I am only saying that it is too soon to be married. Give it some time. Sort out your feelings about Nick West. It might even be wise to wait until after the elections. There could be a lot of trouble when they come up. Wait until afterward; let things calm down some. Maybe when they're over, West will go back to Missouri where he belongs."

"The elections are nearly three months away. That's a long wait, Reverend."

"You'll manage it. If you truly love my daughter, you'll do as I ask, and your love will survive the test of time."

Blake breathed deeply to keep his temper in control. "I'm not worried about that, Reverend. I'd wait years for Sam if I had to. It's just that the last time I planned and waited, the woman I loved died before I could marry her. In these dangerous times, that could happen again, and I don't intend to wait and see. It's true we could marry and end up losing each other, but at least we would have had some time together. And if we love each other, what's the difference if something happens *before* or *after* we're married? It hurts just the same, Reverend. I can attest to that!" He squeezed Samantha's shoulders before turning and walking back toward the courthouse.

Samantha watched after him a moment, then turned to her father. "I thought you would understand, Father. He's lost so much. I won't make him wait, and *I* don't want to wait. Who cares whether or not he likes Clyde Beecher? Mr. Beecher is just a friend, Father, not a relative. And I know Blake will find a way to resolve the problem with Nick West." She stepped closer. "You can't keep us apart, Father. I'm eighteen. I can do what I want."

Walters studied her sadly. "Yes, I suppose you

can." He removed his hat and rubbed at his eyes. "I love you, Samantha. It's just that . . . after that day I carried you home from the print shop, I've realized the horror I would suffer if something happened to you."

"Blake would never let anything happen to me."

"Maybe not deliberately. But he's a troubled man, Sam, a man with enemies."

"And so are you, Father. We both know that from what happened at the print shop. What difference does it make if I'm living at home or with Blake Hastings? He's on *our* side, Father. He only says those things about Mr. Beecher because he's concerned for *all* of us. You can't blame him for not being able to trust people. Please say you'll think about it and that you'll talk to him more about it tomorrow."

Walters sighed, putting his hat back on. "I *will* think about it. But I still don't think you have known him long enough."

"Reverend Walters!" Clyde Beecher hailed them from closer to the courthouse. "The jury! They're coming back inside!"

The reverend took his daughter's arm and hurried back to the courthouse with her. Blake was waiting on the front steps with Samantha's mother. "Figured I'd wait and hear the verdict," he told the reverend, holding the man's eyes challengingly.

The reverend touched his arm. "Blake, I am not against you. I simply have to consider what is best for my daughter. We'll talk more tomorrow evening."

"Don't tell me you two are at odds," Beecher put in. "Is there anything I can do?"

Samantha cringed, worried what Blake would say in reply, but Blake only glared at the man. He grasped Samantha's arm then and pushed her back when he noticed the sheriff bringing Fred Brewster back across the street. The young man was walking bent over, still in a great deal of pain. Blake grinned with pleasure at the sight. Brewster gave Blake a look of savage hatred but said nothing as he was ushered inside, and Blake and the others followed. They stood at the back of the room while the jury proclaimed Fred Brewster guilty of murder and his friends guilty of second-degree murder, malicious destruction of property, assault, and attempted rape.

Samantha felt an arm come around her as the judge sentenced Brewster to be hanged and sentenced the other four young men to twenty years in prison.

"You can't do that!" Brewster shouted, while one of the other young men began to cry. "It's *war*, that's what it is! It's no different from the border wars! People don't get hanged for shooting each other in war."

Judge Bale pounded his gavel. "There is a distinct difference between war and murder, young man," he told him. "What you did was unprovoked, and there is no state of war in the town of Lawrence; nor, I might remind everyone in this room, is there a state of war anyplace in this country! Those who raid and destroy property and rape women and kill farmers along the border are just as guilty of murder as this young man here today. Whenever such people can be caught, they will be arrested and punished."

"Not when they manage to sneak back across the border into Missouri," a spectator shouted.

"Yeah," someone else shouted. "How about a law that will send the bastards back home!"

Someone else agreed, and in moments the whole courtroom was in a shouting match. Blake pulled Samantha out of the doorway, noticing Beecher glance across the room at Nick West. The men exchanged a knowing look while the judge banged his gavel for several long seconds, shouting for order in the court. Blake led Samantha outside, where she covered her ears.

"Oh, Blake, what are we going to do? Look what happened in there. Everything is so ugly and wrong. Maybe Father is right. Maybe we shouldn't get married."

"Don't talk that way. It's been a long, trying day for both of us, that's all." He lifted her chin. "Sam, nothing has changed. Nothing. I still love you and I still want to marry you."

She studied his eyes as people began filing out of the courthouse, some still arguing. Their voices became dim, and her apprehension left her as she read the love in Blake's eyes. Of course it was right. They couldn't let outside forces, not even her father, keep them apart. Why let the ugliness of the hatred around them make its way into the beautiful love they had come to know.

"We won't let them stop us," Blake told her. "I want you, Samantha Walters, and I intend to have you, war or no war, in spite of your father's apprehension, in spite of Nick West."

Clyde Beecher approached them, carrying his usual pompous air. "Will you be joining us this evening, Blake?" he asked. "You should come and bring your friend George. George would be a great inspiration to those who attend."

Their eyes held. "George and I have other plans tonight," Blake answered. "I'll be by tomorrow."

"That's too bad. It's an important meeting." Beecher could not hide the animosity in his eyes.

"I'm sure it is—to you." Blake took Samantha's arm. "Tell the reverend I'll walk Sam home. You and the Walterses can take the reverend's buggy. I want a few more minutes with Sam."

Beecher nodded. "You both must be happy with the verdict. You did a good job today, Samantha." He tipped his hat. "I'll go and tell your father that Blake will be walking you home."

The man left them, passing Nick West as though he hardly knew the man, but Blake suspected differently. West approached Blake, and Samantha clung to Blake's arm, her heart pounding.

"You think this is a setback for proslavery," West said, his eyes drilling into Blake. "But it isn't. This is just the beginning. I'll see you at the hanging."

"It won't be the first one you've witnessed," Blake told him.

West smiled. "And probably not the last. Maybe I'll be lucky enough to attend yours someday."

The man walked off, and Samantha felt a cold shiver move through her. There seemed to be so much against them, so many people and circumstances trying to destroy the love she and Blake shared. But when he moved an arm around her again and began walking with her, she felt safe, protected, sheltered from outside forces. In his arms, nothing could touch her. Surely God meant for this to be. Surely He would see to it that nothing happened to either of them, that they would be able to share this love for many years to come.

"You'll never hang me," she heard Brewster shouting behind them as he was brought back outside. "Bastards! Nigger lovers! It was *war*, don't you understand that? *War!*"

Blake's arm tightened around Samantha. Neither of them looked back.

Six

Blake and George moved through the crowded street, where vendors had set up booths and wagons and women wore their Sunday best even though it was Saturday. Fred Brewster's hanging had turned into a circus, and people mingled and gossipped, the crisp January air doing little to keep most people home.

"You hear that nervous laughter?" Blake asked George. "They're all trying to hide the fact that they're scared to death all of this is going to lead to war, scared they might be the next victims."

"Clancy Jones over at the sawmill says another abolitionist family was attacked two days ago. The woman was raped by several men. They all wore hoods so they couldn't be recognized."

Blake thought of Samantha, not so sure anymore that being in Lawrence meant she was not in the same danger as the border families. "I heard," he answered, scanning the crowd.

He was worried about Samantha, didn't like not being able to be with her, to protect her. He especially didn't like her being around Clyde Beecher. He looked for the reverend, but he couldn't see him anywhere and knew the man probably would not bring himself to witness a hanging. Walters did not believe in revenge, and to him the hanging constituted just another act of violence, in spite of what Fred had done to Samantha. He had called Fred a victim himself—a victim of the prejudice and hatred he had been taught to harbor.

The Reverend Walters believed that capital punishment was wrong. Walters and Blake had got into an argument over the subject, since Blake believed that hanging was too good for Brewster and his kind. Their differences of opinion had led to a heated discussion, which eventually took a turn toward the subject of abolition and how it should be approached. The reverend believed the Christian thing to do was preach all he could, go out among the people and distribute information, to bring in more settlers from the North. Blake agreed, but he also believed that some men responded only to threats and physical attacks.

Walters said that kind of attitude only intensified the violence in the streets and the raids along the border. Soon the argument turned to the subject of Clyde Beecher. Blake declared that it was spies like Beecher who caused the most trouble, and that all bushwhackers should be shot down, including Clyde Beecher. He had let his temper and suspicions get the better of him again, and before he realized what he was saying, he had told the reverend that he didn't doubt Beecher himself sometimes took part in border raids.

Blake's accusations had again incensed the reverend, but this time Blake would not take back his words. Intensified raids and ambushes of innocent people had put most everyone on edge, and Blake's conviction that Beecher was a part of it all made it impossible for him to apologize this time. Before the arguing was over, Walters had ordered Blake out of the house. That had been nearly three weeks ago, and the man's words still rang in Blake's ears.

"You're a good man, Blake, but your heart is full of hatred and vengeance and distrust, and I simply don't believe you're right for Samantha. I think she will understand that herself once she is away from you for a while. I'll hear no more talk for now about marrying. I think you both need time to think about this, to realize everything has happened too quickly. It's the danger of these times that brought you together, and you don't really know your own hearts."

Blake had argued that he loved Samantha, and Samantha, on the verge of tears, argued the same, but the reverend was incensed over Blake's renewed accusations of Clyde Beecher. *"Not only is your own soul troubled,"* he had nearly shouted, *"but you have accused a fine, Christian friend of this family of rape and murder. I won't have it!"* He had asked Blake to leave and not come back until he was ready to apologize for his words against Beecher, and that even then, he wanted Blake to stay away for at least two weeks before seeing Samantha again.

"We will pray for your soul, Blake," the man told him. *"Pray that you will find a way to rid yourself of all the hatred and distrust your father's death has instilled in you. You are welcome in church, for you surely need to hear the word of God and I turn no man away. But I cannot allow you back in my home when I know how you feel about Mr. Beecher."*

Blake still felt fury at the memory of the words. His own stubbornness had kept him away, and he had refused to go to church the last two Sundays; nor would he go tomorrow, even though it meant not getting to see Samantha. But he didn't know how much longer he could stand being away from her. There was no hope of running into her in town, since he already knew her parents intended to keep her at home until after the hanging, something Blake agreed with. They were worried that those who sympathized with Fred Brewster, although few in number, might plot to bring harm to Samantha for her damaging testimony. Sam was only allowed to go to church.

"You looking for Sam?" George asked.

Blake sighed. "No. I'm looking for her father. I thought maybe I could make some kind of amends. I feel like I'm going crazy, not being able to see Sam."

"Why don't you just apologize, Blake? It wouldn't be the end of the world."

Blake took a prerolled cigarette from the inside pocket of his jacket. "I can't this time, George. Every time I see Clyde Beecher, I know I'm right. Walters is being a fool, and I worry Sam will suffer for it. I don't know what the hell to do. Am I being too proud? Too stubborn?"

George grinned sadly as Blake lit his cigarette. "Maybe—a little. But you're also being cautious, and you have a right to be. I think you're right about Beecher, too. All I know is, if I had a chance to see Jesse again, I'd crawl on my hands and knees and kiss the feet of whoever was standing in my way."

Blake took a long drag on his cigarette. "I'm just about to that point," he said as they approached the gallows. "Maybe I'll go over there tonight and try to talk to the reverend. After all this time away from Sam, my feelings for her haven't changed one bit, and I know Sam's haven't, either."

"Then go over there and talk to her father."

"I'd like to take Samantha away with me whether

122

he likes it or not, but damn it, George, I don't want it to be that way. It's her family. I'd like her family to be *my* family. I want to get along with them. I don't want to force Sam to have to choose between them and me." He shook his head. "It's strange that her father and I agree so totally on abolition, but disagree so totally on how to make it come about. And I can't believe he can be so blind about Clyde Beecher."

George shrugged. "Beecher is a clever man. You have to remember he's been a supportive follower since Walters first came to Kansas. Walters has known him a lot longer than he has known you."

"I suppose." Blake spotted several men he remembered from the day of the fight with West, but Nick West himself was nowhere to be seen. "West certainly knows when it's wise to stay home, doesn't he," he remarked to George. "You can bet ninety-five percent of this crowd are abolitionists. While they're all here watching one bushwhacker hang, more men like West and his kind are out there doing their dirty work."

People began to gather around the gallows as the time for the hanging drew near. Some men perched small children on their shoulders, and people jeered as Fred Brewster was brought from the jail to the gallows, struggling all the way. "You're all a bunch of nigger lovers," Brewster shouted, "including that slut Samantha Walters! You'll all regret this! I didn't kill Joe Stetson! It was an accident!"

"Just like the raids along the borders are accidents," someone shouted back.

The crowd immediately joined in, fists raised, shouts of "murderer" and "rapist" mingling with "Hang him high!" The sheriff and three of his men managed to get Brewster up the steps and under the noose, and a minister from a church other than

123

Reverend Walters's Methodist church approached the young man, asking him if he had any last words. Brewster spit on the preacher, and the crowd grew even more angry. The preacher turned away and began to pray for Brewster's soul while men put a black hood over his head and a noose around his neck. Brewster had been given no coat against the freezing January air, and he stood shivering almost violently. Blake guessed it was more from fear and dread than the cold.

The crowd quieted, and two men kept hold of Brewster. "I'm not the only one responsible for this," Brewster spoke up in a muffled voice beneath the hood.

The preacher asked everyone to bow their heads in prayer, after which he led the crowd in the singing of a hymn.

"Wait," Brewster shouted during "Amazing Grace." "I can name names. Don't hang me, and I'll tell you who—" Before he could finish, while the crowd continued singing, a shot rang out, fired from an upper room several buildings away. A bloody hole opened in Fred Brewster's chest, and he slumped, his head catching in the noose, which was no longer necessary. Brewster was dead.

At the sound of the gunshot women screamed and people began to scatter. The sheriff and his men drew their guns, all of them trying to see where the shot had come from. Blake saw another flash, the actual gunshot hardly discernible by then because of the crowd noise, and a bullet whizzed between Blake and George, skimming across Blake's left cheek. Blake jolted backward at the force of the shot, and George called out his name. Another shot was fired, hitting the dirt near George.

"Take cover," Blake shouted at him. "He's trying

to kill us!''

By then the crowd had rushed away from Blake and George, who both scrambled under the gallows, Blake with his gun drawn. Blake heard the sheriff ordering his men to get over to the building from which the shots had been fired. Blake crawled out from under the scaffold to the other side, looking up at the sheriff. "What the hell is going on?"

Sheriff John Tucker ducked down, then jumped off the gallows. "You're bleeding like a stuck pig," he told Blake. "You hurt bad?"

Blake put a hand to his cheek, then noticed the left side of his jacket was already stained with blood. "Nothing that hurts bad. One more inch and it would have been my head." He looked down at George. "You all right?"

George crawled out from under the gallows. "Far as I know." He brushed himself off, looking himself over as though he wasn't sure.

"You'd better get over to the doc's," the sheriff told Blake. He glanced up at Brewster's dead body. "Looks to me like somebody decided to spare Brewster the agony of hanging."

Blake took a handkerchief from his pants pocket and pressed it to the wound on his cheek. "Or maybe somebody was afraid he would shout the wrong names at the last minute."

The sheriff met his eyes. "I thought of that, too. The shootist probably singled you out because you were with a Negro man—or maybe they were aiming for George in the first place. Probably figured if one of their own had to die, then a Negro man ought to die, too." The man pushed back his hat. "Your luck hasn't been too good since you got here, Hastings. Maybe you should move on to another town."

"I haven't done anything wrong here, Sheriff. I'm

working hard at the mill and minding my own business. I haven't even gotten involved in abolitionist activities since I've been here. And as long as Samantha Walters lives in this town, I'm staying. He pressed the quickly soaked handkerchief tighter and looked at George. "Come on. Let's go find Doc Beckett." He looked back at Tucker. "Let me know if your men catch whoever did this," he fumed.

People began drifting back into the street, staring at Brewster's body. The preacher and the hangman finally cut him down, and two other men carried him off, while people began talking among themselves about the possible reasons for the shooting. Some even expressed disappointment that they had been "cheated" out of a hanging.

Blake found the doctor, but he could do little for the wound other than to cleanse it and keep a cloth pressed against it until the bleeding subsided. "The bullet just grazed you," Beckett told Blake. "Took a lot of skin with it. This is going to leave one hell of a scar, I'm afraid. The skin is just scraped away. I can't really stitch it up. It's not like a cut." He shook his head. "You're one lucky man."

"Lucky as far as the wound," Blake grumbled. "But not so lucky that someone is out there taking potshots at me."

"It was probably just a spur-of-the-moment thing for the gunman. I'd wager he wanted to put Brewster out quickly so he wouldn't have to go through the ordeal of a hanging; then he must have spotted George and decided on an eye for an eye: a proslavery man dies—a Negro dies. You were just in the way."

Blake looked over at George. "Maybe." He saw the sorrow in George's eyes.

"Maybe I ought to head on out west," George told

126

him quietly. "Staying with you is just going to keep bringing you trouble, Blake."

Blake gave him a reassuring grin. "Trouble would find me whether I was with you or not."

The sheriff entered the office then, asking Blake how he was doing. Blake got up from the doctor's table and walked to a mirror, studying the ugly gash along the side of his face. "Let's just say this looks pretty good compared to a hole in the middle of my face," he answered. "I guess I'm doing as well as a man who's just been shot at *can* do—which is to still be alive."

Sheriff Tucker removed his hat. "Well, by the time my men raided the building where the shots came from, whoever fired them was gone, naturally. He either rode off or just mingled right in with the crowd. We'll never know who it was. The shot came from the rooftop of Caldwell Supply. Caldwell says he never saw anybody. He's a strong abolitionist, been a solid citizen of Lawrence for many years. He wouldn't lie. There's a covered supply wagon parked behind the place. Whoever it was must have climbed up on it and then onto the roof from there. The roof slopes down close to one story at the back side. At any rate, the alley is so full of footprints, not to mention horse tracks and wagon tracks, that it's impossible to distinguish which ones might have belonged to the shootist."

Blake took the cloth from his face again, noticing that the wound had finally stopped bleeding. He turned from the mirror. "I didn't figure you'd find anything." He looked at the sheriff. "But I'll tell you one thing. My guess is Nick West was behind it."

"West isn't even in town today. He's out at his farm."

"He doesn't have to be here to be responsible. In fact, *not* being here just makes him all the more guilty in my book."

"Could be. I have to say, Hastings, I don't like this feud between you and West one bit. If it keeps up, I just might have to order you to leave town."

Blake's face darkened with anger. "*West* is the one who should leave town. He's got a whole plantation back in Missouri, and he's always lived there. It's pretty damn obvious why he's here, Sheriff."

"I know that. But nothing can be proved." Tucker moved toward the door. "My job has been made a lot harder since that damn Kansas-Nebraska Act went through. I'll just be glad when the voting is over with."

"A lot of us will," George put in.

The sheriff glanced at him, realizing how important it would be to a man like George to have Kansas voted in as a free territory. If the proslavery people swung the vote, George was not safe, even though he had papers to prove he was a free man. He nodded to George and left.

"You want some laudanum for the pain?" the doctor asked Blake.

"Hell, no. It looks worse than it feels. A little whiskey will do." He looked at George. "Let's go to Willie's Saloon and play some cards—try to put this out of our mind for a while. I need a couple of stiff drinks."

George nodded. "You'd better change that shirt and jacket first. You look like hell."

Blake grinned, trying to hide his concern, mostly trying to reassure George he was just fine, since he knew his friend was feeling low over the entire incident. He reached into his pocket and took out some money to pay the doctor. "Let's go," he said then, heading for the door. "Bronson closed the mill for the day because of the hanging. Might as well try to make a little money at poker. Looks like I'll have to buy a new jacket."

Both men left, watching the crowded street. They headed for Blake's boardinghouse to change, after which they would go to Willie's Saloon, where they knew Negroes were welcome. Neither man was aware that Clyde Beecher was watching them. Beecher headed for his horse. He had to ride to Nick West's place and report to him that Brewster had been shot according to West's instructions. The man who had killed him had been paid well to keep his mouth shut and quietly leave Lawrence.

"We can't let the boy suffer those last moments," West had told Beecher a few days earlier. "He might not have been aware of it, but he's one of our own, and I won't give the town of Lawrence the pleasure of hanging him. Besides, he might shout out a few wrong names at the last minute. Several of my own men planted a lot of ideas in that boy's head."

The deed had been done, and West would be happy to know that a good scare had been planted in Blake Hastings and his black friend. Maybe between not being able to see Samantha and knowing his life was on the line, Blake Hastings would get out of Lawrence. That was something Beecher wanted to see happen as badly as West did. The reverend had told Beecher that Blake suspected he was a spy, but Beecher was not about to let Blake know he was aware of the accusation. That would make Blake figure Beecher was just being even more cautious. He simply had to keep proving to Walters by his actions that he was not what Blake accused him of being and

129

keep Walters convinced that Blake was not good for Samantha. Somehow he had to get Blake out of town or arrange his death.

Blake spread out his winning hand and raked in the pot, adding it to a stack of coins and bills beside him.

"Looks like this is your lucky day," another man at the table told him. "First you miss a bullet in the head, now you're taking all our money."

Everyone laughed lightly and anted up for the next hand. Blake liked this place. He and George had discovered that contrary to the establishment where Nick West often hung his hat, this one catered to abolitionists. Anyone suspected of being proslavery, or someone filtered in from Missouri, was quickly put out; and Negroes could get served at Willie's. Only one or two saloons in town would cater to proslavery factions, all of whom were being referred to now as bushwhackers, even if they took no part in the border violence.

Conversation at all the tables revolved around the day's events, and it seemed to Blake he had answered the question of "How are you doing?" about a thousand times. "We'll get those bushwhackers completely out of Lawrence eventually," more than one man told him. "They'll soon learn they'd better get out of town or wish they had."

"Once the vote comes through for a free territory, they'll leave fast enough," another had put in.

Blake took a deep drag on his cigarette and looked at his cards. He thought what a far cry this place was from sitting on the porch swing of the Walters home talking to Samantha. He would much rather be there, feeling her in his arms, tasting her mouth again. Actually, he longed to do much more than that, and another swallow of whiskey only helped stimulate those desires. He was beginning to think maybe George was right. Maybe he should get on his knees and ask her father's forgiveness, find a way back to her at any price. His main problem was his dislike of Clyde Beecher. Walters would expect him to admit he was wrong about Beecher, and Blake couldn't bring himself to do that.

George gave him a nudge then, interrupting his thoughts. "Somebody you know is looking in the doorway," he told Blake.

Blake turned toward the swinging doors to see Samantha looking over the top of them, scanning the smoke-filled room. Her eyes met Blake's then, widening with relief.

"Hey, come on in, honey," one man called out to her.

The remark made her dart away quickly.

Blake threw down his cards. "Deal me out." He quickly scooped up his money and shoved it into his pockets, and George grinned at the thought of Samantha's boldness in coming to a place like Willie's just to find Blake. Blake grabbed his hat and new fur-lined buckskin jacket and hurried outside, where he saw Samantha trying to get past a man who was in the process of making her an offer of a good deal of money if she would go home with him.

Blake rushed toward her, shoving the man aside and grabbing Samantha's arm. "Sam! What in God's name are you doing here!"

She looked up at him with a mixture of relief and embarrassment in her eyes. "Blake!" She hugged him tightly. "I remembered you said this place allowed George to come inside. When you weren't at the boardinghouse, I thought maybe I could find you here. I spotted you, but then I was afraid to go in."

She seemed close to tears. Blake gave the other man a look that told him to get lost or suffer the consequences, and the man walked away. Blake took Samantha aside, stopping to pull on his jacket against the cold night air. "For God's sake, Sam, you should never have come here!"

She looked up at him with misty blue eyes. "Clyde Beecher told us about what happened today. I had to see for myself that you were all right. Please don't be angry, Blake." She reached up and lightly touched his cheek, which was scabbed and slightly puffy. "Oh, Blake, the realization that I could have lost you without seeing you again—"

He put his fingers to her lips, pulling her close. "I've missed you," he told her, his voice gruff with desire. He met her mouth then, the whiskey in his veins making him desire her with even greater intensity. His tongue slaked into her mouth, and she felt an exotic ache deep inside that made her whimper. Blake released the kiss, his whole body trembling. "Let's get out of here," he told her, taking her hand. He led her over frozen mud through three blocks of alleys to a better section of town.

Samantha knew without asking he was taking her to his room at the boardinghouse, and for the moment she didn't care that it was sinfully wrong for her to go there with him. Her blood rushed with strange, wonderful new desires. Being apart from him for the last three weeks had not changed her mind about anything. It had only made her love and want him more. Blake Hastings was everything to her, suddenly her only reason for existing. The realization he had been hurt was more than she could bear, and, right or wrong, she had to be with him.

"Won't your folks wonder where you are?" he

asked, leading her across a quieter street to his boardinghouse.

"They don't even know I'm gone. I snuck out after they fell asleep. I had to see you, Blake. I couldn't stand it."

"Be real quiet. Maybe I can get you to my room without anyone seeing."

They went very quietly inside, closing the front door softly. Blake led her up the stairs quickly and into his room, closing and locking the door. In the next instant he swept her into his arms, turning with her, kissing her deep and hard. He tried to tell himself to be careful. He was feeling his whiskey, and being apart from each other, his being hurt, had made Samantha more vulnerable.

She wanted him. Yes, she wanted him. He could tell by the way she returned his kiss. Should he take advantage of the moment? God, how he wanted to! He left her mouth, kissing softly at her neck.

"I love you, Sam. I missed you so much. I was even thinking of crawling back on my knees and begging your father to forgive me."

"Oh, Blake, I don't know what to do. Father wants to send me away—back East with my brother. He thinks I should get away from Lawrence until the elections are over."

He slowly set her on her feet. "Go away?" He turned away to light a lamp so he could see her better, then pulled her back into his arms. He searched her tear-filled eyes, trying to think clearly. The thought of not seeing her at all for months . . . Still, he reasoned, the way things were now, maybe it was a good idea at that. The important thing was her safety, and he knew after what had happened today that her father was probably right, that being with him only made life more dangerous for her.

Samantha caught the look of resignation in his eyes. The last thing on earth she wanted was to be away from Blake Hastings. If Blake agreed with her father, there would be no fighting it. "Blake, we could get married right away," she suggested, hoping to make him see it her way. "I don't care about the danger. I just want to be with you—to be your wife. If we got married right now—tonight— Father couldn't do anything about it."

How tempting the thought! He wished he hadn't had anything to drink. He waged an inner battle between desire and reason. He sighed, removing his jacket. "Samantha, who would marry us? Every preacher in this town knows your father. They'd know we were only going to them because we didn't have your father's approval; and we both know your father himself would never marry us—not after what happened today." He turned away, unable to look into those big, beautiful, blue eyes and think clearly at the same time. "He's probably right, Sam. You'd be a lot safer back east. I love you enough to know what's best for you."

"No!" Her heart rushed with dread, and she scrambled to think of a way to change his mind. "You don't want me to go. I know you don't!"

"Of course I don't." He turned. "But I also don't want anything to happen to you."

"It won't—as long as I'm with you." She knew deep inside there was only one way to keep him here. Once she belonged to him, her father would *have* to marry them. If she stayed the night . . . here in Blake's room . . . in his bed . . .

She had no idea how the thought had come to her so suddenly, or where she got her courage. She only knew she was desperate to keep him in Lawrence. A tear slipped down her face as she untied and removed her fur cape. She threw it into a chair, then unpinned her hat and took two combs from her hair, letting its dark tresses fall. "I might have to go away, Blake." She began unbuttoning the front of her dress, her heart pounding wildly. "But whether I stay or go, we might never get another chance," she told him boldly. "This might be the worst sin I ever commit . . . but I love you . . . and if something happens to you, I want you to have been my first man. Most of all I just want you to stay here . . . with me."

Blake stared at her in surprise as with shaking hands she pulled her dress from her shoulders and let it fall. She stood there in her camisole and slip, her full breasts cresting temptingly above the lace. Her whole body visibly trembled.

"Sam, don't do this. It isn't right," he tried to argue. "It isn't fair to either one of us."

"Isn't it? We love each other. Something could happen to either one of us any day. I might still have to go away, Blake, but we have tonight." Her cheeks were crimson. "Please, don't make me stand here and undress in front of you like a—" More tears spilled down her cheeks. "Please, Blake. Help me."

The combination of his love for her and the whiskey he had drunk, as well as the sight of her sensuous, virgin body was more than he could resist. He had wanted this all to happen the right way—to marry her and do this on their wedding night. But he realized the love and desire he felt for her would be no different, married or unmarried. She looked so scared and pitiful standing there . . . and so much in love—with him, Blake Hastings. It had been such a long time since he had known this kind of love.

"Sam," he said softly, coming closer. He reached out, gently running his fingers under the straps of

135

her camisole and pulling them off her shoulders. She pulled her arms out of the straps, then closed her eyes and gasped when he moved his fingers along the lace, lightly touching the whiteness of her breasts. He pulled one side away, brushing a full, ripe nipple with the back of his hand. "My God, Sam," he groaned. There was no turning back for either of them.

Seven

The night became one of magical awakening for Samantha. From the moment Blake Hastings's fingers touched her breast, she made up her mind that no matter what happened in the days to come, she was going to possess and be possessed by him, right or wrong.

Never had she felt so full of passion so heated with desire; nor had she ever before thought she could do this without fear. Blake took the fear away, left her little time to think at all as he smothered her with deep, delicious, suggestive kisses while somehow, magically, she found herself lying on his bed, her clothes coming off effortlessly until all that was left were her bloomers. Surely, she thought, this was the way love was supposed to be—to want to please a man the way she wanted to please Blake—to want to take pleasure in him in return, feeling no fear and no shame. Surely God would not have instilled in her this terrible desire for just one man if this were not the man she was supposed to love for the rest of her life.

Blake suspected somewhere deep in the more reasoning part of his mind that he was going to feel like a worthless bastard in the morning. Yes, he loved and wanted her, and she was willing. But he knew he could probably talk some sense into her if not for his own selfish desires. He knew perfectly well he was taking advantage of her desperate desire to be with him, her worry over his being hurt, but right now there was no thinking straight.

She lay on his bed, her full, soft breasts waiting to be touched, tasted. He loved her, and that was all that mattered. More than that, he could die tomorrow, and that would mean someday some other man would have this privilege, know this ecstasy. The thought of another man touching her was made even more unbearable by the thought of Fred Brewster trying to take from her what belonged to Blake Hastings and only caused him to be more determined.

"Make love to me, Blake," she said softly. "I want to belong to you. I'm not afraid, as long as it's you."

He needed no further prompting. He smothered her with kisses, stopping only to unbutton his shirt. He raised himself up to remove it and Samantha's face flushed at the sight of his bare chest. She moved under the blankets, pulling them over her breasts. She closed her eyes when she realized Blake was going to undress completely. Moments later she felt him move under the covers with her.

"Look at me, Sam," he said softly.

She opened her eyes again, keeping them on his own dark, eyes that glittered with love and desire. It seemed she should be afraid, but letting him touch her this way felt so natural and right.

"I love you, Sam," he told her softly, moving against her and running a hand down her bare back.

"I'll love you for the rest of my life."

He met her lips, and she gasped and returned his kisses with hot desire when she felt his nakedness pressing close. Blake pushed the covers away from her breasts and moved his lips down over her neck and chest to gently take a soft pink nipple into his mouth. With a big hand he ever so lightly pushed her bloomers down off her hips.

Samantha shivered with intense desire, clinging to his shoulders and closing her eyes again. A soft whimper exited her lips when he pulled the bloomers past her feet and threw them aside. His lips moved to taste her other breast, and his hand gently explored secret places she was once sure she could never let a man touch. The ecstasy was almost painful, and as his lips trailed over her belly and back to her breasts, his fingers worked in a circular motion that made her lose all sense of reason.

What was this wonderful new feeling he was awakening? In moments she felt a thrilling, unexpected explosion deep inside, a wonderful release that made her cry out his name. He covered her mouth with his own to smother the sound, while he moved on top of her.

"Try not to make too much noise," he whispered, moving his lips to her ear. "I don't want the landlady to know I have a woman in here, especially when it's Preacher Walters's daughter."

"What happened to me?" she whimpered.

Blake grinned, loving her all the more because she had never been touched this way. He was her first, and he was determined now that there would never be another. He kissed her again. "It just means you're ready to become a full woman," he answered. "Please don't be afraid, Sam. I promise that after the first time it just gets better."

"I believe you," she whispered in return.

"I love you, Sam." He smothered her mouth with his own again as he quickly moved inside of her, unable to hold back any longer. He felt her stiffen, knew he was hurting her; but he could tell that in this, as in everything she did, she was trying to be brave, forcing herself not to cry.

He felt her fingers digging into his arms, as he took her rhythmically, knowing he should be more gentle, but feeling such fiery desire that all reason left him. Being with her this way was so exciting and exotic that it was easy to allow a quick release, which he knew was best for her, to save her prolonged pain. He groaned at the utter ecstasy of his own climax, and he reached under her firm bottom to push himself deeper, to feel every last thrill of the act until he was finally spent.

He held her close under the blankets, and she began quietly crying. "Oh, Blake don't let Father send me away," she sobbed, hugging him around the neck. "Not now. I want to stay with you forever. I want to sleep with you, cook for you, be here for you when you come home at night."

He stroked her hair. "Part of me says it's best that you do go away," he told her softly. "But the selfish side of me won't let you go. You're brave and strong, Sam, and I think we can get through this. I couldn't stand to be apart now. If your father won't marry us, we'll go to another town and find someone who will."

She leaned away from him, meeting his eyes. "Do you mean it?"

He smiled for her. "I mean it."

She touched his wounded cheek. "You've got to be so careful now, Blake. I love you so much. I'm not ashamed of what we've done. I'll never be sorry for it, no matter what happens."

"Neither will I." He put a gentle hand to the side of her face. "Are you all right?"

She moved back into his arms, resting her head against his chest. "I feel wonderful. I've never been so happy."

He rubbed a hand down over her hips. "You're so beautiful, Sam. I haven't felt like this in a long, long time. Thank you for loving me enough to give me something I had no right taking."

"I wanted you to take it, to take all of me."

He kissed at her eyes, sweet, warm, gentle kisses. "It's never been this wonderful before, Mrs. Hastings." He kissed her nose. "You might as well get used to the name."

"Samantha Hastings sounds just fine," she whispered. She touched the hard muscles of his chest. His lips covered her mouth in a heated, groaning kiss that made her want him again, in spite of the pain. She felt his velvety-soft manhood quickly grow firm against her belly, and she knew that he wanted to repeat the pleasure they had just shared.

"It's all right," she whispered.

He moved on top of her, grasping her hips and entering her again, both of them losing all track of time and reason. This time she returned his rhythmic motion, arching up to meet him, grasping his powerful forearms as she gave of herself in total abandon.

Blake drank in her exotic nakedness, wondering how he could fit into such a small belly without hurting her. He thrust himself deep, as though to brand her, and after several minutes of the intense pleasure of being inside her youthful body, he drew in his breath at the glory of his release, groaning her name as the life spilled out of him.

Samantha Walters belonged to him now, no matter what her father thought about it. He could even have impregnated her already. Walters would have no choice but to marry them now. He kissed her several times over, happily, hungrily. "Get washed and dressed," he told her then, moving to the edge of the bed.

Samantha glanced at his nakedness, a shiver moving through her at the sight of his virile body. "Right now?" she asked.

"Right now. We're going to your folks' house and get them up."

"Tonight?"

"You heard me. I intend to wake up in the morning with you beside me. We're going to get married tonight. If Clyde Beecher is such a good friend of the family, we'll wake him up, too—get him over there for a witness. We're getting married tonight and you're coming back here to sleep with me."

Samantha's heart pounded with joy, mingled with dread at facing her parents. She told herself it didn't matter. She would be with Blake. He would handle everything. If he wasn't afraid, she wouldn't be, either.

Blake pulled on his long johns and went to the washstand, pouring some water into a bowl. "Come over here and wash." She sat up on the edge of the bed, keeping a sheet over herself and looking hesitant. "Don't worry. I promise not to watch. I just want to hurry up and get it done and get back here with you. We'll go find George and take him with us. He should be there, too."

Samantha rose, coming toward him with the sheet wrapped around her. "Are you sure, Blake? I don't want you to think that I . . . I tricked you or something."

He laughed lightly and pulled her into his arms. "You know good and well you tricked me." He kissed her warmly. "But I don't mind one bit. All you did was make me see how much I need to be with you. I want you right here with me from now on, and we're going to get that straightened out yet tonight."

She smiled and turned away to wash. Blake walked over to straighten the bed, and guilt stabbed at him. Should he have turned her away, let her go back East? Would his selfishness cost her, cost both of them? He sighed and yanked the blankets up over the pillows. The fact remained he had laid claim to Samantha Walters, and there was no use wondering what might have been.

"You sure you shouldn't have worn your gun?" George asked Blake. "Reverend Walters just might take a shotgun after you."

Blake pounded on the door again, while Samantha stood beside him, shivering from nervousness and the cold January air. She realized she would spend the new year as Mrs. Blake Hastings now. "He's the one who is always preaching against violence," Blake was saying.

Through the frosted glass of the door Samantha saw a light moving toward them. Her heart pounded so hard it almost hurt, and Blake moved an arm around her. She could hardly believe what had happened tonight. Somehow she had expected it would happen when she first went looking for Blake. She had *wanted* it to happen. In one sense it seemed so unreal. And yet here she stood beside him, her insides aching from her first experience with a man. It had hurt more than she had let on, but she forced herself to ignore the pain. All that mattered now was that he loved her, that he didn't want her to go away, that minutes from now she would be his wife.

The doors opened, and the reverend held up a lantern, his eyes widening in surprise. "Sam! what on earth—"

"We've come to be married," Blake told him sternly. "Sam would rather you married us, but if you won't, we'll go to some other town and find someone to do it. I love your daughter, Reverend, and this is the way it's going to be."

Samantha saw her mother approaching from behind her father, hurriedly tying a robe closer around herself. "Howard? What is it?"

Walters stood staring at Sam and Blake, anger in his eyes. "It's our daughter," he answered, obvious fury in his voice. "It seems that while we thought she was sleeping, she snuck off on us to shame herself—"

"Don't say it, Reverend," Blake interrupted, stepping closer with a threatening look in his eyes. "You know in your heart the kind of person your daughter is. I have nothing but the deepest respect for her. I love her and she loves me, and if you hadn't done your best to keep us apart, this would not have happened. Sam came to find me. She told me you wanted to send her away. We both knew we couldn't bear that. I'll tell you flat out I've already laid claim to her, and a damn piece of paper doesn't make a bit of difference except to make it legal in the eyes of others. Now, are you going to marry us or not? We don't have all night."

"Oh, dear," Milicent fussed. "Samantha, how could you—"

"I've done nothing wrong, Mother," Samantha

replied. "I love Blake. When I heard he was hurt, I had to go to him. And once I saw him again, I made up my mind nothing and no one was going to make me leave Lawrence and Blake." She moved her eyes to her father, who still stood staring at her with a look of disappointment and astonishment. "Please, Father. Let me be happy. See Blake for what he is—a good man who loves your daughter. The things that have happened to him haven't been his fault, and if he should die tomorrow, I won't regret one minute of tonight. Please marry us and give us your blessing. With so much danger around all of us, we can't afford to have disharmony in the family. We all need each other. Blake can help you in your work, and he has no family, Father. *We* can be his family. If I love him, you should love him, too."

Walters watched them both, the cold night air beginning to chill the hallway. Milicent touched her husband's arm. "Howard, they're in love. Have you forgotten how we felt when we first loved each other? It's obvious Blake will be good to her."

Walters breathed deeply, then stepped back. "Come inside before we all catch our death." All three of them came into the hallway and Walters set down the lantern, turning it up for more light. "Can't you at least wait a proper length of time and have a church wedding?"

"No," Blake answered matter-of-factly. "I told you, Reverend, we have already consummated our love. I don't intend to go back to my room tonight without Samantha, and I don't intend to have her talked about. Your friends don't need to know the sequence of events. Just tell them we came to you tonight to be married and you married us. That's all they need to know. We thought of getting Beecher to witness it, but George is a free man. He can do the honors. If Beecher doesn't know how it happened, that's one less person to worry about telling others. George can be trusted."

"What about a ring?"

"We'll go shopping for one tomorrow."

"You don't have a license," the reverend reminded them.

"That's something else no one needs to know. We'll get that tomorrow, too, and you can sign it. It will simply say you married us tonight instead of tomorrow. No one will see the license but us."

Walters seemed to soften, a look of resignation coming into his eyes. "I see you've thought of everything."

"I didn't mean for it to happen this way. Neither one of us did. But it's done now and there's no changing it. Just marry us, and Sam will go and get a few of her clothes."

The reverend's eyes showed a strange sadness then. "You have to understand that I see her as my little girl, Blake. Someday you will have a daughter, and when some man comes along wanting to steal her away from you, you'll know how I feel tonight."

Milicent dabbed at misty eyes, and Samantha touched her father's arm. "Father, you aren't losing me. You're just making me happy. Just because I'll be Blake's wife doesn't mean I'll stop being your daughter. I'm *not* a little girl, Father, not anymore."

The man sighed deeply. "No. I suppose not." He raised his eyes to Blake. *"You* have seen to *that!* You had better take good care of her, Blake. There you stand, carrying another scar from some man's bullet. I can't help but worry."

"Being here makes her no safer, Reverend. You know damn well I'm right. You can't expect to take such a firm, public stand for abolition without

146

putting yourself and your family in danger. Just because you don't believe in violence doesn't mean those against you don't."

The reverend nodded. "I know." He put out his hand. "I will marry you. But I want your promise that you will never again speak against Clyde Beecher in front of me or in my house."

Sam's heart pounded as the air hung silent for a moment. George knew how hard it was for Blake to take the man's hand then. He shook it. "I will say no more about him. But unlike you, Reverend, I don't intend to tell Beecher any more about my personal comings and goings than necessary."

"That's your decision. Come into the parlor. I have a Bible there."

Blake gave Samantha a reassuring smile. She felt warm and loved, already anxious to get back to Blake's room. Was this really happening? She wondered how she looked. There had been no time to primp. There were no flowers. Still, neither one of them needed the usual props and amenities. All that mattered was that they become husband and wife.

They spoke their vows, and the reverend prayed over them. Milicent could not help the quiet tears over her "baby" suddenly becoming a woman. Samantha hurried upstairs to pack some of her clothes, and after more tears and warm hugs, she left with Blake and George. George congratulated Blake when they reached the boardinghouse. "I'm happy for you, friend," he told him.

"I just wish I could be witness to your own wedding, George—to Jesse."

"I don't hold much hope of that ever happening." George looked at Samantha. "You take good care of this guy," he told her. "You have your hands full."

"I don't mind." She took George's hand. "Thank

you for coming with us, George. And you're just as much my friend now as Blake's. As soon as we get a house of our own, we'll make arrangements for living quarters for you. Nothing is going to change as far as your friendship with Blake."

George grinned, squeezing her hand. "Sure, things will change some. They're bound to. I understand, and I don't blame Blake one bit."

Blake touched George's arm. "Don't go making any rash decisions. Until the trouble in this town is settled, I just might need your help a time or two."

"I have a feeling *I'm* the one who might need help. But you know where I am."

The two men shook hands again. "I'll see you at the sawmill day after tomorrow," Blake said. "Do me a favor and tell Bronson I got married and won't be in tomorrow."

George's grin widened. "He'll understand that, I'm sure." He nodded to a blushing Samantha and walked off into the darkness.

Samantha turned to Blake. "I wish George could be as happy as we are right now," she said. "I feel so sorry for him. His life has been so sad."

"Maybe someday he'll find someone he cares about as much as Jesse. I suppose it can happen more than once for any man—like it did for me." He pulled her close. "I love you, Sam." He picked up her bag of clothes and walked her to the door and inside, leading her up the stairs. "I have some explaining to do to my landlady in the morning," he teased.

Samantha laughed lightly. He opened the door to his room, setting the bag inside, then turning to pick her up in his arms. "It's not much for the moment, but welcome home, Mrs. Hastings. All I want the rest of tonight is to sleep with you in my arms, to wake up next to you in the morning." He kissed her lightly.

"You need time to heal."

"I heal fast," she whispered.

He grinned, thinking how easily she stirred his every desire. He carried her inside and kicked the door shut.

"So, our little shooting incident didn't scare off Blake Hastings," Nick West said as he lit a cigar.

"Just the opposite," Clyde Beecher answered. "He and Samantha Walters just ran right into each other's arms. Now that she's his wife, he won't be leaving Lawrence."

West sat thinking, absently stroking at his thin mustache. "That probably means Hastings will become more active in Walters's efforts to win the Free-soil vote."

Beecher kept his own thoughts unspoken. West wouldn't like it if he knew Blake Hastings suspected him of being a spy. West would probably cut him off from the generous amount of money the man paid him to keep eyes and ears open. Besides, even though Hastings had married Samantha, there was still no real danger. Reverend Walters still had full faith and trust in him, and that was all that counted.

Both men sat in the privacy of West's farm home north of Lawrence. Beecher looked around at the fine oak trim and oak bookcases in West's office, thinking how someday, when all the uproar over slavery and free states was over, he would start spending all the money he was making and have a nice place of his own—maybe find some pretty young thing to share it with him. There were plenty of women around who would marry a man for his money. He realized he wasn't much to look at, with a nose that was too big and a face marked with pits from a bad case of measles as a child. But the whores liked him well enough. Maybe he'd find a whore to come live with him!

"Are you going to get rid of Hastings all together?" he asked West. "As long as he's alive, he's a menace."

West leaned back in his leather chair and put his feet up on his desk. "I don't think so. I've already come too close a couple of times to being linked to violence. I don't want that." He took another puff on his cigar, watching the blue smoke curl into the air. "Hastings wants my life. Let him come and get it. Let him be the one to suffer the consequences of violence." He looked at Beecher. "The man isn't going to kill me outright. He has a wife now. He doesn't want to end up in a noose. He knows the only way to get me is if I start something first so he can call it self-defense." He grinned. "I'll just surprise him by being completely polite to him and staying out of his way."

"What about him joining forces with Walters?"

West laughed lightly. "Let him. I have men working night and day on bringing in more proslavery people from Missouri. No matter how hard that preacher works to win the vote, it isn't going to happen. Maybe most of Lawrence is made up of Free Staters, but there are plenty of proslavery people in the rest of Kansas. With the extras I'm pulling in from Missouri, we can still swing the vote." West brought his feet down, leaning forward with his elbows on his desk. "I think we're going at this thing backward."

Beecher frowned. "I don't get your meaning."

"I mean that we can still do a few things to scare some of the outlying settlers into voting our way; but we can get away with a lot more *after* the elections. Just think for a minute. If the vote goes our way, we can *legally* set up some proslavery laws—a proslavery territorial government—penalties, maybe even imprisonment for the more radical Free Staters. Get my meaning?"

Beecher began to smile. "Yes, sir, I get your meaning."

"Once we vote in our own men, people like Walters and Hastings can be charged with treason and arrested if they continue to work against slavery. Hastings might even get careless and shoot someone—get himself hanged. There are all kinds of possibilities. I might have a chance at legally putting Hastings out of business and shutting him up once and for all about his accusations that I had his father killed."

Their eyes held. *"Did* you have him killed?" Beecher asked.

West's eyes sparkled. "You really expect me to answer that?"

"I guess not."

West laughed again, setting his cigar in an ashtray. "Let's just say I was not fond of the man. He bought and freed a pretty little slave girl I had planned on bringing home for my own pleasure." He rose from his chair, walking to a window. "But, the past is past. I personally never laid a hand on the man. If some of my men got a little carried away, that's their problem. It was none of my doing." He turned and looked at Beecher. "And now I have found another little Negro girl who's prettier than the one I was originally going to buy. In fact, I actually miss her. I think I'll just go back to Missouri for a while and spend a few weeks with her—drop out of Lawrence and dispel people's suspicions about me. I can't be blamed for anything if I'm not around now, can I?"

"Good idea," Beecher answered.

151

"Even you should lay low for a while," West told him. "My border raiders have a pretty good idea which settlers to keep harassing. They can keep up the dirty work while I'm gone. In the meantime, now that Hastings is closer to the reverend, you'd better keep your own nose as clean as possible. Stick close to town. Don't do anything to give the reverend anything to suspect. Maybe eventually you'll even win over Blake Hastings. I'll come back to Kansas in a few weeks, bring more voters with me. After the elections, everything will change. It's ones like Walters and Hastings who will be on the defensive then. We can go after all of them with the full blessings of the territorial government."

Beecher grinned as he rose and put on his hat. "I anxiously await the day."

West came closer and put out his hand. "You've done a good job, Beecher. I'll be in touch with you as soon as I get back from Missouri." He shook the man's hand, then walked around his desk to open a drawer. He took out a wad of money, handing it across the desk. "This should tide you over until I get back."

Beecher took the money eagerly. "I should say so," he answered.

"That money is one of the main reasons why we can't end slavery in this country, Beecher. Where would the big plantation owners like myself be if they had to start paying their help? Abolishing slavery would destroy the entire economic system of the South."

Beecher stuffed the money into a pocket. "You just send a messenger when you get back and let me know when you want to see me again. You know where I'll be."

West grinned. "In that little shack, living like the

152

poor, devoted church leader."

Beecher grinned. "The poor Christian with a few thousand dollars buried under his house, you mean."

Both men laughed, and Beecher left. West walked to a window to watch him ride off, contemplating the pleasure he would take in seeing that the entire Walters family as well as Blake Hastings were punished for their traitorous actions once Kansas was voted in as a slave territory. They would all regret being so outspoken against slavery; and that big black friend of Blake Hastings would be in his own tub of hot water.

He turned to go to his bedroom and pack some clothes, surprised that he actually missed Jesse March. He hadn't had a decent round in bed with a woman since leaving her. He decided that when he came back to Kansas next time, he would bring Jesse with him and keep her here at the farm. After the elections he could take her into Lawrence and flaunt her in front of Blake Hastings. Maybe that would get the man's dander up and make him do something foolish to get himself arrested and imprisoned. Blake was a lot like his father when it came to owning slaves. He would take one look at sad little Jesse and want to buy her; only West was not about to sell her at any price to someone like Hastings.

He took a carpetbag from the closet. This was a good time to leave for a while. Let Hastings stay in Lawrence and dig his own grave.

Eight

Samantha turned to snuggle against Blake, resting her head on his shoulder and moving an arm around his middle. There were times when she still found it hard to believe she was waking up in his bed every morning, that she could freely enjoy being with him this way.

They had been married two whole months already, and she had not regretted one moment of it. She prayed that the relative peace they had found since marrying would last forever. Blake had discovered that Nick West had gone back to Missouri, and although she knew her husband still held a deep hatred for the man, she hoped that with West gone, Blake would learn to forget about vengeance. After all, he was married now. They had rented a cozy, four-room frame house from Jonas Hanks, a faithful member of Reverend Walters's church whose family had outgrown the house. Hanks had built himself a bigger one.

Samantha loved her house, and she worked hard at keeping it clean and tidy, trying to keep some semblance of peace and order within the confines of her home, where she felt protected from the unrest of the outside world.

Although the cold winter and now a blustery March had not ended the border wars, Blake himself had not been involved in any more confrontations or shootings. He reasoned that whoever had shot at him the day Brewster was shot had left town and wouldn't be back. Blake was doing well at his job at the sawmill, and even George seemed to be happy and settled. Blake had painted and cleaned out a small shed behind the house and had installed a wood-burning heating stove in it for George so he could live close by. George had bought a bed and some used furniture, and Samantha had made curtains for the one and only window. She worried that the shed was too primitive, but to George it was a castle, and he seemed perfectly content.

Samantha knew she was being foolish to think that the quiet love she shared with Blake and the peace they had found here in their little house could last forever. The elections would be held in a week, and the streets of Lawrence remained in upheaval. Samantha knew Blake was trying, for her sake, not to get too involved, other than helping at the print shop. Joe Stetson's wife, determined that the death of her husband would not stop publication of the newspaper, had helped the reverend, George, and Blake get the printing machines back into working order, teaching Samantha how to set type, showing Blake how much ink to use, reordering broken equipment and in general, taking over her husband's job. The Stetson's fifteen-year-old son Mark also helped; and now an abolitionist newspaper was again being printed and distributed every week. With the elections so close, anything could happen now.

What frightened Samantha most was, if the vote did swing to the proslavery faction, people like her father, herself and Blake could be in a dangerous predicament.

"What are you thinking about?" Blake asked.

Sam glanced up to see that his eyes were open. "I didn't know you were awake."

"Kind of hard for a man to keep sleeping with a beautiful woman wrapped around him."

She smiled, nestling back into his shoulder. "I was just wondering how much longer we'll go without any big trouble. The elections are coming soon. It scares me a little."

Blake sighed, turning to hold her closer. "It scares me, too. More and more border people are coming into Lawrence, scared half out of their wits. Sheriff Tucker says the border raids have escalated again, people reporting cattle stolen, barns burned, hooded bushwhackers warning them they had better vote for slavery for Kansas. The land belonging to Free-soil sympathizers who leave is being taken over by proslavery families from Missouri, people just pretending to settle in Kansas. You watch how fast they all run back to Missouri after the elections are over. Once they put men into office who they know will do their bidding, they'll go back to where they came from, satisfied that Missouri will not be totally surrounded by free states and abolitionists." He kissed her forehead. "All you and I can do is take one day at a time."

"I know." She kissed his chest, running a hand lightly over his strong arm. "What about Nick West, Blake? You have hardly mentioned him since he left town."

He moved a hand along her leg, rubbing at her thigh. "I'm going to do my best to put it all behind me, for your sake. I just hope he stays in Missouri."

She hugged him closer. "Thank you," she whispered.

Blake moved his hand around to caress her bottom, thinking how firm and velvety it felt against his fingers. Everything about her was beautiful, desirable. He had once wondered if a man ever got tired of a wife, if he got so used to her that she didn't excite him anymore. But he had none of those feelings with Sam. He figured it was because he loved her so much, that what he felt for her was so much deeper than merely physical that he could never grow tired of her. She had turned into a provocative lover, tantalizing and pleasing and eager, but with the deeper fulfillment of sharing souls and hearts.

He had worked hard at giving up his thoughts of vengeance against Nick West. He was not positive he could completely forget the matter, but he had a wife now who needed him. Sam was more important than getting revenge against someone as worthless as West. He was trying to learn to live by her father's preaching that vengeance belonged to God alone. Maybe Reverend Walters was right—that all they could do was spread God's word and work peacefully for the free vote and that those who dealt in the ugly horrors of slavery would get their just punishment from God, if not in this world, then in the next.

Still, he was not firmly convinced God didn't intend to use men to do some of that work for him. He knew it wouldn't take much for him to revert to his belief that a little physical persuasion was the only way to get a job done. But for the moment it was Sam's "physical persuasion" that made him put aside all such thoughts. Waking up to her in the morning always made him want her. She was all soft and warm and sleepy then. Making love always seemed a little sweeter.

He breathed in the scent of her hair, his hand moving back over her belly, then down to explore her lovenest, where he found the moistness he always found there in the morning.

"Blake, it's getting late," she protested weakly.

He moved his lips down to nuzzle at her neck. "We just talked about how we can only take one day at a time," he answered, pushing her gown to her waist. He moved on top of her, his hardness pressing against her.

She smiled softly, closing her eyes and opening herself to him. He entered her in one hard thrust, making her draw in her breath. It was always this way in the mornings, most of the time not even removing her gown. It was just a sweet, pleasant way to wake up. It was in the afternoon or evening that they did much more. Blake had taught her to put aside all her inhibitions, to explore and allow herself to be explored, to realize that this was just one facet of their love that needed expressing and that there was nothing wrong with anything they wanted to do. Sometimes she felt so wanton and bold, yet she knew she was pleasing him immensely and she took her own pleasure in return.

She arched up to him in sweet rhythm, feeling the building ecstasy as he moved inside her in that magical way that brought the throbbing release deep in her belly and just made her want him more. She felt it now, gasped his name, moved almost wildly then as though she could not get enough of him. He grasped her hips, rising to his knees and pushing deep, holding off as long as possible to give her the full enjoyment of him.

Samantha felt his own life pulsing into her, and she prayed that maybe this time it would take hold.

She wanted more than anything to give him a child. She knew that a baby would be even more insurance that he would put aside his hatred and vengeance and not do anything to risk his life.

He relaxed, lying down beside her again. "I love you," he told her, kissing at her hair. "I'd like to stay here all day, but I'd better get to work." He moved away from her, sitting up. "Are you staying home today?"

"I'm going over to Mother's."

"Fine. Just don't go walking the streets with flyers or go over to the print shop. Not without me. We'll go help out after I get home today."

"Blake, I'm perfectly capable—"

"Not without me. We made an agreement." He rose and picked up his longjohns, going into a small room off the bedroom to wash.

"I try to stay out of trouble and forget seeking vengeance against Nick West—you don't go walking the streets alone or help Mrs. Stetson alone. Remember?"

She sighed, pulling the covers over herself. "Yes." She waited for him to finish washing.

Blake emerged wearing his underwear. "And if Beecher shows up at the house over there, you don't let him talk you into going alone with him anyplace for any reason."

"Blake, you said yourself you followed him several days in a row, and he never did anything underhanded. You must know by now—"

"I still don't trust him. He's been good as a saint lately, but remember that Nick West is out of town. I have a feeling they both made an agreement to lay low for a while. If Kansas gets voted in as a slave territory, which it just might, you'll find out quick enough who the bad guys really are."

160

The statement brought the quick, tight feeling to her stomach that it always did. "I know," she said quietly. She rolled to the edge of the bed and sat up. "I'll fix your breakfast as soon as I wash."

Blake watched her walk into the washroom herself then. She pulled the curtains shut, and he was instantly angry with himself for causing her unnecessary concern. Whichever way the election went, there was going to be trouble; but for now life had been happy and relatively peaceful. For all he knew it would last. The morning had started out sweet and happy. He should have left it that way. He pulled on a shirt and walked to stand beside the curtain. "I'm sorry, Sam."

He heard the sound of her wringing out a washrag. A moment later she pushed the curtain aside and embraced him. He rubbed a hand over the soft flannel gown she still wore. "I just wish it was all over," she said quietly. "Why do things have to be this way? It seems like it's all we ever talk about. Even though we've found peace with each other, there's that ugly black cloud hanging over us—hanging over Lawrence." She looked up at him. "I'll be so happy when the day comes that we can talk about something besides slavery and states' rights. I want to talk about farming and building a house and . . . and babies."

He kissed her forehead. "I want the same things you do. In the meantime, I know how independent and determined you can be, Sam. It's just that I made a promise to myself and to your father that I would make sure nothing else happened to you. I admire your bravery, but you are also my wife now. I don't ask you to do or not do certain things just because I think I have the right to direct your life. It's just that I love you. I don't know what I'd do if something happened to you. I guess all the other losses I've known just make me be more protective. I'm afraid I'll wake up one morning and you won't be there in bed with me.''

She looked up at him, her eyes misty. "I'll always be here. And it's the same for me, you know. I don't want anything to happen to you, either.'' She reached up and touched the white, still-prominent scar on his left cheek. "Every time I look at this, I am reminded of how close I came to losing you before I ever even got to have you for my own.''

He thought of the night she had first come to him, forcing aside her pride and disrobing in front of him in a successful effort to get him to keep her father from sending her away. He always smiled at the thought of it, fully realizing that of all the things she had done, that had to be one of the bravest.

He leaned down and met her mouth in a deep, sweet kiss. She returned it with equal zest, always loving the taste and smell of him, always relishing the comfort of his strong arms, knowing that as long as they were around her, nothing could happen to her.

North of town Nick West was also waking up. He had just got back to Kansas late the night before, this time bringing his mistress with him. He rose from bed, going to the door and opening it to catch the scent of coffee. His cook and housekeeper, Hetta, already had breakfast started. She was good at her job, had kept the place tidy while he had been gone.

West had hired Hetta out of a saloon, an aging prostitute who was grateful for the chance to finally get out of the saloon and live a more normal life. Hetta couldn't care less about the issues of slavery or

162

abolition; and because of the life she had led, she knew when to keep her mouth shut. She had shown no surprise when Nick showed up last night with Jesse. West figured the woman understood that Jesse's position was no different from some of the young girls who found themselves forced into prostitution. They learned to like it after a while, just like he was sure Jesse had.

Still, he couldn't trust her completely—not just yet. He had locked his pretty little slave in the next room, chaining one ankle to the footrail of the bed. He had been too tired that night to take any pleasure in her, but he was rested now. He walked over and unlocked the door, giving no heed to his nakedness. After all, Hetta had seen all there was to see in her sordid life. He noticed Jesse was awake as he closed the door.

"Well, now, did you sleep well?" he asked her.

Jesse turned away, hardly able to stand looking at him. She knew that under normal circumstances, Nick West could be considered handsome for a white man, in spite of his advancing age. But she had known only the cruel side of him, and she had the scars from beatings and cigarette burns to prove it. The man was clever, always careful not to leave marks where he could easily see them when he took her; or to scar her pretty face or breasts. In Nick West, Jesse March had realized her worst nightmare in being a slave.

Her former owner had been relatively good to his slaves, giving them decent quarters, not working them until they dropped, feeding them well. West dressed her well, fed her well. He did not expect hard physical work from her, but he expected her to be at his beck and call whenever he had a physical need. He seemed very taken by her, determined that she

163

should submit willingly to him, should show desire and eagerness when he bedded her. The only way he had got her to at least pretend those things was to torture her until her spirit was broken. Even then, he did not trust her not to try to run away.

She twisted at the cuff around her ankle. "Take it off, Nick," she asked him. "I can't enjoy anything with this on. It hurts."

He smiled, turning to get the key from the drawer of a dresser across the room. He came over and unlocked the cuff, then took the blankets from where her foot stuck out and threw them back, exposing her nakedness. "You're the prettiest Negro girl I've ever set eyes on," he told her, "and there have been plenty of them. You please me the most, Jesse."

She felt the sickness in her stomach, but she smiled for him. The memory of the pain he could cause would stay with her forever, and now she would do whatever he wanted just to keep from ever feeling it again.

"Then come let me please you some more," she said aloud, thinking what pleasure she would take in sinking a knife into his heart.

He moved onto the bed and she closed her eyes, wondering what he would think if he knew that the only way she could bear this was to imagine it was George Freedom doing these things to her. How she had loved him! George had been her first man, and in her heart he had been her only man. Nick West couldn't take that from her. She wondered what had ever happened to George, or if he thought about her anymore.

Blake and Samantha walked through the streets toward the church, George beside them. Samantha hunched her shoulders into her thick, blue wool cape, keeping her hands in a fur muff against the damp, cold March air and wondering if spring would ever arrive. Blake liked her in blue, said it made her blue eyes look even prettier. She wore a blue dress of heavy cotton with several slips for warmth; a satin-lined fur bonnet was tied under her chin to protect her ears from the cold. Her heart rushed with a mixture of excitement and dread. This was election day, and her father's church was one of the locations where voting would take place.

The street was already filling with people, and excitement hung in the air. Here and there they could hear men arguing over slavery, taking the issue down to a last-minute decision. Somewhere in the distance a band finished playing "The Star-Spangled Banner," then started in again with a marching tune. The street was filled with vendors peddling their wares, and an almost circuslike atmosphere prevailed. It reminded Blake of the day Fred Brewster was to be hanged. He hoped this day would not bring the violence that one had.

"Wish I could vote," George spoke up.

"Maybe some day Negroes will win the right," Blake answered.

George grinned and shook his head. "I doubt that day will ever come. First they'd have to end slavery all together in this country, and I don't think it will ever happen, no matter how much some people want it."

"Don't be such a pessimist," Samantha told him. "I happen to believe it *will* happen, the same as the fact that someday women will *also* be able to vote."

"And you're a dreamer, Sam," George answered.

They approached a platform, where a man named Andrew Reeder stood talking to onlookers. Reeder had been sent to Kansas by President Pierce to govern

165

the territory, and he had very cleverly not voiced his feelings either for or against slavery. Although Samantha guessed he was a Free-soil man at heart, most people had no doubt that whichever way the wind blew today, Reeder would go with it. He simply urged people to feel free to vote, to keep some semblance of law and order, and to peacefully accept the outcome.

Several other platforms had been erected, used by both proslavery and Free-soil men running for office. All the candidates had been traveling the territory as extensively as possible to urge people to vote for them, all of them taking the risk of being shot down by enemy factions. Most were now in Topeka, but supporters used the platforms today to speak for their favorite candidates and try to win last-minute votes.

Blake scanned the crowd as they walked, and Samantha felt his grip tighten on her hand. "Look who's back," he said to George.

George turned to see Nick West driving a buggy down the street, moving slowly because of the crowd. "Just in time for the elections, I see," George answered.

Blake kept his eyes on the man as he came closer. Samantha felt the tension building. "Blake, remember the promises we made each other," she urged. "Let's just get over to the church. We promised Father we'd help watch the election booths."

"I know. We'll make it," he answered, keeping his eyes on West, who smiled and nodded as he drove by.

"A rather cold, damp day for coming out to vote, isn't it," West called from his carriage. "My, you're looking very pretty, Mrs. Hastings, in that lovely blue color." He moved his eyes to Blake. "You know how to pick them, Blake."

166

The man drove on, and Blake watched after him, all the old feelings of hatred beginning to burn inside him. "I didn't think we were lucky enough to be rid of him for good," he commented. He looked down at Samantha, seeing the worry in her eyes. He moved an arm around her and started walking again. "Let's get over to the church."

They moved through the crowds, Blake watching people closely, aware that today anything could happen. No one needed to tell him that half the people he saw didn't belong here. People didn't need much in the way of identification. They just needed to swear they had settled in Kansas and to describe their location. A lot of the people he noticed as they made their way up the street were obviously not common, peaceful settlers. The crowd was made up more of men than families, and some of those men wore guns and struck a menacing pose. He wore his own gun today, and he kept his wool jacket pushed back on the right side, freeing his holster in case he needed to use that gun quickly.

He had not even wanted Samantha to come out into the streets, but he knew there was no use in trying to make her stay home today of all days. This was the day she and her family had worked so hard for. He kept her close beside him, holding no doubts that border ruffians and bushwhackers composed a good share of the people here today. The theme of popular sovereignty that Congress had enacted through the Kansas-Nebraska Act had come to be called "squatter sovereignty," because of all the people who had come to Kansas to "squat" just long enough to get in their vote. Blake had no doubt the results of today's elections would not reflect the views of most of the permanent citizens of Kansas Territory.

Samantha's father welcomed them eagerly when they arrived, asking Blake to help keep people in line. He glanced at the six-gun Blake wore at his side and frowned.

"Don't ask me to take it off today, Howard," Blake told his father-in-law. "There's too much tension in the air. I intend to be ready if there's trouble."

The reverend just sighed, having learned that there was no arguing with his new son-in-law. He had learned that the night Blake had come to practically order him to marry him and Samantha. He liked Blake very much, and it was obvious Samantha was blissfully happy, but he still worried that Blake Hastings was going to make a young widow of his daughter. Still, Blake had made major strides in settling down, and he had not brought up the subject of Nick West or Clyde Beecher since the wedding.

Blake kissed Samantha's cheek. "You stay here inside and hand out ballots. George and I will be right outside keeping an eye on things."

"Be careful," she urged.

He gave her a smile and a wink, and Samantha moved to sit down beside her mother behind a table stacked with voting ballots. She breathed deeply in an effort to dispel her concern over how this day might turn out. A rough-looking man who needed a shave stepped up to the table. "Let's have a ballot, little girl," he told her, a look in his eyes that told her she would not want to come across him alone in a dark alley. She handed him the ballot and he winked at her, walking over behind a curtain to cast his vote.

"I'm worried, Mother," she told Milicent. "I don't like the looks of some of these people."

"Nor do I, Sam, but there is nothing we can do about it. Just hand out the ballots and pray for the best."

168

Sam gave another ballot to a younger man, then glanced past him, straining to see outside the door and catch a glimpse of Blake. She noticed him standing with his hands on his hips, watching the crowd. Her Blake, always ready to defend against the worst of them! Lord knew he was skilled with guns and fists, but if the territorial laws got changed, that might not be enough for him and her family. Their very future depended on which way the vote went today.

Samantha lowered the newspaper, which Blake had left work to bring to her. He knew he should be at the mill, but this could not wait. He watched the change in her face, from happy and contented to deep worry, and a little fear. "My God, Blake, what are we going to do?" she said in a near whisper. She met his eyes. "After all our work, all the risks we took . . ."

"The risks are much greater now. This is bad, Sam. Maybe I should take you completely out of Kansas."

She stiffened. "You'll do no such thing. I'll not run from this! And you know Father won't. I won't leave my parents to face this alone."

He pounded his fist on the tabletop. "Damn it, Sam, I'm just thinking of you, *and* George *and* your folks."

"We *can't* just run, Blake. And I can't believe that Governor Reeder or the President—either one—will stand for this! Over sixty-three hundred votes, Blake, and according to Kansas records only twenty-nine hundred men were *eligible* to vote! It *reeks* of fraud and ballot stuffing! No man in his right mind can let this pass as legal!"

"Can't he? You just watch what happens as soon as word gets around that Kansas had been voted in as

169

slave territory. The border raiding will only get worse, and Reeder doesn't have one bone in his back! Anyone can see that. The bushwhackers are threatening everyone and everything that gets in their way, including Reeder himself. They have *elected officials* behind them now! Reeder *will* let this pass, Sam, and if he does, the President is going to rely on the man's decision. Do you really think President Pierce wants to offend any state or territory? These are dangerous times, Sam. Presidents are as vulnerable to a bullet as anybody else! He's not going to raise one finger to change what has happened!"

Her eyes teared and she turned away. "He *has* to. Reeder and the President both should order another election. People should be screened. They should have some kind of proof of how long they have lived in Kansas. They—"

"Stop it, Sam! We've lost! Get it through that pretty little head of yours. We've *lost,* and from here on you can't go walking the streets handing out abolitionist material. You can't work down at the print shop putting out the newspaper. Everything you do now could be considered treason."

"I can't believe this is happening," she said, her voice breaking. "We worked so hard—"

Blake came around the table, grasping her shoulders from behind. "I know, Sam. The whole thing makes me sick. Men like Nick West will have their heyday now." He turned her to face him, looking at her sternly. "I know you still aren't convinced about Beecher, but now more than ever I want you to be careful around him, Sam. I wish I could convince your father of that. If the new government creates laws against abolitionist movements, your father will be one of the first ones to be handed over by Clyde Beecher. He might not physically do the dirty work, but he'll drop the right names to the right people. Beecher has a long list to work with."

"Oh, Blake, it's so hard to believe—"

"Believe it! I don't want you voicing any radical abolitionist ideas around him from here on. You just pretend you've accepted the vote and don't intend to try to actively interfere."

A tear slipped down her cheek. "Blake, I'm not made that way, and neither are you. Nor will I run from this. You know in your heart how wrong this is. You know most of Kansas's solid citizens are against slavery. This whole election is a *lie*, and we can't leave it this way! You can't honestly tell me you could turn your back on what has happened and just walk away from it. I know you better. You'll stay and fight this, because you know it's the right thing to do. You'll fight it for the sake of people like George. We don't need any more slave territory, Blake. If we let this stand, the horror of slavery will just keep spreading, and there will be no hope for the ones who are still suffering the way George once suffered."

She detected tears in his eyes. "Damn you," he said, pulling her close. "None of it is as important as not losing you," he told her.

"Some things *are* more important than our own selfish wants," she said sadly. "What frightens me most is that you might not be able to fight this with just words. You're in more danger than I am, Blake." She broke into tears and he held her close, stroking her hair. He glanced again at the headlines of the morning paper, which she had laid on the table. PROSLAVERY CANDIDATES WIN CONTROL OF TERRITORIAL LEGISLATURE!

"Don't go back to work just yet," Samantha asked him. "Stay and hold me for a while." He picked her up in his arms and walked into the sitting room,

171

lowering himself into a big rocker while keeping her on his lap. "Please try to keep doing it Father's way, Blake. Please don't get involved in the violence."

"That depends on what happens from here on, Sam. You want to stay and fight this, and you're probably right to do so. But I can't guarantee I'll be as passive as your father. It just depends on how far I get pushed, and whether or not anyone threatens you or George or your family."

"Maybe Reeder or the President will declare the elections invalid. Maybe you're wrong about them letting this stand."

"I hope I am, honey. But I don't think so."

"Take me to Mother's when you leave. I should be with them today."

"I will. Just watch what you say around Beecher."

She kissed his neck. "I'm sorry I got you into all of this."

"You?"

"If you hadn't nearly run me over a few months ago, we might never have gotten together. You might be heading west with George, or still working back in Missouri and not be mixed up in this."

"Loving you is worth any sacrifice. I wouldn't trade one day of it. And even though I don't like the risks involved, I would have been a little bit disappointed if you had agreed right away to leave Kansas. Much as I hate the risk of anything happening to you, your stubbornness and bravery are two of the reasons I fell in love with you in the first place. We'll stay, Sam. We won't leave your parents. But we've got to be even more careful in everything we do from here on. A lot of the proslavery squatters and border ruffians have remained here, intending to make sure the vote stands and their people run Kansas's territorial legislature. I expect a whole new

172

list of laws is going to be thrown in our faces real quick."

"We might have to obey them, but that doesn't mean we have to agree with them. We'll just have to stand together. There are a lot of people who feel the same way we do."   .

He kissed her hair. "I just hope they're all as brave as you. People have a tendency to run away with their tail between their legs when you need them most."

She moved to kiss his cheek, and he turned, meeting her mouth in a hungry, desperate kiss, both of them wondering how long the love and happiness they had found in each other's arms could last amid the bitter hatred and rivalry building not only in Kansas but in the entire country.

Back at his own house Clyde Beecher saddled his horse to ride out to Nick West's ranch to tell him the good news. He smiled at the memory of Howard Walters literally weeping over the headlines that morning. What a fool Walters was! The course of events over the next few months was going to be interesting indeed. Maybe now Nick could find a way to get his hands on George Freedom.

"That nigger's days are numbered," Beecher muttered absently to his horse as he mounted up. "And so are Blake Hastings's days—and those of that pretty little wife of his!" He headed out, feeling smug and victorious.

Nine

July 1855

The Reverend Walters finished his fervent prayer and opened his eyes to scan his congregation. He saw the deep fear in the eyes of some. People fanned themselves against the summer heat, and a few flies were making pests of themselves, only adding to the jumpy nervousness felt by many.

"Well, my friends, we have received the news," Walters told them. "Our new proslavery legislature has met in Pawnee, and they have made new laws that prohibit abolitionist activity. They have even kicked out of office the few abolitionist legislators who managed to get themselves elected and replaced them with their own puppets."

The man wiped at his brow with a handkerchief, refusing to take off his suit jacket because he was in the pulpit. "These are dark times, my friends," he went on.

Blake shifted uncomfortably, not from the heat, but from his uneasiness now at Walters's continued abolitionist preaching. George, already afraid, had stopped coming to church. He feared he would be in even more danger if he was known to attend any gatherings where abolition was preached.

"This is a time of testing," Walters continued, his voice rising. "This is a time when we must either adhere to our Christian faith and do what we know is right, against all danger; or we turn our faces away from God and admit we do not have the faith we have heretofore professed to have. I, for one, will not turn away. I, for one, know in my heart that those who think they can own men like cattle, those who believe it's all right to beat and torture another human being, to work him to death, to tear babies from the arms of their mothers, to separate husbands and wives and use human beings for their own profit or pleasure—these people, my friends, do the work of Satan, not God! They will one day get their just punishment, as those who stand up for freedom and equality will one day get their just *rewards!*"

Blake moved his eyes to Clyde Beecher. He sat at the front of the church just behind Walters, who now considered Beecher an assistant lay pastor. Beecher was watching Walters carefully, his dark eyes unreadable. The pitted marks in his skin seemed more prominent today, and Blake wondered if it was the heat, or the way the sun shone through a window onto the man's face—or perhaps it was because beneath that calm look on his face the color was rising. Yes, *that* was it!

Blake kept watching him while Walters preached, slowly sensing the anger and deceitfulness that lay just beneath the surface of his professed friend and fellow Christian. In the seven months he had been married to Samantha, he could not help having occasion to be around Beecher often. There were times when he actually began to believe he might have been wrong about the man. Beecher could be so

176

sincere, and, contrary to what Blake had expected, he had not turned on Walters and his family and followers since the elections. He continued to preach abolition right along with the rest of them, seemingly unafraid of the consequences. But did he have friends in high places, people who knew he was only putting on an act in order to provide them with names of traitors?

Beecher's dark eyes turned to Blake, and Blake met the look squarely. Words did not have to be exchanged. Each knew what the other was thinking in that look, and Blake prayed for the day when Clyde Beecher would slip up, and he could prove to the reverend that his good Christian friend was really his enemy. He suspected that if looks could kill, Clyde Beecher would be shooting him down this moment.

"We are going to test these new laws," Walters was saying, "and we are going to test our own faith. As the psalm says, 'Yea, though I walk through the valley of the shadow of death, I shall fear no evil, for Thou art with me.' It tells us, 'Thou preparest a table before me in the *presence* of mine enemies.' Throughout the Bible we are told to trust in the Lord, and victory will be ours. I happen to still believe the word of God. Do you? Is your faith strong enough to bear up under what lies ahead?

"I will not cease preaching the word of God, my friends, and that means I will not cease preaching against the abomination of slavery! You must remember that we are not alone. Throughout the town of Lawrence, abolitionist movements continue to be waged. Eventually, through hard work, we can come together and show the trash who came here from Missouri to cast their illegal votes who *really* runs Kansas—and what Kansans *really* want! The elections were a travesty, and although for now the

President of the United States has seen fit to declare those elections legal, he will soon learn the error of that decision! Already Governor Reeder, the very man the President himself appointed to come here to oversee this new territory, a man who even went so far as to declare the elections legal, showing that he was willing to try to support the new legislature—even Reeder has been kicked out and replaced by a proslavery man. Surely the President will see that our new government is nothing more than a dictatorship, illegally elected, making illegal appointments and creating laws that defy the very Constitution of the United States!''

Whispers moved through the congregation when one family got up and walked out. It was obvious they were afraid to be caught listening to the reverend's "treasonous" remarks. Blake reached over and grasped Samantha's hand reassuringly. He glanced at her, thinking how pretty she looked in her pink gingham dress, a little straw hat perched perfectly on top of her lustrous dark hair. He met her blue eyes, eyes that he sometimes got lost in, eyes that had made him wilt at her pleading the night she came to him and asked him to make a woman of her. So beautiful she was, but so independent and sometimes too brave for her own good, just like her father. Just sitting in this church now was a form of treason.

Walters held out his hands in a calming gesture. "Don't let these things destroy your courage and conviction," he pleaded. "Some people let fear control their lives. They let it make them turn from God. Be strong, my friends, be brave. Remember that God is on *our* side!"

Blake watched his father-in-law, wondering if he

was one of the greatest men he had known, or a naive fool.

"My friends," he went on, "the new legislature cannot have everyone in Lawrence arrested! Every day Free-soil supporters come here to find shelter, to be with those who believe as they believe—that slavery is wrong—and that someday, somehow, we will defeat the mockery of a government that now runs Kansas! Lawrence is rising to the occasion, becoming the heart and soul of the abolition movement, which, my friends, will not be stopped."

The reverend went on to quote several scriptures that spoke of being of strong faith, of trusting in God to guide and protect, ending with the fact that Christ went to the cross rather than turn from God and his faith. "Now the cross has been brought to us," he told them. "Are you willing to shoulder it, to drag it with you to Calvary? Or will you take the easy way, and hope to be able to explain your actions to God when you meet him in the Hereafter? I personally do not want to have any explaining to do. Anything we must suffer here on earth for standing up for what is right, is worth not having to explain our actions later before Christ."

He closed with a long prayer, after which Mrs. Hanks, Blake and Samantha's landlady, began playing a hymn on the piano. People rose and began singing, including Mrs. Hanks's husband and six children. Blake glanced at Beecher again. He sang with as much gusto as the others, his eyes lighting up as though he glowed with faith. Blake wondered if that glow came from the thought of how much money he might be making as an informer.

The service ended, but there was little in the way of visiting and laughter afterward. People filed out quietly, and Blake suspected that each week the reverend was going to find fewer and fewer people sitting in his pews.

Beecher walked up to the reverend, shaking his hand and telling him what a fine sermon he delivered, that he admired his bravery.

"They can make their laws, my friend," Walters told him. "But just let them try to make them work here in Lawrence. Our movement is too strong here, Clyde, and we have to make it even stronger."

"You know I'm behind you," Beecher answered, as Blake and Samantha approached. Beecher turned his dark eyes to Blake. "And why hasn't your friend George been coming to church, Blake?" he asked, his eyes feigning concern.

Blake controlled a strong urge to grab the man and threaten him with his life if he didn't admit he was really a spy. "He decided it was best for the time being to keep to himself as much as possible. Except for work, he doesn't leave his place much."

"But he's a free man. He has nothing to worry about."

Their eyes held. "Doesn't he? This is a proslavery territory now, last I heard. *Some* men don't much care if a Negro is carrying papers or not." Blake took Samantha's arm and led her out of the church. "Your father is risking his life now. I hope he knows that, Sam."

"We have to stand behind him. He's right, you know."

"Well, being right doesn't always mean you'll win in the end."

"Father is planning a meeting tonight. The whole town is becoming united now, Blake. Most of the proslavery people and those who are afraid to stand up for their beliefs have left Lawrence. This is

180

becoming a stronghold for Free-soilers and abolitionists. Don't you see what that means? We're safer here than anyplace else. It's just like my father said. They can't come here and arrest the whole town of Lawrence. Mother told me this morning that as soon as Father and the others get a little more organized, they're going to hold a convention, elect their own representatives and adopt their own constitution, one that outlaws slavery. They'll write the President and plead with him to declare the first elections invalid. If we stand firm, the current legislature will eventually crumble. Too many Kansans are against slavery and don't want to be considered a slave territory."

Blake felt the recurring fear of losing Samantha, but he knew how much she believed in her father's cause. "I hope you realize that if they do that, and if the President refuses to recognize your father's new government, Kansas will have a civil war on its hands."

They stopped walking, and she looked up at him. "They'll win, Blake. I have to believe that."

He shook his head. "Why do you insist on learning everything the hard way?"

She smiled lightly. "I stuck my neck out marrying *you*. I haven't regretted *that* for one minute. I didn't learn any hard lessons there. It's all been wonderful."

He sighed, putting an arm around her shoulders and turning to walk again. "You can't compare that to what's happening in Kansas, Sam. You weren't risking your life when you married me."

"Wasn't I? You could have been a wife beater."

He laughed lightly. "The way you talk sometimes about getting so involved in Kansas politics, I wonder if maybe I *should* give you a good thrashing."

"You just try it."

"No, thanks. I've seen you in action." He gave her a light squeeze. "You just remember, Sam, that your father can be right as hell, but he also believes in abstention from violence. Proslavery men won't stop at just words. They have the law on their side. And there are plenty of abolitionists who are also not afraid to get physical. The border raids aren't *all* committed by bushwhackers, you know. Plenty of jayhawkers cross the border into Missouri and do just as much damage. If this abolitionist movement against the current government continues to grow, the fighting won't stop just at the border. It will affect all of Kansas."

"Well, why don't you wait and see how our own convention goes. If we can get the support of the President, there won't be any bloodshed."

"Presidents are not known to admit they've been wrong about anything. Pierce already declared those elections valid and has supported the new government. If he recognizes new elections, which, I might add, would now be considered treason, people would think he was weak and unable to make up his mind. In these times he can't afford such opinions. Besides, he has a whole country on the brink of war. He's not going to give any extra attention to a western territory with a small population."

"Blake, please don't talk that way." She stopped and looked up at him again, her eyes wet with tears. "He just has to help us. He's our only hope."

He sighed, pulling her close. "I'm sorry, Sam, but I just don't see it happening. You just be sure to remain close to me all the time and stay inside when I'm at work."

"You'll go to the meeting tonight, won't you?"

How he wished he could get her out of Kansas, but

she had stubbornly refused to leave her parents. "Yes, if you insist on going, I'll take you. You just remember that those meetings are now considered treasonous." He held her close for a moment, remembering the sight of his father hanging in the shed, put to death for standing up for what he thought was right. He hoped his wife did not have the hardest lesson of all still ahead of her. She had already suffered enough at the hands of Fred Brewster.

November 1855

George drove Blake's flatbed wagon to the supply store, carrying in his pocket a list of items he needed. He felt somewhat apprehensive, even though he was a free man in this town of mostly abolitionists. He still could not get used to being able to go where he pleased, and he was accustomed to Blake always being with him. But Blake and Samantha had gone to Topeka with Sam's parents to attend a territorial convention being held by abolitionists and Free-soilers. Over the summer the movement by the Free-soilers to form their own government and defy the current one had grown to near warlike proportions. Half of Lawrence was empty of its citizens, people gone to Topeka to voice their opposition to the current government. The convention was being held in Topeka because it was more centrally located and a greater number of abolitionists from other parts of the territory could attend.

George pulled the wagon to a halt, pushing on the brake and climbing down from the seat. He hoped there would be no trouble in Topeka for Sam and Blake, and that they wouldn't be attacked by bushwhackers on their way there or back. He wondered sometimes what he would really do without Blake to turn to. He told himself he had to stop depending on him. After all, Blake was married now. He knew Blake and Sam wanted him to stay, didn't mind having him live in the shed behind their house, but he wondered if maybe it was time to be moving on, to test this new, wonderful freedom completely on his own.

He tied the two draft horses Blake had recently purchased in hopes that he would be able to buy a farm sometime soon and settle there with Samantha in peace. He would need the horses for plowing. George had agreed to take care of them while Blake was gone, and letting them pull the wagon to the supply store was good exercise for the animals.

He turned to go inside the store when he heard his name suddenly called, a soft, almost frightened sound that came from a woman several feet to his right. George turned in the direction of the voice, noticing a fancy black buggy parked several feet away in front of a barber shop. A young Negro woman sat in the seat. His heart began to beat a little faster as he walked closer, curious, sure the woman had spoken his name, thinking that voice sounded familiar. His eyes widened as he came closer, and a chill seemed to surge through his veins. "Jesse!" he gasped.

Jesse March quickly looked around as though frightened, then looked back at him with tear-filled eyes. "I wasn't sure it was really you. Oh, George, I never thought I'd see you again!"

His own eyes misted as he came to stand beside the buggy, wanting to grab her and hold her close, yet suddenly unsure what he should do. Jesse! She looked as pretty as ever, sitting there dressed as fine as a rich white woman, wearing a deep-green velvet dress and matching cape. "I can't believe this!" he said, breaking into a smile. "How did you ever end up here in Lawrence, Jesse? I looked everywhere for you after I got freed—me and a friend of mine, a white man."

A tear slipped down her face. Oh, how handsome he still looked! No finer looking man walked the face of the earth! If only they could be together again, but now . . . "You're free?"

He grinned wider, stepping closer and grasping her hand. "Yes, Jesse. I've got the papers to prove it."

She smiled through tears. "I'm so glad for you, George."

His smile faded. "You?"

She turned away. "You don't want to know."

"Who bought you, Jesse? I'll buy you back. Between me and my friend, Blake Hastings I know we can come up with the money."

She looked at him, fear and shame in her eyes. "If you knew, George, you wouldn't want me back. And he . . . he would never sell me anyway."

A silent rage began to build in George's soul. There was only one reason she would think that he wouldn't want her. . . . "I've never stopped loving you, Jesse. Nothing that's happened to you matters. All I care about is—"

"Get the hell away from that buggy, nigger," a voice roared from the front of the barber shop. George jumped at the sudden barked order, turning to see Nick West stepping away from the door. "What the hell do you think you're doing, holding Jesse's hand! She's my personal property!"

George just stared at the man a moment, letting it all sink in. So, it was *West* who had bought Jesse! He glanced at Jesse again, who just stared at her lap, looking both ashamed and terrified. He knew without asking how West was using her, and he felt sick inside. He knew that if Jesse was Nick West's lover, it had not come about willingly. What had the man done to her? What had she suffered?

His heart raced with a mixture of anger and fear. He knew that even though he was free, a Negro man still had his place, even in a town full of abolitionists. And the new territorial laws were on the side of men like West.

"I happen to know Jesse well," he said, bravely stepping closer to West. "In fact, I love her. We were going to marry at one time, but then she got sold off."

"That's right, nigger. She got sold—to *me!* Your feelings for her don't mean a damn thing! I happen to be very fond of Jesse myself. And Jesse is very fond of *me,* aren't you, honey?" The man moved his steely blue eyes to Jesse, a threatening look telling her how to answer.

Jesse swallowed. "Yes," she said.

George looked up at her, seeing her tremble, then looked back to West. "A person feels enough pain, he or she will do or say just about anything for that pain to stop," he growled. "I know. I've been there myself!"

"Then you know a nigger's place, especially one who's still owned. Now get away from that buggy. I ever catch you near Jesse again, I'll have you *shot!*"

George stood there indecisively for a moment, wishing Blake were with him. Blake would know what to say, what to do. "I . . . I'll buy her," he told West. "I'll pay whatever you want. I'll find the money somehow."

West just chuckled, as more people gathered around to watch the confrontation. He realized he was not surrounded by friends. Lawrence was becoming a mecca for abolitionists, and he knew the day was coming when he would have to stay away all together. He decided it was probably time to go back to Missouri again, but he would not stop supporting the proslavery sympathizers with money and guns. He turned to one of his men, who had come to town with him to get a haircut too.

"Go get the sheriff," he told the man, who quickly left. West looked back at George. "She's not for sale, not for any price."

George stepped even closer, his fury obvious now.

"George, please don't," Jesse spoke up, wondering if she had found him again only to watch him die.

"It isn't right," George answered, his voice low and threatening, his eyes still on West. "What have you done to her, West? Did you whip her? Burn her?"

"Shut up, nigger," West growled, his eyes menacing. "You shut your smart mouth or I'll have you arrested!"

"For what? For knowing the truth about you? Sell her to me, West! Let her go free, or *you're* the one who will be shot!"

Some onlookers stepped back, afraid of the huge man, some almost gasping at the dangerous threat. Even though most wanted a free territory, deep inside they could not tolerate a black threatening a white man, even if that man was a slave owner.

"You'd better watch what you say, nigger. You'll end up in a lot of trouble," West warned.

George charged at the man, and Jesse screamed as he grabbed West by the lapels and slammed him against the wall of the barber shop. "*Sell* her, you white trash," he snarled. "*Sell* her to me! She's mine! She belongs to *me!*"

"Get your hands off me, you big nigger," West gasped.

"Hold up there," came another voice. "Let go of

the man, George, or I'll have to jail you." Sheriff Tucker approached, gun drawn.

"He's a no-good slave owner," George answered. "He's got my woman! I want her back!"

Jesse could hardly see what was happening for the tears in her eyes. She whispered George's name, terrified of what would happen to him. He suddenly turned, bringing West around with him so that the man was between himself and the sheriff's gun. "It's not right, Sheriff! I know that woman in his buggy. We were supposed to be married once."

"She's . . . *mine!*" West told the man, his voice strained. He grasped at George's wrists, but George was much too powerful for him. "I've got . . . legal papers," he gasped. "Get this nigger . . . off of me!"

"Let him go, George! You can't do this. Mr. West owns her, and you know that under the new laws I can't do anything about that. Now let go of him or I'll throw you in jail!"

George envisioned West pawing over Jesse, shaming her, humiliating her. He drew back a fist and landed it in West's groin. West went down, and George kicked him under the chin, sending him sprawling. In an instant several men leaped upon George, grabbing hold of him as best they could. It took six men to get him off West and hold him away from the man. George strained at the hold, growling that West had no right to mistreat Jesse.

"A man can do whatever he wants with his own slaves," West's man answered as he stooped to help his boss. The man looked at the sheriff. "You'd better remember the new laws in this territory, Sheriff. Get that nigger the hell out of here, or Mr. West can easily arrange to have him hanged for treason, talking out against slavery like that!"

George still fought but was unable to handle the

mob of men who held him. They wrestled him to the ground and rolled him onto his belly, some of them actually sitting on him.

"Put these on him," the sheriff said, handing some handcuffs to one of the men. "Maybe a few days in a cell will calm him down."

George growled and squirmed more as his hands were forced behind his back and the cuffs were locked on. Jesse covered her face with her hands, weeping. What would happen to him now? How cruel to see him again, only to know he could never touch her again, make love to her again. What hurt most was George finding out about her, and the fact that he might suffer for wanting to help her. Why had she called out to him? If only she hadn't been so surprised to see him—had had time to think before calling his name.

"Jesse . . ." he moaned then, his face in the dirt.

Nick West's man helped Nick into the buggy, where Nick sat bent over and groaning.

"You see that nigger sits in jail a while, Sheriff," West's hired hand called out. "No nigger has the right to attack a white man. Now all of you know why they have to be kept in their places! You turn them all loose, none of us will be safe!"

"Get us . . . out of here," West gasped. "They're all abolitionists."

The man turned the shiny black horse that pulled the carriage and drove off.

"Bring him to the jail," the sheriff ordered the men holding George.

"Let me go," George begged as the men allowed him to stand. "I've got to get Jesse."

"You've got to mind your own business, George," the sheriff told him sternly. "We don't believe in slavery, but it's the law in this territory now, and

189

you'd best be remembering that. You go interfering too much, and you might find yourself being hauled off some night by proslavery men who don't give a damn about your freedom papers! You've got no right to that woman, and Nick West and his kind can make a lot of trouble for you!"

The men forced George across the street toward the jail, shoving him into a cell and locking the cell door. "Forget West and the woman, George," one of them told him. "You go anywhere near either one of them, Nick West will be putting a noose around your neck." The men left, closing an outer door and leaving George alone in the cell, his wrists still cuffed behind him.

George got up and paced, fighting an urge to break into tears like a child, feeling the horrible frustration of knowing Jesse was in Nick West's hands and he could do nothing about it. "Jesse . . ." he groaned. "Damn it, Jesse! I'll kill him someday!" He closed his eyes, his breathing heavy. A tear slipped down his cheek, and he wished Blake would get home. Blake would know what to do about this.

Nick West's carriage made its way out of town, and Jesse sat quietly crying, wondering what would happen to George, if she would ever see him again. She gasped when West suddenly grasped her knee painfully, squeezing as he spoke. "What the hell do you think you were doing—talking to that big nigger stud, letting him hold your hand!"

"Please don't," she protested, grimacing with pain.

He let go of her knee, turning to grasp her around the throat while the other man drove the buggy, thinking the whole thing quite funny. He grinned when West held Jesse's throat with one hand and punched her in the face with the other. "I'll teach you to make eyes at him," he growled. "Was he better than *me*, Jesse? Huh?" He hit her again, but Jesse made no sound. "Your actions cost me some pain, woman, and you're going to *pay* for it! You have apparently forgotten you're my personal property! As soon as we get home, I'll refresh your memory!" He turned to his man. "Stop the buggy!"

The man did as he was told, and West took a piece of rawhide from the bed of the buggy. "Go tie her to the back. She can walk the rest of the way!"

The man took the rawhide. "Must be a good six or seven miles, boss."

"You don't need to tell me how far it is. I said to tie her to the back of the buggy, and you don't need to go especially slow on the way home."

The man's eyebrows arched. "Yes, sir." He climbed down, reaching up and lifting Jesse down. He tied the cord tightly around her wrists, then led her to the back of the buggy and secured the other end of the cord. He climbed back up and got the horse into motion again.

"We're going back to Missouri," West told him. "Our work is done here for the time being. I've got the telegraph operator paid off. He'll take and send messages for me without the wrong people knowing about it. Beecher will keep me informed on the abolitionist movement here. I think we need to organize better, maybe find a way to teach Lawrence a lesson—as well as people like Reverend Walters and that bunch over in Topeka. The bastards! What makes them think they can get away with declaring their own little government and making their own rules? They'll *all* pay for it!"

He glanced back at Jesse, who was struggling to

keep up with the buggy. He grinned, turning to look ahead again. "George Freedom will pay, too, for what he did to me today! And Jesse will pay for never telling me about him. The next time she sees him, he's going to belong to *me!* Maybe I'll even chain him up and bring him to our bedroom to watch. That would be worse punishment than a whipping, don't you think?"

"Whatever you say, boss."

West lifted his chin smugly, still trying to calm down. He knew without question that if others had not gotten George off him, the huge man would have easily killed him. He touched his aching jaw, feeling the swelling there.

"He's going to regret he ever threatened me. The law is on *our* side now!"

Jesse struggled to keep up, the tight, pointed-toe shoes West had made her wear that morning already hurting her feet.

Ten

Blake carried in the luggage after having un-hitched the buggy he had rented and bedding down his black mare for the night. "I'll return the buggy in the morning," he told Samatha wearily. "The draft horses look fed and well tended, and the wagon is out back. George must be sleeping. I'll give him the news in the morning."

Samantha met his eyes, seeing the mixture of sadness and anger that had been there since the convention ended. "I put wood in the stove," she told him. "Do you want to light it and see if it's enough?"

He rubbed at the back of his neck. "Sure." He picked up a lantern from the kitchen table and carried it to the sitting room. "It's going to take a little while to warm it up in here, we've been gone so long." He opened the potbelly stove and lit the kindling, standing and staring silently at the flames for several minutes until it began burning hard. He added a little more wood, then closed and latched the door.

Samantha untied and removed her bonnet, walking over to touch his shoulder. "I'm sorry, Blake.

You know Father tried to fight it."

"Hypocrites," he seethed, rubbing at his arms then in a warming gesture. "They call themselves abolitionists, and then they make it a law that Negroes won't be allowed in the territory! They're all *cowards*, that's what they are! They think that if there aren't any Negroes in Kansas, their troubles will go away! They won't *have* to deal with the slavery issue, because there won't be any slaves around to worry about! I still can't believe it. We go all the way to Topeka, probably got our names on a list of traitors, help work for a new constitution, elect abolitionist men to defy the government, and then they turn around and say Negroes won't be allowed to step foot in Kansas Territory! They're all a bunch of two-faced, lying hypocrites!"

"Blake, you have to remember this is all new to them. A lot of them are scared to have gone as far as they have. They have families!"

"Well, so do *I!*" He faced her, and the hurt in his eyes pained her heart. "I also have a best friend who is Negro, and I don't intend that he has to leave Kansas and struggle on his own! He's proven himself a good citizen, Sam. He works hard and keeps to himself."

"And Father already said he would call a special meeting to ask the townpeople to let him stay. They'll make an exception for George, I'm sure."

He snickered. "So what if they do? Do you realize how all that is going to make him feel?"

"I know, Blake. I wish I could change it, but I can't." She touched his arm, feeling his tension. "But the important thing is, we've gone so far as to create a new constitution and elect our own people. We knew this wouldn't work out perfectly overnight, and I think George will understand that, too. First let's concentrate on overthrowing the current government. Let's see how President Pierce reacts to our petition. Not allowing Negroes in Kansas was just added to assure the President that there would be less reason for fighting if they were banned all together. That clause can be changed, and it will be, in time."

He studied her blue eyes, sighing deeply. "You're always so sure things will work out, Sam, but I'm not. I feel like I'm just falling deeper and deeper into a bottomless pit, like I'm going to lose you and George and everything that is dear to me."

She put her hands against his chest. "You aren't going to lose me, or George. You're just tired from the long trip. Why don't we go to bed and talk about all this in the morning? We'll have George come over for breakfast. There is plenty of time to straighten this out. At least we made a stand against the proslavery government. We can win this, Blake. You saw how many people were there. Once we get Kansas back to a Free-soil territory, we'll work to abolish the law that bars Negroes. It's just a desperate attempt to be recognized. You know that."

"I know this is all getting out of hand." He turned to check the stove once more, then picked up the oil lamp and walked into the bedroom, setting the lamp on a small table and sitting down on the edge of the bed to remove his boots.

Samantha untied her fur cape and began unbuttoning her dress. The room hung silent as she removed the dress and sat down on the other side of the bed to unlace her high-button shoes. She knew how badly Blake felt about the way things had gone at the convention. He had even spoken before the hundreds who had attended, arguing vehemently against including the clause in the new constitution that all Negroes be banned from Kansas. The movement had surprised her, too. Her father had also argued against it, but the rule had passed. People were convinced that the clause would encourage the President to recognize their government as the only legal government for Kansas.

She felt Blake moving under the covers, cursing at the cold. Samantha hurriedly undressed and pulled on her flannel gown. She turned down the lamp and moved under the covers, snuggling against Blake for warmth. The pleasant smell of burning wood filled the air from a little smoke that had escaped when Blake was making the fire.

"That's a nice, familiar smell," Samantha commented. "It tells us we're home."

He turned toward her, pulling her closer. "I'm sorry I've been such a bear to live with," he said. "It just makes me so damn mad."

"I know." She kissed his neck. "Blake, don't let this destroy what we have together. Please try not to let it get in the way . . . not here . . . in this room."

He sighed again, kissing her hair. "I try not to. But sometimes, like tonight, when I put up the horse and checked on the draft horses, I wonder if we'll ever have our own place, be able to live normal, peaceful lives, if I'll ever get to use them to plow land on my own farm, Sam. I always thought that if I bought a farm, George would stay on with us, help with the farm—maybe that he'd even find a woman of his own someday and they could live on our property. Now they're telling us he can't live anywhere in Kansas Territory!"

"We'll talk the people of Lawrence into making an exception."

"That isn't the point. The point is—"

She put her fingers to his lips. "Blake, not in this room, remember?" She touched his hair. "We've been so busy these last two weeks we haven't—" She

196

moved her hand down over his powerful shoulder and bare chest. "This room is just for our own little world, Blake; a world apart from what is going on outside these walls. George can't enter here, abolitionists and bushwhackers can't enter. No one! It's just ours. Do you realize we'll be married a whole year in just another month?"

He grasped at her hair, moving down to meet her mouth in a kiss that had a desperate feel to it. He moved on top of her, the kiss lingering until he moved his mouth to kiss her neck. "I think about it all the time," he told her softly, "about how hard this has all been on us, how it sometimes makes me feel so far away from you."

"Well, I'm right here, Blake, and we're alone and safe in this little room. I can think of a wonderful way of getting warm."

She felt him softening. "You can, can you? Why don't you tell me how we can do that?"

She smiled, studying his handsome face in the soft light. Blake never let her turn the lamp completely down, always worried about an attack on Lawrence she was sure would never happen. *"If anyone ever barges in here in the middle of the night, I don't want to have to fumble around with a lamp,"* he had told her early in their marriage. *"Besides, I like to be able to see you when I make love to you, see you sleeping beside me when I wake up in the night."*

His rifle always sat propped beside the bed. He had taken another rifle and his six-gun along on the journey to Topeka, worried their little entourage would be bushwhacked on the way to the convention. She hated what was happening as much as he, but she was determined not to let that ugly world into her bedroom.

She moved her hand down to gently touch that

197

part of him that belonged only to her now. This virile, handsome man was her own private property, and she would not let bushwhackers and politics steal him away. Those things had become as much an enemy as another woman might be. She stroked and caressed until his hardness made her feel on fire, and she knew that for a little while she had managed to soothe his anger and frustration and bring back the Blake she had married.

"Does this help?" she asked, teasingly pulling at him.

He grasped her hand. "You'd better be careful, Mrs. Hastings, or I won't last long."

She smiled, leaning up and kissing his shoulder. "Sometimes I wish it could last all night long."

He met her mouth at the seductive remark, unbuttoning his long johns while he kissed her hard and deep, running his tongue into her mouth suggestively. Already they both felt warmer. He nibbled at her ear then. "Get your drawers off, woman," he told her, moving off slightly to remove his long johns. He could never resist her gentle touch, the still almost-innocent way about her. And tonight he had a sudden need to remind himself she was right here in his bed, well and safe. She was right. The outside world could not enter here. She felt so good beside him. It made him feel so loved.

Samantha quickly removed her bloomers and gown, snuggling under the covers beside him again. He covered her mouth with a pressing kiss, loving the way she could sometimes behave like the most wanton woman. She groaned and moved her tongue into his mouth when his hand touched secret places she had offered to him alone. He worked magic with his fingers, bringing a moan to her lips. He loved the feel of her sweet moistness, the knowledge that every part of this woman belonged to him.

He felt her shudder with a climax, and he moved on top of her, entering her in one hard thrust that made her cry out. She pushed against him so that he could bury himself to her depths, and she whimpered his name as he moved in teasing circles, feeling his own pride and ecstasy at the knowledge that he pleased her greatly. She had a way of bringing out every ounce of his manliness, making him feel virile and sometimes kingly. She was so independent in so many ways that it made him feel proud to know that when it came to this, she belonged totally to him, Blake Hastings. It was he who had captured her, his name she carried.

He raised up, grasping her slender knees, the blankets falling away. His eyes left her face to drink in her naked beauty. Samantha felt a great pride in knowing she could please this man, took her own pleasure in his perfect, rhythmic movements. She grasped the brass rails at the head of the bed and raised her hips to meet him, feeling like a harlot and not caring. She *was* a harlot with Blake Hastings. He made her feel wild and free.

He moved his hands down along her thighs and grasped her hips. She opened her eyes, seeing in his own dark eyes the look of a conquering warrior. She let go of the bed rails and moved her hands along his powerful arms, his captive mistress. His eyes closed, and his jaw flexed in reaction to ecstasy as his life surged into her.

He slowly lowered himself then, pulling the covers up over his shoulders. "I want to stay inside you," he said softly. "I want to feel it again. It makes it seem like everything is all right. And it's been such a long time . . ."

"Everything *will* be all right, Blake."

He sighed deeply. "I want it to be. You're all I've got, Sam. You and George." He rested his head beside her and she gently stroked his thick, dark hair, sure she felt a tear drip onto her neck.

"Oh, Blake, my darling . . . don't. We'll be all right."

Her own tears came then, both of them suddenly needing the release to all their worries. They clung together and wept, finally falling asleep before making love again in the wee hours of the morning.

Blake got up from the kitchen table to answer the back door. He found Jonas Hanks waiting there and stepped back, inviting his landlord inside. Samantha quickly poured another cup of coffee.

"What brings a bank teller around here so early?" Blake asked the man jokingly. "I thought you kept banker's hours."

Jonas smiled and nodded, bidding them both a good morning.

"I was just about to go roust George out of bed," Blake added. "I'm surprised he isn't here already. He's usually up and over here for breakfast by now. We've got to get to work."

Jonas rubbed at his wrinkled cheek, his narrow blue eyes showing a strange sadness. Samantha set out a cup of coffee for him, always finding it amusing that such a short, tiny man could have a wife twice as big as himself and six children to boot. "Please sit down and join us, Jonas," she told him.

Hanks looked at Blake. "I appreciate the invitation, but this isn't just a visit—not at this hour."

Blake sobered, and he felt a strange alarm. "What's wrong, Jonas?" He smiled nervously. "We didn't forget last month's rent, did we?"

The man removed his hat. "I just thought I'd come tell you right away this morning. I saw that Sam's father was back, so I knew you were, too. You'd best get over to the jailhouse, Blake. Your friend George is there."

Samantha watched the fear and anger rise in Blake's eyes. "What the hell for? Is this how they intend to enact the new law? All of a sudden George is a criminal?"

"What new law?" Jonas asked.

"We formed our own constitution, Jonas," Samantha explained. "I'm afraid that to show the President we don't want any trouble, our newly elected legislators decided to ban all Negroes from Kansas."

Jonas frowned. "That's ridiculous. It's hypocritical!"

"Of course it is," Blake fumed. "Did Lawrence get word of it already? Is that why George is in jail? I figured at the most they'd just tell him to leave town."

Jonas's brow wrinkled with concern. "It's got nothing to do with that, Blake. The way I hear it, there was some kind of confrontation a few days ago between George and that Nick West—something about a Negro woman West had with him. I guess George got all hot under the collar, attacked Mr. West, insisted West let him buy the girl from him, something like that."

Blake looked at Samantha. "Jesse!" he said in a near whisper. "It must have been Jesse! George wouldn't react that way over anyone else. My God! Nick West must be the one who bought her!"

"We'd best go over there, Blake," Sam answered, setting the coffeepot back on the stove.

He ran a hand through his hair. "No. You stay here. This is a personal thing for George." He looked at Jonas. "He being treated decent over there?"

"Far as I know. I don't think there's going to be a trial or anything. West never came back to press charges. I think he's a little bit afraid to be in Lawrence now because of all the Free-soilers and abolitionists moving in. There aren't many people in this town who like to see a man flaunting his slaves. At any rate, I think Sheriff Tucker is just holding George until you come for him. He figures you can talk some sense into him, keep him under control. He's afraid George will do something really stupid if he lets him go on his own."

Blake sighed, turning to take his jacket from a coat tree near the door. He pulled it on, then took his wide-brimmed leather hat from the tree. He glanced at a worried-looking Samantha. "I'll be back in a while," he said, then turned to Jonas. "Thanks for coming to tell me right away."

"I figured you'd want to get him out of there. I'm the one who brought your horses and wagon back to the house the day it happened. I've been tending the horses and keeping an eye on things ever since. It's been five days."

"Damn," Blake muttered, heading for the door.

Samantha called out to him to be careful. She saw the hurt and sadness in his eyes, and she knew how sorry he was for poor George. If she were some man's slave, Blake Hastings would risk life and limb and his entire future to get her back, she was sure. That must be how George felt, and Blake knew that. She could tell by the look in his eyes that he was already thinking how he would feel if it was Samantha who needed help. He turned and hurried away.

*　　　*　　　*

Blake kept his eyes on George, seeing the agony in his friend's eyes as Sheriff Tucker opened the cell door and let Blake inside, closing and locking the door behind him. George looked down then, resting his elbows on his knees. "If you came to let me out, you'd better think twice about it," he told Blake. "The minute I'm out of here, I'm going to get Jesse."

Blake sighed deeply, removing his hat and walking to sit down on the cot beside George. "My suspicions are right then? Jesse is with Nick West?"

George put his head in his hands. "I came into town for supplies, and there she was, sitting in his fancy buggy, waiting for him to get a haircut. He had her all dressed up like a fancy white woman." His hands moved into fists. "A *kept* woman!" He got up and walked to the cell bars, grasping them tightly. "If you could have seen the look on her face, Blake. Shame, fear—terrible fear. I know her, Blake. She didn't go down without a fight. He's beat her to where she just gave up." George whirled, looking even bigger in the small cell. "I can't just leave it, Blake! I've got to try to help her! Think how you'd feel if it was Sam!"

Blake rubbed at the back of his neck. "I'd want to do the same thing you're thinking. The trouble is, there's a big difference between me and you."

"You mean that I'm a *nigger* and you're a *white* man! You can get away with more than I can!"

Blake had ever seen George so full of hate and fury. He had never shown such resentment of whites. "I'm afraid that's *exactly* what I mean, George," he answered, rising. "Except you're *Negro*, not a nigger! You've never called yourself that, and don't be doing it around me or insinuating that that's how I look at our relationship!"

George seemed to wither slightly. He turned away again. "I'm sorry. I just feel like I'm going crazy, that's all. Maybe I *am* going crazy. Do you know what it's like to sit here helpless while the woman you love is being raped by some other man?" His voice broke on the words. He swallowed before continuing. "That's all it is, you know. Just because he owns her and she's black and has no rights, he thinks that makes it okay. A man like that, he'd probably think the rape of a white woman is some terrible thing, but he can do it to—" He gripped the bars again, hanging his head.

Blake stepped closer and touched his shoulder. "George, I want to get you out of here, but I can't do it unless you promise to stay close to me and not go gunning for Nick West. There might be other ways around this. Let me try first. I care about you, George. I don't want to see a noose around your neck."

The man turned, tears in his eyes. "What the hell am I going to do? He said he wouldn't sell her, Blake. Not to anybody for any price. This is my Jesse we're talking about. Back in Missouri before she got sold, we were already in love. I was her first man. We were going to see if we could marry. If we couldn't, we were going to run away together, maybe try to get to Canada. My owner must have got wind of it, because all of a sudden she was just gone. I didn't figure I'd ever see her again, and now—" A tear slipped down his cheek. "I can't let it lay like this, Blake."

Blake rubbed at his eyes, "I know." He threw back his head and sighed, pacing again. "Right now, just tell the sheriff you'll stay close to me and won't do anything foolish and go breaking the law. We've got more troubles than Jesse."

"What do you mean?"

Blake met his eyes. "We've stuck our neck out, George—held our own convention, elected our own

204

men. Under current Kansas law, we're all traitors now. Most of us are centered in Lawrence, so the whole town is in danger. We drafted a letter to the President, asking him to recognize the true wishes of Kansas citizens to be a free territory and to declare the former elections invalid and the current government illegal. Unless he goes along with it, we're all susceptible to arrest. Sam's parents naturally want to fight this all the way through, and Sam won't leave them, which means I have to stay in Lawrence for the time being."

"So? You already figured on that."

Blake hesitated, hating to tell him. "George, they made up a law banning all Negroes, free or slave, from Kansas."

George just stared at him a moment. "From the whole territory?"

"The whole territory." Blake could see the bitter irony of it showing in his friend's eyes.

"So, they call themselves abolitionists. They want to free all slaves and not allow slavery in Kansas—but they also say no blacks are allowed in their territory. I guess it's pretty easy to say you're against slavery when you know that no freed slave is going to come and live in your backyard!" He snickered, turning away and wiping at his eyes again. "That's what I call being real brave."

"I know it stinks, George. Sam's father and I tried our best to get the law repealed, but most people insisted that it stay. They reasoned that maybe we could prove to the President that there won't be any more trouble if we're allowed to stay in power. With no Negroes around, a lot of the problem is obviously eliminated."

George laughed a bitter laugh of resignation. "Instead of facing the problem, they get rid of it.

205

How brave of them."

Blake felt ashamed of his own race, hated having to tell George about the ridiculous law. "Look, George, first the new constitution has to be recognized by the President before they can enforce *any* law. That buys us some time. And Reverend Walters wants to hold a town meeting asking people to make an exception for you because you've been living here already. You support yourself; you don't bother anyone."

George's eyebrows arched. "I'm in jail for disturbing the peace and attacking a white man. That's all the excuse they'll need to make me go, and you know it. Besides that, I'm going to go and get Jesse and head north, so it doesn't matter."

"That's suicide! I told you to let me see what I could do first."

"*You?* You *hate* that man, and he wants you dead. You think he's going to discuss it with *you,* make any deals with *you?* You're dreaming, Blake. It's as dangerous for you to try to do something about it as it is for me. I won't have you getting hurt or killed over my problems. You've got a new wife depending on you now and *I've* depended on you long enough. I'm a free man, Blake. This is *my* problem, and I'll find a way!"

Their eyes held. Somehow they had always known that somewhere along the line it would come to this. The country wasn't ready for Negro men to be free, let alone for a Negro and a white man to be best friends. "Let's go home," Blake said, the sadness evident in his voice. "We'll talk then about what to do about Jesse. Let's just get you out of here first."

He called the sheriff to come and release them. Tucker warned George that if he got in the same kind of trouble again, he'd be in jail a lot longer. He released the man in Blake's custody and sent them

206

both on their way.

When they arrived home a worried Samantha hugged Blake in relief, then turned to embrace George, surprising him with the spontaneous hug. In awkward embarrassment he grasped her arms and stepped back, looking sheepishly at Blake, who only grinned. "Sit down, George. Sam will make you some breakfast."

"Oh, George, was it Jesse? Is that why you attacked Nick West?" Samantha asked.

George sighed, taking a chair, the sudden embrace from Sam making him want Jesse all the more. It had been a long time since he held a woman, made love. The frustration of knowing Jesse was with West made him feel almost sick. "Yes, ma'am, it was Jesse. I'm going to get her away from him if it's the last thing I do."

Samantha glanced at Blake, and he saw the terror move into her eyes. "George, you can't just take her," she reminded him. "I know how terrible it must be for you, but we still live in a country where slavery is allowed. She belongs to Nick West, and Kansas is a slave territory now. We're going to try to change that, but—"

"I'm going to get her, Sam," he interrupted. "Nothing you or Blake say will change my mind." He rubbed at his curly dark hair with a big hand. "I don't mean any disrespect, and I know you're both concerned about me, but I'm going after Jesse. Maybe I can sneak her away. If I can, we'll head north into Canada." He looked at Samantha. "And I don't want either one of you involved. It could mean prison or the noose. Once I'm gone from here, you two just tell people you don't know where I headed. Just tell them I heard about the new law against Negroes, so I left."

Blake hung up his hat and coat, then took George's

for him. Samantha turned to the stove, putting on a piece of ham, her heart heavy. Everything was so unfair, and it seemed no matter how hard they fought to change that, things only got worse.

"Look, George, we have to try the right way first," Blake said, sitting down across from him. "I'll ride out to West's place and see if I can talk to him."

Samantha's heart tightened at the words.

"Like hell you will," George answered.

"We've got to *try*, George. Give me a few days. Sam's father and I will talk to everyone in town, explain the situation, see how much money we can raise to buy Jesse's freedom. A lot of Reverend Walter's parishioners don't like this new law banning Negroes at all. Most people in this town will support you, George. Give them a chance to help you. I know you think you're alone in this, but you aren't. We'll work on it all week, as well as Sunday morning in church. I have some savings of my own—"

"No! That's for that farm you want for you and Sam."

"Jesse is more important," Samantha answered for Blake. "If it was me instead of Jesse, wouldn't you give Blake every dime you had if it might help me?"

George closed his eyes, shaking his head. "You know I would."

"Well, it's the same for us. Let Blake try it his way. If it doesn't work, we'll still have our money; if it does, it will be well worth giving it up. We'll just have to start saving all over again, but at least you'll have Jesse. Maybe you'll be allowed to stay here, and eventually this whole ugly mess will be over and we can buy a farm together. I have no doubts Jesse and I would end up great friends."

George leaned back in his chair, meeting her eyes. "You would. Jesse is a fine woman. She can't help what's happening to her now. I know her, Sam. West had to treat her awful bad to make her stay with him like that. I saw her in town, in his buggy—all dressed up. I'll never forget the fear in her eyes when she thought West might see us talking. He's made her his personal—"

Sam saw the agony in his eyes. She reddened at what she knew he was going to say. "I'm so sorry, George." She looked at Blake. How she hated the thought of him confronting Nick West. She knew how just looking at the man stirred Blake's anger. Would he do something rash, get himself shot? She wanted to argue that he shouldn't go, yet she knew there would be no stopping him. George was his best friend. Blake's own father had died freeing slaves. Would it be the same for Blake?

"Remember our agreement to try to do things the peaceful way," she told him. She saw the bitter hatred return to his eyes.

"Easier said than done when it comes to West. I can only try. I told you the kind of scum he is. Now you know."

"I never doubted that part for a moment."

Blake turned to George. "It's settled then. We'll work hard all week at raising money. Samantha can call a meeting of the town women. Her father and I can work on the men. Sheriff Tucker and I will ride out to West's place with it. Having Tucker along should help keep the peace. Besides, considering how West and I feel about each other, I'd better have a witness to whatever happens." He leaned across the table and touched George's arm. "We'll do our best, George. Just hang on."

George breathed deeply, his eyes misty. "You've done too much for me already."

"No more than you'd do for me if the situation was

reversed. You just relax and eat a decent breakfast. We've got to get over to the mill and make some money if we're going to have any to buy Jesse with.''

George smiled sadly. "I expect so.'' Their eyes held. "Thank you, Blake.''

Blake snickered. "Don't thank me. I have a feeling that if I had been here and seen what you saw, I'd be going after Jesse even if she was a complete stranger. The idea of *any* young girl being at that man's mercy is enough to make me try to get her out of there.''

"Like father, like son,'' George said ominously.

Samantha put a hand to her stomach, which suddenly felt tight and sick. Like father, like son. Nick West had had Blake's father hanged for doing the very thing Blake would try to do now. How she wished they could have stayed in the bedroom, lying close in bed, clinging to each other, shutting out the rest of the world. But it was morning now, time to face that world and its ugly realities.

Eleven

A cold north wind carrying stinging sleet whipped at their faces, as Blake and Sheriff Tucker approached Nick West's farm north of Lawrence. Blake pulled his hat a little lower over his forehead, bending into the wind as he headed his horse down a slope toward the ranch house, which was obviously recently built. He felt a lingering fury over the fact that West had come to Kansas just to establish a residence and help gain votes for the proslavery representatives.

A few horses and cattle grazed in corrals, but other than that, the farm did not look very busy. Yellowed corn stalks, their ears picked and stored for feed two months earlier, stretched for several acres, looking dry and bleak.

They approached the house, and Blake turned to check his saddlebag, as he had done several times along the way, making sure it remained tightly secured in the bitter wind. It contained one thousand dollars in donations. Back in Lawrence, Jonas Hanks held a paper listing every contributor and how much they had given so that if this attempt at buying Jesse March failed, the money could be returned. Blake prayed that by some miracle he could bring Jesse back to George, realizing what George might try to do next if this mission was not successful.

A farm hand headed toward them before they could dismount. The collar of the man's deerskin jacket was turned up against the cold. "What's your business?" he called out to them.

Blake rode closer to the man. "I'm Blake Hastings and the man with me is Sheriff Tucker from Lawrence."

"I know who you are. What the hell do you want?"

Behind the turned-up collar and wide-brimmed hat Blake recognized the man as one of those who had been with Nick West the day Blake got into a fight with him, one of the men who had held him while Blake landed a hard fist into his gut. He held his temper in check as he answered the man. "We've come to talk to Nick West."

"What about?"

"It's none of your business. Where's West?"

"He's gone. Went back to Missouri."

Blake's heart fell at the words. "When?"

"Over a week ago."

Blake glanced at the house. "Mind if we have a look for ourselves?"

The man glowered at him, weighing his decision. "Go ahead," he finally answered. "Me and two other men are the only ones here. Left us to watch the place. There's a woman keeps house for him—a whore from town. She won't be much use to you, but go ahead and see for yourself. West is gone. Probably won't be back till next spring, if he comes back at all. Search the outbuildings if you want. You'll find his fancy buggy gone."

"You know anything about a Negro woman he kept here?"

212

"Jesse? Sure. He took her with him. Said he had a buyer for her—some big plantation owner in Georgia he met a few months ago. The man made an offer, but West wouldn't sell her at the time. Told me before he left that he decided maybe he'd wire the man once he got to Missouri and take him up on his offer. Said Jesse was getting to be too much trouble."

"Did he say how much the man had offered. Mention his name?"

"Never gave a name, but he did say he could get a good fifteen hundred dollars for her, now that she's, uh, broke in, so to speak." The man grinned, and Blake wondered where he got the strength to keep from killing him. He turned his horse and trotted it back to the house, where he dismounted. Sheriff Tucker followed suit.

"What's up?"

"Dead end, apparently," Blake answered. "West went back to Missouri, according to that son of a bitch over there. He says West intends to sell Jesse to some man from Georgia. Let's go check out the house." He walked up onto the porch and knocked on the front door, noticing the lovely frosted design on its glass. A moment later a woman opened the door, giving them a look that told them they had better have a good excuse for being there. She recognized Sheriff Tucker, and her eyebrows arched.

"What is it?" she asked.

"We want to take a look around inside," Tucker told her. "The ranch hand out there said it was all right."

"What are you looking for?"

Blake thought how hard she looked, her face showing lines from too much liquor and tobacco. Her hair was an ugly dyed black, and she was heavy around the middle.

"We just want to make sure Nick West is really gone, as well as the Negro woman he kept here," Tucker answered.

The woman stepped back. "Hurry up so I can close the door. It's cold." The men stepped inside the well-kept home, noticing the expensive Oriental rugs that decorated a polished wood floor. "Look all you want." The woman moved her eyes over Blake hungrily. "Name's Hetta. I don't remember seeing you around Lawrence."

He removed his hat, his cheeks red from the cold. "I'm Blake Hastings. I've only been in Lawrence a little over a year. Spent most of that time married."

She grinned at the meaning of the remark. "Well, I've been working for Mr. West longer than that, so I guess I never would have met you in any of the saloons." She looked at Sheriff Tucker, who was peeking into one of the bedrooms. "What are you two looking for, anyway? Illegal guns or something? If West is up to anything against the law, you sure won't find any proof of it in *this* house."

"He ever in charge of any of the bushwhacker raids that you know of?" Tucker turned and faced her.

Hetta stiffened. "No. None that I'm aware of. I just keep house for him, Sheriff. I don't nose into his personal or political affairs."

"I'd say his mistress is a pretty personal matter," Blake answered. "You must have known her. He must have had her in this house."

He noticed a defensive look come into her eyes. "What if he did?"

"Did he abuse her? Force her?"

She put her hands on her hips. "Look, mister, when it comes to how men handle their women, I don't interfere. Does anybody ask you if you abuse or

214

force your wife?"

"Don't compare a wife to a bought and paid-for slave! I've brought money along to buy her off of West. We were hoping we'd find both of them here."

"Well, you won't. Mr. West took Jesse back to Missouri. He told me he was going to sell her to a man from Georgia. Said he'd take her on to Georgia himself—wanted to stay out of Kansas and Missouri both for a while, till things cool down over the elections."

"He wanted to get as far away from the man who loves Jesse, that's what," Blake sneered. He looked over at Tucker. "He must have been afraid George would come after her."

"Come here a minute, Blake," the sheriff called.

Blake walked over to a bedroom door and Tucker motioned him inside, pointing to a spot on the brass footrail of the bed that had been worn to a silver-gray tarnish. "Could be from a chain. Why just one spot like that?"

"Damn," Blake muttered, his hands moving into fists. He turned and went to the doorway. "Did West chain her to the bed?" he asked Hetta.

The woman shrugged. "It's none of my business what goes on behind closed doors. Like I said, I just keep house."

"You must have helped take care of her," Blake fumed, his voice rising.

Hetta folded her arms. "All right—so she was kept chained. It was just one ankle, and he never beat her or anything like that. She was well fed and kept clean. West was even giving her reading lessons— brought her some children's books to amuse herself. She was only chained because she was a slave, and Mr. West was afraid she'd try to run away. He was

215

very fond of her."

"Then why would he sell her to the man in Georgia?"

"How do I know? Maybe because she was trouble. Maybe he's getting tired of her. I've been around the business of buying and selling women all my life. What's it to you, anyway? She's black. You got a liking for Negro women?"

Blake stepped closer, and the look in his eyes made her back off. She wondered for a moment if he might hit her. "My best friend is a Negro man, and he was going to *marry* that woman until Nick West bought her and took her away! I'm trying to get her back for him!"

"Well, that won't be possible. She's gone. If I know Nick West, he won't tell who he sold her to, because he won't want the man to have any trouble over it."

Blake looked her over, disgust in his eyes. "I never even got to meet her, but I'll tell you one thing. I have no doubt she's ten times the woman *you* could ever hope to be, you stinking slut!"

"Blake!" Tucker moved across the room. "Let's get out of here."

Blake stood glowering at Hetta, who held his eyes with her own hard glare, trembling slightly at the insult. "Yes. *Do* get out," she fumed. "Get the hell out!"

Blake turned and stormed out, his heart aching for George. How could he tell him Jesse was gone? Just knowing she was here, even though in the hands of Nick West, was some little comfort. At least then George knew her whereabouts. Now she would again unwantedly elude him, and hope of finding her would fade once more.

Blake mounted his black mare, turning the animal in an angry circle while he waited for the sheriff to mount his own steed. Tucker reined his horse away from the hitching post. "I'm sorry, Hastings."

Blake thought about how he'd feel if it were Samantha. His eyes showed his terrible pain. "So am I. Just don't tell George about the mark on the bedpost."

Tucker nodded. "I won't say a thing."

Blake jerked his horse around again, longing for nothing more than to kill Nick West. "Let's go," he said, kicking his horse's sides and riding off.

George was standing anxiously at the kitchen door when Blake rode around the back of the house. In spite of the cold, the door stood open, George staring through the screen with a look of horrible disappointment and hopelessness on his face when he realized Jesse was not with Blake. Blake dismounted and tied the mare, coming to the door. He opened the screen.

"I, uh, left the money with Tucker," he told George, meeting his eyes. "All but my share. He'll see it gets back to the people who contributed."

George closed his eyes and turned away. Blake looked at Samantha, seeing her sorrow mixed with relief that at least he had returned safely. He came inside and closed the door, unbuttoning his jacket. Before he could remove it, Samantha walked up to embrace him. She stood for a moment in the comfort of his strong arms, surrounded by the fleece lining of the jacket, thinking how safe she felt when she was close to him this way. How she wished it could be the same for poor Jesse.

"Does he want more money?" George asked, his back to them.

Blake gently pushed Samantha away, taking off

his jacket. She took it from him and hung it on the coat tree. "He wasn't there, George. He took Jesse and went back to Missouri." He sighed deeply, hanging up his hat. "According to a farm hand and the woman who keeps house for him, West said he was going to take Jesse on to Georgia where he was going to sell her to some plantation owner he met a few months ago. No one knows who it is, and you and I both know West would never tell us."

George shook his head. "My God," he groaned.

"I'm sorry, George. Even if she had been there, West would never sell her for less than fifteen hundred dollars. The ranch hand said West had already been offered that much. I know it sounds like a cruel compliment right now, George, but . . . she must be very beautiful."

George nodded, his back still to them. "She is." He turned to face them, tears on his cheek. "Why did God let me see her again? I could have somehow learned to live with it, never knowing at all. But to see her again, to know how she was suffering—how she'll suffer even more being traded off like a harlot—" He closed his eyes and breathed deeply, wiping at the tears. "I can't let it go now, Blake."

"You have to, unless you want to die or take a chance on being brought back into slavery. You stay away from Nick West, George. He'll destroy you."

"What difference does it make? I'm already destroyed," the man groaned, stepping closer. "I can't go on living this way. What good is my freedom if I can't enjoy it with Jesse? I've got to take the chance, Blake. You'd do the same damn thing. I've got to go after her."

"Damn it, that's suicide!"

"I've got no choice!"

"But I can't help you, George! I can't leave

218

Samantha—not for the length of time it might take to find her, let alone the fact that we'd never have enough money between us to buy her!"

"I don't expect you to go with me. This could take weeks, maybe months. But I'm going to find Jesse, and I'm going to get her back even if I have to *steal* her away! *Nobody* is going to stop me, and I'm going to do it on my own. I can't depend on you forever, Blake, especially not now!"

They all stood looking at each other, the room suddenly quiet. It was obvious the decision had been made and no one was going to change George's mind. "You figured on doing this all along, didn't you?" Blake finally asked.

George nodded. "I knew there wasn't much hope you'd come home with Jesse. I thought maybe at least she'd still be up there at West's ranch and I could get her away from there. Now the search is going to be a little harder, but I'll find her—one way or another."

"A Negro man riding into a southern plantation looking for a Negro woman?" Blake rubbed at his eyes. "You'll end up wearing a ball and chain."

George grasped the back of a chair. "Maybe. But it wouldn't be any worse than what Jesse must be suffering. I can't just settle on a farm with you and live my happy little life while I know Jesse is out there somewhere suffering pain and humiliation."

Blake pulled out a chair and sat down wearily. "All right. Let's say you manage to find her, you even manage to sneak off with her—where will you go?"

"Canada." George pulled out a chair, sitting down eagerly, his eyes lighting up with new hope at the mere thought of finding Jesse. "There's places in Canada where runaway slaves are safe. I could get a message to you—let you know we're okay."

Blake leaned back and reached inside his pants

pocket, pulling out a wad of bills. He put them on the table. "Keep my share."

"No, sir, I'm not—"

"Keep it!" Blake commanded. "You'll need it. You might end up doing a lot of traveling, with no time for work. You'll need money. When do you plan to leave?"

"First thing in the morning. With any luck, I'll find out West changed his mind. Maybe he's got Jesse on his farm in Missouri."

Their eyes held, both realizing that after tomorrow they might never see each other again. "You've got to be damn careful if you intend to go anywhere near Nick West."

"I won't have to. Once I get there, I'll sneak into the fields, find some of the other slaves, see what they can tell me. West doesn't have to know I'm anywhere around."

Samantha walked over to where George sat, touching his shoulder. "It's so dangerous, George. We'll be so worried, sitting here wondering if you're all right."

He sighed deeply. "If I can find a way to contact you before we get to Canada, I'll do it. But once it's done, you both might be better off *not* hearing from me for a while. West or some of his men might try to harass you, get you to tell them if you've heard from me, know where I might have gone with Jesse."

Blake grinned sadly. "Do you really think we'd tell?"

George scooted back his chair and rose, eyeing both of them lovingly. "No. I, uh, I love you both. Maybe someday, a long time from now, we can all be together and live in peace."

Samantha's eyes teared. "Maybe. I'll be praying for that." She embraced George, and Blake stood up to embrace them both. George sniffed, pulling away after a moment and breathing deeply for control.

"I'd better go pack a few things," he said.

"I'll have breakfast before dawn," Samantha told him. "You be sure to come and eat with us before you leave."

He nodded.

"What about a horse?" Blake asked him. "You can take Midnight if you want."

George shook his head. "Thanks, but I had a feeling I'd be doing some traveling. I saved back enough money from what I gave you for Jesse to buy a horse. Got one off Jules Cade over at the livery while you were gone—a nice-looking paint."

Blake ran a hand through his hair, his arm still around Samantha. "Well, it's obvious your mind has been made up for a long time."

"It has—ever since I saw Jesse in town ten days ago." His eyes teared again. "I'm going to find her, Blake, or die trying. Life just isn't worth living this way."

Blake reached out, and George took his hand, squeezing it. Neither man needed to say what he was thinking or to try to express how deeply each cared for the other. It was all said in that one gesture, and in the look they exchanged. George turned and left, closing the door softly. Blake leaned against the door. "Damn it all," he moaned. "Damn all of them to hell!"

Samantha and Blake worked harder than ever on an abolitionist newspaper. Now that the ugliness of slavery had been brought down to a personal scale because of George and Jesse, both were determined to continue doing what they could to at least make

Kansas a free territory. Perhaps it would be a start to one day abolishing slavery everywhere.

PRESIDENT PIERCE FAILS TO RECOGNIZE NEW ABOLITIONIST LEGISLATURE, today's headline read. Samantha felt the sick feeling of hopelessness churn in her stomach as she set the type. "Kansas's proslavery voters have once again elected J. W. Whitfield, a strong proslavery man, as congressional representative for Kansas Territory. We, on the other hand, stand strong behind Andrew Reeder as our own representative, the man originally appointed by President Pierce to govern Kansas, the man our spineless President quickly replaced with Wilson Shannon, another proslavery man, as soon as the first illegal elections were held. Our President seems incapable of understanding the true wishes of Kansas citizens, or of understanding that Kansas is facing a civil war. Until the President allows honest elections in Kansas, we must hold fast and be true to our convictions. We will not be run by outsiders and bushwhackers."

Samantha found no typographical errors. She leaned back in her chair, wondering about George. It was late December. George had been gone over a month now, and there had been no word. She knew that worry over his friend was eating at Blake, who had been more quiet than usual ever since his departure. When he made love to her, it seemed part of him was not with her at all. No matter how hard they tried, the fighting outside their doors had entered their bedroom, unbidden, unwanted, eating at them like an infection. How she hated it.

She looked up when Blake came inside, a grave look on his face. "There's big trouble brewing," he told her. "You might have quite a story for the newspaper."

222

Reverend Walters came in from the back room. "What's happened, Blake?"

"Men are gathering in the street. Sam Clay has been shot."

"Sam! He's one of our most ardent supporters!"

"Well, he's a *dead* supporter now. He got into some kind of land dispute with a proslavery man over near the Wakarusa. The man shot him."

Walters sighed deeply, shaking his head. "That's a terrible loss."

"That's not the worst of it. Some of Clay's neighbors witnessed the whole thing—reported it to the Douglas County sheriff. He won't do anything about it. Says it was a legal shootout, even though there are witnesses to testify that Clay was unarmed."

"Everyone knows the county sheriff is proslavery, bought and paid for by the new government," Samantha put in. "Of course he won't do anything about it."

"Well, a lot of people are gathering in the street ready *to* do something about it! There's a vigilante group forming out there, preparing to march on the home of the murderer and burn it down."

"Good God," Walters muttered. "That will only make things worse."

"You might as well face it—both of you," Blake told them. "Things *are* going to get worse. You aren't going to be able to continue your fight through peaceful means. The violence might even come right to Lawrence. If those men out there do what they say they're going to do, there is going to be a retaliation by the proslavery men. They know Lawrence is our stronghold. The best way to beat us is to bring the fight right to us."

"Blake, you . . . you aren't going to join those men in burning the killer's house, are you?" Samantha asked the question with great trepidation. "Anyone involved in that will most surely be labeled a traitor of the worst kind. A vigilante!"

Blake walked to a window, watching an angry crowd gather farther up the street. "Sam, we're already traitors. Just publishing this newspaper makes us traitors. Preaching against slavery makes us traitors. You knew that from the beginning."

"Please try not to get directly involved in the violence, Blake."

He turned and met her eyes. "I don't know how much longer I can hold back. The day is coming when I'll have no choice, Sam." He moved his eyes to Walters. "It might be the same for you."

"Never. I'll never raise my hand against another human being," the reverend objected.

"What if that human being is raising his hand against *you?* If God wants you to fight this, Howard, you'd better use every resource available!" He walked over to Samantha, taking her hand. "Come on."

"Where are we going?"

"Home. It's getting late. You can finish in the morning."

She looked at her father helplessly. "Go on with you," he told her. "Get him home and keep him there." She grabbed her coat and Blake helped her get it on. They walked outside, where dusk was fast falling. Samantha could hear the angry shouts, could see that some men were already on horseback with lit torches. Blake turned her away.

"We'll take the back way. I don't want you around that mob. Beecher is over there egging them on. You can bet he'll remember the name of every man who takes part in this and report it to just the right people, like that county sheriff."

"Blake, Mr. Beecher just gave that splendid

sermon against slavery in church last Sunday."

"And he's the biggest liar and hypocrite who ever walked. You mark my words." He held her arm, keeping watch warily all the way home. Samantha could feel his worry and tension, and she knew that not hearing from George was only making things worse. She felt some relief when they got home. At least he was not going to join the vigilantes. He hung up his coat and hat and put some more wood in the stove, then turned when Samantha touched his back. He grasped her arms.

"I feel so many things slipping away, Sam," he told her.

She reached up and touched his face. "Not me. I'm right here."

He leaned down and met her mouth. She reached around his neck, and he hoisted her up so that she wrapped her legs around him. He carried her into the bedroom, both of them suddenly wondering how much time they had left before the world outside would take even this from them. He laid her back on the bed, moving a hand under her dress, kissing her throat.

"I want to make love to you, Sam," he groaned. "I want to feel every part of you, be inside you." He covered her mouth in a hungry kiss, and they managed to become lost in each other. This time she felt his full attention was with her, that for one brief night they might again keep that other world out of this room.

They made love almost savagely, clinging desperately to each other into the late hours of the night, while outside the mob of abolitionist vigilantes grew to uncontrollable proportions. They mounted their horses and headed out, their torches lighting up the night sky.

Twelve

It was midmorning when Blake came charging through the back door, startling Samantha. She lowered her knitting when he came into the sitting room, his breathing heavy as though he was in a hurry. He tossed one of his saddlebags onto a chair. "There's big trouble coming, Sam. I'm not going to sit back and wait for it this time!"

Her chest felt tight as she rose from her chair and set the knitting aside. "What is it?"

"Scouts tell us the Douglas County sheriff is on his way here to arrest the men who were involved in burning Walt Harding's house! He's mustered the help of a gang of proslavery raiders. Our own men are gathering in town right now."

He walked to a buffet and opened one of the doors, reaching inside to take out some ammunition for his rifle. "They intend to ride out and meet that Missouri rabble before they can reach Lawrence. They're coming up from the south—almost to the Wakarusa River. They've got to be stopped."

"Blake, they haven't done much so far against those of us who just preach against slavery. But those who get involved in the violence are much more likely to be pointed out as traitors."

"Well, I for one am tired of sitting around waiting for things to happen. If those sons of bitches make it to Lawrence, a lot of innocent people will be hurt! We're better off going out to meet them." He rose and faced her. "I've held back all I can. If you and your father want to make a stand against slavery and against the new government, it's time to take some action instead of just using your mouths and printing newspapers!"

He saw the terror move into her eyes. "Do you think there will be . . . actual fighting . . . shooting?"

"Most likely. We're hoping that when the bushwhackers see us standing together, ready to fight, they'll back down. It's one thing to go out and attack people in their homes, Sam, like what happened to Harding. I'm sorry his house was burned, but the fact remains he killed Sam Clay in cold blood and he should have hanged for it! As far as I'm concerned, the men who burned his house were dealing out justice. They don't deserve to be arrested."

He shoved the ammunition into the saddlebag, then carried it into the bedroom to pack a few clothes. Samantha followed. "I'll pack you some food," she said quietly.

"Fine. I left my other saddlebag on the kitchen table. Give me enough for three or four days. With any luck it will only be one or two. We'll send those bastards packing! It pisses me off that the county sheriff would use no-good, murdering Missouri border raiders to help him do his job. It only shows who is *really* behind the new government!"

"You . . . you really feel you have to do this. Go and meet them with guns?"

Blake hesitated in his packing, turning to meet her eyes. He sighed, walking closer and grasping her arms. "Sam, I don't feel like I'm really doing anything in this fight if all I do is sit around listening to sermons and helping print newspapers. And this thing with George is driving me crazy. I've got to either get more involved or get the hell out of Kansas; and I can't even do that now. You have your parents to think about, and now I have George. He might try to contact me. We're in this now, Sam—up to our necks. We were in deep when we attended the convention in Topeka, and now we're even deeper."

Their eyes held, and she nodded. "I know. I also know how restless you've been." She searched his eyes pleadingly. "Please be careful. Please try to avoid actual conflict."

He leaned forward, meeting her lips lightly. "I'll do my best. This is partly for your sake, Sam. I don't want the sheriff and his men to get into Lawrence. They might try to do more than arrest the men who burned Harding's house. They might get to people like you and your folks. So far Lawrence has been our stronghold. They haven't followed through on their threats to come here and arrest everyone involved in the movement."

He turned to quickly finish packing, closing his saddlebags and walking into the kitchen to pick up his rifle. He opened it to make sure it was clean and loaded. "I'll go pack my gear now," he told her. "Put some food in those saddlebags."

Samantha put a hand to her aching chest after he walked outside. Blake and an unorganized gang of abolitionists were riding out to meet a mob of border ruffians who might be more ruthless than Blake and the others were anticipating. To imagine Blake hurt or dead . . . She shivered, wondering if she had done the right thing in continuing to fight the new government. In doing so, she had gotten Blake just as involved. She had known all along that a man of his character and temperament could not stay in this fight long without getting caught up in the growing violence. Worry over George had only made him even more edgy. She told herself to stay strong. Blake didn't need to see his wife showing any weakness. She knew instinctively that this time there would be no arguing with him. He came back inside, stamping snow from his feet.

"This is a hell of a time of year to have to be camping out," he muttered. He bent down to brush snow from his pants.

Samantha turned with the saddlebags, forcing back an urge to cry. "Will you be back for our first anniversary?"

Blake straightened, love and apologies filling his dark eyes. "My God, it's only a couple of weeks away, isn't it?"

She handed out the saddlebags. "There are plenty of potatoes here, some bread and some canned beans and peas, a little sugar and flour, some cookies. You . . . didn't give me much warning or I could have done a little better job."

He stepped closer, taking the bags and laying them on the table. He drew her into his arms. "I'll be back," he promised. "This may turn into nothing but a standoff, Sam. So far, the new government hasn't dared to come into Lawrence and arrest anyone. That's why we're going out to greet the sheriff before he gets here. We want to continue to keep them out of the city."

She wondered if she should tell him she thought she might be pregnant. She decided against it. For one thing, she still wasn't sure herself; after all, she was only a week late. Why give him one more thing to worry about while he was away? It might cause him to get careless.

"I want you to go and stay with your folks while I'm gone," he told her. "And if the bushwhackers should somehow get through, you stay clear of Clyde Beecher. Try to get your folks to join up with Jonas Hanks. Maybe all of you could gather together at the Free State Hotel. You'd be safer there."

She hugged him tightly. "With you out there, they'll never get into town," she answered. She looked up at him and he met her lips, kissing her hungrily, both of them wishing there was time to do much more.

"I'll make this up to you when I get back," he told her.

"Just come back alive and well," she answered. "That's the best thing you can do for me right now."

He kissed her forehead. "I sent Mark Stetson over to your folks to tell your father to come and get you." He sighed deeply, pulling back and buttoning his buckskin jacket. He adjusted his hat and grabbed up the saddlebags. They watched each other quietly for a moment as he hesitated at the door. "I love you, Sam."

"And you know how much I love you. God be with you."

His eyes looked misty as he turned and headed out the door. She stood at the screen, oblivious to the cold, watching him tie the bags onto his gear and mount up on Midnight. He gave her one last look and waved. She waved back, but the lump in her throat was too painful for her to speak. She watched him ride away, realizing that war and violence were coming ever closer to their own doorstep.

It became known as the Wakarusa War, a standoff between the new proslavery government and the "treasonous" abolitionist government. To Samantha's relief, the confrontation at the Wakarusa River did not lead to all-out battle. Kansas's federally appointed governor, Wilson Shannon, a fierce proslavery man in his own right, managed to mediate the situation and prevent bloodshed; but the die had been cast. Several Free-soil men in Lawrence, including Samantha's father and Blake, as well as several of the men who had burned Walt Harding's home, were declared traitors by the proslavery government. Reverend Walters's *Free Soil* newspaper, as well as another Lawrence newspaper, were declared to contain treasonous propaganda, and the Free State Hotel was condemned as a gathering place for the worst of the traitors.

Still, no arrests were made, but Lawrence shored itself up, ready for the worst. Its determined citizens continued to fight the new government and to dare it to enact its brazenly illegal laws. In spite of being condemned, Samantha's father continued to print his newspaper with Blake's and Samantha's help.

It was mid-January when Samantha sat near the heating stove, unwrapping an anniversary gift from Blake. She still thanked God every day that he had come home alive and unhurt, which made this moment all the more special. She opened the gift box and pulled out a fur-lined woolen cape. "Oh, Blake," she gasped, holding it up. "It's beautiful! After giving so much money to George, how did you ever afford it?"

He grinned, reaching out to touch the thick rabbit lining. "I had my own little separate savings for this. I've been wanting to get it for you ever since you admired it in the millinery shop almost a year ago. I couldn't think of a better gift for the middle of winter."

She rubbed her cheek against the fur. "How thoughtful of you." She met his eyes, her own misty. "I don't have a gift for you. With everything in such turmoil, prices have gone up. The money you give me for food and other bills doesn't seem to go so far anymore."

He watched her lovingly, always enjoying the way her lips moved when she spoke, the way her lovely blue eyes danced. Today she wore blue again, a lovely velvet dress she knew he loved to see on her. The neckline showed just enough of her firm bosom to remind him she was just as beautiful and desirable as the day he married her.

"You don't really think I need a gift, do you?" he asked. "Just being together in peace is good enough."

She folded the cape back into the box and set it aside. "Actually, I do have something to give you, but I can't give it to you just yet."

He frowned. "What is that supposed to mean?"

She took a deep breath, wanting to shout the words. "You'll have to wait about seven more months. I'm giving you the one thing you want most of all—a family of your own."

She watched his dark eyes, first showing slight confusion, then beginning to light up with the realization of what she was telling him. But just as quickly they showed something close to sorrow. She felt a panic rising deep inside. "Blake, you *want* a baby, don't you?"

He leaned forward, putting his hands on the arms of her chair. "I want that more than anything in the world. It's just . . . My God, Sam, we're all liable to be arrested at any time!"

"They wouldn't arrest *me*. You said yourself that no women have ever been arrested. And they certainly aren't going to do it when they find out I'm pregnant. Besides, we're relatively safe here in Lawrence. If they haven't done anything to us by now, they probably won't. They must know the President might be giving consideration to our pleadings. They're waiting for him to make the next move." She grasped his arms. "Blake, I know it's bad timing, but . . . I can't control when these things happen, no more than I can control my desire for you when you lie next to me in the night."

He knelt in front of her, taking her hand. "It's the best gift you could ever give me, Sam. God knows I've never done anything to keep it from happening. Maybe I should have been more careful, knowing how dangerous things are."

"Blake, being pregnant is my *protection!* Don't you see? God gave us this baby so that I couldn't be arrested. And soon, President Pierce will straighten all this out and we'll be free to live our lives as we see fit. You'll see."

He decided not to spoil what he felt was a hopeless dream. "Maybe you're right—about the baby protecting you. Are you sure about it?"

"I've never been this late," she answered, feeling embarrassed at mentioning such a thing. "And I've been feeling sick lately, especially in the mornings. Mother told me that's a pretty sure sign."

"When would he be born?"

"He?"

He grinned, squeezing her hand. "He or she."

"I guess around late July."

He touched her chin, leaning up to kiss her lightly. "Any harm in celebrating our anniversary the same way we celebrated on our wedding night?"

She felt the warmth spread through her at the words. "No harm at all."

He grinned the handsome grin that always made her feel a little weak. No matter what the outside forces, this special love they shared had not changed. His eyes dropped to the soft crest of her breasts above the enticing neckline of the blue velvet. He leaned forward and lightly kissed their soft, white fullness. She grasped his head, a pleasant chill of excitement moving through her. She wound her fingers into his thick hair. "I love you so much, Blake."

He moved his lips to her throat, kissing it lightly before rising and picking her up out of the chair. He carried her into the bedroom, laying her back on the bed.

"No more hard work for you," he told her. "No more going to the newspaper office. You've got to be more careful than ever now, stay away from danger—"

"Blake, I'll not change one thing I'm doing. Not just yet. I'm not an invalid. I'm just pregnant." The words brought a light flush to her cheeks.

He began unbuttoning the front of her dress. "Just the same, you do what I say. This baby means more to me than anything in this world." He stopped short, suddenly grinning wider. "My God, Sam, you're going to have a baby!" She laughed as he lay down beside her and pulled her into his arms. "What can I say? Thank you, Sam. I just wish . . ." He held her tighter. "I just wish all the fighting and political wars were over. I wish George would come back or get in touch with us. This is a hell of a world to bring a baby into."

"I know." She relished the scent of him as she rested her head against his chest. "But he or she will have us to love and protect him. We'll shelter him

235

from any harm, Blake. God is giving us a baby. He'll make sure nothing happens to it—or to us.''

She moved her lips to meet his mouth, whimpering when a big but gentle hand reached inside the now-open dress and under her silk chemise to grasp gently at her full breast. His kiss lingered, deepened, as he massaged her awakened nipple lightly with his thumb.

Samantha relaxed and enjoyed the delicious warmth that flowed through her as he began removing her clothes seductively, piece by piece. How she enjoyed his gentle touch. This was a time for celebration. Again, they must not allow the outside world to interfere with this.

She watched him boldly as he undressed himself, then closed her eyes as he began moving over her with delicious kisses, reminding her she was Blake Hasting's woman and making her glad this was the man she had chosen. They needed nothing more now but to be one.

They relished the sweet ecstasy of being united, both glorying in the fact that this could still be so wonderful, that this could still help them shut out the rest of the world. A new dimension had been added to their rich love. Blake Hastings was the father of the baby growing inside of her; and she was going to be a mother. No outside forces could change that. She was carrying Blake's child, and she had taken his seed joyfully. Surely this was a sign of good things to come.

Eighteen fifty-six brought increased activity by the stubborn, determined Kansas abolitionists and Free-soil supporters. Against Blake's wishes, Samantha worked long hours at the printing office, keeping the citizens of Lawrence and supporters in outlying areas abreast of the latest happenings. Blake took turns with other brave men in riding out to deliver the newspaper to more distant farmers and ranchers.

More elections had been held, and the free-soil Kansans elected a new governor, Charles Robinson, as well as electing new, even more determined men to their own legislature, an act condemned by the President of the United States as one of blatant rebellion.

PRESIDENTIAL PROCLAMATION WARNS AGAINST BORDER RAIDS AND VIOLENCE, the headlines of the *Free Soil* read by mid-February. "President Pierce continues to support our illegal proslavery legislature and congressional representatives," the story continued. "We must do our best to support an abolitionist candidate in this year's presidential election. Perhaps then the political picture in Kansas will be one of justice and fairness."

The raiding along the borders of Kansas and Missouri had become more frequent and much more violent, with death and property losses mounting. "Bleeding Kansas" was indeed becoming red with blood, and people from both sides of the issue were clamoring at the President to help bring law and order to Kansas Territory and to Missouri's border. Blake fumed that just issuing a proclamation was not going to solve anything. The territory remained torn because the President was not brave enough to declare the original elections invalid. As long as the proslavery faction had Pierce's approval and support, Blake knew the battle to make Kansas a free territory was going to be an endless foray, but his own courage and conviction were bolstered when he finally received word from George in late February.

Samantha looked up from setting type when Blake

came to see her unexpectedly on noon break from his job at the sawmill. "I checked at the post office again, and look what was there waiting for us," he told her, looking happier than she had seen him in a long time—except for the night she told him she was pregnant. "It's a letter from George!"

Her face lit up, and she turned in her chair. "Oh, Blake, read it quickly!"

He pulled up a chair beside her and tore open the envelope. "Thank God I taught him to write," he said with a light laugh. "He hasn't completely mastered it yet, but he can do it good enough to let us know . . ." He stopped to scan the letter, and to Samantha's relief, his face showed only joy.

"My God, Sam, he did it! It says here he found out from some of the field hands that West never sold Jesse at all! He says Jesse told him that he just wanted us to *think* he sold her to keep us off his back . . . Let me see if I can make this out. The sentences are kind of run together. Next time I see George, I'm going to light into him about forgetting to use periods and capital letters."

Samantha could see the affection in his eyes. How she wished it was safe for George and Jesse to come here and be with them. She wondered sadly how long the fighting over slavery was going to continue, how long it would be before they saw George again. "Hurry, Blake," she said anxiously. "What happened?"

"Well, from what I can figure, he apparently waited until West took Jesse with him into town. Soon as West went inside a bank, George rode up and scooped Jesse onto his horse and rode off with her. They apparently got quite a distance away before West discovered what had happened, enough of a head start to avoid being trailed. He says they traveled mostly at night, stuck to the back country, finally made it into Canada. He's somewhere north of Minnesota. Says he can't tell me exactly where—doesn't want us to know just now. He sent the letter from America. He must have gone back across the border to send it so no one would see a Canadian postmark. He says when it looks like things are more settled in the States, he'll get in touch again, but that he'll probably never be able to bring Jesse back into the country."

His smile faded some, as both of them felt a sudden sadness, in spite of the good news that George had made it to Canada and had his Jesse with him. "My God, Sam, if slavery is never abolished in this country, they'll never be able to come back. Jesse March is Nick West's property." He met her eyes. "We'd better burn this."

Her eyes misted. "Blake, at least he's safe in Canada, and he's with the woman he loves. He got her away from Nick West."

Blake looked at the letter again. "Yes," he said rather absently.

"Blake, what's wrong?"

He sighed deeply. "Nothing, I guess. Everything that has happened . . . I don't know. I guess it's made me suspicious of everything. George just riding off with her like that and not being chased and caught—it almost sounds like it was too easy. For some reason I suddenly have this crazy feeling maybe George isn't safe at all." He looked at the letter again. "Maybe they aren't even in Canada."

"Blake, you're too much of a pessimist sometimes." She rubbed at his shoulders. "My darling, you know George's handwriting. Is that it?"

He studied the letter some more. "Yes. It's his writing."

239

"Well, then, why are you worried? It's his handwriting, and George wouldn't lie to you. It all makes sense—the length of time it took for him to get back to us and all. That's about how long it would take to escape to Canada. Why would he write us this letter if anything had gone wrong?"

He ran a hand through his hair. "I suppose you're right." He smiled again, but not with his original eagerness. "I guess we just have to hope and trust that everything is all right." He looked at the familiar, somewhat childlike handwriting again. "He knew we'd want to hear from him. It makes sense that he wouldn't want us to know exactly where he is, in case someone should question us about it."

He rose, carrying the letter to the wood-burning stove at the corner of the room. Its belly was full of hot coals to heat the printing office. He opened the door, scanning the letter once more before tossing it inside and adding more wood. He closed the door and faced Samantha. "He said Jesse was okay—just said she needed a lot of loving to get over her ordeal with West." He smiled sadly. "George will gladly give her that." He rubbed at the back of his neck, turning to look out the window at the muddy street. "I wish we could have met her."

Samantha walked to where he stood, touching his back. "They'll be all right as long as they stay in Canada," she tried to assure him.

He sighed deeply. "*If* they're in Canada."

She rested her head against his arm. "Blake, you saw the letter in George's own handwriting. Someday this will all be over and they can come here to be with us, or at least tell us exactly where they are."

He moved an arm around her shoulders. "Maybe so. In the meantime, be sure not to mention any of this to Beecher. As far as he knows, we still haven't

240

MORE PASSION AND ADVENTURE AWAIT... YOUR TRIP TO A BIG ADVENTUROUS WORLD BEGINS WHEN YOU ACCEPT YOUR FIRST 4 NOVELS ABSOLUTELY *FREE* (AN $18.00 VALUE)

Accept your Free gift and start to experience more of the passion and adventure you like in a historical romance novel. Each Zebra novel is filled with proud men, spirited women and tempestuous love that you'll remember long after you turn the last page

Zebra Historical Romances are the finest novels of their kind. They are written by authors who really know how to weave tales of romance and adventure in the historical settings you love. You'll feel like you've actually gone back in time with the thrilling stories that each Zebra novel offers.

GET YOUR FREE GIFT WITH THE START OF YOUR HOME SUBSCRIPTION

Our readers tell us that these books sell out very fast in book stores and often they miss the newest titles. So Zebra has made arrangements for you to receive the four newest novels published each month.

You'll be guaranteed that you'll never miss a title, and home delivery is so convenient. And to show you just how easy it is to get Zebra Historical Romances, we'll send you your first 4 books absolutely FREE! Our gift to you just for trying our home subscription service.

BIG SAVINGS AND FREE HOME DELIVERY

Each month, you'll receive the four newest titles as soon as they are published. You'll probably receive them even before the bookstores do. What's more, you may preview these exciting novels free for 10 days. If you like them as much as we think you will, just pay the low preferred subscriber's price of just $3.75 each. *You'll save $3.00 each month off the publisher's price.* AND, your savings are even greater because there are never any shipping, handling or other hidden charges—FREE Home Delivery. Of course you can return any shipment within 10 days for full credit, no questions asked. There is no minimum number of books you must buy.

heard from George. He left Kansas to head west and that's all we know."

"I won't say a word."

Blake looked down at her. "I miss him, Sam. I won't feel right about this until I see him again face-to-face and know he really is all right."

George shivered in the cold stall. The little bit of hay he had managed to scrape up to cover himself for warmth was damp, some even mixed with horse dung. The vicious whipping and beatings Nick West had subjected him to, along with little food and nothing for warmth but the now-ragged shirt and pants he wore were causing him to weaken and get sicker every day.

He thanked God that at least Jesse was still at the house. In spite of knowing what Nick West was doing to her, she was at least warm and well fed, living in the comfort of his plantation home. Someday, somehow, he would get out of this and he would take Jesse away.

He struggled against tears of hopelessness. Was he a fool to think he could save Jesse now? Not only was he chained by a wrist and an ankle to the wall of the horse stall, but even if he could get free, he was so weak he could never get far if he tried to run. Nick West had seen to that. He almost wished West would have hanged or shot him when his men caught up with him and Jesse and dragged them back to West's plantation in Missouri. But no, killing him would not have been as delightful for West as torturing him in front of poor Jesse. He could still hear her wrenching sobs as West forced her to watch him being whipped and beaten. For weeks George had stubbornly refused to write the letter to Blake that

241

West wanted him to write, telling Blake everything was fine. West didn't want Blake to come "nosing around."

"We'll take care of Blake Hastings in our own time and our own way," he had told George. "I don't want any surprises from him. As long as he thinks you're all right, he won't be bothering me."

George knew that writing the letter eliminated all hope of Blake coming to help him. But pain and hunger had a way of making a man change his mind, and on the promise of decent food and some warm blankets, as well as a little more freedom once he was stronger, George had written the letter, sealing his own confinement back into slavery. Nick West had destroyed his freedom papers. George decided that he *had* to write that letter, for it was the only way to get his own strength back, in case an opportunity arose in which he could free Jesse and run away with her. Dying was not going to do her any good. Maybe, at the least, he could find a way to get word to Blake about what had really happened.

He heard the barn door open again, and he wondered if someone was coming to use the whip on him again. He was hardly aware of what time of day it was, or how much time had passed since he had been brought here. A man called Cal appeared at the door to the stall. He tossed a couple of blankets to George, along with a loaf of fresh-baked bread.

"The boss says to start treating you a little better. He wants you to get stronger. He's gonna need another hand in the fields come spring."

George pulled one of the blankets over his legs, then grabbed the bread and bit into it.

Cal grinned. "Maybe now you'll learn your place, nigger. You know what will happen if you try anything funny. You just remember that Mr. West

242

doesn't kill runaways. That's too easy. He makes them *suffer*—and every time you try something, that pretty little nigger gal you've got an eye for will suffer, too. You remember that!''

George just glared at him, chewing on the bread. Cal laughed lightly and left, closing the barn door again and leaving George sitting in near darkness. George swallowed the bread, wishing he had some water to wash it down with, wondering if Blake had received his letter yet. Would he believe it, or would he by some miracle read between the lines? He leaned against the stall, praying Jesse was all right, hoping West wouldn't sell her before he found a way to again try to help her.

Thirteen

"Something doesn't feel right tonight," Blake said quietly.

He lay gently rubbing Samantha's softly swelling stomach, both of them pleasantly weary from making love. Blake was more careful with her now, afraid of doing something to harm her or the unborn child she carried. Samantha was seven months pregnant. Her stomach was still not huge, but she wore full dresses or loose shirts over skirts she could no longer button. Her belly had a roundness to it now when she lay on her back, and Blake loved the look of her—soft, pregnant with his child, looking more radiant and beautiful every day.

"I feel it, too," she answered. "I think it's just the strain of the constant threat from the authorities. And it's been three months since we've heard anything from George."

"I don't like the fact that Clyde Beecher was gone so long. He claimed he was going out into border country to preach to settlers and to deliver more newspapers. He sure strutted his stuff in church

Sunday, putting on an act of bravery and conviction. As far as I can remember, he's never left Lawrence before. I can't help thinking he wasn't doing what he told your father he was doing. But then it does no good to try to tell your father that."

"Did he say something to make you more suspicious?"

Blake sighed sleepily, turning and moving an arm across her chest. "You know Beecher. He's a careful man. He did ask if I had heard from George. When I told him no, he gave me kind of a strange look—said he could hardly believe my good friend hadn't sent me some kind of letter by now. I got the impression he was feeling me out, almost like he knew I was *supposed* to get a letter. I had my mind made up that George was all right until I talked to Beecher. Now I have my doubts again."

"It could just be coincidence that he asked about George, Blake. I still have trouble picturing Mr. Beecher as a spy. Maybe you'll get another letter soon from George that will give you more details. The first letter *was* in his handwriting, you know."

"I know. But I'm surprised West or one of his men hasn't come to me to try to bully me into telling if I know where he is. If Jesse was so special to Nick West, then once she was stolen away, George would be the first man West would suspect. Somebody would have questioned me about it, considering my relationship with George. Don't you think it's strange that I never heard from anyone?"

Samantha ran her slender hand along his hard-muscled forearm. "I suppose it is. But then a man like West wouldn't want to come to Lawrence and try to threaten anyone right now. He'd have too many enemies here. He must know that. For all we know he just went ahead and hired men to start searching. I just hope George can stay one step ahead of them. I doubt they'd let the Canadian border stop them." She turned to face him, kissing his cheek. "Blake, George is probably still running. He could be almost to the Pacific Coast by now, for all we know. That's probably why you haven't heard from him."

"Maybe. But it's pretty hard to do much traveling in Canada in the winter. I think it's more likely they found a place to hole up. If they're on the move, they would just now be getting good enough weather for it. In the meantime, a thousand things could have happened to them over the winter. West's men might even have found them."

"Blake, you've got to stop visualizing the worst." She drew in her breath and smiled, taking hold of his hand and moving it to her stomach. "Here, feel this. It will help you get your mind off George and back to a happier subject. Do you feel it?"

A sweet, warm comfort engulfed Blake when he felt his baby moving inside Samantha's belly. "Yes," he answered, grinning. "Our lovemaking probably disturbed him."

She laughed lightly. "I don't doubt that. *She* was probably all ready to go to sleep."

He leaned down and kissed her belly, then rubbed it gently. "Well, now it's time to go *back* to sleep, little one," he said, pretending to talk to the baby.

"Not quite yet. I have to wash and put my gown back on first. I'll be right back," Samantha told Blake. She rose, thinking how nice it was that she didn't freeze now every time she got out of bed. May had been warm and sunny, and even the nights had been pleasant. Spring always made her happier—a sign of life and new hope. She wanted to believe that it might also bring peace to Kansas, and news from George.

Blake rolled over and pulled on his long johns, then took a cigarette from the night stand and lit it. He lay back in bed, quietly smoking, wishing he could feel better about both George and the baby. He still had reservations about George's situation and the authenticity of his letter. If he were unmarried, he would go do some checking himself. But now there was Sam and the baby . . . the baby . . . What a hell of a time to bring a baby into the world!

Samantha came back to bed. "I see a very distant look in those eyes, Blake Hastings," she told him, reaching over to turn down the lamp a little more. "You've got to stop worrying about George, and about our baby, too."

He took a deep drag on the cigarette, listening to the sound of crickets outside, then reached over to knock some ashes from the cigarette into an ashtray. "I can't help it," he answered, laying back again, studying the soft glow of the cigarette. "It's nice to have spring, but warmer weather means both sides are going to be a lot more active. The fighting is going to get a lot worse. I wish to hell the President would send in some federal troops to keep an eye on things. He tells us to stop fighting, but he doesn't do a damn thing to help accomplish that. He's got no spine. Our baby might be born into all-out war!"

"Well, come November we can vote for someone who will support us."

"If a candidate supporting abolition even gets nominated."

She rubbed at his shoulder. "We're doing it again, Blake. We're not supposed to talk about these things in the bedroom. How about if I change the subject to my brother, Drew. My parents got a letter from him today. He was here visiting for a month the summer before we met, but last summer he stayed in school.

248

Now he says he might stay on at school through this summer again so he can finish sooner. He wants to be a lawyer."

"I'd like to meet him."

"Well, someday you will. Father says the way things are right now in Kansas, he might as well stay at Harvard. If I know Drew, he's in a great quandary right now, wondering if he should be here with us. He's a very fine, responsible person. Father said he'd write and tell him he'll be a bigger help when he returns a full-fledged attorney. He's afraid if Drew comes home now, he'll get wrapped up in what's going on here and never make it back to school."

"Well, maybe we should send *you* to New England to be with *him*. You shouldn't be here either, you know."

"We've been over this before. I'm not leaving my parents. Drew wouldn't have stayed on at school if he truly realized how bad things were getting here. I don't think he's really aware of how far things have gone, and what he doesn't know won't hurt him. He can stay where he is, and I'll stay where I am."

Samantha's eyes closed. The constant chore of having to make vital, daily decisions, as well as her pregnancy and the worry over George and what was going to happen next, all combined to make her tire more easily lately. "It wears a person out," she said sleepily, "feeling so constantly torn. Poor George. If only we would hear from him. I know how much you miss him."

"You just worry about yourself and the baby. And I really do want you to start slowing down, Sam. You're working too hard. I don't want to risk anything happening to this baby. It's mine, too, you know, and if I want you to take it easier from now on, I think you should do what I ask. This is your first child. You have no idea how hard or easy this pregnancy will be on you."

"Well, so far I've been fine. But I will do as you ask, my husband." Her words became slightly slurred from a relaxed sleepiness. She vaguely remembered Blake saying something more, just before the pleasant and much-needed sleep finally claimed her. Blake lay awake a while longer, still feeling a strange uneasiness. He reached over and crushed out his last cigarette, then turned to pull Samantha into his arms and let sleep claim him also.

How long they both slept before their rude awakening neither of them could be sure. Blake woke up first, hearing nothing, but again sensing something was not quite right. Just as he sat up there came the sound of several windows being broken at once. Someone let out a rebel yell, and flames shot up along curtains and walls all around the house.

The noise startled Samantha awake, and at the same time Blake was pulling her out of bed.

Samantha gasped and coughed as the house quickly filled with smoke. Blake had already found her robe and threw it around her shoulders, then left her to grab his loaded rifle beside the bed.

"Blake!" Samantha screamed, unable to see him. She felt his arm come around her again.

"We've got to get out here!" he shouted. She pulled at him, wanting to save some of her things, the rude awakening and the panic of the fire keeping her from thinking straight.

"There's no time!" Blake said, jerking at her.

"The baby clothes . . . all the clothes I made for her—"

Blake grabbed her firmly under the shoulders. "Forget about them," he told her, every wall of the house in flames now. He dragged her past the sitting

250

room, stopping long enough to tear a heavy bureau away from one wall and reaching into the hole it hid to take out the money he kept there. In that one quick moment, Samantha had disappeared.

"Sam!" he screamed. He cursed himself for stopping for the money and he threw it down, screaming Samantha's name again.

He heard an almost kittenlike cry and headed back into the bedroom, where a confused Samantha was trying to pound out some of the flames, getting her hands burned in the process. The hem of her robe had caught fire. Blake threw down the rifle and grabbed her to pull her to the floor. He quickly snuffed out the flames with his hands.

He felt again for the rifle, relieved when he found it right away. He kept hold of it as he picked up Samantha in his arms and headed for the front door, which was also in flames. He stood back, holding on to Samantha as he kicked hard three times until the door flew open. The fire seemed to spread faster and harder then. He ducked through the doorway, quickly checking Samantha when they got outside to be sure her hair or robe had not caught fire.

When he was certain that she was fine, he turned with her still in his arms, his heart breaking at the sight of their cozy little house already burning brightly, beyond saving. Strangely, what hurt the most was the thought of the bedroom burning, the one room where Samantha had said they would always be safe. In the distance there came the sound of war whoops and rebel yells, thundering horses and gunshots. Several other buildings and homes were on fire.

Blake frantically tried to think where to go. He looked up the street toward the church and parsonage and saw they were both on fire. Sam's parents!

Had they gotten out? He headed in that direction when he heard the sound of a horse thundering up behind him. He turned just in time to feel the blow of a club at the side of his head. He heard Samantha's scream near his ear and he staggered. He continued to cling to Samantha with one arm as he pitched to his right, catching himself with his other arm as he fell. He rolled onto his back, still holding Samantha, who landed on top of him.

"Stay put!" he shouted, refusing to let the blow overcome his senses. He let go of Samantha, terrified that all of this was going to make her lose the baby, but having no time to see if she was all right. He left her and scrambled for his rifle as the horseman came back at them. To Blake's dismay he saw Samantha standing and facing the man, holding a rock in her hand. She threw it hard, and it glanced off the side of the head of the man's horse. The animal reared and squealed just as the man was about to grab at Samantha.

"Sam, get out of the way!" Blake shouted, positioning his rifle.

Samantha ducked out of the way just in time to avoid the animal's hooves as it reared up high, throwing its rider. The horse's eyes were wild, the side of its head bleeding.

In the two or three seconds it had taken for the man to fall, Blake realized that killing him would be the worst thing he could do—maybe even what someone *wanted* him to do. With the new laws making people like himself considered traitors, he could easily be hanged. The assailant was starting to rise, and he reached for his own six-gun. Before the man could gather his senses, Blake landed the butt of his rifle across his head, knocking him out cold. The man sprawled onto his face. Blake kicked him onto his back, and in the bright light of the fire he could see it was one of West's farm hands, the man who had greeted him at the ranch several months before when Blake went looking for Jesse—the same man who had held Blake so West could beat him. More than anything Blake wanted to hold the barrel of his rifle to the man's head and pull the trigger, but he suspected that spies were everywhere this awful night. If he shot this man he'd be dragged off by bushwhackers and hanged without even so much as a trial.

He turned to Samantha, who just stared at him in wide-eyed terror. She looked strangely ghostlike, silhouetted against the orange flames of their little home. Everything they had worked for and accumulated over the past year was going up in flames. It was only then Blake realized that the shed out back and the horse stalls were also on fire, and he had no doubt that his prize black mare and his two draft horses had been stolen.

Samantha was looking past him, then toward the parsonage. She began shaking her head. "Mama!" she cried. "Blake, the parsonage! The church!" She ran past him, and he caught her arm.

"Get back into the shadows," he told her. "And stay with me! Whatever you see or whatever happens, don't let me out of your sight!"

She looked at him, just then realizing she stood there in only a nightgown and that Blake was wearing only his long johns. Both of them were barefoot. Somehow Samantha had lost her robe. She was beginning to feel the pain of the burns on her ankles and hands, and a violent trembling overcame her as she realized the enormity of what was happening.

Blake picked her up again, carrying her into the

shadows, afraid for her to be seen by the bushwhackers. Were they after specific people, or just out to sack Lawrence? It seemed that everywhere people were running and screaming. Several other homes and buildings were on fire, and the night air was filled with rebel yells and gunfire. Blake made his way carefully toward the parsonage, his heart pounding at what he might find, yet more worried over what this might do to Samantha in her condition.

Samantha stared at the parsonage as they came closer. Everything was burning brightly, totally engulfed in flames. Blake found a stump in the moonlight and sat down on it, holding her close. "Sam, I can't go looking for your parents or try to help them unless you promise to stay right here on this stump. You can't go wandering around by yourself, understand? One of those bushwhackers might come along and hurt you or ride off with you. Promise me you'll stay here and lay low."

He could feel her shaking. "I'll stay right here," she answered, her voice sounding small and far away.

He rose and carefully set her on the stump. "I'll try to find help for us, a blanket or something for you." He laid the rifle across her lap. "Don't be afraid to use this if you have to."

Their eyes held, their faces lit up by the fires of Lawrence burning. "Blake . . . our home." Her whole body jerked in a sob as she turned her eyes to the parsonage. "Mama . . . Father—"

He pressed his hands to either side of her face. "Stay here. I'll see if I can find them. Maybe they got out."

Samantha watched anxiously as he walked away. She wondered how she would have gotten through this night without Blake. She would probably be burning alive in their house right now if he hadn't gotten her out of there. She sat torn between the horror of knowing her own home was burning and the terror that her parents might have been killed. Shouts and gunfire could still be heard amid the bright flames that glowed everywhere, and she realized that this was indeed war, and it had finally come to their very doorstep, had invaded their lives, their private bedroom.

She shivered, forcing back an urge to cry from the pain of her burns, suddenly feeling very cold in spite of the warm night. Blake disappeared for a moment, and she felt a sudden panic until he reappeared again. He was still alone. He came toward her then, sweeping her up into his arms. "Hang on to the rifle. I think the horse shed out behind your folk's house is untouched. Maybe we can hole up in there in the straw, find a horse blanket to cover you with."

"My parents . . ."

"I didn't see them anyplace. I can't know if they got caught inside until the flames die down. Right now I intend to get you out of sight until the bushwhackers leave. It's too dark and there is still too much shooting to try to find your folks tonight, especially with you in your condition. We'll have to wait until morning light."

"But . . . they might be looking for us."

"Then they'll find out tomorrow that we're all right. I can't take the chance on the wrong people spotting you and singling you out." He walked rapidly, his voice determined. She knew there was no arguing. He set her on her feet under a tree near the horse shed. "Stay right here until I check things out."

He left her then, keeping the rifle with him this time. Samantha watched as he approached the horse shed carefully. He kicked open the shed door and moved inside. After a minute or two he returned to her. "Come on. It's all right. Your father's bay gelding is still in here."

Samantha came closer, and he put an arm around her and helped her into the shed, closing the door, shutting out the sight of the flames and muffling some of the sounds of screaming and shooting. "Over here," he told her, leading her to an empty stall. "This one seems clean. Get down on the straw there."

She obeyed, wincing with pain. "Blake, my ankles and hands . . . they're burned." Her eyes began to adjust to the faint ray of moonlight that came through a small open window at the back of the shed. She saw him set the rifle aside. He took a blanket from where it was draped over the wall of the stall and brought it over to her.

"Do you think you can stand it until morning?" he asked her. "I don't know what else to do, Sam, where else to take you. We have to wait until morning, see whose houses are left standing and where we might get shelter." He covered her carefully, feeling her trembling. "Sons of bitches," he muttered. "I'd like to kill them all!" He sat down beside her, moving an arm around her. "What about the baby?"

"I'm all right . . . I think. I just feel numb, except for my burns. Oh, Blake, I'll never be able to rest. It hurts too much." She felt the panic rising again. "What about Mother and Father? Blake, what a horrible way to die! What will I do if they're both dead! Why are they doing this? Why?"

He pressed her head against his chest. "You know why, Sam. I told you things would get worse. I should have acted on my instincts earlier tonight when I felt something was wrong." He kissed her hair. "Try not to think the worst about your folks, Sam. We might find out in the morning that they got

ut just fine. Concentrate on trying to relax. Think
f the baby, just the baby—and the fact that we're
afe."

Wrenching sobs overcame her, and she thanked
God that at least she had Blake. "Our home . . . the
baby's things . . . Mother and Father . . ."

"Hush. We're alive. We have each other, and
you're still holding on to that baby. That's all that
matters for a moment." He kissed her hair, her
forehead. "Just be still, Sam."

They clung to each other as outside the shooting
subsided. Rebel yips and shouts grew dimmer, until
all that could be heard was the crackling and
popping of burning buildings, the sounds of some of
them collapsing. Now and again there came a
scream, and it sounded like men were organizing to
try to put out fires. Blake heard someone shout
something about buckets. He realized he could
probably go out and help now, but Samantha seemed
to have managed to fall asleep, most likely, he
figured, from emotional exhaustion. He was not
about to disturb her, even though he wanted to get up
and fetch a blanket for himself.

He rested his head on the hay, weary, angry, feeling
like crying himself. He remembered then dropping
the money he had tried to save. It was gone now. He
would be a father in two months, but now he had no
home, little money, not even any clothes or food. His
horses were gone, probably never to be seen again,
and he wasn't sure how he would get back on his feet
after this blow. If the mill had also been burned, he
had no job. Worst of all, Sam's parents might be
dead. If he found their burned bodies in the house
tomorrow, how was he ever going to tell her? How
would such news affect her? On top of all their other
losses, would they lose the child they so dearly

wanted? The baby might be all they had left.

A tear slipped down his cheek. "Don't let her lose the baby," he whispered, wondering if God had listened to the prayers of anyone who lived in Kansas lately.

Samantha felt the flames, saw them in front of her eyes. She reached out for Blake, but he was on the other side of the flames, himself engulfed in the inferno. "Blake!" she screamed, trying to get to him, but her legs would not move. She gasped from the acrid smoke and unbearable hot air.

"Sam, it's all right," someone was telling her. "You were just dreaming."

She gasped, moving from dream to reality, opening her eyes. It took her a moment to remember where she was. The horse shed! Her father's bay whinnied in the stall next to them. The fire! Last night was not a nightmare then. Why else would they be in this shed? She looked at Blake, her eyes wide with terror. "My parents!" She touched his chest, which was cool, and she realized he had stayed there with her all night without a shirt or any covering. "Blake, you must be so cold."

She drew her hands back then because of the pain she felt when she touched him. By the light of early dawn she could see that part of her palms and forearms were a vivid red with burns.

"My God, Sam, I've got to get you some help," Blake told her.

"We've got to find my parents first," she pleaded.

"Not until I see that you're taken care of. You and that baby come first. I'll get you someplace warm and find myself some clothes. Then I'll start searching." He rose and helped her to her feet. "Can you walk?"

"It isn't that," she answered. "It's just hard to hold

this rough blanket with my hands hurting so. Pull it around and hook it over my arms on both sides like a shawl."

He helped her with the blanket, then found another and put it around his shoulders. "Wait a minute," he told her. "There's no sense in you walking with those burned ankles. We'll use your father's bay."

He hurried to take the horse out of its stall, then put a bit and bridle on it. He hoisted Samantha onto its back so that she sat sideways, and she managed to grasp the horse's mane with her right hand, which was not as badly burned as the left, to help her keep her balance. Blake picked up his rifle and took hold of the reins, carefully opening the shed door and looking out first before exiting, then led the horse outside into the morning sunlight. "So," Blake muttered, "they finally decided to teach Lawrence a lesson. I wish the President could see this." Both of them felt the horror of the devastation before them.

"Blake, please just go over there between the parsonage and the church," Samantha pleaded, her heart aching fiercely at the sight of the burned-out parsonage. It was obvious nothing was salvageable. "Mother and Father might be someplace near."

"Knowing them, they're probably in town helping anyone who needs it," he told her, praying he was right but almost sure he was wrong. If the Walters were alive, they would be close by, looking for their daughter. He glanced farther up the street at their own little house. There was nothing left but a pile of black embers. The shed George had lived in and the horse barn were also gone. He looked up at Samantha, who had followed his gaze, and the look in her eyes tore at his guts.

"We tried so hard to keep this out of our house, our

bedroom," she said quietly.

Angry bitterness filled Blake's soul. The attack had made him suddenly feel like a failure. Everything he had worked for was gone, and he had a baby on the way. He said nothing as he led the horse around between the parsonage and the church. There was no sign of the Walters. Blake prayed that if they were still in the house, their bodies were hidden under rubble, fearing that to actually see them might be so horrifying as to make Samantha lose the baby. It would be bad enough just having to tell her the bad news, without her seeing it for herself. To his relief he saw no bodies.

"They probably burned the print shop, too," Samantha said, her voice sounding strangely calm and accepting. Blake suspected she was only pretending, that on the inside she feared the worst for her parents.

"We'll head into town and—" Blake did not finish the sentence. He saw Clyde Beecher coming hurriedly toward them then, his face showing surprise and near disappointment when he saw them, rather than relief.

"There you are!" he called out to them, now putting on a look of concern. "My God, are you two all right? I hurried over to check out your house and saw no sign of bodies, thank God! I couldn't imagine where you had gone."

"You've already been to our house?" Blake asked.

"Why, yes. The first thing I did this morning was check the parsonage and church and your house. After all, Samantha's parents are very important to me."

Blake looked him over. He seemed unscathed, his clothes showing no sign of a struggle, his hands not the slightest black from helping someone or search-

260

ing through burned rubble. He glanced over at the burned-out parsonage. "Tell me, Beecher. Did *your* place get burned?"

The man immediately took on a defensive pose. "No. I feel very blessed that my home was left untouched. In fact, I thought if I found any of you I would offer my home as refuge. Lord knows the Walters have done enough for me."

Blake could hardly control his fury. He was still firmly convinced that Clyde Beecher had had something to do with the raid. He glanced around at the burned homes of people he knew, all of them had been very active against the new government. He moved his dark eyes back to Beecher. "Yes, the Walters *have* done a lot for you; more than you deserve, I expect."

Beecher frowned. "What do you mean?"

"I mean, it's obvious that whoever attacked this town last night was after people who were the most active in the antislavery movement. I'd say you should be right up there at the top of the list, but you were left untouched. I wonder why."

Beecher began to color deeply. "Just what are you insinuating, Blake?"

Blake stepped closer. "You know *exactly* what I am insinuating, Beecher!" he sneered.

"Blake!" Samantha called out to him, still not convinced Clyde Beecher could be a spy. "Not now, Blake. I've got to do something about these burns, and you've got to look for my parents."

Beecher sniffed and straightened his shoulders, looking deeply offended. "I don't know where you get your ideas, Blake, but I have never done anything but fully support Samantha's father and his movement. I know that you have never liked me, and I can't imagine why; nor do I have an explanation as to why my home was not burned. Considering what I suspect you are thinking right now, I wish it *had* been. It pains me deeply to know you actually think I would be capable of . . . of spying! That's what you're insinuating, isn't it?"

Samantha almost felt sorry for the man. The look on his face was one of utter astonishment and deep hurt. He looked up at her. "Samantha, I know that he is your husband, and I suppose he had a right to his own thoughts. But you have known me much longer. Do *you* believe these accusations?"

"I—"

"Leave her out of this!" Blake fumed.

Beecher looked sadly at Blake. "In spite of your hideous, uncalled-for accusations, Blake, my home is still open to you—for Samantha's sake. You both obviously need shelter right now. I can give you some clothes and help you find something more permanent. You've got to get your wife cleaned up and do something about those burns I see on her hands."

"I'll see to her myself. I wouldn't stay in your house if it was the last building left standing in Lawrence—nor would I trust you for five *minutes* alone with Samantha!"

"Blake!" Samantha reddened at the remark.

Blake started past Beecher, who grabbed Blake's arm. "It's times like these when a man needs his friends, Blake," Beecher told him. "Don't do this. Samantha's parents meant everything to me. They would want me to help you."

"Get your hand off me," Blake warned.

At the look in Blake's eyes, Beecher let go, thinking how pleasant it would be to have Blake Hastings in a compromising position, like tied to a whipping post. How tempting it was to tell him what had really happened to his friend George. Maybe, in the not too distant future, he would find out for himself. Now that the plans to burn Blake and Samantha Hastings alive in their own house had failed, other measures would have to be taken.

"You talk in the past tense about my parents," Samantha was saying. "Why? Are they already dead, Mr. Beecher?" She felt the painful lump rising in her throat at the question.

"No. I mean, I don't know. I didn't mean to speak as though they were. I am only saying that since we can't find them for a moment, I would like to help."

Blake started forward with the horse again, and the big animal lumbered past Beecher, who looked pleadingly at Samantha, thinking to himself what a fine actor he was. He could see that Samantha felt sorry for Blake's remarks. "Let us know if you find anything, Mr. Beecher," she called out to the man.

"I will," he answered. "I surely will." Beecher turned away, smiling to himself. "Say what you will, Blake Hastings," he muttered., "Your time is coming, and so is your wife's." He decided to once again examine the parsonage. He knew where the reverend and his wife slept, knew just the right places to set a fire that could easily trap them. He hoped West's men, with whom he had met along the border a few days earlier, had correctly understood what they should do. He had drawn a careful map of Lawrence, pointing out the houses that should be burned. West would not be happy to know Blake and Samantha had escaped, but there was more than one way to skin a cat.

He shoved his hands in his pockets, curling his nose against the stink of still-smoldering wood. He caught another smell then, not sure what it was but positive it was not wood. He kept sniffing, walking closer to the back corner of the house, above which would have been the Walters' bedroom. He had smelled that smell before, when he visited a burned-out farm after one of West's raids. A person did not soon forget the smell of burned human flesh. He followed it, deciding it seemed to be coming from a pile of rubble that included a potbelly stove, smoldering wood, and bedsprings.

He kicked at the smelly mess, managing to shove back the springs just a little and opening a small hole in the array of black wood. He saw it then, a human hand, charred so black that it was difficult to tell if it belonged to a man or a woman.

Beecher breathed deeply with satisfaction. "Well, they managed to do one thing right," he thought. "There will be no more sermons about abolition from the Reverend Walters, nor is there a church left in which to give them." He kicked away a little more of the rubble so the bodies would be easier to find, glancing toward the direction Blake and Samantha were headed. "I'll let you find them yourself, Hastings," he muttered. "Maybe you'll remember the stink of it and wish to hell you had got out of Kansas when you still had the chance."

Fourteen

"Somebody is going to pay for what's happened here," Blake fumed as he led the horse into a half-burned-out Lawrence. "I'm going to see that it happens! Men like Clyde Beecher are going to be found out for what they really are. It's time to rid Lawrence of its own traitors!"

Everywhere Samantha looked she saw groups of men rallying, arguing about the best way to retaliate for the bushwhacker attack. She felt a rush of hopelessness and terror. Not only had she and Blake lost everything, and her parents might be dead, but Blake was talking as though he intended to get directly involved in the violence. She knew this was not the time or place to try to reason with him, and she felt the terrible loneliness of a sudden invisible wall between them. The fighting had come to Lawrence—had come into their home, into their personal lives.

Blake stopped and turned to look up at her. "I can't just sit back and let this happen anymore, Sam. I'm not made that way." He saw the fear and desperateness in her eyes, but he was too full of a need for vengeance to say what he knew she wanted to hear—

that he would remain opposed to violence. "Keep an eye out," he said then, turning away and going forward with the horse. "Watch for your parents."

Both of them searched the crowds carefully, but the Walters were nowhere to be seen. A sick fear engulfed Samantha, and touching, painful memories began to plague her, time she had spent at the parsonage and in the church with her parents, brave people who did not believe in violence, yet knew that they were risking their very lives to fight for what they thought was right.

She wondered how she was going to break this news to Drew, and if she would be able to convince him it was useless to come home right now. She missed her brother and thought how comforting it would be to have him here, especially if something had happened to their parents. But she had Blake, and what good would it do Drew to come home now? Her father had wanted him to stay and finish school, and she hoped he would do just that.

For all the men gathered to argue revenge, there were as many women wandering the streets and weeping, several people, men and women alike, still in their nightclothes. A few buildings were left standing, but many others lay in smoldering ruin. It was a devastating sight, and Samantha knew the shock and horror of the past night would not leave them for a long time to come, nor would recovery be easy. But these were dedicated, determined people, and there would very definitely be a violent retaliation for what had happened here. Would Blake be a part of it? This was surely the last straw.

She drew her blanket closer, aching just to find shelter, a bed, some ointment for her burns, a place to get cleaned up. A few pieces of straw still clung to her flannel gown and in her hair, and she knew she must be a mess. Poor Blake was walking through the streets in his underwear, with only a blanket around his shoulders. His face and arms were black from smoke. The town was in such a mess that people hardly noticed one another in conditions that would have been embarrassing in normal times.

"There's Jonas Hanks," Blake said to her then. He called out to the man, who was helping a store owner clean up some debris in front of his establishment, which, luckily, had escaped with only minor damage. Jonas turned, his eyes widening at the sight of them. The man was black from soot.

"Blake! Samantha!" He walked up to them. "Don't tell me—Your house is burned?"

"Completely," Blake answered. "So is the parsonage and church. Have you seen the reverend or Mrs. Walters?"

Jonas's eyes saddened. "I'm afraid not." The man ran a hand through his hair wearily, looking as though he had probably been up most of the night. "Thanks to the help of six kids, we managed to keep our house from completely burning. It's still livable. We have that much to be grateful for." His eyes moved over Blake's half-dressed form. "My God, Blake, did the two of you lose *everything?*"

Anger and frustration were evident in Blake's eyes. "I'm afraid so. We got out with exactly what you see us in now. My horses were stolen, too. We took this one from Sam's father's shed. I didn't want Sam to have to walk, not after what she's been through in her condition. She's got some burns, too. I've got to find help for her, Jonas."

Jonas reached out and touched his arm. "You take her right over to my house. The missus will see to her. We'll put a couple of the girls together so you can have one of their bedrooms until you figure out what you're going to do."

"I hate to put you out, Jonas."

"After what has happened? We don't have any choice but to help each other now. I'm glad to do it, especially considering Samantha is the reverend's daughter." He took the reins from Blake. "Come on. We'll get her over there right away. I'll see about finding some clothes for the both of you. Mennan's Clothery survived the fires. In the meantime, my oldest daughter probably has some dresses that would fit Samantha."

Samantha could feel Blake's tension, even from the distance. His pride had been wounded. He didn't like depending on others, but with most of their money gone, he would have to do just that for the time being. "I'm grateful to you, Jonas. I'll try to make some other arrangements as soon as possible."

"Well, that might be a while. Everyone is going to have to rebuild, which means you'll be waiting in line, the only remaining hotels and boardinghouses being filled to the brim now." The man shook his head. "How planned do you think this was, Blake? Who do you think was behind it?"

Blake's eyes blazed with a need for revenge. "It was *very* well planned. Take a look around. Only the homes and businesses of the most active abolitionists were hit. Someone told those men just which buildings to torch, and I don't doubt they intended that a lot of our leaders die in the process. I'm firmly convinced Clyde Beecher had a hand in it."

"Beecher!" Jonas stopped walking, looking up at Samantha, then back to Blake. "You serious?"

"Completely. I know you think I'm crazy, but I know I'm right. We'll talk about it later, after I get Samantha settled."

The two men started walking again, Jonas

shaking his head. "That's awful hard for me be believe, Blake. The man has preached some fine sermons. He's worked faithfully against slavery all these months, right alongside the reverend. I have to disagree with you."

"Think what you want. No one is going to change my mind."

They rounded a corner, and Samantha felt heartsick at the damage that had been done. A few people stared at them with blank looks on their faces, and one woman sat weeping on the steps of her burned-out home. Jonas headed toward his own house, which still looked intact, although part of one corner was black from fire.

"I'm just awful sorry about your losses, Blake," Jonas told them. "I'll round up a couple of men and go over to the parsonage, take a look around. We'll see what we can find."

"Thanks, Jonas. And I, uh—I'm sorry, but a lot of my money burned up with the house. All I have is what I had in your bank. Take it easy on buying clothes. When Sam is feeling up to it, we'll just buy material and she can make more. Cheaper that way." He made a gesture of hopelessness with one hand. "I'm afraid I don't have a dime on me."

Jonas waved him off. "Don't worry about it. We all have to pitch in for the time being. A man can't afford to be too proud at a time like this, Blake."

They reached the house, and Blake helped Samantha down from the horse. He quickly carried her inside, where Mrs. Hanks immediately began giving orders, telling her eldest daughter to get some of her things out of her room and move them in with her sister for the time being. Blake carried Samantha into the bedroom, which was one of two on the main floor of the big, rambling, two-story house. The other lower

269

bedroom belonged to Jonas and his wife, while the rest of their brood of children all slept upstairs.

Blake laid Samantha on the bed, leaning over her to kiss her lightly. "I'm sorry I was short with you earlier," he told her. "I'm sorry about a lot of things. I should have got that money into the bank like you told me to do. I was going to get around it it—"

"Blake, the money doesn't matter right now. I'm more concerned about you, what you have in mind to do. I need you, Blake. You might be all I have left."

Her eyes teared, and he put a big hand to her face. "We don't know that yet. There are a lot of things we have to talk about and decide, but not right now. You just let Mrs. Hanks help you clean up and dress those burns. I'm going back to the parsonage with Jonas. I'll be back in a while."

She grasped his hand as he started to rise, paying no attention to the pain of her burns. "Be careful, Blake. They want you dead, you know."

"I'll be careful."

"Do you think they'll come back?"

"I have no idea, Sam. My guess is that they're through for a while. They've left their message. If they come back too soon, they have to figure we might be ready for them. They don't want to be caught and identified, not if there were deaths involved. But I did recognize one of them—the one who tried to attack us last night."

"Who was he?"

"One of Nick West's men."

Her eyes widened. "Are you sure?"

"You don't forget the face of a man who held you while he let someone else beat you up. Besides, I also saw him at West's ranch the day I went to try to find Jesse."

"Oh, Blake, it's all so ugly and frightening. I never

270

really thought they would come right to Lawrence like this. No one is safe! I'm worried about the baby now."

He put a gentle hand to her stomach. "You just worry about hanging *on* to the baby. You think you need a doctor?"

"No. I have Mrs. Hanks. The doctor must be terribly busy with people who are hurt worse than I am." Their eyes held, and a tear slipped down the side of her face and into her ear. "I love you, Blake. Please don't do anything foolish."

He leaned forward and kissed her cheek, just as Mrs. Hanks came back into the room with a pan of warm water, her daughter following her carrying rags and an ointment. "I love you, too," Blake answered. "But I can't make any promises right now. We've lost everything, and I intend to get some of it back."

He rose and left, his words burning in her heart. Samantha looked at Mrs. Hanks, her eyes tearing more. "I'm so afraid for him, Mrs. Hanks."

The woman came to her side, setting the pan of water on a nightstand. "Be afraid for yourself, honey," she answered. The stout, kind-looking woman dipped a rag into the water and wrung it out, and Samantha noticed how worn her hands looked, probably from scrubbing clothes for her big family. "You just concentrate on that baby. Let's get a clean nightgown on you and wash you up. I have some ointment for those burns, you poor child."

Samantha put a hand to the buttons of her gown, hesitating. "He's different, Mrs. Hanks. I can see it in his eyes, feel it when he touches me. He's going to get directly involved, and I'm going to lose him. Our baby might never get to see its father, and I might have no one left."

271

"You'll have the *baby*—a part of your husband. But don't be thinking the worst, Samantha, not right now. It might not be nearly as drastic as you think, and they might find your folks are just fine," the woman tried to assure her. "You just remember for now that Blake Hastings is a proud man, with a need to protect his own and to right the wrong that's been done to him. You can't interfere with a man's pride, Samantha, or demand that he swallow it forever. Sometimes you destroy him that way, and he's no longer the man you married. That *is* part of the reason you married him, isn't it?"

Sam closed her eyes. "Yes," she answered quietly. She unbuttoned her gown, hardly aware then of the pain of washing and dressing her burns. She could think of nothing but Blake, out there in the shattered town of Lawrence. She worried that the bushwhackers would come back; and for a moment, she was afraid of what Blake and Jonas would find at the parsonage.

Mrs. Hanks helped her put on a clean gown and left her to rest, telling her she would bring up some tea and bisquits in a little while. Samantha rolled to her side, letting the tears come, praying fervently that her parents were all right, and that nothing would happen to Blake. The horror of the past night settled over her then, the memory of their burning house piercing her heart like a sword. Gone! Everything was gone—perhaps even her beloved parents! Was she also losing Blake? She had never felt so horribly alone, nor had she ever felt this kind of fear. No one was safe now. No one.

Samantha awoke to the muffled sound of voices coming from somewhere in the house. She thought she heard a woman crying, and her heart rushed with

272

dread. She looked around the room, taking a moment to remember where she was, wondering how long she had been asleep. Her head ached from a sick dread that had engulfed her even in sleep, and from the ugly dreams that had returned.

She managed to sit up to gather her thoughts, the pain in her hands reminding her of her burns, which were now protected by gauze. She thought she heard Blake's voice then, and she started to rise when she heard his familiar footsteps coming down the hall toward her room. She drew the blankets over her legs, waiting apprehensively.

The door opened slowly, and Blake looked inside the room. A sick feeling moved into her stomach at the sight of his worry-drawn face, dark, tired circles under his eyes. "I wasn't sure you were awake yet," he told her. He stepped farther inside, wearing a new blue shirt and denim pants. His boots looked as if they belonged to someone else, but Samantha cared little at the moment from whom he had borrowed them. She was only concerned with the look on his face. Their eyes held, and tragedy was evident in his own dark eyes, which showed a deep sorrow in knowing he was bringing his beloved wife the worst news possible, except perhaps to be told her own husband or child were dead.

"You . . . found them," she managed to say, her voice sounding strangely far away. Dread gripped at her insides like a vise. Blake came inside the room and closed the door, coming to stand beside the bed.

"I might as well say it straight out, Sam." His own voice betrayed the strain of the day, as well as his own grief. "We . . . did find them . . . both of them . . . under the rubble. I'm so damn sorry, Sam." His eyes were instantly watery, and one tear slipped down his cheek. How he hated telling her such awful news. He watched the mixture of feelings pass through her eyes—instant disbelief, followed quickly by horror, and then the terrible sorrow.

"My God, Blake," she uttered, the words whimpered. She covered her mouth and turned away, moving down into her pillow and breaking into deep, wrenching sobs that tore at his heart. His own grief, and his sorrow for her sake, were enhanced with worry over how this news would affect her physically.

He sat down carefully on the edge of the bed, reaching out to touch her shoulder. "I've told Jonas to see if the doctor can come over and give you something to help you sleep the next couple of days."

"I don't want to sleep," she wept. "I want to remember!" Her hand moved into a fist as she grasped at the sheet. "I want to lie here and remember everything about them. I . . . want to get up . . . and go right back out there and start up the newspaper again! It's for Father. I have to do it for him!"

"You aren't going to do anything right now but rest. I'll take care of the funeral arrangements."

"Blake . . . my God, what's happening! How could they do this? How?"

He gently squeezed her shoulder, but she could feel his anger. "Because they're ruthless bastards who think their precious belief in slavery is worth more than human lives," he nearly growled.

Her sobs deepened again. "Mama," she muttered. "What if . . . they suffered, Blake. What if they . . . felt the flames! If only there was something we could have done."

"I know. I tried, Sam, but the place was already too far gone when we got there last night." He moved onto the bed, lying beside her and drawing her into his arms. "Most people who die in fires die from the

274

smoke long before the flames get to them. I doubt they felt the fire." He held her firmly as more sobs came, feeling his own panic over what this tragedy might do to her. "Sam, they're most certainly with God now. Few men work harder to stand up for Christ's teachings than your father did; and he did it without violence. They're in a better place now, where there's peace and tranquility—none of the hatred and fighting they had to put up with here. Your father would only say he had died for a good cause."

"It isn't fair. He never hurt a soul in his life."

"I know it isn't fair, and I'd give anything to change it for you. At least they weren't burned badly and left alive."

The reality of it kept sweeping over her in great waves of horror. Her parents were dead! What made it worse was the horrible way they had died. She had not been able to give them a last good-bye, to hold them once more, to tell them she loved them.

"Oh, Blake, they'll never see their grandchild," she wept.

He leaned over her, wanting to weep himself, but too angry for tears. He would never forget the sight of the burned bodies, the stench of it. He was glad they had not found them earlier, when Samantha was still with him. What he couldn't understand was how he had missed them the first time he searched the house. It was almost as though someone had kicked aside the rubble so that they were suddenly easier to find.

A bitter hatred engulfed Blake when he remembered leaving Clyde Beecher at the site earlier that morning. Had Beecher found the bodies and deliberately left them for Blake to find, maybe hoping Samantha would be with him to view the horrible sight? He would not be surprised. He decided that for the moment he would not mention his suspicions to Samantha. He did not want to bring up the condition of the bodies. Her own imagination was vivid enough.

"Oh, Blake . . . what are we going to do now? We have no home . . . hardly any money. My parents are dead."

"We're going to take one day at a time. Today you're going to stay right here while I make some arrangements."

"No." She turned to face him, the devastation in her beautiful eyes tearing at his heart. "Let me go with you. I can't . . . just lie here, Blake. Not now. I'll go crazy lying here waiting for you." She wrapped her arms around his neck. "And I'm afraid to let you out of my sight. You might never come back!"

"I'll come back, Sam. I'll always come back."

The words had an ominous ring to them, as though they meant more than just going across town to make funeral arrangements. She clung to him, telling herself that he would never leave her, not now, not in her condition. Surely he would not let his anger and hatred make him go off and do something foolish. She swore secretly that she would not let him do such a thing. She had convinced him once not to let *her* go away. Now she would have to make sure it wasn't Blake who left instead, that it wasn't Blake who would lay his life on the line like her father had done. With Blake it would be even more dangerous, for he wouldn't stop at talking. She sensed he wanted and needed direct action now, and it terrified her.

"Don't leave me, Blake. Please don't leave me now."

He kissed her hair, but he did not answer.

* * *

276

The next several hours were the worst of Samantha's life. Her legs felt like rubber, and she wondered how she managed to stay on her feet. She clung to Blake's arm most of the time, realizing she should be in bed after the shock of the past night, yet unable to bear lying there alone. Blake was her whole world now, all she had left.

They borrowed Jonas Hanks' buggy so that Samantha could stay off her feet as much as possible. They first drove to the telegraph office, which to their relief was still in operation. The telegrapher informed them that federal troops had been requested to come and help protect Lawrence, but most townspeople did not expect any help. "We'll have to form our own little army. We'll get them for this, that's for damn sure," the man told Blake, little knowing that one of his own co-workers was a proslavery man who sent secret coded messages between Nick West and Clyde Beecher.

Blake was strangely quiet, giving no reply. Sam wished she knew everything that was going through his mind, yet decided she might be better off not knowing. They sent a wire to her brother, urging him to stay where he was, since there was absolutely nothing he could do about what had happened, and his parents would be buried before he could arrive.

"It probably won't do any good," Samantha told Blake. "He'll want to come, for my sake if nothing else."

"I gotta say, Mrs. Hastings, you're holding up awfully well," the telegrapher told her. "Most women in your condition would be withering away in bed right now after last night, let alone losing your folks. I'm real sorry about what happened. I lost a barn myself, but I was lucky enough to save my house."

Sam struggled against a need to scream and wail. "I'm . . . glad for you," she answered. She stood there feeling lost and unreal. She wore one of Mrs. Hanks' large, roomy dresses, feeling worn and plain and fat.

Blake handed the telegram to the man, taking some money from his wallet. "Never mind," the telegrapher told him. "I heard you saying on your way in that you took the last of your savings out of the bank this morning. For the next day or two I'm not taking any fees. An awful lot of people have to wire relatives, and most of them also lost a lot."

Blake scowled, hating charity but deciding that if it was being done for everyone, it was all right. "Thank you," he answered. "I'll check back tomorrow and see if there is a reply." He took Samantha's arm and led her outside. Their next stop was the mortician. Her parents' bodies were already in nailed coffins, which Samantha touched lovingly, again overwhelmed by the realization that she would never see them again.

Silenced. Her father had finally been silenced. She had never been so aware of the danger that lay in standing up against slavery. If this could happen to Lawrence and to Kansas, it could happen to the rest of the country. What kind of world were they bringing their baby into? Her child would have only her and Blake and its uncle Drew.

She felt a terrible emptiness when she touched her mother's coffin. In spite of still having Blake, there was something intensely personal about losing parents, especially her mother, something she felt she could not share with Blake. It felt strange and horribly lonely to suddenly not have a mother and a father, those dependable, loving people who had nurtured her from birth, two people she had

278

foolishly taken for granted would always be there. Their deaths had left a sudden void in her life, and she felt unreal and out of place.

"I suppose you will want Mr. Beecher to deliver the eulogy," the mortician said to Samantha, interrupting her thoughts.

"No," Blake quickly replied. "Find someone else. Anyone! Clyde Beecher is not going to pray over two people he helped kill. I don't even want to see him at the funeral."

"Blake!" In her grief and confusion, Samantha could not deal with the thought of Beecher being a traitor. To her the man suddenly represented a link to her parents. He had shared so much time with both them and with her, before she married Blake. "Everyone will expect—"

"I'm sorry, Sam. I know what a bad time this is for you but I will not have Clyde Beecher at this funeral! If he comes and delivers the eulogy, then *I* won't be there!" He saw the hurt look in her eyes and he stepped closer, grasping her arms. "Sam, you've got to go along with me on this. Please think about the things that have happened, how Beecher fits in. How will you feel if you find out I'm right? How will you feel if he speaks over your parents' graves and you find out later that he is the one who betrayed them?"

"Beecher?" The funeral director looked at Blake in shock. "Are you saying the man is a *spy?* My God, man, he's the most devoted member of Reverend Walters' church! He's assistant pastor!"

"I don't care if he can make a halo glow around his head. He's no good in my book, and someday you people are going to find that out."

"Oh, Blake, what are we supposed to tell him?" Samantha asked, her eyes, already red from crying earlier, again brimming with tears.

"I'll tell him myself, and I'll tell him why. You don't have to worry about it."

"Blake—"

"I won't talk about it anymore, Sam."

She turned away, touching her father's coffin then, feeling shut out of real life, even feeling her own husband's anger at a time when she needed his understanding. Why couldn't he realize Clyde Beecher was a fine man? She had long ago given up even considering him as a traitor. It was a subject she simply avoided around Blake, but now there was no avoiding it. In her mind it was going to be embarrassing trying to explain to people why Beecher wasn't there. Would her father's friends and parishioners turn on her, be angry with her?

She gave no more argument as she struggled through the rest of the arrangements, agreeing to a Presbyterian minister to conduct the funeral, a man with whom her father had also been closely associated. The funeral director said his wife would take care of flowers.

"I can't pay for a headstone, not right now," Samantha told the man. "We lost a lot of money in the fire, and there is nothing salvageable that we could sell. Father, of course, had very little money, except for a fund he had set aside for helping continue Drew's education. Simple wooden crosses will do. Father would like that just fine."

Blake felt the pain of suddenly being unable to provide for her. The sawmill, and his job, were gone. Samantha could feel the tension in the air when she mentioned having little money, and she sadly felt the strange wall between herself and Blake growing thicker and higher.

"Tomorrow at two then," the mortician repeated. "A simple burial with wooden crosses. Reverend

Vickers will conduct the funeral, and I'll post a couple of men to stand watch and keep Clyde Beecher away." The man glowered slightly at Blake on the words, thinking Blake must surely have lost his mind in the shock of the raid.

"You won't need the men," Blake told him. "I'll handle Beecher. He won't be there. I guarantee it."

It all sounded so cold and matter-of-fact to Samantha. How she wished she could at least see her parents once more, take one last look at their faces. But she knew there was a reason for the caskets already being nailed shut. Blake did not want her to see the bodies, nor did she want to remember them any way but alive and well and smiling. A sudden, deeper grief engulfed her then, and she looked at Blake with devastation in her eyes.

"Blake—"

She looked so pale that he grasped her arms. "What is it?"

"My God! The fire! I don't even have any pictures . . . nothing to remember them by! Nothing! All I have is my memories. What if someday I forget how they even looked!"

Her voice was full of panic, and he felt her trembling.

"Samantha, you won't forget. I promise you that. I have no pictures of my parents, but I've never forgotten my father. Besides, it's the loving spirit that matters. I never even had the opportunity to know my mother, yet I often feel her with me. She died just to give me life, and your parents died for a good cause. You aren't going to forget them, and you will always feel their presence. I promise you."

"But it's so . . . so unreal . . . like a horrible dream . . ."

He put an arm around her, turning to the mortician. "I think we're through here. I'd better get her home." He led her outside and to the buggy, sensing that she was near collapse. "I never should have let you come with me," he told her. "You should be back in that bed."

She turned, grasping his arms. The agony in her eyes was torture for him. "I just . . . Seeing those coffins . . . it wasn't real until then. And when I thought about there being no pictures left—"

He pulled her close, holding her tightly. "Sam, you forget I understand how it feels. My own father died tragically, for the same cause. I can help you through this. All I ever had these last few months was you. Even my best friend is gone, maybe for good. At least you have a brother left—and we have the baby." He kissed her hair. "I know you don't like to appear weak, but *I* know how strong you are. We've *got* to think about the baby. You don't know how this will affect your pregnancy. Please, let me take you back and put you to bed."

She met his eyes, his face a blur through tears. "Come with me. Hold me for a while. I just don't want to lie there alone."

He sighed deeply. "I'll stay with you a while, and I'll be with you tonight."

She rested her head against his chest. "What comes after the funeral, Blake? What do we do then?"

"I don't know. I have to find a way to make some money. God knows there won't be any jobs around here for a while. I hate to leave, in case I hear from George, but we might have to."

"We have to at least wait and see if Drew is coming. And I'm not even sure I *want* to leave, Blake. When I think of what happened to my parents, it just makes me more angry. It makes me want to take up where they left off." She looked up at him, her face looking tired and drawn. "We've come so far, Blake, worked so hard. We can't let them defeat us. We can't let them make us run."

He touched her face. "Sam, if we don't leave, this could happen again. The next time it could be us. You know I'm not going to sit back and allow it."

Their eyes held, both of them feeling trapped, torn between what was right and wanting to flee to safety. "I know," she answered. "It's you I'm worried most about—not me."

Pain was evident in his eyes. "I love you so," he said softly. "But there's something . . . "

She touched his lips. "Not today. I have you here today, and that's all I need to know. There's something you've been trying to tell me for a long time. You've held it back because of the baby, and because you knew my parents and I didn't want any violence. You've heard from that John Hale, haven't you? There's something he wants you to do." She searched his eyes. "And you want to go find out for yourself about George, don't you?"

He grasped her arms. "You've had enough heartache for one day. We'll talk after the funeral." He helped her into the buggy and climbed up beside her. She pictured her parents' burning, crying for help; felt the cold emptiness of their sudden deaths. Her loneliness only deepened at the knowledge that something was brewing in her husband's heart— something that had been stirred into action by the raid on Lawrence. He was sitting next to her, but she sensed his mind was far away, and it seemed as though he was not really there at all. She wondered if Kansas's ugly, bloody civil war was going to destroy her marriage just like it had destroyed their little home, and her parents. She thought back to that day she had kicked Fred Brewster in the leg. She never dreamed back then that things would go this far, that the border violence would come this close to home.

She leaned her head against Blake's shoulder, and he moved a strong arm around her. She decided she could not think about the future right now. It was too miserable a thought. She would just think about today, and today Blake was still here beside her.

Fifteen

Clyde Beecher opened the door to his small cabin, his eyes widening in surprise when he saw Blake standing outside. All defenses came alert at the threatening look in Blake's eyes, which glowed with a strange, fiery anger by the soft light of the fire from Beecher's fireplace; his tall, broad frame was silhouetted against the dark night beyond the doorway.

"Blake! What brings you here?" Beecher spoke up, deciding that whatever Blake thought he was, he was not going to do or say anything to feed that suspicion. "I don't believe you've ever visited me."

Blake did not miss the quick defensive fear that first showed in Beecher's eyes, but the man had just as quickly put on a pleasant, rather sad face as he stepped aside to let Blake enter. "I want you to know that I understand your cruel words this morning. You've been through something terrible, and in these times, people find it hard to trust others. They say things they don't mean—"

"I meant every word," Blake interrupted. He refused to step inside, but he took inventory of the two-room structure nonetheless, quickly perceiving that Clyde Beecher was far from being tidy. His cabin had the smell of a house seldom cleaned, a house that had collected soot from the heating stove, as well as cooking smells—the same smell he had often detected on Beecher's clothing.

Beecher's half-smile faded. "You all but accused me of being a spy this morning, Blake." He put on a look of terrible hurt. "I've devoted every moment of my free time to helping the abolitionist cause. How can you even suggest that I could have had anything to do with what happened last night, let alone that I could have been responsible for the death of a great man like Howard Walters?"

Blake leaned on the doorjamb. "Tell me something, Beecher. Just exactly what is it you do for a living? In all the time I've known you, you've never held a steady job of any kind. Just odd jobs here and there—hardly enough for a man to live on."

Beecher folded his arms. "Not that it is your business, Blake, but to begin with, you can see that I live a simple life. I don't need much. I have sacrificed a finer life in order to have more time to devote to the cause. You know yourself I have spent most of my time preaching, helping Howard, delivering copies of the *Free Soil*, running errands for the church. All I need is enough for food and a few clothes."

"You don't even need that. You ate most of your meals with the Walterses."

"Always on invitation. When a man devotes his life to Christ, Blake, his needs are taken care of. Jesus Christ never needed a steady job. God provided for him."

Blake felt sick at the hypocritical comparison. "Maybe so. But I don't think it's God who's providing for *you*, Beecher. I think it's someone else!"

Blake caught the look then: the desire to kill.

286

Another man might have missed it, but not Blake. Beecher shook his head, sighing deeply. "I don't know where you get your ideas, Blake. Look here." He pointed to a crate full of Bibles. "You ask how I make my living. I only recently found new employment, where I am able to spread God's word and make money at the same time. I have been risking my life, traveling into border country to sell these Bibles to the poor souls who have suffered so pitifully at the hands of bushwhackers. That's what I was doing the last few days before this terrible attack on Lawrence."

"You travel the border country, a man alone, a professed radical abolitionist—and you come back unscathed." Blake took one step inside, his big frame seeming to fill the room. "I find that pretty hard to believe. I also find it hard to believe that last night no one burned your cabin, in spite of the fact that you were as close to Howard Walters as any man could be!"

Beecher arched his eyebrows. "Someone apparently made a mistake."

Blake grasped the doorknob and leaned closer to the man, his eyes menacing. "That's right, Beecher, and it was *you!* If you wanted to come out of this looking like a saint, you should have had them burn *your* house along with the others!"

The man's eyes blazed. "I've had about enough of this, Hastings! How dare you make such suggestions, after all I've done for the cause! My God, man, I've lost my best friend! You have no idea what I am suffering!"

Blake grasped the front of his shirt, jerking him forward. "How much did Nick West pay you to point out the right house to burn?" he growled.

Beecher's face was deep red with exasperation. "What in God's name are you talking about! Have you lost your mind?"

"One of the men who attacked me and Samantha was part of West's bunch! I don't have any solid evidence yet—*yet*, Beecher!—but somehow I'm going to prove that you've been working for West all along! But that's not why I'm here. I came to tell you that I don't want you anywhere around tomorrow at the Walters' funeral!"

Beecher sucked in his breath in shock, dropping his arms. "You can't tell me where I can and cannot go! Howard Walters was my best friend! He was the greatest man I have ever had the privilege to know. I intended to talk to Samantha about delivering the eulogy. Why, it's—it's preposterous to even *consider* not attending his funeral!"

Blake gave him a light shove. "Well, you'd better do more than consider it! As far as I'm concerned, you're responsible for the death of Samantha's parents. I'll not have you stand over his grave and deliver a sacreligious, hypocritcal speech about how much he meant to you!"

Rage was evident in Beecher's eyes, his face beet red. "How *dare* you talk to me that way! What would people think if I wasn't there?"

"I don't give a damn *what* they think! Say you were sick, for all I care. But I'm telling you right now, Beecher, if you show up at that funeral, I'll tell everyone there exactly what I think about you! Maybe most of them won't believe me, but, by God, I'll put the idea in their heads! The way people in this town are feeling right now about proslavery bush-whackers, I don't think you want them to even *suspect* you could be a spy! If you want to be able to remain in Lawrence, you'd better stay away from the funeral tomorrow! We've arranged for another

288

preacher to do the service."

Their eyes held, Beecher's jaw flexing in humiliation and anger. "Does your wife feel the same way you do?"

"My wife is in too delicate a condition and in too much grief to know how she feels about *anything!*"

"She *doesn't* believe it, does she?" Beecher answered, holding up his chin proudly. "Samantha thinks you're crazy to think such a thing. She's known me a long time. She would never believe that I would betray her family! This should be *her* decision, not yours!"

"She has already told me to do what I think is best."

"But she thinks it's wrong!"

"Leave Samantha out of this. This is between you and me, and I'm telling you again—stay away, or you'll wish you had!"

Beecher drew in his breath, straightening his shoulders. "All right. I'll stay away, in spite of the deep hurt it will cause me. But I'm only doing it out of respect for Howard and Milicent Walters, and of course, for Samantha. It's obvious that if I show up, you will create a scene. I don't intend to have such a humiliating thing happen at such a sacred ceremony, nor do I intend to upset poor Samantha even more than she already is. But you're wrong, Blake—dead wrong about me."

Blake glared at him. "I hope to hell I am!" he growled. He turned and left, and Beecher shut the door. His hands moved into fists, and he lashed out with one arm, knocking a plate from the table.

"Bastard!" he growled. He turned and looked at the door. "You'll find out soon enough what side I'm on, Blake Hastings! You're going to make a mistake somewhere along the line, and you'll find yourself in Nick West's hands—as well as *mine!* You won't be so high and mighty then, you son of a bitch!"

Samantha buttoned the black muslin mourning dress loaned to her by the Hanks' eldest daughter, Loretta. The dress had a tiered skirt and a matching black jacket. Because Loretta was just slightly heavier than Samantha, the dress fit Samantha's thickening waist without any problem, and the jacket helped hide her heavy belly.

"Is this all right?" she asked Blake, who stood near the bedroom window reading a letter.

"Hmmm?" He looked over at her. "It looks fine."

He turned back to the letter, and Samantha watched him. He looked handsome in the black suit he had rented from Mennan's Clothery but his eyes looked so tired, and strangely unreadable. She had always been able to tell what he was thinking, until the last two days. She thought perhaps it was just because she was not herself. Neither of them was the same. The attack and the shock of losing everything, as well as her parents' deaths, had changed them both. She only hoped it was temporary. Time had a way of taking care of such things.

Blake sighed, folding the letter and shoving it in his pocket. "I'll get out the rest of our money and we'll buy you some clothes when you're up to it," he told her. He turned to face her, and she thought how lying with him two nights ago, just before the raid, seemed like such a long, long time ago. The man before her now was a different Blake.

"What is it, Blake? Who was that letter from?"

He just stared at her a moment. "I picked it up at the post office today. Since our house was burned, they didn't know where to deliver it." He ran a hand through his hair. "We'll talk about it later. Let's just get through today first." He looked her over. "You even look pretty in black."

She felt a nameless fear, didn't like the look on his face. What was the letter about? Who was it from? He seemed so full of hate and bitterness now, so much like the very men who had taken part in the violence Kansas had suffered these past months. Would he join them?

"I don't feel very pretty," she said aloud, going to a mirror. She tucked in a strand of hair that had fallen from where she had rolled it up at the sides, then picked up a black straw hat and pinned it on the top of her head. She pulled the little veil over her red-rimmed, puffy eyes. "Now I know why women wear veils at funerals. It's so no one can see how terrible they look. Thank goodness Mrs. Hanks had more than one black hat."

He came up behind her, moving his arms around her from behind. "You could never look terrible. As far as having to borrow these clothes, I'm sorry, Sam. It won't be forever. I'll buy you what I can for now, and I'll find a way to get more money."

She worried about the last words. *A way to get more money.* . . . As though he was plotting a way to get it quickly. Blake Hastings was her protector and provider, and she knew he felt as though he had failed at both, even though he couldn't help what had happened.

"The important thing is that we're here together, Blake—alive and well." She held out her hands. "I even buttoned my own dress. I know the burns still look kind of bad, but they were more superficial than we thought. They don't hurt nearly as much as they did yesterday. And we have friends, shelter, and a

291

little money in the bank."

She looked at him in the mirror, and she could tell he knew she was only trying to think of things to make him feel better about what had happened. He met her eyes, and both felt the awful tragedy of it, both fought the need to break down. This was not the time, and nothing could be changed. Nothing.

"Blake—what if Mr. Beecher comes to the funeral? And you know he'll come."

"He won't. I took care of it."

She frowned. "What do you mean?"

"Exactly what I said." He let go of her and walked over to the bed to pick up a hat. "He won't be there and there won't be a scene. If anyone asks, just tell them he told us he was sick."

She put a hand to her stomach. "You . . . you didn't hurt him or anything, did you?"

He put on the hat. "I simply paid him a visit and told him to stay away."

"And he agreed?"

"Not at first. Then he decided he'd rather not make a scene. Besides, he doesn't want the rumor spread that he's a spy, which is what I told him I'd do if he showed up."

"Blake, it isn't right. He should be able to come to the funeral."

His eyes narrowed, and for the second time in as many days she saw a side to him she had never seen before—determined, angry with her—a look that told her that although he respected her independence, when it came to this subject, he intended to wield his husbandly rights. "I don't want to talk about it again," he told her. "And I don't want you contacting him to apologize for your husband's actions."

She frowned. "I would never undermine your

decisions that way, Blake. You know me better. But that doesn't mean I have to agree with you."

"No. It doesn't. But someday you'll see that I was right. I just hope you don't learn it the hard way. In the meantime, you do what I ask and stay away from the man, understand?"

She sighed, lifting the veil. "I understand." Her eyes teared. "Blake, I need you today. I need the Blake I married, not the angry, demanding man who's standing before me now."

He seemed to soften then as he came closer and pulled her into his arms. "I'm sorry, Sam. There are just so many things to think about now. I have a wife, a baby on the way—and we don't even have a place to live or any clothes. I can't find work, and I don't know who to trust except the Hankses—not to mention the fact that George is still out there somewhere, maybe not as safe as we think." He sighed deeply. "How do you feel? Are you sure you can go through with this?"

"I don't have much choice."

"You could stay here. People would understand."

"No. If Drew could be here, I might consider it. But I won't have my parents buried with neither of their children present. Just stay close to me, and try to rid yourself of your anger. I feel like there's a wall between us, and it frightens me. It makes it hard for me to take comfort from you."

He rubbed her back. "We'll work it out. You just remember that no matter what I do or say, the fact remains that I love you more than anything on this earth, and somehow I'm going to make up for what has happened."

Someone knocked on the door. "It's time to go, Samantha," came Mrs. Hanks's voice. "Are you two ready?"

293

"Yes," Blake answered. He took Samantha's arm and led her to the door. He stopped, leaning down to lightly kiss her lips, both of them wondering when they would ever get back to normal again, feel the need and urge to make love again. Their whole world had been turned upside down. Blake pulled the veil back down over her face and they went out, climbing into the Hanks's three-seater buggy that would take them to the cemetery. Since the church was gone, the funeral would take place at the gravesite.

George walked behind the plow horses, struggling to keep up because of the heavy leg irons he wore. They had been cuffed around his ankles so long that the painful, bleeding rawness they had initially caused had turned to tough, leathery skin. He still felt weak, after a bout with infection from another cruel whipping he had suffered over a month ago, inflicted by Nick West himself after he caught George talking to one of the female slaves. He was forbidden to talk to anyone. The chain linking his ankle cuffs was extra long so that he could walk in normal strides, but the leg irons were never removed, discouraging any ideas of trying to run away.

George pushed hard on the plow, taking his anger and frustration out on the hot, laborious task he had been assigned. He growled at the two draft horses when they veered in the wrong direction, jerked them back into place, the reins digging into his shoulders, which were sore from still-healing lash marks and from too much sun. He wore no shirt, and flies and smaller bugs nipped at his sweating body.

He tried to keep his wits about him, hoping that somehow, someday, he would find a way out of this, a way to help Jesse. The whipping West had given him had been made even more painful by the fact that West had brought Jesse along to watch. That had hurt almost more than the whip itself. He wondered how horribly disfigured his back must be now, after already being so badly scarred. He would not soon forget lying for days on the floor of the stall, being visited three times a day by one of West's men, who would throw saltwater on his back to keep it clean. That was not the kind of pain a person soon forgot, if ever, and he spent most of his time alone just thinking of the several ways he would make Nick West suffer if he ever got the chance.

But would that chance ever come? Would Blake somehow find out he was not really in Canada? He had seen Clyde Beecher come to West's farm. Blake suspected Beecher of being a traitor. Now George knew it was certain. If only Blake would follow the man; if only Beecher would slip up, maybe ask about him. That would make Blake suspicious.

Farther to his right several Negro women worked in the hot sun, planting corn. There was no visiting, no singing. Rules were strict here—West saw to that. There wasn't a slave he owned who had not felt the whip, or suffered starvation, or been chained. Not far from him a woman collapsed, but he dared not go to help her.

He barked at the horses, clinging to the handles of the plow, ignoring the biting flies and the heat. Only four more rows and he would be done. He noticed with alarm then that Nick West was coming down the field road in his fancy buggy. The man stopped at the end of the row George was plowing and waited, and George wondered what he had done wrong now. He thought with relief that at least Jesse wasn't with him.

"Hold up," West told him when George reached

the end of the row. West climbed out of the buggy, holding out a canteen. "Have a swallow," he told George with a sly grin. "Pour some over your head and shoulders. You look like you could use some refreshment."

George just glared at him, slowly reaching and taking the canteen, waiting for some kind of trick. "Go ahead," West told him. "You have my permission." George quickly drank down nearly half the canteen's contents, then poured the rest over himself, gasping with the relief of the cool wetness. West just snickered as he watched, then took back the canteen. "Not even a thank-you?" he asked.

George thought how he would have traded the water for the chance to sink a knife into Nick West. "Thank you," he said grudgingly, his voice low.

West adjusted his hat, looking around the field. "I don't know how you people do it, working out here in this heat. It *is* awfully hot for May, isn't it? But great weather for planting corn. We should have a good crop this year, plenty of feed for the livestock, let alone the market."

"What is it you came out here for?" George asked. "You don't generally come visit your Negroes just to talk about the weather."

West laughed lightly. "All right. I came out here to give you some news." He stepped back, tossing the canteen into the buggy, then putting his hands on his hips in a pompous gesture. "I just thought you'd like to know that the city of Lawrence was attacked night before last. Some of my men took part in the raid. They just got back this morning with the good news. They attacked in the wee hours of the morning, when people are usually sleeping their deepest. Mr. Beecher was a great help in letting them know which people were making the most trouble in the abolition movement. That Reverend Walters you know—he was high on the list—and of course, your good friend Blake Hastings and his charming wife.''

George felt light-headed from the heat and the horror of the news. "What happened to Blake and Sam?" he asked.

"Well, they are most likely dead, as are the Reverend and Mrs. Walters.'' With great delight West watched the changes in George's eyes, from shock to grief to bitter hatred.

George held himself in check. He wanted dearly to lunge at West, to wrap his big hands around the man's throat until he turned purple and died. But maybe that was what West wanted. Maybe he was just telling him this news to get a rise out of him so he could punish him again.

"I don't believe you," he said quietly.

West shrugged. "Believe what you want. My men set fire to both houses while everyone inside slept. I'm told that by now half of Lawrence is burned to the ground. I'll be getting word from Beecher soon, no doubt. He'll tell me for certain. Who knows? Maybe your friends didn't die. Maybe they're just horribly burned and disfigured. That would be too bad, wouldn't it? I mean, Blake Hastings was quite a handsome man, and his wife quite beautiful. Beecher even tells me she was pregnant.''

"Sam? And you set fire to their house, in her condition?"

West took a thin cigar from his pocket. "Don't be expecting Blake Hastings to come to your aid, George. He's either dead or too badly injured to do anything. Same goes for his wife's parents. And, of course, since Hastings is the only one who can testify that you are legally a free man, you don't have any hope of leaving my, uh, *employ*, shall we say?''

The draft horses jolted slightly, and George grasped the reins, jerking them back. West noticed how the big Negro's muscles rippled at the movement, realized what George Freedom could do to him if he had the chance. He loved the feeling of power he had over these people, even the big, strong ones like George, who were completely helpless under his rule.

"You bastard!" George seethed. "At the least you probably caused poor Sam to lose her baby!"

West lit the cigar. "If that's all that happened, they should feel lucky. I'll know soon enough." He puffed the cigar. "If they *did* survive, it won't be for long. I want Blake Hastings dead, and I'm going to see that it happens. I just thought you'd like to know the latest news." He turned and climbed into the buggy. "Oh, by the way, George—speaking of losing babies. I'm afraid your little Jesse is awfully sick herself right now. Seems she went and let herself get pregnant. It was mine, of course," He frowned, making a clicking sound. "I couldn't very well have a little mulatto running around the house now, could I? I hired a nigger woman from another farm to come over and get rid of it. Jesse will be all right—in time."

George let the horror of the words move through him, dropped the reins to the plow horses and headed for the buggy. West grabbed his whip and held it up. "Ah—ah, George. You don't want to feel this all over again, do you?"

"What did you do to Jesse?" George asked, his fury making him feel like he might explode, tears coming to his eyes.

"She'll be just fine. It will teach her a lesson, letting herself get pregnant like that. I thought I had taught her all about timing and such things. When the day comes I want children, I'll marry a decent white woman and have *white* babies. In fact, I just might have to sell Jesse pretty soon and look for a respectable wife. Jesse has pretty much worn out her usefulness to me, but she's still beautiful enough that I could get a pretty penny for her. What do you think? Should I sell her?"

George felt the panic rising. If West sold her, he might never find her again. Still, she would at least be out of his clutches. But would she be worse off with someone else? "I think you should go to hell," he seethed, a tear slipping down his cheek. "Let me see her, West. Just let me see her so I know she's all right."

"Don't be a fool. Besides, she's over the worst of it now. The bleeding and sickness have stopped. She's just weak. She's at the house, being well taken care of. I'll decide what to do with her when she's fully healed.

"You murdered your own child," George growled.

"I got rid of a little half-nigger bastard," West sneered. "What would I want with a kid like that? I bought Jesse for pure pleasure, not for making babies." He tipped his hat, the cigar between his teeth as he talked. "Get back to work." He turned the carriage and drove off, leaving George standing there feeling helpless and heartbroken.

Could Blake and Sam really be dead? And what had poor Jesse suffered? He closed his eyes, throwing back his head. "Jesse . . . " he groaned. West had hired some witch to get rid of Jesse's baby. She could have died. God only knew what she had gone through, or if she might still risk death. He fell to his knees, wondering when God was going to deliver him from this hell. If Blake was dead or badly injured, he would not be coming to his aid. Jesse was living in hell, and he couldn't do a damn thing about it; and if Blake was dead, George would have no way of proving he was a free man, if the opportunity ever again arose.

He could not stop the tears of frustration. Hatred and anger ate at him like a cancer, bringing him literal pain. He wept for several minutes, until he heard the field foreman shout at him to get back to work. Feeling weary and spent, he got back to his feet, dragging the chain and cuffs with him as he walked behind the horses and picked up the reins. Tears ran down his face through dirt and sweat as he turned the big animals and started a new row.

"'Behold, I show you a mystery,'" the Presbyterian pastor read from the Bible. "'We shall not all sleep, but we shall all be changed, in a moment, in the twinkling of an eye, at the last trump: for the trumpet shall sound, and the dead shall be raised incorruptible, and we shall be changed . . . O, death, where is thy sting? O, grave, where is thy victory? The sting of death is sin; and the strength of sin is the law. But thanks be to God, which giveth us the victory through our Lord Jesus Christ.'"

The man scanned the crowd for a moment. "Howard Walters himself would want you all to remember this next passage. Remember it well, my friends, for it gives strength and hope to those of us who have vowed to continue our work for the abolition of the sin of slavery." He looked again at the Bible in his hands. "'Therefore, my beloved brethren, be ye steadfast, unmovable, always abounding in the work of the Lord, forasmuch as ye know that your labour is not in vain in the Lord.'"

He again looked at the crowd. "Yes, my friends, we

must be steadfast and unmovable. We must continue the work of the Lord. We must not let the fight end here and leave victory to those who committed the heinous crimes of two nights ago. Howard and Milicent Walters gave their lives for what they thought was right. They gave their lives just as Christ gave his. Can *we* do less?''

Samantha stared at the coffins, nailed shut. The awful emptiness again consumed her, the realization that she would never see her mother and father again; never hear her father's voice in the back room of the print shop, or hear him preach; never be able to turn to her mother when she needed her loving advice. In spite of her love for Blake, and his strength and tender love, the loss of her parents left her with a frightening loneliness, as though she had somehow lost part of her own identity. She had always been Howard and Milicent's daughter. Now she was just Samantha Walters Hastings. She knew it would take some time to adjust to the fact that she was her own person now.

She had thought herself so grown up and independent when she daringly married Blake. Now, suddenly, she felt like a vulnerable little girl again. It would have been so much easier if her parents had died naturally, at a nice old age, when she herself would have been older. But she realized now that even though she was a married woman with a baby on the way, a big part of her was still the little girl who had belonged to the Walters household.

If only there were at least a picture! She prayed that the years would not fade the memory of her parents' faces. She shuddered at the realization that soon they would be lowered into the dark depths of the earth, forever silenced. She could not hold back the choking sobs then, and Blake's comforting arm came around her. She wept against him, wondering how she would have stood up to this horror if she didn't have him.

She thought of Drew. Thank God she still had a brother. Maybe Drew had a picture. He had sent a telegram, telling her to put flowers on the caskets in his name and that he would reimburse her when he arrived. Drew was coming to Lawrence, in spite of her plea that he stay at school. He wanted to visit the graves and pay his respects, and he wanted to meet Blake. Most of all, he wanted to know who had been behind the deaths of his parents. Samantha hated the thought of his leaving school just before the beginning of the summer curriculum, but Drew was as stubborn and determined as his sister. She knew there would be no arguing the issue, and she could not deny she would be very happy to see her brother right now.

The guest preacher delivered a touching eulogy, accenting the fact that Howard and Milicent Walters had sacrificed safety and all things familiar and comforting to come to Kansas from their home in New England—coming into a new, restless, blood-torn territory to try to bring peace, to try to halt the growing evil of slavery in America.

"They could have stayed in New England and just talked about how terrible slavery is; but instead, they came here themselves, urged friends to also come here and settle, just to add their numbers to our own so that Kansas might win the vote against slavery. It is true," the preacher continued, "that alas, the vote was lost. but we have made great strides in fighting the illegal elections, and one day, my friends, if we stick to the teachings of Reverend Walters, we will get that vote turned around. We will have our chance for new elections, and we will win! When we do,

Howard and Milicent Walters will be watching and cheering from their rightful place in heaven with our Lord Jesus Christ."

Several "amens" were whispered throughout the crowd. Samantha was comforted by the fact that it seemed a good share of the citizens of Lawrence were here at the graveyard, hundreds of people come to pay their respects to someone who had only been with them for a little over two years. Her parents had made a deep impression on the people of Lawrence.

"'Therefore we are always confident, knowing that, whilst we are at home in the body, we are absent from the Lord,'" the preacher read again. "For we walk by faith, not by sight. We are confident, I say, and willing rather to be absent from the body, and to be present with the Lord . . . We must all appear before the judgment seat of Christ; that every one may receive the things done in his body, according to that he hath done, whether it be good or bad."

He looked at the crowd again, a light breeze blowing his thinning hair. In the distance, a half-burned Lawrence lay in ugly ruin, some of the buildings still smoldering. Clyde Beecher was nowhere in sight. Samantha wondered what Blake had said to the man, and she couldn't help feeling a little sorry for him, considering how close he had been to her father. She wanted to be able to believe Blake. Her husband was a good judge of character, a man who had seen more of the world than she, who knew people much better. She hated arguing with him about Beecher, hated the wall it created between them. Yet she found it difficult to believe Beecher could be the evil traitor Blake made him out to be. She decided she would not talk about it anymore, for she hated the look in Blake's eyes every time she brought up the man's name, and she respected her husband's wishes and decisions. She only wished there were some way to prove one way or the other where Beecher's loyalties lay.

"Ashes to ashes, and dust to dust," the preacher was saying. He threw some dirt onto the coffins, then nodded to Samantha to do the same. Blake held her hand, while with the other she picked up some dirt and threw it onto the coffins.

"I love you, Mama," she said quietly. "And I love you, Father. We won't quit now. We're going to win this."

Several other women in the crowd were weeping, and men were dabbing at their eyes. Mrs. Hanks led everyone then in the hymn, "In The Sweet Bye and Bye," and the preacher delivered a closing prayer. People began to disperse, and Mrs. Hanks moved among the crowd telling fellow parishioners they were welcome to come to the house for a while and express their sympathy to Samantha.

"She and her husband lost everything, you know," the woman told someone nearby. "They'll be staying with us for a while."

Lost everything. The words were so ugly. What would happen now? What did Blake mean about finding a way to make money? And he still had not explained the letter he had been reading. Was he going to expose himself to danger? Would she lose her husband, too? She would not want to live if that happened.

She remained at the gravesite until everyone but the preacher and Blake and the men assigned burial detail were the only ones left. Jonas Hanks told Blake he would walk the family home and leave the buggy for Blake and Samantha.

"We'd better go now," Blake told her.

Samantha shook her head. "Once I leave, it's over.

304

They'll be gone forever."

"They already are, Sam. It's just going to take you some time to realize that, and to heal. Standing here isn't going to bring them back."

Memories flooded her again, and again the tears came, the awful reality covering her like a black cloth. Blake caught her, picked her up in his arms. "No, Blake."

"It's time to leave, Sam. You're going back to the room and you're going to take some of that medicine the doctor gave you to relax you."

"I can't leave."

He kept walking with her, kissing her forehead before setting her into the buggy. Blake's own heart pained his chest, memories of his father's simple burial on the farm coming back to haunt him. He had buried the man alone. There had been no fancy funeral, no preacher to say words over him. He picked up the reins and got the buggy into motion, heading toward the Hanks home. Samantha started to turn.

"Don't look back," Blake told her. "We'll come back after the graves are covered and when you're stronger. We'll plant some flowers over the graves."

Samantha looked ahead, grasping his arm. "Yes. Mother liked daisies and morning glories. I feel most sorry for her, Blake. She wasn't one to go out and pound the streets or deliver speeches. She just quietly supported my father because he was her husband."

"She was a fine woman, and so are you. You have your mother's goodness and you father's spirit and determination."

They drove through town, where a few people nodded to them, some shouting out to Samantha they were sorry about her parents. Clyde Beecher watched from the doorway to the telegraph office. He turned to the telegrapher paid by Nick West to keep quiet about telegrams sent back and forth between himself and Beecher—telegrams in a code only Beecher and West understood, but which the telegrapher knew had to do with bushwhacker raids.

Beecher approached the man, who others in town did not know was a proslavery sympathizer. "Got a message for West," Beecher told him, looking around to be sure no one had come inside. "W and X survived. Y and Z are out. Buried today. Will keep tabs. Let me know next move." He signed the note "YE," using the third letter of his first and last name: Clyde Beecher. The idea was to confuse anyone who might see the message and try to discover who had sent it. W and X were the codes for Blake and Samantha.

The telegrapher nodded. "Got it." He looked up at Beecher's pitted face. "You going to wait for an answer?"

"No. I'll be back later. You just be sure to keep your mouth shut."

"Yes, sir, Mr. Beecher. I understand."

The man began sending the telegram, and Beecher left. He had a feeling that Blake Hastings was not going to let this go easily. He was a man with a temper, and that temper had been pushed too far. He was going to retaliate in some way, and when he did, Beecher intended to be ready to catch him at it. Maybe Blake Hastings would set his own trap. After the insult Blake had handed him, he would like nothing better than to have the man in his clutches. He could hardly wait to find out how Blake would react when he discovered his nigger friend George was a prisoner on Nick West's plantation in Missouri. By the time he did, Blake himself would be in the same predicament. Beecher was determined to see to that.

Sixteen

Samantha stirred when she felt Blake come to bed. She had no idea what time it was, only that it was dark, and the room was warm. She could hear crickets singing outside the open window, and occasionally a bug would hit the screen. She wore only a sleeveless cotton nightgown because of the heat, and she had thrown off the covers. When she felt Blake's arm come around her, she touched it lightly, her burns hurting only if she rubbed them against something.

"You're awake?" Blake asked softly.

"Yes. Just now. I felt you come to bed." She drew in her breath and moved his hand to her belly. "Feel it? I think it's your son who really woke me up."

He held his hand firmly against her fullness, feeling the strange rippling movement. "Thank God you've hung on to him," he told her, kissing her hair. "And I'm glad to hear you calling it him instead of her."

"I decided to give up the argument for now."

She could feel his smile, and she stared out at a half moon. "Do you think we're safe tonight, Blake? What if they come back?"

"They won't for a while. They must know we have men keeping watch now. Fact is, I get my turn at three o'clock this morning. Mrs. Hanks set an alarm clock in her room."

Samantha turned. "I don't like the thought of you out there roaming the streets in the dark."

"Everybody takes their turn."

Their eyes held in the soft light of a lamp turned low. "Make love to me, Blake," she whispered.

He leaned closer and kissed her mouth lightly. "You don't really mean that—not after the funeral."

"I do mean it. You're all I have left. And now that I know how fine the line is between life and death, how quickly we can lose those we love, I don't want to waste one precious moment. I don't want you to go out there tonight without making love first."

He sighed deeply, stroking the hair back from her face. "Sam, you've been through so much today, cried so many tears. This has all been such a strain on you. I worry about the baby."

"Please, Blake," she whispered.

He studied the blue eyes that he loved so dearly. Her face looked milky white and almost silken in the soft light, her lips full and inviting. How he loved her! How he hated what all this was doing to her. He reached down to remove his knee-length long johns, preferring to sleep naked but afraid they could get rousted out of bed at any time. He pushed up her gown, moving on top of her, knowing that this time their lovemaking would not be an act of lustful passion, but more a reminder that they were both alive and still together, a union of souls—or, in these times, very possibly a last act of love.

He met her mouth in light, biting kisses, moving tongue and lips over her cheeks, her eyes, back to her mouth. "We have to be quiet," he whispered. "The

Hankses are right across the hall."

He entered her quickly with no preliminaries. This was all either of them needed tonight, the union. He moved slowly, quietly, thrusting deep, moving in gentle circles, reminding her in the most tantalizing ways that he most certainly was alive and well and still her husband. But she sensed the edge to him, the slight hardness that had not been there before the raid. She knew that what she was doing was a futile attempt at making him change his mind about whatever it was he had planned. She had been able to claim him and hold him once by an act of passion. But this time would be different.

He met her mouth again, grasping her under the neck and thrusting his tongue deep while at the same time he pushed himself inside, his life spilling into her. She didn't need her own release tonight. She had only wanted to feel Blake inside her, to help him free himself from some of the pent-up anger and frustration.

Still, he seemed tense as he moved off her. "I wasn't much of a lover tonight."

"I didn't need you to be. I just wanted you— wanted to be a part of you." She moved to nestle her head in his shoulder. "I feel so apart from you, Blake, ever since the raid."

"It's too fresh in our minds. Besides, I have a lot to think about. They stole everything from us, Sam, and I'm going to get it back."

"How? Please don't leave me in the dark, Blake. What was in that letter? It has something to do with that, doesn't it? Are you going away? Will you be in danger?"

He sighed, kissing her forehead and sitting up. He moved off the bed and went to the washstand. "You're better off not knowing all the details." He poured some water into the bowl and washed himself, then pulled on his long johns. He came back to sit down on the edge of the bed, reaching over to the nightstand for a cigarette. He took the glass chimney from the oil lamp and bent close to light his cigarette on the flame.

"The letter was from that John Hale, wasn't it?"

"Yes," he answered, putting back the lamp glass. "It's the second letter I've received from him. I never told you about the first one."

"He's got a job for you—a dangerous one?"

"I'd be well paid, and we need the money."

"I'd rather be poor and have a husband beside me than be rich and alone."

He took a long drag on the cigarette. "Well, it sure as hell won't make us rich. It will just help, that's all. Right now I need work, Sam. I can go back to work for Hale—make regular shipments like I always did. But first he has a special job for me."

"You'll be working for jayhawkers, won't you! Blake, that's just as bad as being a bushwhacker!"

He stood up, pacing a moment, coming back to the bed and sitting on the edge of it to face her. "Do you think I care about that anymore?" He tried to keep his voice to a near whisper. "This is *war* now, Sam! Can't you see that? For the time being there's no way out. Your brother is on his way here, and you're bound and determined to carry on your father's work in his memory. We don't know what the hell has happened to George, and we can't leave Lawrence until we *do* know! We're *stuck* here, Sam, and I can't just wait for something else to happen! I have a chance to make some badly needed money *and* get a little revenge at the same time, don't you see?"

She leaned toward him, her eyes misty and pleading. "I see you becoming just like them. I see

310

hatred and vengeance in your eyes. I just buried my parents today, Blake." Her voice broke on the words, and she put her head down on his arm. "I can't lose you, too. You're all I have."

"You *won't* lose me. I know my way around, Sam."

"You had George to help you before," she sobbed. "You weren't working alone." She raised her face to meet his eyes. "And before . . . there was just you. You didn't have a wife . . . a baby on the way."

He reached over and crushed out his cigarette. "That's exactly why I have to do this. It's *for* you and the baby. Hale is paying me in advance so I can send you the money. No matter what happens, the money is yours."

"You tell yourself it's for me. But it's really for *you*," she told him through tears. "It's because you can't stand what happened. You feel like you didn't do enough, but you *did*, Blake. You got us out of that house before we were burned alive. You saved me from that man who rode down on us. You—"

"We lost *everything*, Sam!" He got up from the bed. "And your parents died. I sensed something was wrong that night before we went to sleep. I should have *acted* on that! I might have saved the house *and* your parents. Now there's nothing left but to somehow make up for it, and I'm not going to be satisfied just handing out newspapers! It's time to hit *them* before they hit us again."

"And innocent people will suffer on their side, just the same as on ours," she argued.

He sighed, running a hand through his hair. "The men who ride for John Hale don't operate that way." He came back to the bed, grasping her arms. "Besides, I won't be involved in the actual raids. That's all I can tell you now, Sam. It's dangerous for

311

you to know any more. All you have to do is tell people I've gone back to work for Hale Freighting. Whether I actually will or not, I'm not sure yet. I don't like leaving you alone for days at a time, especially not now. But this one job will pay well, and you should be safe here with the Hankses. I don't think there will be another raid anytime soon, especially once we retaliate. Men are guarding the town. Everyone is more alert now. I think I can safely leave you here for a while."

She could see there was no arguing with him this time. His mind was made up, and he could be just as stubborn as she. "They finally did it, didn't they?" She touched his face. "They invaded our most private lives, took away our little sanctuary, drove a wedge between us."

He grasped her hand. "Sam, this is something I have to do. It's got nothing to do with how much I love you. However long we might be separated, our love for each other can never change. It can only deepen. And whatever I do, wherever I go, we'll be together in spirit—and I'll damn well come back."

Come back. Somehow the words didn't help. She rested her head against his chest. "I've never been so afraid in my life," she told him. "It would be so much easier if I had Mother and Father to turn to while you were gone."

"I know, and I'm sorry, Sam. I know this is a damn rotten time to leave, but this can't be put off. The sooner I'm done, the sooner I'll be back." He gently rubbed her back, kissing her hair. "Someday this will all be over. We'll have that farm, Sam—our own house again . . . lots of kids. We're going to grow old together, I promise you that."

She wept against his chest. "Only God can make

that kind of promise." She hugged him tightly. "I love you, Blake. I need you so."

He tangled his hand in her thick hair, breathing deeply of its scent, wanting always to remember it. "I need you, too. You might think that I don't, but don't forget that in the beginning *you* were all that *I* had. This is all either of us has for family now, Sam—each other . . . the baby. I want you to promise me that while I'm gone you'll stay away from active politics and you'll get plenty of rest. What I'm doing will take all my alertness, and I can't be worrying about you. Just this once, do as I ask and stay close to this house."

"I will. You . . . talk as though you're leaving soon."

"Tomorrow morning, soon as I'm finished with my night watch."

She sat up straighter, and he felt torn at the desolate look on her face. "So soon! You won't even get any rest."

"Time is important. I already wired Hale earlier this evening that I'd be in Independence by the day after tomorrow. I'll take the train. That's all I can tell you. When the job is done, I'll explain it all. It shouldn't take me more than five days. I'll be back within the week."

Their eyes held. "It will be the longest five days of my life," she answered. "We haven't been apart since we got married, Blake."

He leaned closer, meeting her lips, lightly at first, then more hungrily. Both of them suddenly realized this could very possibly be the last night they spent together. He laid her back, smothering her with kisses. "I'm so sorry, Sam," he groaned.

*　　　*　　　*

At his own cabin, Clyde Beecher opened the door to see the telegrapher standing on his porch. "What are you doing here?" Beecher asked him. "Someone might see you talking to me."

"No one noticed. I made sure of it. I figured I'd better come over here soon as I went off my shift and let you know."

Beecher looked past him, scanning the darkness beyond, then let him inside and closed the door. "Let me know what?"

"That Blake Hastings—he came over this evening and sent off a message to John Hale in Independence. Hale's a strong abolitionist. I think Hastings used to work for him."

Beecher's eyes lit up. "What was the message?"

"He said, 'Be there by Saturday.'"

Beecher frowned. "That's it?"

"That's all. But I figured it had to mean something, what with the raid and all—and Hale working underground. You know nothing would make Blake Hastings leave his pregnant wife now of all times, unless it was real important. They're up to something, Mr. Beecher."

"Yes, it certainly sounds that way." Beecher reached into his pocket and pulled out some coins, handing them to the man. "Thank you for the information."

"You want me to wire a message to Mr. West?"

"Yes, but I have to think about it first. I'll be by in the morning." Beecher opened the door to let him out, then closed it, a broad smile lighting up his face. "Well, well, Mr. Hastings. It looks as though you're going to make this easy for us after all."

He walked to an old desk given to him by the reverend and sat down to compose a message for West, trying to decide how to word it. "W coming to

Indep. Watch for shipment. Must be stopped. Be there myself in two days."

He leaned back and studied the message. Yes, he would leave himself in the morning and head straight for Nick West's plantation. He would have to be careful. Find out if Blake was going by train—take a separate train so Blake wouldn't know he was also heading east. One thing was sure, if Blake Hastings was going to be captured and killed, he wanted to be in on it. He'd finally get back at Blake for all his insults. Not only that, but Little Miss Samantha would be completely vulnerable once her husband was out of the picture.

There had been a time when he thought he might court Samantha, maybe convince Howard Walters that he was proper husband material for the man's daughter. But although Samantha had always been friendly toward him, it was obvious she had no interest in him romantically. Probably thought him too old and ugly for her. Besides that, she had been nearly as active against slavery as her father. She, too, would learn a good lesson. It was time to show them all that those who spoke against the government and dealt in other traitorous activities should expect their just punishment. Man or woman, young or old, those who broke the law had better be shown for once and for all that they could not get away with it or the abolition movement would never be stopped. With Blake gone, maybe there was some way he could later woo Samantha out of Lawrence. She would be too well guarded to have her arrested right in town, but if he could get her away . . .

Blake stepped out onto the porch with Samantha, carrying a bag of personal toiletries and a few articles of clothing. He wore his six-gun, and also carried a rifle. He faced Samantha, his heart aching at the sight of her. She looked so forlorn, her belly swollen with his child, her eyes sunken from the strain of the past three days.

Again a little voice inside asked him if he was doing the right thing. Part of him told him to stay here with his wife, but another part—the proud, stubborn side of him—told him to go and do something about the wrong that had been done to them. Besides, the best argument was the one hundred dollars he would be paid to deliver guns to a fiery abolitionist called John Brown. He had met the man at the showdown along the Wakarusa a few months ago, and if anyone could properly retaliate for what had happened at Lawrence, John Brown and his sons and followers could.

Blake wouldn't take part in the raiding himself. He was only to deliver the guns and ammunition, which John Hale would provide. He had burned the letter from Hale, according to Hale's instructions, so that no one would discover his mission. All Hanks knew was that he had a chance to make some money by working for a while again for Hale Freighting, and that he was leaving today to do just that. The Hankses were good, dependable people, and Blake knew Samantha was in good hands. At least he wasn't leaving her completely alone, although from the look on her face, one would think just that.

He knew the horrible loneliness of losing one's parents, but it was a personal loneliness that his presence or absence was not going to help. Only time would heal those wounds—and the baby. Once she held that baby in her arms, she would have a new direction in life, something new to treasure and love, and a lot of her loneliness would vanish.

At the moment he could only hope he would be with her for the birth of the baby. He had assured her he would be back in less than a week, but he knew just how dangerous this job really was, especially now that the fighting had grown more violent and heated. Every shipment that left John Hale's supply house would be suspect. He wasn't even sure right now just where he was to deliver the guns. Hale would tell him that when he got to Independence.

He sighed deeply, moving his arms around Samantha. "I might as well get going. The sun is up."

"Blake, you look so tired. You hardly slept at all last night."

Their eyes held on the remark, both remembering why he had not slept. The few hours he was supposed to be sleeping they had spent talking and making love. "I've gone without sleep plenty of times. I'll be all right."

She studied his handsome face. "It's dangerous for you to be tired. You've got to stay alert."

He leaned down and kissed her lightly. "No one is going to bother me on the way there. I'll be on a train full of people. It's after I get there and do what Hale needs done that I'll be in danger. But I've done all this before, Sam. I know what to do, what routes to take, what to watch for—and Hale is good at disguising his shipments."

She paled slightly. "Oh, Blake, it's guns, isn't it?" she whispered.

He put a finger to her lips. "I'm just delivering a load of feed—just a normal shipment to a regular customer. Period. I just happen to be in the freighting business again, that's all. Remember that, and don't get such a worried look on your face whenever someone asks you where I've gone. You'll

317

give it away. Be my strong, brave Samantha—and please, act natural."

She breathed deeply, nodding. "I'll try. And if there's any way you can get a message to me, at least let me know you arrived in Independence all right, please, Blake?"

"I will." He leaned down to kiss her once more, drawing her close, the kiss lingering hungrily until they heard the screen open.

"Oh! I'm sorry," Mrs. Hanks spoke up.

Samantha reddened at being caught in the embrace. Blake pulled away, grinning. "It's all right. I was just about to leave."

"Well, I packed you some sandwiches to take along. I'm told the food at the train stops is nearly inedible." The woman handed out the sack full of food, and Blake took it.

"Thank you, Mrs. Hanks," he told her. "You and your husband have done too much for us. I promise to make it up to you."

"Nonsense! You needed help, and we helped you. The Good Lord would expect it of us. Besides, I will enjoy Samantha's company while you're gone, and the girls love having her here. We'll all be just fine while you're gone, and we'll be praying for you."

Blake nodded. "Thank you, ma'am. Tell Jonas good-bye for me. I know he's got guard patrol this morning."

"Yes, it's a shame, isn't it, the way we're being forced to live now. Lawrence has become almost a prison for us. It's just so sad." The woman's eyes teared, and she touched Blake's arm. "God go with you, Blake. Hurry back." As she turned and went back inside, Blake looked at Samantha.

"Be careful, Sam. And stay close to this house."

"Please let me come to the train station with you."

"No. We already discussed it. A tearful parting there would just make things look more suspicious. People don't need to see you down there looking at me as though you think you'll never see me again." He kissed her forehead. "And quit thinking it. I'll be back."

Their eyes held. What was there left to say? He was leaving, and that was that. "I love you," he said then, his voice breaking slightly.

She did not reply, but he could see the answer in her eyes. He knew she was too choked up to speak. He turned away, stooping to put the sandwiches into his bag, picking it up again, along with his rifle. He looked at her once more, his own eyes red and moist. He wondered if he would ever forget the sight of her this morning, the look on her face—wondered if he would regret what he was doing.

"Good-bye, Sam." He turned and walked away, heading for the train station.

Samantha watched him slowly disappear. He turned once to wave, and she waved back, wondering if this was the last time she would see her beloved Blake. They had had so little time together, and most of that time had been spent campaigning, working for the cause, living a life of turmoil and danger. Their dream of settling peacefully on a little farm seemed more remote than ever.

She turned to go inside when she saw a familiar horse and rider approaching. She had seen Clyde Beecher at her father's house often enough to know the man from a distance. She quickly turned away and breathed deeply, dabbing at her eyes. She still did not agree with Blake about Beecher being a spy, but the suspicion had been planted. She knew Blake would not want Mr. Beecher to see she had been crying. He might suspect the danger her husband

319

was subjecting himself to. As she heard Beecher's horse come closer, she pressed her hands to the sides of her hair, hoping she didn't look too upset.

"Samantha!" he called out. "You're up early. I supposed after all you've been through, you and Blake would still be resting this morning."

Samantha wondered suddenly why Beecher himself had come around so early. If he thought they would still be sleeping, why was he here? It was a strange time to come visiting. Could Blake be right? Did Beecher come just to see what Blake was up to?

"Life goes on, Mr. Beecher. You know me. I'm not one to sit around feeling sorry for myself. I'm very sorry you were sick yesterday and unable to attend the funeral. You must have been quite ill."

Samantha hoped that Beecher believed that she knew nothing about Blake visiting him and warning him to stay away from the funeral. She wanted the man to think that she had every confidence in him. Most of all, she didn't want him to think she had anything to do with keeping him away, for indeed, she still felt badly about that.

"I, uh, I was," he answered, apparently surprised she didn't know the real reason. "I feel badly about it, Samantha. You can just imagine. Reason I'm up and about so early is that I was on my way to the cemetery to pay my respects. I wanted to get there early so I'd have some time alone." He removed his hat, leaning forward in his saddle, his eyes looking misty. "This is such a terrible loss. I am afraid I feel rather out of place now—no leader, no church. I am thinking of starting a church of my own. I take it you intend to continue your father's work?"

"Yes—eventually. Blake wants me to wait until the baby is born."

Beecher looked up the street in the direction Blake

had walked. "Was that Blake I saw?"

She watched his eyes, wishing she could read them, wishing she could be sure about him. "Yes. We lost everything, Mr. Beecher, as you well know, and there's no work for Blake in Lawrence now. He's taking the train to Independence to see if he can get his old freighting job back. He expects to be back within the week."

"I see. I'm surprised he's leaving you alone."

"I'm not alone. I'll be staying here with the Hankses until he gets back. We don't have much choice right now. Blake needs the work."

He put his hat back on. "Well, I hope he has good luck. And I hope he gets back soon. I'll be leaving myself today."

"Oh?" A tiny alarm rose deep inside Samantha. "Where are you going?"

"I decided that our brave and faithful followers outside of Lawrence should be told what has happened to their beloved leader. They should know about your father, and someone should make sure they don't lose faith. As soon as I return, I'd like to start raising funds for a new church. I hope I can count on you to help."

"Of course. And thank you for going out to talk to the others. Be careful, Mr. Beecher. Things are much more dangerous now."

"I appreciate your concern. It's the same for your husband. It takes a brave man to take a job that involves crossing that border, let alone being an abolitionist, riding into slave territory. Blake must want the work awfully bad."

Samantha wondered if he was just fishing for more information. She hated herself for being so distrustful. "With a baby coming, it's more important than ever. As far as the danger, Mr. Beecher, I suppose

321

we're all in danger now, no matter what we do. We can't stop living because of it. Thank you for paying your respects to my parents. And I . . . I'm sorry for the way Blake talked to you the morning after the raid. He was just upset. These are trying times, Mr. Beecher. We're all on edge, and Blake is a man who finds it difficult to trust anyone."

"I understand completely. I hold no ill feelings toward either of you. You mean very much to me, Samantha. Your father was my closest friend and a great man. If there is anything you need while Blake is gone, you be sure to come to me—although as I said, I will be gone myself for a few days. I'm sure you'll be fine here with Jonas and his wife. And I'd like to express my deepest sympathy. The loss of your parents has been felt by the entire community."

His voice broke on the last words, and he took a handkerchief to his eyes. "I will see you in a few days."

Samantha nodded and watched him ride away, heading toward the cemetery. She turned to go inside, her feelings over the man torn, her mind and heart too full of worry for Blake to even care at the moment.

Beecher did ride to the cemetery, but he did not stop at the graves of Howard and Milicant Walters to grieve. He would simply wait there until the first train headed east left Lawrence. Then he would take the next train. There was no big hurry. West would receive his telegram this morning and he would assign men to watch for Blake. By the time Beecher arrived at West's plantation, the man would probably have Blake Hastings there as a prisoner. How he looked forward to watching Blake suffer and die!

Seventeen

Blake helped stack gunny sacks full of seed for corn into a huge freight wagon inside John Hale's warehouse. The false bed of the wagon held rifles and ammunition, to be delivered to John Brown and his followers, who were determined to strike back in retaliation for the attack on Lawrence.

"You sure Brown knows what he's doing?" Blake asked Hale, stopping to take a rest.

"He's a man who will seek the proper revenge," Hale told him. "The man is a little bit crazy at times, but he knows how to stir up his followers. He'll get the job done."

Blake leaned on the wagon's tailgate. "I just hate to see any innocent people die, like Samantha's folks. I'm all for revenge, after what happened, but against the right people. One place he *should* hit is Nick West's farm in Missouri. I'd gladly shoot down West myself. Trouble is, Brown doesn't dare ride that deep into Missouri. West is well protected and he knows it. Brown will have to settle for the border. I just hope he knows who the true culprits are."

Hale, a stocky man with thick, dark hair and a burly build, folded his arms. "You having misgivings about this, Blake? You've done it before, with no qualms. That sweet new wife getting to you?"

Blake grinned. "Could be. She doesn't believe in violence, even after what happened. She's got my mind going in circles, but I needed the money this time, so I decided not to worry about what these guns will be used for. All I want to do is get them where they're supposed to go."

Hale nodded. "Pottawotamie Creek. You'll find John Brown at the south end. He has a temporary camp set up there. If you don't make it in three more days, he's going ahead with what he has. He already has weapons, but they're outdated. With these rifles he can build his own little army."

"Army? You make it sound more and more like war."

"It *is* war, Blake, and I think it's going to get a lot worse before it gets better. Eventually the whole country is going to be involved. Hell, there has even been physical violence in the United States Congress! I just read in the papers where some senator from Massachusetts was beat unconscious with a cane by a representative from South Carolina, just because the senator spoke out against slavery! He supposedly insulted the representative's uncle, another senator, but I'll lay odds the root of the ruckus was simply the high feelings for and against slavery. If our men in Congress are getting into physical battles over the issue, where does that leave the rest of the country? Several southern states are already talking secession. God only knows where it will end."

Blake thought about Samantha and the baby. "Yes. I suppose God *is* the only one who knows." He sighed deeply. "We'd better finish loading this thing so I can be on my way."

"I just wish you didn't have to do this alone," Hale

told him, picking up another sack of seed. "Too bad George can't be with you. It always helps to have a lookout and a second gun."

Blake climbed up onto the wagon and took the sack from him. "I just hope he's really in Canada. I still don't feel right about the whole thing. Keep your eyes and ears open for me, will you, especially if it concerns West and his men."

"I'll do that." Hale grunted as he turned and picked up another heavy sack into the wagon. He leaned on it, meeting Blake's eyes. "You realize, I hope, that if I get a wire that you never made it, I can't do anything about it. A lot of people suspect what I do, but no one has been able to prove it yet. If you get caught by the wrong bunch, I can't come searching for you. I'd give myself away."

Blake nodded. "I understand. You ought to get yourself out of Independence and reestablish yourself farther north. You can't hold out here much longer without big trouble."

"I'll worry about that when the time comes."

The two men finished loading the wagon, then turned to each other, grasping hands. "God go with you, Blake."

Their eyes held, both of them realizing the danger. "I'm not sure which one of us needs His protection more," Blake answered, "but I guess He's big enough to watch out for both of us."

Hale nodded. "It's got to be done, Blake. I don't like violence, either, but if that's how they're going to operate, we've got no choice. Eventually the pro-slavery faction is going to lose in Kansas. By the time the territory becomes a state, it will be a *free* state. Those of you who believe that have to hang on and keep at it."

Blake sighed, releasing his grip. "Yeah, I suppose." He turned, climbing up into the wagon. He adjusted his hat, then looked back at Hale. "I'll wire you when the job is done and I'm back in Lawrence. I'll spend a few days with my wife, then bring the wagon and team back and do a few regular runs for you. I need the work, John."

"It's here for you. It isn't easy finding drivers who'll cover the border area. Everybody is too afraid."

Blake shrugged. "People have to have their supplies, war or no war. As long as it's still a lot cheaper by wagon than by train, you'll have customers. Thanks for advancing my pay on this one. I wanted to be sure Sam got the money, in case I don't make it back."

Hale nodded and stepped back. "Good luck, Blake." He walked to the wooden sliding door to the warehouse and opened it. Blake snapped the reins and whistled, getting the team of six huge draft horses into motion. The horses and freight wagon lumbered out into the sunlight, few people paying much attention as Blake drove through town heading west, unaware of being watched by six different men from various vantage points. Nick West was one of those men. He watched from the upstairs window of a whorehouse.

Once the big wagon was out of sight, West shoved a woman from his lap and walked out onto a balcony, giving a nod to a man across the street. The man signaled others, and all went for their horses, mounting up, then waiting for their leader to join them. Moments later Nick West rode up to them, smiling victoriously. "Hang back the rest of today and tonight," he told them. "We'll let him get a good distance from civilization first."

The men nodded in agreement, and all six of them

rode out at a casual gait, following the deep wagon tracks.

"Sure as hell looks like he's carrying more than seed," one man commented.

West glanced at the tracks. "I'd like to expose Hale right here in town, but then I might not get my hands on Blake Hastings personally. It will be much more enjoyable this way. Why wait for the law to do what we can do a lot faster? Besides, if there *are* guns in that wagon, I want them for myself."

Blake stretched out beside his campfire, his rifle beside him. He was feeling more relieved on this second night. By tomorrow he would deliver the guns to John Brown at Pottawotamie Creek, and he would be free to go back to Samantha and wire Hale that the job was finished. He just hoped he could sleep with one eye open as he had last night.

Fatigue was taking its toll. He realized he should have gotten more sleep the night before he left Independence, but that was water over the dam now. He had not had a decent night's sleep since. Just one more night and he didn't have to worry about raiders. John Brown would have his guns, and Blake would drive a wagon full of seed into Lawrence, a perfectly innocent freighting job.

It bothered him a little that John Brown was considered somewhat of a fanatic, and he continued to wrestle with his conscience over what he was doing. Still, it felt good to be doing something productive, something that would make up, at least a little, for his losses. Revenge would be had, and he would have some badly needed money in his pocket, or, more to the point, in Samantha's pocket. He had wired the money ahead, not wanting to carry it on him in case he got caught.

This was for Samantha and the baby, and that made it all worth it. If he never made it through this, Sam would have some money to build a future on. He just hoped she would have sense enough to go back to New England with her brother and the baby. She'd be so much safer there, and although he had not met Drew, he did not doubt he could depend on the young man to watch after his sister. That was another consolation. Drew should arrive in Lawrence any day now.

The night was alive with singing insects, and there was no other sound in the darkness beyond the light of the fire. Once in a while one of the horses snorted and scuffled, but there was no sign of any unsavory characters lurking in the shadows. Blake lit a cigarette, taking a deep drag, wishing he hadn't eaten so much. After not eating all day, he had cooked up a pan of potatoes and salt pork. His full stomach was not going to help him stay awake. He sat up straighter, deciding he had better take the same precaution as he had with George the night they were attacked by West's men—make up a false bedroll and sleep in the wagon.

He got up, finding some brush and scooping up dirt in order to make a form under his blanket, using a small sack of corn as a pillow. When he was finished, he threw his cigarette stub into the fire and studied the fake bedroll, deciding it looked authentic. He climbed into the wagon then, shoving his rifle under the tarp that covered the seed and then scooting under it himself to sleep on top of the seed bags. It was a comfortable enough bed, although he didn't care for the stuffy air under the tarp. Still, it was better than risking being shot up in his sleep.

He thought about Samantha, struggling to allow

himself only light sleep. He prayed she was all right, was sorry he had to leave her at such a crucial time. He realized how lonely and scared she must be, but what else could he do? He thought of their last night together, how they had gently made love, how sweet and delicious and giving Samantha was. He prayed all this turmoil would be over soon, and they could finally live a peaceful, normal life.

His eyes drooped, and he took a deep breath, forcing them to open again. He decided to turn his thoughts to George, consider all the possibilities of where his friend might be, or if perhaps he never got out of Missouri. Should he leave Samantha again to try to find him? Did he dare ride onto West's plantation to see if George had ever been there? Trying to keep his thoughts running failed to stave off the much-needed sleep. Soon his eyes drooped again, this time staying closed. Again his thoughts moved to Samantha, his beautiful, gracious, brave Samantha. In the next moment those thoughts changed to dreams, as he drifted off into a deep sleep.

He would never be sure how long he slept when he jumped awake at the sound of a voice. He was lying on his stomach under the tarp, and he grasped his rifle.

"Give him a good kick," someone was saying.

"Get ready," someone close by whispered. "Don't forget the last time we sent men out to get rid of the bastard."

Blake gripped his rifle, trying to determine how many there were. He wished George was with him now. Should he just lie there, or should he jump up and start firing?

He heard the sound of several thuds. "Jesus Christ, it's a fake," someone muttered. There was a momentary silence. He heard shuffling footsteps then, realizing someone must be directing the men outside silently.

"Come on out, Hastings," someone called. He recognized Nick West's voice. "We know you're in that wagon. My men are right underneath, so you can't possibly get to them with that rifle I know you've got on you."

Blake tried to determine the direction of the voice. It seemed to be coming from the darkness straight across from the wagon. He hunkered to his elbows under the tarp, pointing his rifle. "You've got no call attacking me, West," he called out, cursing himself for falling asleep. "A lot of people know I'm out here hauling freight for John Hale. I'm on my way to Lawrence with a load of seed. You going so broke that you have to steal seed?"

"Not at all. It's not the seed I'm after. It's what's hidden under it that I want—along with your hide, of course."

"There isn't anything in here but corn, you bastard! Come and check it out for yourself, or are you too yellow to step into the light of the fire and deal with me man to man?"

Blake felt movement on the wagon then. He whipped around onto his back, throwing back the tarp and firing at the two figures that were climbing into the back of the wagon. Both men cried out and fell off the wagon. Blake whirled, getting to his knees and firing at another man who was climbing up the back of the wagon. There came a scream, followed by loud curses. Another shot rang out, and Blake felt the sting in his side, followed by a hard blow between his shoulder blades that numbed his whole body.

He felt more movement then, but could do nothing about it. Someone yanked his rifle out of his hand. "Tie his hands," he heard West ordering. Blake wondered why the man didn't just kill him and have it over with. "Get him down from there!"

Blake felt his hands being drawn behind his back and someone binding them tightly with rawhide. He was lifted, then thrown off the wagon. He landed hard on his back, which was already badly injured from the first blow. He cried out with excruciating pain, then felt a booted foot against his throat.

"Just lie there and relax my friend, while my boys go through that wagon" came West's voice.

"You dirty son of a bitch," Blake growled. "Can't you ever fight your own battles, you yellow bastard!"

"Lou, rip open that seed!" West ordered. "Spill it all on the ground! Buck, you help him, but first send those draft horses on their way! Both of you—find the guns. Use hatchets if you have to. Once you get them out of there, torch everything else!"

Blake lay helpless and seething with fury as through blurred vision he saw West's men ripping open bags of seed and scattering them everywhere, destroying everything. Several shots were fired, and he heard horses running off.

"Boss, my wrist!" one of the men said, coming closer. "The bastard nearly shot my hand off."

"What about Penny and Hal?"

"I think Penny is dead. Hal took a bullet in his upper right chest. He's hurtin' bad."

"I'll get help for you and Hal as soon as I get back. Do you think Hal will make it that far?"

"Hard to say."

"Wrap that wrist and see what you can do for Hal. We'll load Penny up onto his horse and take him back with us. I want no evidence left here. This is just another bushwhacker raid as far as the law is concerned. It will be a cold day in hell before they figure out where to look for Blake Hastings." West

331

kept his foot on Blake's throat as he talked.

"Just so I get a piece of him," the injured man answered.

"Don't worry, you'll all get your turn." West looked down at Blake. "You're in for some stiff punishment, my friend. You've killed one of my men. Fact is, you as much as admitted killing several other of my men a while back. Maybe when you were in Kansas, you could get away with that—as well as getting away with smuggling guns—but not in Missouri, Hastings. Not in Missouri! You're in *my* territory now, under my jurisdiction. Your personal little battle against slavery is over. We silenced the Walterses. Now we'll silence you—and eventually, that spunky little wife of yours."

Blake strained against him, feeling the agony of helplessness. "You keep away from Samantha!" he hissed.

West chuckled. "You aren't in much of a position to do anything about that now, are you?"

"You're scum, West! You're a murderer, a traitor, and a thief! I hope you enjoy . . . burning in hell!"

West finally removed his foot, grabbing Blake by his leather vest and jerking him up. Blake grunted with black pain. "I won't burn in hell, Hastings, because I believe God is on *our* side," he growled, keeping his face close to Blake's. "God never meant for *niggers* to be treated the same as whites, didn't you know that? We're the superior race. It's ones like you, who sell your race short, that are going to burn in hell! But I'm not going to send you there quickly, my friend! You're going to know your *own* hell right here on earth first! I'm going to pay you back for insulting me in front of all those people back in Lawrence—for all your underhanded, traitorous work to fight slavery, for calling a nigger like George

Freedom a *friend!*"

He gave Blake a shove, while the two men of his who were left uninjured began hacking away at the wagon bed.

"What do you know about George?" Blake seethed, managing to stay on his feet.

West just grinned. "You'll find out soon enough." He looked toward the wagon. "Hurry it up, boys. We've got to get out of here."

"How did you know about this?" Blake sneered. "It was Beecher, wasn't it? He's been working for you all along!"

West's eyebrows arched. "I commend you, young man, for your insight. You suspected Mr. Beecher almost from the day you met him. Strange that you were the only one. I'll bet your wife still trusts him."

Blake glowered at West, feeling sick at the mention of Samantha. What did this maniac have in mind for her? "Sam knows better now," he fumed.

"We'll see . . . in time. But not to worry for the moment. Your little woman is still safe and sound in Lawrence, for the time being. Mr. Beecher will be meeting us at the plantation."

Blake eyed the man narrowly, telling himself to be glad that he was at least not going to be killed on the spot. As long as he was alive, there was hope that somehow he could escape. He managed to turn his head to watch the ransacking of the freight wagon. His every movement brought agony because of the blow to his back and the pain burning in his side from a flesh wound.

West's men broke open the bottom of the wagon, finding the guns. Blake decided not to bother telling them that all they would have had to do was remove a few well-placed boards under the wagon to find them. He hoped they had destroyed some of the weapons with their hatchets.

"They're here, boss, just like you said," the one called Buck told him.

"Take as many as you can strap to the horses," West ordered. "They'll come in handy for our own raids. Load some of the ammunition into your saddlebags. Burn everything else once you're through."

The man with the injured wrist returned, his wrist wrapped in gauze. "Tie this off, will you?" he asked West. "I'll see what I can do for Hal."

West did as asked, and Blake looked down at his side, noticing his shirt was soaked with blood. "You'd better do something about me, or I won't be alive later for whatever you've got planned."

"I know what to do for you, mister," the injured man answered. He walked up and kicked Blake hard in his wounded side. Blake cried out and crumpled to the ground.

"What the hell do you think you're doing?" he heard West shouting. "I want him *alive!*"

"The son of a bitch nearly shot off my hand!"

"Get over there and help Hal! Lou! You get over here and wrap up Hastings's wound. Let Buck finish the packing. I'll load Penny's body onto your horse, Buck. We'll let Hastings ride Penny's horse."

"Yes, sir."

The words all sounded distant to Blake. Was he dreaming all of this? Where was Samantha? He wanted her here to take away the pain. No! She shouldn't be here! Was she really still all right in Lawrence? Where was Beecher? What was going to happen to Sam? If only he could get his hands out of their bindings. The brutal kick brought on a fierce nausea, and in the next moment he lost most of the supper he had consumed earlier.

"Jesus, boss, he went and got sick," someone nearby was saying. "Do I still have to bandage him?"

"Yes" came the terse reply. "Clean him up and douse that wound with whiskey. Wrap it good and tight. I want him alive and conscious when we reach the farm. I ought to *cut* off Jude's hand for kicking him like that. When he suffers, it's going to be at *my* hands, and at the right time."

Blake groaned as someone moved his body, apparently to get him away from his own vomit. Then another person doused him with water, forcing some into his mouth and telling him to spit. His shirt was torn open, and an ugly sting came on the wound. Blake's thoughts drifted. He wondered if Samantha was putting whiskey on his wound. After a few minutes it began to feel better, as he felt his middle being firmly wrapped. The tight gauze acted as a kind of brace for what he was sure was a cracked rib—maybe more than one.

"Sam," he muttered.

"Name's not Sam," someone close by growled. "Name's Lou. Now get up, you nigger lover. It's time to go." Blake grunted as he was helped to his feet and led to a horse. "Get on up there. Get your foot in the stirrup. I'll give you a hoist."

Blake struggled to obey, unable to grab the pommel because his hands were tied behind him. He forced himself to climb up, leaning forward as the man behind him gave him a boost. He was afraid that if he failed, he'd be hauled back tied belly-down over the saddle, a miserable way for even a healthy man to travel, let alone someone with wounds like his. He felt his chest grate against the pommel, but managed to swing his right leg over and find the other stirrup. He straightened, hoping he could remain in a sitting position without passing out.

"Use that lamp under the wagon seat there. Douse the wagon and the rest of those guns with the oil," West was ordering. "Use some of that brush from his bedroll and set it on fire from those hot coals. Throw them onto the wagon."

Blake waited in black pain, moving in and out of reality. He became more alert when flames suddenly whooshed up from the wagon, causing his horse to whinny and shuffle sideways. He nearly fell off.

"Get back," West was ordering. "What's left of the ammunition is going to blow pretty quick."

The men all mounted up. Blake saw a dead body draped over the horse ahead of him. One of the other riders looked as bad off as he did, hanging over in the saddle as though he might not make it. Blake figured it must be the man he had shot in the chest. He wished it had been Nick West.

Someone grabbed the reins to his own horse and they all rode off. A few minutes later Blake heard several explosions. He knew it was his wagon and the ammunition West had left behind. West was right. People would consider it just another bushwhacker raid, and who would know where to look for Blake? It didn't really matter, except for poor Sam. An urge to cry welled up in his soul at the thought that he might never get to see his child. West most certainly meant to kill him eventually, although God only knew what he had in mind to do to him first.

He fought back the feelings of helplessness and despair, letting fury and a stubborn refusal to admit defeat replace them. He was alive. That was all that mattered. Maybe he would at least find out the truth about George. If he was a prisoner on West's farm, maybe somehow he and George could escape together. He told himself to stay alert, not to give up. Where there was a will, there was a way. He must not think about how hopeless the situation looked at the moment. And he must not think about Samantha. He had to concentrate on the present situation, gather his thoughts.

One thing was certain. If he ever managed to get out of this, there was one man he hated more than Nick West, and that was Clyde Beecher.

Samantha sat up with a jolt, not even sure at first what had awakened her. A cry? Yes. Hadn't she heard Blake calling her name? She touched her forehead to find it was wet with perspiration. Blake! She looked around the room, realizing she was still in the safety of Loretta Hanks's room. She had only been dreaming, or had she? It seemed so real.

Her heart was still pounding, and she wondered if pregnancy made a woman have bad dreams. She threw back the covers and sat up on the edge of the bed, breathing deeply, unable to let herself go right back to sleep for fear of falling into the same dream. She wasn't even sure what it was, except that she remembered Blake's face, could still hear him calling out her name.

She got to her feet, putting a hand to her belly, thinking again how the baby was all she had now of Blake. She walked to a window and looked out into the darkness. Was Blake in trouble? Was that why she had had the dream? Was it possible for two people to be so close that when one was in trouble or in pain, the other could sense it?

"Oh, Blake, hurry up and get back here," she whispered, then moved to a bureau, where she had put the letter she had received earlier in the day—only two days after Blake had first left. He had arrived by train the same day and had already sent one of

John Hale's men back with the letter and the hundred dollars Hale had paid him in advance. Samantha realized then how dangerous Blake's task truly must be, since he had so quickly sent the money ahead.

She took out the letter, opening it and turning up an oil lamp to read it again. *My darling Sam,* he had written. *I arrived safely and all is going as planned. With any luck, I will be arriving in Lawrence with a freight wagon two or three days after you get this letter. Considering the danger of raiders, I am sending the money directly to you. Put it in the bank and use it sparingly. If I don't return, please obey my last request and return to New England with your brother Drew. Do this one thing for me, Sam, for our baby.*

I love you, Sam, more than my own life. If your brother gets there before me, stay close to him and wait for me. Trust no one else. God bless you and the baby. I miss you already. Someday this will all be over, and we'll have that peaceful little farm and lots more babies. All my love . . . Blake.

She refolded the letter, her eyes tearing. Never had she known such loneliness. The first time he had left, before they were married, she had missed him terribly, but she had had her parents to turn to. And that was before Blake Hastings had made a woman of her and she knew the beauty and ecstasy of having a man at her side who loved her and took pleasure in her. Now her parents were not here, and the tender comfort of Blake's arms had been taken from her. She had no one, no one but the precious baby. Would the child ever know its father?

She put the letter back in the drawer and went back to the window, sitting down in a wooden rocker, wondering what on earth she would do if Blake never

338

came back. What a horrible emptiness that would leave in her life. And how would she be able to even find out what had happened to him? She couldn't just up and run back East without knowing. Either way, how could she live without him? She would never love this way again, never want another man the way she had wanted Blake.

She felt the baby move, and she touched her belly again. The baby. Blake wanted it to survive and grow up in peace. She would have to take it back home with Drew like he asked. She would do it for Blake.

But when? If Blake didn't return when he claimed he would, how long should she wait for him? How was she to know what had happened to him? She closed her eyes and put her head back, rocking gently, her mind whirling with indecision. She told herself then that she didn't have to decide anything right now. Drew would be here any day, maybe even tomorrow; he would help her through this. In three days or less Blake would come driving that big freight wagon into town, and her worries would be over. Her anxiety earlier was just due to a silly dream, and possibly her pregnancy. Blake was all right. He had to be.

John Hale put down the book he was reading, thinking he had heard a noise downstairs in the back room of his store.

He got up to investigate, taking a hand gun with him. Because he knew he had many enemies, he had taken to sleeping in a room above the store in order to keep an eye on things. He held up an oil lamp, going down the stairs and searching through the store, finding nothing.

He sighed and shook his head, realizing that the

danger of the times was making him more jumpy lately. It irritated him that he had so much trouble sleeping now. He suspected his underground activities to help fight slavery were becoming too well known, and like Blake had told him two days ago, perhaps it was time to get out of Independence. If he didn't, he would die from lack of sleep.

Tonight had been another one of those restless nights. Once he reached his room upstairs he picked up his pocket watch from the stand where it lay and looked at the time. "Four A.M.," he muttered. "Wouldn't you know? In two hours I have to be up."

He suddenly realized he was bone weary. Now that he had checked downstairs and found nothing, he decided it was foolish not to get those last two hours of sleep. He had awakened at two and had been reading ever since, which had helped bring on the desired sleepiness. He set the pistol on the stand beside the bed, then turned the lamp low and crawled under the covers. He let his eyes close, breathed deeply to relax, telling himself that after tomorrow everything would be fine. He would get the telegram from Blake saying the guns had been delivered, using the special code they had devised so as not to actually mention the guns. John Brown would visit sweet revenge on some of the men who had raided Lawrence, and the proslavery people would know that the abolitionists were not going to just lie still and wait to be attacked.

Finally the much-needed sleep came over him. He did not hear the almost undetectable sound of a man climbing the stairway to his room, wearing only his stockings so that he would make no noise. The man had waited for hours, crouched behind a stack of filled potato bags in the back room of Hale's supply store. He had come into the store earlier, mixing with customers, making his way to the back room and never leaving. Hale had closed late, and the man waited until he was sure Hale was sleeping soundly.

He had already tried this once, only to reach the foot of the stairs to hear Hale cough and clear his throat. He had hurried back to his hiding place, and a few loose potatoes had fallen, causing John Hale to come downstairs to check out the noise. Hale had apparently been satisfied that it was simply a matter of gravity that had made the potatoes tumble, and he had gone back to bed.

Again the intruder had come out from his hiding place and made his way to the stairs. This time he noticed the lamp in the upper room was turned down low, and he could hear John Hale snoring. He smiled. At last he would be able to accomplish his mission for Nick West and murder John Hale in his sleep.

He crept to the top of the stairs, waiting a moment and watching Hale sleep. He came closer, taking a six-gun from his holster and approaching the bed. He reached across a snoring Hale and carefully picked up the extra pillow that lay beside the man. Quickly he pushed it over Hale's face and shoved his gun under the pillow, pulling the trigger before Hale ever knew what was happening. The pillow muffled the shot just enough that it would take people a while to realize it was a gunshot they had heard. At this hour of the morning, people didn't generally think too clearly.

He didn't remove the pillow, not caring to see the results of his heinous crime. The blood that was quickly soaking the pillow under Hale's head told him all he needed to know. He shoved his gun back into its holster and hurried back downstairs, picking up his boots and quietly leaving by the back door. He kept to the dark alleys and the shadows, and minutes

341

later he was mounting his horse, which he had left tied in a heavy stand of trees outside of town. He rode off, using the bright moonlight to head for Nick West's plantation, where he would pick up his much-deserved reward. West would be delighted to learn that John Hale was finally dead.

Eighteen

Blake was barely aware of his surroundings as he rode blindly with West and his men. Around dawn the men stopped to bury the one called Penny. The pain in Blake's back and side was close to unbearable, but he refused to wilt in the saddle, still worried he'd be thrown over it belly-down if he did.

The sunrise brought warmth, but did little to help Blake, who needed water and medical attention badly. Flies buzzed around his sweating brow, and his hands were not free to brush them away. By midmorning the pain and injuries finally overcame him and he drooped forward, then slid out of his saddle, hitting the ground hard. That was all he remembered before waking up in a bed. Someone was gently washing his face and neck, and his hands were free.

Blake opened his eyes, seeing through blurred vision a black woman bent over him. He remained calm, telling himself to think, get his bearings. What was he doing in a comfortable bed? The last he remembered, Nick West and his men had beat and shot him and were bringing him to West's plantation —most likely for further torture before killing him.

343

He realized he must be in West's home, as he looked around the finely furnished bedroom, with velvet draperies at the windows and a thick green carpet on the floor. He was lying in a four-poster, canopy bed.

"Are you feeling better, Mr. Hastings?" a woman asked him in a near whisper.

He focused his gaze on the woman again, and was struck by her beauty. She began toweling off his face and neck.

"I got you all cleaned up and put new bandages on that wound, but I don't think you even knew what was going on," she told him. "There isn't much I can do about that terrible bruise on your back. Can you move?"

Blake just stared at her, then swallowed. "I need . . . some water," he finally spoke up.

She turned and poured some from a pitcher, then put a hand under his head and helped him drink. She put back the glass, then adjusted his covers. He moved his legs and arms, trying to sit up, but the pain in his back and side were still torture.

"Just lie still," the woman told him, touching his shoulders. She leaned closer. "The longer you take to get well, the better," she whispered in his ear. "Nick just wants you to lie here long enough to make sure you'll live, just so he can torture you later."

She leaned back again, picking up a bottle of alcohol and wetting a rag with it. She began rubbing it over his chest, and Blake realized then that he was wearing only his long johns. He watched the beautiful Negro woman a moment longer, gathering his thoughts.

"You're Jesse March . . . aren't you?" he asked then.

She glanced toward the door, and when she looked back at him, he noticed for the first time the fear and hopelessness in her eyes. "Yes," she answered.

He realized now why George had been willing to risk his life for her. She was beautiful, gentle, exquisite. He closed his eyes. "My God," he groaned. "What happened to George? He came for you. I got a letter . . . said you were both in Canada."

Her eyes misted. "The letter was a fake," she said quietly. "My George is right here on this plantation, a slave again. Nick keeps him in cuffs and chains, works him like a draft horse. It's been bad for him, Mr. Hastings." A tear slipped down her cheek. "Real bad. We tried to get away . . . but Nick caught us. He had George whipped. It was terrible. George almost died."

Blake grasped her hand. "I'm going to get both of you out of here, Jesse."

She shook her head, smiling dejectedly through tears. "You don't know what you're saying," she answered. "It's impossible. You're his prisoner now. Nick will never let you leave here alive." She pulled her hand away, glancing at the door again. "There are too many of them, Mr. Hastings. This place is too big and too well protected."

She began washing him with the alcohol again. "Call me Blake," he told her. "And I will find a way. Now that George and I are here together, we'll figure something out."

She sighed, setting aside the alcohol. "I'm glad to meet you, Mr.—I mean, Blake. When George and I were trying to run away, he told me about you, said you were his best friend. I never knew a black man could call any white man a good friend. You must be a fine person, Blake, and I wish this could all be different—that we could all just be happy together. George said you had a beautiful wife, a brave lady who preaches against slavery."

345

Blake's own eyes misted at the thought of Samantha. Would he ever see her again? "Yes. Her name is Samantha. She's going to have a baby."

"I'm glad she's all right. Nick told me you two had been killed in the raid on Lawrence."

"We got out with just some minor burns."

She shook her head. "You should have stayed in Lawrence, Blake. Nick says you were hauling guns for jayhawkers."

Blake winced as he tried to move again. "I had to do something after the raid. We lost everything. Somehow I had to get back at them . . . and I needed the money. At least Sam has that."

"But it's going to cost you your life," she said softly, wiping at her eyes. "Nick is going to kill you. This is so cruel . . . letting you rest like this. Like . . . fattening up a pig for the slaughter."

"I'll think of something. I have to."

She shook her head. "It's no use, Blake. You don't know how cruel he can be."

His eyes moved over her, and he realized the hell she must have suffered these past months, tortured into submitting to a man she hated. "I think I do know," he answered. "West had my own father hanged for helping slaves. I've had more than one run-in with the man. I—"

"Well, well, you're awake and talking, I see," Nick West said, coming into the room. He gave Jesse a menacing look that made her quickly move away from the bed. "You were supposed to call me the minute he woke up, Jesse," he told her.

"I was just about to," she answered, holding up her chin.

West walked over to the bed, looking Blake over, then glancing at Jesse and back to Blake. "Beautiful, isn't she?"

Blake held his eyes, wishing he was at full physical strength. After meeting Jesse and knowing what was happening to her, and now knowing George had been tortured and held prisoner here, he hated this man more passionately than ever. "Very," he answered.

West puffed out his chest. "Now do you see the advantages of owning slaves? I am a rich man because of my slaves, Blake. They keep this place going—good workers. I buy only the best. And there's the advantage of being able to keep the beautiful ones like Jesse right here at the house, in my own bed. Women like Jesse are much better than a nagging, demanding wife. And unlike a wife, I don't have to wait until she's in the mood. Jesse never says no, do you, Jesse?" The question was asked with a sneer, and Jesse looked away.

"What's wrong, West?" Blake asked cuttingly. "Can't you find a willing woman? Or is it that . . . none of them can stand you?"

Jesse's eyes widened with fear for Blake at the cutting remark. This friend of George's knew no fear, and she felt sorry for him, knowing that Nick would never let him live. She already knew from George what a fine man Blake Hastings must be, and she knew how hard it was going to be on George to watch his friend die.

West's eyes had narrowed to tiny slits of hatred. He came closer to the bed. "You have one day, Hastings. I brought you here to stop that side from bleeding and make sure you were decently healed and alert enough to feel the full brunt of the pain I intend to inflict on you." He leaned closer. "I think a good whipping would be fitting, don't you? If you want to befriend niggers, you can just live like one for a while." He grinned, standing straight again. He looked over at Jesse. "How about it, Jess? Isn't he a handsome nigger?"

Jesse held West's eyes. It was obvious she wanted to say something derisive, but Blake could tell she had learned long ago to keep her comments to herself. She simply turned away and walked out of the room. West looked back at Blake, and out of the corner of his eye Blake saw someone else walk into the room. His rage grew deeper when he saw that it was Clyde Beecher. The man grinned as West kept talking.

"You might like to know that by now John Hale is dead." West folded his arms behind his back, looking up at the ceiling. "I have a suspicion he'll be found sometime this morning, murdered in his sleep." He looked down at Blake, feigning sadness. "Such a shame, considering how hard the man worked for abolition. But then, when one deals in such dangerous undertakings, he has to expect his life could be in danger. Of course, since Hale was most likely the only one who knew what you were up to, no one is going to know what on earth could have happened to you, are they?"

Blake felt sick at the remark. John Hale—dead! Nick West was even more evil than he had thought. Surely death was all that lay ahead for him, too.

"You murdering bastard! Why don't you just kill me and get it over with!"

West just smiled. "Enjoy the comforts," he told him. "Jesse will bring you some food. And, uh, I *will* get around to killing you, my friend, in due time. I want you to think about it for a while. You have until tomorrow morning. After that, life won't be so luxurious. And if you're wondering about your friend George, I'll be sure to bring him around tomorrow to see his old friend . . . hanging from a whipping post. Oh, and you'll have another ardent admirer there." He turned. "Mr. Beecher is looking forward to watching. I might even let him participate. I think he deserves it, don't you? After all, you did treat him rather shabbily. It seems you have a habit of insulting all the wrong people, Blake. Now we want to pay you back. After that, Beecher will head back to Lawrence to, uh, check on your wife." He chuckled, turning then to go out of the room.

"Bastard!" Blake screamed at Beecher as loudly as his strength would allow. "You leave Sam out of this! She's pregnant, Beecher! West, get back in here! Do what you want to me, but leave Sam alone! She can't do you any harm, you goddamn yellow-bellied bastard!"

Beecher clicked his tongue in mock scolding. "You've got to learn to control your temper, Blake. It's always been your downfall, you know."

The man walked out behind West. Blake heard West barking some orders, and two men came inside the bedroom to keep an eye on Blake. Blake closed his eyes, breathing deeply to stay in control and keep his head. Sam! He had to get out of here! She had asked him not to do the job for Hale. He should have listened to her! His mind reeled with a need to kill Nick West and Clyde Beecher! His insides ached at the realization that poor John Hale had been murdered. And George! He had suffered another whipping. The man's back was already a scarred mess.

Worse than all of it, if he didn't surve this, what would happen to Sam? He could only pray she was smart enough now to remember his warnings about not trusting Clyde Beecher. But the man was so clever and devious.

He had to do something! He tried to rise again,

managing to get to a sitting position. He could barely move his arms for the deep injury between his shoulder blades. He tried to get to his feet, but dizziness took over. In the next moment two men were jerking him back into the bed, making him cry out with the pain.

"Stay right in that bed, Hastings," someone growled at him, "or you'll find yourself chained."

Blake obeyed. He realized he was no good to anyone in his present condition. All he could do was lie here and pray that a little rest and food would bring him enough strength by tomorrow to do something about his predicament. Somehow he had to help George and Jesse, and he had to get back to Sam before something happened to her!

He tried to calm himself, tried to forget the pain by concentrating his thoughts on Sam—her beautiful face, the feel of her beside him, her gentle words of love. What had he done? It was all gone now, the little bit of peace they had found, the special, personal hideaway of their little bedroom, where they once thought they were safe from all outside dangers. Sam—all alone, waiting for him, carrying his baby. He never should have left her. Why had he let his hatred and need for vengeance take control of his better sense?

"Sam," he groaned. He tried not to think about the fact that Jesse was probably right. There was no way out of his present predicament. Nick West was going to kill him, and there wasn't a damn thing he could do about it.

Samantha sat on the front porch of the Hanks home, watching the street for a team of horses and a freight wagon. She knew it was really too soon to expect Blake to come, but she had no idea what his mission was. Perhaps he would get back sooner than expected.

She wore one of her new dresses, a pretty blue calico that matched her eyes. It was gathered under her breasts, which were getting fuller, and the full flow of the dress shrouded her pregnant condition. Her dark hair was drawn up at the sides, and she wore a bit of rouge, wanting to look as nice as she could for Blake's homecoming, even though she realized it probably wouldn't be for another couple of days.

People on horseback and in wagons passed busily in the street, and the air was filled with the sounds of hammers and saws. Lawrence was already rebuilding. Its stubborn citizens were not going to let the raid make them leave or give up their determination to make a stand for an abolitionist government. Just this morning Jonas Hanks had told Samantha and his family that a town meeting would be held later in the day to discuss what to do next and to draft another letter to Washington, calling for new elections.

Samantha took hope in the attitude of the townspeople. She was sure that they would eventually win this battle, and when they did, her parents would surely know about it. She could feel them near, took strength in their memory. If only Blake would come down the street now, all in one piece, she would know for certain that everything was going to be all right.

She felt the baby move and she put a hand to her belly. "Papa's coming home soon," she said softly. She watched the street, noticing a familiar figure walking toward her. Her heart quickened as he came closer, for it was as though her father had returned from the dead. She realized then that it was not her father, but her brother Drew, older, more manly than she had remembered him.

She gasped with joy and rose. How could her brother have grown and changed so much? Other than being taller and having more hair, he was a replica of their father. She realized then that it had been nearly two years since she had seen him last. He was twenty-one now. "Drew!" she called out.

Drew spotted her and walked faster, setting down his bags on the lawn and leaping up onto the porch to take her into his arms. "Sam," he said lovingly, hugging her close.

"How did you know where to find me?"

He smiled through tears. "Apparently everyone in town knows who Samantha Walters Hastings is. It was easy." He kissed her cheek and drew back, his eyes watery. "Sam, what is going on? Mom and Dad . . . and this town—half burned. My God, Sam!" He stood back and looked her over. "You look like you're all right."

"I had a few burns." She showed him her hands. "They don't hurt anymore." Her own eyes teared. "Oh, Drew, you should have just stayed at school— and yet I'm so glad you're here."

They hugged again, and she took more hope in the day. "You didn't really think I'd stay away after hearing the sad news, did you? I still can't believe it's all true." His voice broke on the words, and for several minutes they both just stood holding each other and crying.

"I'm so sorry you had to come here to this," Samantha finally told him.

He pulled away, taking a handkerchief from his pocket and wiping at his eyes. "It's all so incredible."

"Not if you know what has been going on here, Drew. We tried to keep it from you. Father just wanted you to stay in school."

352

"He should have sent you back to New England. You could have stayed with the preacher family I'm living with in Massachusetts. They would have gladly taken you in."

Samantha shook her head, leading him to the swinging bench on which she had been sitting. They both sat down. "I wouldn't have gone, Drew. I've worked just as hard as Mother and Father did on getting some fair elections and getting Kansas established as a free territory. Besides, by the time things began getting really dangerous, I had already met Blake."

Drew looked around. "Yes. He must be quite a man to capture my bull-headed sister. Where is he? I'm anxious to meet him."

Samantha took a handkerchief from a pocket of her dress. "He isn't here, Drew. I'm not at all sure where he is."

"What! He left you?"

She shook her head. "Not the way you think. It's a long story, Drew. Blake is a wonderful man—handsome, good, brave. I love him more than my own life, and he loves me just as much. But after the raid . . . it was hard on him. We lost everything, Drew, everything—clothes, home, personal possessions, money, our horses . . . everything. Blake is a proud man, a good provider. He found a chance to earn some money quickly. In fact, he's already sent me a hundred dollars."

She met her brother's eyes, her heart paining at memories of her father whenever she looked at him. "But he's into some dangerous business, Drew. He wouldn't even tell me exactly what he had to do, but I know it has to do with working for jayhawkers. He used to work for a man called John Hale—in Independence. Hale is a staunch abolitionist, and so was Blake's father. He was hanged for his beliefs."

"Hanged!" Drew turned away. "I never dreamed things were this bad out here, Sam. I mean, back in New England the papers are full of the fights going on in Congress over slavery, but my God, here it looks like people have already gone to war!"

"In a sense they have, Drew. You can see with your own eyes what happened to Lawrence. Blake, I'm afraid, is a man who is not unfamiliar with violence himself. I think he took this job as an act of revenge, and I think he's smuggling guns to jayhawkers."

Drew shook his head, rising. "He shouldn't have left you."

"He had to, Drew. Someday you'll understand it all. We were almost penniless. And when a man has so much stolen from him, he feels a need to do something about it. A lot of men in town have been talking retaliation. And it's not as though he just up and left me. He left me with a good family, and he knew you would be here any day. And like I said, he already sent the hundred dollars he was to earn for the job. I got a letter from him. According to that, he should be back in two more days."

Drew sighed, grasping a support post and turning to face her. "I guess I can understand some of it. When I think about our folks—" His eyes teared anew, and he turned away. "My God, Sam, I'll never get to see them again—talk to them again. At least you continued to be with them all this time. It's such a terrible, lonely feeling. I feel so guilty, not coming back out here last summer to see them."

Samantha rose, walking up to touch his arm. "Drew, you did exactly what they wanted you to do. They didn't want you here. They were even going to send me back, but I didn't want to go because of Blake. Later Blake and I both considered leaving, but

I didn't want to leave Mother and Father because I knew how dangerous things were getting; and we both felt we should stay in case we heard from Blake's Negro friend, George Freedom."

Drew frowned. "Negro friend? Where is he? Why did you have to wait for him?"

Samantha breathed deeply, leading him back to the bench. "Maybe I'd better start from the beginning." She sat him down, and Mrs. Hanks came out then at the sound of voices. Samantha introduced her brother, and after several minutes of conversation, Mrs. Hanks went inside to make them some tea. Samantha took her brother's hand, feeling less lonely now that he was here. She began telling him what had happened, all about Blake, including the incidents with Nick West and Blake's suspicions of Clyde Beecher.

"That's the main reason I'm worried," she told Drew. "Blake thinks Nick West was behind a lot of the raiding, and I'm afraid maybe somehow he found out what Blake was up to. Clyde Beecher left the same day as Blake, and he hasn't returned."

Mrs. Hanks brought out a tray of tea and set it on a wicker table beside the bench. Samantha put a finger to her lips, warning Drew to say nothing about their conversation until the woman had poured the tea and left again. Drew took a sip of his tea, shaking his head. "Father wrote me several times, praising Clyde Beecher as a true man of God and a great help to him. I find it hard to believe he could be a traitor."

"I have the same trouble. But Blake is a man of the world. He seems to understand people well. Until he returns, we have to remember that he could be right. We have to be careful what we say around Mr. Beecher if he should happen to come visiting. But as far as I know, he's still away. He told me he was going

355

to visit some of our supporters in the outlying areas and tell them about Father and about the raid."

Drew ran a hand through his hair. "Everything is so crazy and unbelievable. I've got to think about it all. Maybe if Blake doesn't show up, there is something I can do to try to find him."

"Oh, Drew, I wish you would! But not alone. You should find men to help you. Father was well liked here. It would be easy for you to enlist some help. It's much too dangerous out in border country now for a man alone."

Drew glanced at the doorway. "I take it you don't want to talk about Beecher in front of Mrs. Hanks?"

"No. As far as I can tell, Clyde Beecher thinks I don't believe Blake, and in a sense, I don't. But I don't want Mr. Beecher to think that I even might believe he could be a traitor or he might be more defensive around me if it's true. If he knows anything about Blake, maybe he'll slip up in some way if I continue to be friendly to him. Besides, if it's true, he could be very dangerous. He's less dangerous if he thinks I believe he's a man of God."

She sipped some of her own tea. "Listen to me. Now I'm sounding suspicious, like Blake." She looked down at her cup. "I hate what this is doing to all of us, Drew. It has taken away my happiness, separated Blake and me. No one knows who to trust anymore. Blake said once that if this whole country goes to war over the issue of slavery, brother could be fighting against brother. It's so sad, and so frightening."

She drank some more tea, and Drew watched her, thinking about how beautiful and womanly his sister had become since last he saw her. Blake Hastings had turned a little girl into a lovely woman. It was obvious she enjoyed being his wife, obvious the man was good to her.

"I never even told you you're prettier than ever," he told her aloud.

She blushed slightly, smiling. "When we were little you used to call me an ugly little pig."

"That's when you used to pester me all the time and try to steal away my toys."

They both smiled. Drew took her hand. "If you feel up to it, we'll go visit Mother and Father's graves tomorrow."

She nodded. "Yes, I'd like that. I haven't been back since the funeral five days ago." She sipped some more tea. "Sometimes it seems so unreal. I keep thinking they are going to just show up. Father was so dynamic, so brave, Drew. And Mother was so quietly supportive. It isn't fair. It just isn't fair."

Her throat ached again at the thought of it, and Drew squeezed her hand. "Are you feeling all right? It's a miracle you didn't lose your baby after that raid."

"I'm all right, thank God. This baby might be all I have left of—"

"Don't be thinking like that, Sam," he told her sternly. "At least not yet. From the things you've told me, Blake sounds like a resourceful man who handles himself real well. Give him another few days before you go to worrying yourself too much."

She breathed deeply. "The worst part is that if he doesn't show, I don't have the slightest idea where you should go looking for him."

"Well, I expect this John Hale would be the first man I should see. If Blake is missing and was doing a job for the man, Hale would surely be glad to tell me what route he took. Maybe the man would even go along with me."

"He might. Blake talked like he was a good man."

Samantha noticed Jonas Hanks coming up the street then, seeming to be in quite a hurry. She set aside her teacup and rose, putting a hand to her chest. Jonas never usually came home this time of day.

"Sam!" he called out to her, hurrying closer. Sam thought how if not for the age in his face, he would look more like a young boy approaching, his build was so slender. He came up the steps, then stared at Drew strangely.

"He looks just like Father, doesn't he?" Samantha said. "Jonas, this is my brother, Drew."

The two men shook hands, Jonas greeting Drew warmly and telling him he was welcome to stay at the house. "It will be good for Sam to have you here," he told the young man. "This has all been a terrible strain on her, especially in her condition. And now with Blake gone—"

The man moved his eyes to Samantha, and she knew something was wrong. "What is it, Jonas?"

He sighed deeply, nervously twisting his hands. "A man from the telegraph office came over to the bank today, looking for Tom Barker. Tom was at the bank seeing about a loan to replace some of the equipment he lost at his newspaper office. He's planning to get out a new edition today or tomorrow, but it won't be easy, what with the raiders destroying part of his press." Jonas's eyes showed sorrow and worry. "Well, that's beside the point. At any rate . . . Sam, that man Blake was supposed to be working for, that John Hale, he was pretty well known in Independence—suspected of doing underground work for abolitionists. Blake wasn't supposed to do something for the man that involved jayhawkers, was he?"

Samantha paled slightly, and Drew grasped her arm. "Why do you ask?" he said to Jonas.

Jonas glanced at Drew, then at Samantha. "Well, that John Hale—he was found murdered earlier today. Independence telegraphed the news here to Mr. Barker for the newspaper. I imagine they don't realize there might not even be a paper for a couple of days yet." He saw Samantha go even whiter. "I'm sorry, Sam. I just thought you should know. Apparently somebody shot Hale in the head while he slept."

Samantha felt faint. "Dear God," she muttered.

Drew led her to the bench to sit back down. "Now don't get all worked up," he told his sister. "By the time that happened, Blake would have already been on his way to make whatever shipment he was supposed to make. Just because Hale has been killed doesn't mean Blake is in danger."

"Oh, Drew, you know that it does. Oh, dear God, dear God! Anything could have happened to him. Anything!"

"You don't know yet that he won't show up here tomorrow or the next day sound as a dollar," Drew assured her. "And if he doesn't, I'll go looking for him, Sam."

Samantha wilted into her brother's arms, glad for the fact that at least Drew was here. Still, it would be little comfort if something had happened to Blake. Blake! Had he been murdered, too? Or was he perhaps lying wounded somewhere, needing her, calling for her?

She remembered her dream last night, when she thought she heard Blake calling for her. Maybe it had all been more real than she had thought. How she hated this helpless feeling! At the moment the only thing she could think of that would be worse than learning Blake was dead would be for him never to return and never to be found; to never know what had really happened to him. How could she possibly go on without him?

Blake, her handsome, loving, gentle husband, so brave and determined. Would he become another casualty of this ugly civil war? And that was what was happening no matter if Washington had officially declared the country at war. It *was* war, and Blake was involved as deeply as her parents had been, as deeply as John Hale had been. Now her parents were dead, and so was Hale. Had Blake been added to the list of casualties?

She heard the sound of a heavy wagon lumbering by, and she quickly pulled away from her brother to look, her heart leaping with anticipation, but it was only a wagon full of lumber for rebuilding a house across the street. Her heart fell, and somehow she knew Blake would not be coming today, or tomorrow or the next day. Perhaps he was never coming back at all.

Nineteen

"Let's go, Hastings," one of West's men ordered Blake, nudging him in the neck with the barrel of a rifle. "Up and at 'em."

Blake rubbed sleep from his eyes, wondering how he had managed to fall asleep at all. He had lain awake until the early morning hours worrying about Samantha, trying to decide how he could get out of this. If he was his normal physical self, he would have tried, but he still could barely move his arms. He grimaced as he sat up. "Does the criminal get to relieve himself before he's executed?" he asked sarcastically.

The man stood back. "Over there in the corner. Make it quick. West is waiting for you out in the barn."

Blake eyed the man with a great desire to kill him. He could barely get to his feet, and his back and shoulders felt on fire. He had eaten only a small amount of food the night before, and it was obvious he would get no breakfast. He half stumbled into the small room that contained a chamber pot and wash bowl. He realized then that he had slept only a few hours over the past four days, had eaten only the one small meal since his supper night before last. He had hoped there would be a window in the washroom through which he could escape, but he knew his condition would make it impossible to run or to fight anyone. His whole body screamed with pain, and he walked partially bent over because of his back injury.

He returned to the bedroom, thinking how he could bear all of this if only he knew Samantha was all right. Surely by now Drew was with her. Maybe she had even heard about John Hale's death. That would warn her to be extra careful. He walked up to his "keeper," holding the man's eyes. "You sure you want to be a part of this? West has no right doing any of this." He saw a hint of doubt in the man's eyes.

"Let's go" was the only answer.

"West is a maniac, can't you see that?" Blake asked him. "War is one thing—shooting people down in battle can be accepted. But this is different. Torturing someone for the pleasure of it is evil."

The man moved behind him, jamming the rifle barrel into his ribs. Blake grunted with pain. "Get moving," the man ordered.

Blake walked into the outer room of the elegant home, where Jesse stood waiting with another man. She wore a lovely, deep purple dress of light cotton, white lace decorating the front of the dress in one center panel. Her hair was gracefully piled on top of her head, and it was obvious Nick West had ordered her to look her best today for the "entertainment." Blake saw tears in her eyes, but she held her head proudly.

She was even more beautiful than Blake had remembered from the night before, and he thought what an ugly shame it was the way she had to live. If only she and George could be together, what a magnificent couple they would make. Jesse was obviously a proud, intelligent woman, and George certainly equalled her.

"May God be with you and end it quickly," she told him. "I'm so sorry, Blake. Nick says I have to come."

Their eyes held. "I understand," he told her. He headed out the door then, still wearing only his long johns. He was herded toward the barn, and on the way he took a quick inventory of the layout of the house and outbuildings, just in case . . . just in case he lived and escaped and had the chance to come back here. It was obvious the place was well guarded, but if a man knew the layout, and if he came at night . . . with a knife . . .

He saw Clyde Beecher standing outside the barn door then, wearing that vicious smile Blake had grown to hate. "Good morning," the man called out. "Pretty day, isn't it? The Indians would say this is a good day to die. I suppose that applies to white men, too."

Blake said nothing. He knew Beecher wanted him to shout out all sorts of obscenities, but he realized that would give the man added pleasure. Whatever was going to happen, he was not going to give them the satisfaction of his curses, nor was he going to plead with them. Just before going inside he stopped and turned, looking at the man who had brought him here. "What's your name?" he asked.

The man looked surprised at the remark. "Wilson. Ted Wilson."

Blake nodded. "Ted Wilson. I'm Blake Hastings. Sometimes it makes things different to look at a man as just another person—to know his name. You have a wife, Ted? Family?"

The man looked taken aback. "Yeah," he answered. "A wife and two kids."

Blake searched his eyes. "I have a wife, too. She's expecting. She's waiting for me right now back in Lawrence. Lost both her parents in the raid. I'm all she's got left. That should make you feel real good about what's happening here. West is real good at torturing helpless, unarmed men. It takes guts to do that, doesn't it, Ted?"

The man stiffened. "Shut up and get inside! Once your flesh is whipped raw, I'm the one who's going to take you out on the prairie and blow your head off."

Blake stared at him a moment, realizing he truly had no way out of this—no way, except for reaching whatever might be human in this man called Ted Wilson.

"Stop trying to save yourself, Hastings," Beecher told him then. "You'll soon learn it isn't smart to insult people like myself and Nick West."

Blake turned to look at him, his eyes blazing. "You're a dead man, Beecher! Even if I die today, it's too late for you. I've told too many people about you. You're going to be found out for what you really are, but the worst for you won't be here on earth. It will be after you die—when you make your report to God. He isn't going to be very happy with you using religion as a cover, is He?"

"Get the hell in that barn," Beecher sneered.

"The fires of eternal hell, Beecher," Blake taunted. "That's what lies ahead for you. I'm not afraid to die, Beecher, but *you* are, aren't you? You and West are both afraid of it!"

Beecher drew in his breath, grasping the gun from Ted Wilson and ramming th butt of the rifle into Blake's lower back. Blake stumbled forward with a grunt, unable to put out his hands to stop his fall because of his stiff arms. "Now get him inside," he heard Beecher growling.

"Let's go, Hastings" came Ted's voice. The man jerked him up, and Blake cried out with the pain in his shoulders, now enhanced by a second blow to his back. For a moment everything seemed blurry as he was led inside the barn. He could smell animal manure, felt hay and soft dirt under his feet. Then came the most excruciating pain of all. Men pulled his arms over his head, a movement that made him scream almost constantly for several minutes while they tied his wrists securely and left him hanging from a beam, his toes barely touching the floor. Because of the injury to his upper back, the position was agony.

He told himself he had to get through this. Maybe, just maybe, West didn't intend to kill him. He could stand whatever lay ahead as long as he was left alive, for as long as he was left alive, there was a chance of escaping and getting back to Sam. He had to think about Sam, only Sam.

He shivered from pain, opening his eyes to see Jesse standing off to the side, a man on either side of her. Nick West and Clyde Beecher both stood in front of him, and to his left he saw George, in leg irons, cuffs on his wrists. He wore only cotton pants, and even from the front Blake could see traces of newer whip marks at the tops of his shoulders and around the front of his ribs. He stood silent, his eyes teared.

"George," Blake muttered.

George just shook his head, then looked down.

"We told George this morning that his good friend had finally come," West spoke up. He puffed on a thin cigar, walking up to George. "Go ahead, George. You have something to say?"

George looked back up at Blake. He swallowed before speaking. "How did you get here? You ought to be back in Lawrence with Sam," he said, his voice shaking.

"Didn't West tell you," Blake grimaced. "Most of Lawrence was burned. Sam's folks are dead, and we lost everything." He gritted his teeth against the pain. "I took a job for John Hale . . . needed the money. When that was done, I was going to come here . . . see if West had you. I suspected your letter was fake. I'm sorry, George . . . sorry I didn't act on my suspicions sooner."

George looked him over as though this was the last time he would see him alive. "It wouldn't have mattered. If you'd come here looking for me, you'd have ended up right where you are now."

West grinned. "There, you see," he asked, stepping closer to Blake then. "George understands. He knows it's useless to go up against a man like me. He learned the hard way, and now you will, too. I thought it only fitting that George get to watch." He took the cigar from his mouth, pressing it out against Blake's left armpit. Blake grunted and stiffened, but refused to cry out. Never had he known such hatred.

George looked away, feeling sick at what would happen to his friend. He knew the feel of the whip. He glanced over at Jesse, who looked at him only for a moment, her eyes full of love and sadness. She dropped her eyes, and George knew she was afraid to let her eyes linger on him for too long.

"Get those bandages off him," West was saying to one of his men, who walked up to Blake and took out a knife, quickly ripping off the gauze that was wrapped around Blake's middle. Blake wondered if perhaps he was already in so much pain that he wouldn't feel the whipping quite as much. One thing he knew for certain—men didn't usually die from whippings. Was that all West had in mind for him? Was Wilson just taunting him when he said he was supposed to shoot him? He swore with all the fury that welled inside him that if he lived through this, he would find a way out of here, and Nick West and Clyde Beecher would pay dearly!

West handed a whip to Beecher, who curled it up in his hand, stepping closer to Blake. "Some last thoughts for you to contemplate before you pass out," he told Blake. "When we're through with you, you'll be taken someplace far away and shot. No one will ever be able to link your death to Nick or this farm. Your friend, George, will remain here in Nick's employ." He grinned then. "And I will return to Lawrence . . . and to your lovely wife."

Blake gritted his teeth, jerking at the ropes that bound him, pain searing through him with every movement. "Sam can't do any harm to your damn proslavery movement," he growled. "Her father is the one who needed to be silenced, and you've done that! There are plenty of other people working a lot harder now for abolition than Sam. Leave her alone! She's going to have a baby!"

Beecher rubbed at a pockmarked cheek. "Well, you see, the law governing Kansas makes no exceptions for women, not even pregnant women. A traitor is a traitor, and there is no doubt that Samantha has participated in traitorous activities. Of course, it would be dangerous to try to have her arrested in Lawrence—too many supportive friends there. I'll have to find a way to get her out of town first, but that shouldn't be too difficult. She still trusts me. I think it's time all you traitors suffered some kind of punishment, don't you?" He frowned. "Oh, but jail can be such an awful place for a woman, can't it— thrown in with prostitutes and all sorts of lowlifes."

In blind rage Blake kicked out unexpectedly,

catching Beecher between the legs. The man doubled over, and instantly West was there to grab the whip out of Beecher's hand, ordering two of his men to get Beecher out of the way. He landed a hard fist several times against the wound in Blake's side that Jesse had so carefully dressed the day before, and it started bleeding again. Blake could not keep from crying out, and George started forward but was shoved back by the two men who guarded him. "Watch it, nigger, or West will open up your back again," they warned.

"That should take the devil out of you," West was growling at Blake. He stepped back, taking a handkerchief from a pocket of the silk jacket he had worn for the occasion and wiping Blake's blood from his fist. "Apparently I'll have to take my round first. As soon as Beecher is able to stand, he'll finish, and I daresay he'll be twice as vicious after that kick. That was pretty stupid, Blake!"

"What's the difference?" Blake answered, panting from agony. "You're going to kill me anyway."

"That's right. It's just that in your particular case, I wanted the luxury of watching you suffer first—and of letting your good friend George watch, so he knows what happens to white niggers who try to help him."

West moved around behind Blake, and Blake glanced at Ted Wilson. The man looked away, shuffling his feet nervously, and Blake knew he was not fully in favor of what was happening. But he was only one man, and it was certain he was not brave enough to try to stop the others. Blake moved his eyes to George then, his jaw flexing with pain and anger.

"Keep your faith, George," he told him. "Someday there will be no more slavery, and you and Jesse will both be free."

George raised his chin, managing to give Blake a

supportive smile, although tears were running down his cheeks. Blake heard the first lash then, felt the metal tip of the whip tear into his back. The second one wrapped around him, biting into his wound. With each snap his body jerked, but he refused to utter a sound. He just kept his eyes on George.

Yes, now he knew what this was like. Now he was in George's shoes. Now he knew why, if he ever survived this, he would continue the fight against slavery, even if it meant going to war. By the time West handed the whip over to Beecher, Blake had completely lost count of how many times its sting had cut into his flesh. He could feel blood running down into his long johns, soaking them at the hips. Was there any skin left for Beecher? Not that the man would care.

"You bastard!" Beecher growled, wielding the whip, bringing new pain when he lashed it around Blake's legs, opening brand-new ribbons of blood. A blessed unconsciousness soon overcame Blake. He did not hear George's sobs, or hear Jesse cry out for Beecher to stop. West ordered Jesse back to the house. "Take George back out to the fields," he told the men who watched over George. Finally he ordered Beecher to stop and had Blake cut down. He turned to Ted Wilson.

"Load him up in a wagon," he ordered the man. "Cover him up good so nobody knows he's back there. Drive him far from here, preferably across the border. Dump him off in Kansas and put a bullet in his head. People will chalk it up to a bushwhacker raid, but they'll never know he's been here. Just make sure he's dead."

"He'll be dead from the whipping," Beecher sneered, limping around Blake's prone body to get a good last look. "Wilson won't have to shoot him," he said with a delighted grin. "He's already lost enough blood to kill a man."

"When it comes to Blake Hastings, I want to be sure," West answered. "He's too goddamn stubborn."

Several men hauled Blake's body to a straw-filled wagon, throwing it into the back of it. They covered him with more straw, dirt, and even pieces of manure filtering through into Blake's cuts. Wilson loaded his rifle into the wagon, then hitched two horses to the front of it. He climbed up into the seat.

"You know what to do," West told him.

"Yes, sir, I know what to do."

West nodded, lighting another cigar. "You're a good man, Wilson. Report back here when it's done, and you'll have a nice bundle of money waiting for you. You can buy the wife and kids anything they need. Just don't tell them how you got the money. What they don't know won't hurt them, but what they do know *could* hurt them. You remember that, and remember . . . this isn't personal. It's war, Wilson, war, and people like Blake Hastings are the enemy." He slapped the rump of one of the horses, and the animal bolted forward, taking the second horse with it. Wilson kept hold of the reins and snapped them, and the wagon clattered out of the barn into the open.

Outside George stopped walking to turn and watch the wagon. He knew Blake was in it, knew he was riding to his death. He sniffed and wiped at tears with his forearms, his wrists still bound. In that wagon was his last hope of being found and helped. More than that, in that wagon was the best friend he would ever have. Blake's father had given his life for abolition. Now Blake would follow in the man's footsteps, just as Samantha would surely follow her parents' road to defeat.

He stared at the house a moment. Jesse was there, but how long would it be before West sold her and he completely lost track of her again? She had looked so beautiful this morning, yet so pitiful. Only a dog like West would make her stand and watch what had been done to Blake. He remembered the shame and agony of his own whipping, that Jesse had been forced to witness that, too. But there had been a look in her eyes that day, a look that had given George strength. It told him that men like Nick West might be able to beat and destroy the body, but he could not destroy soul and spirit. George had tried to instill that same thought into Blake as their eyes held while Blake was whipped. One spirit that would not be defeated was the spirit of freedom. Men like West only made that spirit stronger in the souls of his people and those who risked their lives to help them.

One of the men with him uncuffed George's wrists then. "Get back to work, nigger," he told him.

George bent down and picked up a hoe, looking again in the direction of the wagon, but it was out of sight.

Ted Wilson drove the wagon for several miles, nervous about the bleeding body of the helpless man lying under the hay in the wagon bed. He had done a lot of things for Nick West, and had been paid well. But he had never shot a man in cold blood. Lately he had been having second thoughts about some of the things that were going on, and the look in Blake Hastings's eyes that morning, the man's remarks about having a wife and a baby on the way, had not helped his quandary.

Wilson's wife knew he was involved in bushwhacker activities, and she was against such violence. All Wilson had done so far was ride in bushwhacker raids, helping destroy the crops and homes of abolitionists. It had seemed right, at the time. After all, it would be disaster to free all slaves, wouldn't it? Negroes didn't know how to live without being owned, without everything being provided for them. They had no education, no way to survive on their own. They would surely turn into thieves and murderers and rapists. At least that was what men like Nick West preached.

Still, Wilson's own wife had befriended a few Negroes, and she said they were some of the finest people she knew. Jesse March certainly seemed like an intelligent, gracious lady, in spite of the way Nick West used her. And he couldn't forget the genuine care and sorrow in George Freedom's eyes as he watched Blake Hasting being whipped. The look both men had exchanged spoke of deep friendship, deep respect.

He headed the team up a hill, stopping at the top of it and taking inventory of the horizon beyond. He was in open country now, not likely to run across anyone who knew him—anyone at all for that matter. It was only three or four miles to the border. A little way beyond that he would dump the body.

He got the team into motion again, inwardly praying that when he reached the right spot, Blake Hasting would already be dead. That way he could absolve himself of having anything to do with his death, even though he still felt partly responsible simply by not giving aid to the man. But he didn't dare do that. If he did, and Blake survived, his own family would suffer the wrath of Nick West.

Indecision gripped him as he neared the border. He drove the wagon through a stream, and it bounced and jolted over some rocks and up the opposite bank. He heard a groan from under the hay, and his stomach turned at the sound. He drove the wagon harder then, anxious to get this over with, disappointed that Hastings still lived.

He reached a grove of cottonwood trees, halting the wagon and climbing down. He came around behind the wagon and lowered the gate, reaching out to grasp Blake's ankles. He took a deep breath and pulled, hearing another groan. He noticed with a shiver that sliding the body had left a trail of blood along the bottom of the wagon. He brushed away some of the hay and grimaced as he grasped Blake under the arms, feeling ill at the feel of open flesh and warm blood on his hands. He pulled then, quickly stepping back and letting Blake's body fall face forward to the ground.

He looked at his hands, covered with blood, then ran to a nearby stream to wash them off. When he returned, Blake still lay where he had left him, looking lifeless. It seemed to Ted that it was very unlikely Blake would live out the day. He certainly was not going to get any help out here, and before long his wounds would be infected from the dirty hay.

He climbed up onto the wagon and rearranged the hay that had not fallen out with Blake's body, scattering it around so that the blood did not show. He decided that if anyone did notice it, he would tell them it was from a slaughtered cow he had delivered. He climbed over the seat and picked up his rifle. His instructions had been to shoot Blake Hastings if he was still alive when the body was dumped. He got down from the wagon and walked to the back of it again, cocking the rifle and pointing it at Blake's head.

He noticed Blake's hands go into fists, his body beginning to twitch from pain. Flies were beginning to land on the open wounds. The sun was hot, and Blake had lost considerable blood. "The hell with it," Wilson muttered. "You're as much as dead, Hastings. I'm not going to have this on my conscience." He gently released the hammer of the rifle, climbing back into the wagon and driving off, leaving Blake's nearly lifeless body to lie in the hot sun, the manure in the hay and Blake's own blood attracting even more flies. There remained only the sound of locusts and buzzing flies, and an occasional agonizing groan.

In spite of the hot day, a chill swept through Samantha as she and Drew stood over their parents' graves. Again she suddenly felt the sensation that Blake needed her. She looked across the eastern horizon, more worried, praying that by some miracle he would show up today. She was haunted by John Hale's murder. Whoever killed him might easily have known about Blake's shipment.

"I still can't believe it," she said aloud, kneeling beside the graves. "I can still hear Father preaching, still see Mother sitting in the front pew listening proudly, smell her pies baking on Sundays."

Drew stared in tears, taking a handkerchief from his pocket. "I'm just so sorry we never got to talk again, sorry I didn't come out sooner."

Samantha rose, touching his arm. "Drew, we've been over that. You were doing what they wanted you to do. Father left that special fund back East for you to use to finish your schooling, and you must do it— for him."

He nodded. "I know." He blew his nose and wiped

374

at his eyes. "But I'm not going back until you find out if Blake is all right—and not until after the baby is born. If we don't know anything about your husband by then, you're coming back with me, Sam, and I won't have any arguments. I won't leave you out here alone. Blake would understand. He would know where to look for you if you left Lawrence."

Samantha turned away. "He's got to come back, Drew. I can't even begin to imagine what I'll do if he doesn't." She walked a few feet past the graves. "I'm worried. I have that feeling again, like Blake is calling for me. If he doesn't return today, you've got to gather some men and try to find him." She turned to face him, her eyes pleading. "You could start in Independence, like you said the other day. Find some people who worked for John Hale. See if any of them know about Blake taking out a shipment for him and what route he might have taken."

"I'll do whatever you want, Sam. But I won't know where to even begin to look if nobody in Independence knows anything. Hale might have been the only one who knew, and now he's silenced forever. It does make me wonder about Blake."

Samantha's chest felt tight with dread. "If you can't find anyone who knows anything, there is one place you must check, Drew; but you'd have to be so careful."

"Nick West?"

She came closer again. "He's a dangerous man, Drew, very dangerous. Don't go there without plenty of men, plenty of witnesses. And while you're there, ask about a Negro man named George Freedom. Try to talk to the other slaves if you get a chance. They're the only ones who would tell you the truth, if they aren't too afraid. George is a very big man, tall and broad and powerful, and quite handsome. Some of the men around here would know him if they saw him. If he's there, Drew, use your knowledge of the law to get him out. He's legally a free man. I just pray to God he's really in Canada with Jesse like his letter said."

Drew breathed deeply, feeling the sudden new weight of possible bloodshed on his shoulders. "Well, I expect most people in Independence would know where this Nick West's plantation is, seeing how wealthy and important he's supposed to be." He removed his hat and ran a hand through his hair, which was damp from perspiration. "Sam, you've got to face the fact that I might not come up with anything."

Their eyes held. "I know," she answered. "But we at least have to try. You keep in touch with me by telegraph and I'll let you know if Blake has shown up here."

He nodded. "Maybe he'll come riding in today."

Oh, how she wanted to believe that! But intuition was plaguing her. If only she hadn't had the dream. If only she didn't have this tense feeling today that Blake was again calling for her.

"He has to," she answered, looking almost like a little girl.

Drew came closer, drawing her into his arms. "He will, Sam. I'll just bet he'll show up today and I won't need to get up a search party at all."

"Oh, Drew, everything is so different, so changed," she said, resting her head against his chest. "Blake and I were so happy. With him gone, it's like part of me has died. I've lost too much too quickly."

"You've still got the baby. That's the important thing. No matter what has happened to Blake, you're carrying his child, and nothing can change that, nothing can take that baby from you. It's a gift from

Blake, a part of him you'll always have."

She closed her eyes, shivering again as a hawk flew overhead, giving out a mournful call. It seemed to be reflecting Blake's voice, calling her name.

Blake was only vaguely aware that he was lying in the hot sun. Something kept biting at him, but he couldn't move his arms to get it away. His pain was so deep that he was more numb than in agony, and his nostrils were filled with the smell of hay and manure . . . and something else, something he could not name at first.

Blood, he thought. That was what he smelled. Blood and raw flesh . . . his own. He knew that he was dying, and part of him wanted to just go ahead and relinquish this life, give it up and slip off into the bliss of death. But something deeper stirred in him, something that kept the pulse of life surging through him. That something was bitter rage, and the distant knowledge that Sam needed him.

He tried to move, and that was when he became more aware of just how badly hurt he was. Just one small movement brought a rush of pain, and it seemed that hundreds of flies buzzed in his ears. Flies! Were they all landing on him? Was that the biting he felt? Were they eating at his flesh like that of a dying animal?

"God help me," he groaned, thinking what a hideous way this was to die. By the time he was found, he would be so bloated and unrecognizable, no one would even know who he was. And Sam . . . Sam would never know what had happened to him.

Apparently West had ordered him dumped someplace remote. He remembered now, remembered West telling him he'd be taken far from his plantation after the whipping. He groped through his memory for the details. Yes. West had said he would be shot. That man, Ted Wilson, was supposed to do it.

Shot. So why was he lying here still alive? Was someone still coming to do him in?

He heard voices then, horses. Had West brought him here to torture him even more before he was killed? The horses came closer, but he couldn't move to turn and look to see who it was. He could hear men talking a strange language he had never heard before. Now he could see the legs of the horses, saw the legs and feet of men who dismounted. They wore buckskins, moccasins, and they continued to converse in a strange language.

Indians? He had never had much experience with Indians. There were few left in Missouri. Occasionally a few Pawnee came into northern Kansas from Nebraska to hunt buffalo. Was that who these Indians were? The Pawnee could not always be trusted. They had done some raiding, and he knew the government was trying to negotiate a treaty with them.

Someone brushed at the hay around him, knocking flies away. Blake groaned, too weak and in too much pain to try to explain. If these Indians were here to kill him, he hoped they would do it quickly. Someone close by him sounded as though he was giving orders, although Blake could not understand him. He heard others running about, talking rapidly.

"What are you called?" the one kneeling close asked him in English.

Blake swallowed. "Water" was the only answer he gave. His thirst was agonizing because of the loss of blood. The one close by shifted slightly, and in the next moment some cool water trickled over his mouth. He stuck out his tongue and gobbled some down his throat.

"Not too much just yet," the one near him said. "We will talk later."

Blake moaned with black pain then as several hands grasped his legs and arms and moved him onto a stretcherlike device. Someone poured water over his back and legs, then draped cotton cloth over him to keep the flies off his wounds.

"We will let the women clean him properly back at camp," the one who spoke English told someone else. "When he can speak, we will find out who he is." There was a hesitation. "Only white men would do something like this to his own kind." He barked another order in his own tongue, and Blake felt himself being tied securely onto the stretcher. One end was lifted so that his head was raised, and moments later the contraption bounced and jolted over the ground, every movement bringing agony to Blake. He wondered if these wild people meant to help him, or hurt him.

Twenty

Samantha walked up the steps of the Presbyterian church, where she often went to pray now that her own church lay in ashes. All day she had felt watched, and she turned to look behind her, but she saw no one suspicious.

She entered the church and closed the door, walking to the altar and kneeling there to pray for Blake. She also prayed for Drew, who had gathered several men to investigate Blake's disappearance.

God had to protect Drew. If she lost him, too . . . She sighed, touching her belly, reminding herself she had the baby . . . the baby—not only a part of Blake, but even a part of her parents. She looked up at the cross that hung at the front of the church. Surely God wouldn't have let Blake die, but there had been more news that made her wonder, if he wasn't dead, was he involved in something so heinous that he couldn't or wouldn't come back to her?

She shivered at the news Jonas Hanks had brought home this morning. The violent abolitionist John Brown had attacked the homes of suspected pro-slavery families along Pottawotamie Creek. Five men had been dragged from their beds and brutally murdered. In spite of what had happened at Lawrence and to her parents, it didn't seem right. What good did all that violence do, except to spawn even more bloodshed? Setting a home on fire just didn't seem as devious as dragging a man from his home and hacking him up in front of his terrified family. Surely Blake couldn't have been a part of that massacre!

That became her first prayer. Was there a side of him she didn't understand? Would his need for revenge make him do such a thing, without even being certain that the men involved were indeed part of the group that had raided Lawrence? It seemed the whole world had gone crazy. Even men in Congress were becoming physically violent. What hope was there for the entire country, let alone Kansas, if those who were supposed to be in charge could not agree on the issues?

She bowed her head, praying fervently that Blake had not been with John Brown, that there was some simple reason he had not returned. Maybe it was just a longer journey than he had anticipated. She prayed he was not hurt, or dead, yet John Hale's death and John Brown's raid kept moving in to undermine her faith. Was there a connection? And if there was, where did that leave Blake? Had Hale been working with or for Brown, perhaps supplying him with weapons? If Blake was the deliveryman, had he remained with Brown to take part in the bloody raids?

She looked up at the cross. "I hardly know what to pray for," she said quietly. "There is so much. I want You to protect Kansas . . . Lawrence. I want You to help us all find the road to peace. I want You to please help and protect my brother and bring him back safely, with good news about Blake. Most of all I want Blake to come home, safe and sound. I want to know he didn't take part in those awful murders. Mostly, I just want him to be alive."

She closed her eyes, resting her elbows on the kneeling rail. "It all seems like too much to ask, even from you, Lord Jesus. I suppose we must be ready to die, if it means helping stop this ugly sin of slavery. But Lord, You brought Blake to me, let me love him. You allowed our union, allowed his seed to grow inside of me. Surely you didn't mean to take him from me so quickly."

"Samantha!"

Samantha jumped, startled at hearing her name shouted. She turned to look toward the doorway to see Clyde Beecher coming toward her. "Mr. Beecher!" she exclaimed, rising.

The man hurried closer. "I heard you might be here. You've got to come with me, Sam, right away! It's Blake!"

Samantha's chest tightened at the words. "What's wrong? Where is he?"

"He's at a settler's house just outside of town. He's been hurt bad, Sam. I was visiting these people, on my way back from riding the circuit, when some of John Brown's men brought him there and left him off."

"John Brown!" Samantha felt almost sick with alarm. "Mr. Beecher, did Blake take part in that awful massacre?"

"I'm not sure, but he must have. All I know is that he's badly hurt and calling for you."

Samantha thought about her dreams, the sensations she had experienced that Blake needed her. Suddenly it didn't matter if he did take part in the raid. At least he was alive! But for how long?

"I'll go and tell Mrs. Hanks right away. We can use

their buggy—"

"There's no time for that, Sam, and I already have my own buggy. We'll be lucky if he's still alive when we get back. Please, Sam, if you want to see your husband at all before he . . . before he departs this world, you'd better come with me now. I can come back and explain to the Hanks family after I leave you with him."

Her eyes teared. "Oh, my God. Is it that bad?"

The man's eyes filled with what seemed true sorrow. "I'm afraid it is. Just come with me now. I've already sent for the doctor."

A tiny alarm sounded in Samantha's brain. Blake had told her never to trust this man—never to be alone with him. But in her confused and lonely state, just one small flicker of hope that Blake could be alive was all she needed. And she had never been able to fully believe that Mr. Beecher could be the villain Blake thought he was. He looked so worried and concerned right now. And how kind of him to come and get her right away!

"Let's go then," she said, rushing past him to the door. She did not see the relieved smile on Beecher's face. He hurried behind her, glad that at this particular time of morning there was no one close by the area to see him helping Samantha into his carriage and riding off with her. He had followed her here, finally catching her alone. He quickly took a back street out of town, feeling more jubilant at every moment.

Beecher drove the buggy for nearly two miles before the alarm in Samantha's brain began to sound louder. This was a deserted, rarely used road, an original route east that had been replaced by a better road not long ago. They drove past several farms, stopping at none of them. "How soon will we be there?" she asked, fighting a building panic, beginning to hope beyond hope that Beecher was telling her the truth.

"Just another half mile or so," he told her.

"How . . . what happened? Was he shot? Stabbed? Beaten?"

"Gut shot—the worst way to die," Beecher told her. "Thank God I found you in that church. If you were praying to find him, then our prayers are answered. But I'm afraid if you were praying for his life, I'm not sure the Lord can give that to you."

Again he sounded sincere. Beecher's closeness was beginning to bring her an uneasy feeling. They drove for what she was sure was another half mile, but she saw no house in sight. Suddenly Beecher turned the buggy, heading down an embankment, where Samantha saw an enclosed coach waiting, three men lounging near it. One stood up and waved to Beecher as though expecting him.

"What . . . what's going on?" Samantha asked. "Who are those men? Where is Blake?"

Beecher reached the coach, then wrapped his arm around Samantha, nuzzling her neck. "Blake is dead," he said coldly.

Samantha jerked away from him, her mind spinning with the horrible statement, feeling a mixture of horror at the news and from the currently more pressing issue of getting away from Clyde Beecher. She turned to meet his eyes, seeing for the first time what Blake had seen months ago, the eye of an evil man, a traitor, probably a murderer. She slapped him hard, jumping down off the buggy, but in the next moment two of the other men had grabbed her. She screamed as one of them forced her arms behind her, and she felt handcuffs being fastened securely and painfully around her wrists.

"What are you doing?" she screamed. "Where am I going?"

Beecher jerked her around. "To prison, my sweet Samantha, where all traitors belong." He moved one hand to rub it over her breasts and stomach. "Maybe your little baby will be born there."

Her eyes widened, and she suddenly spit in his face. "*Spy!*" she screamed. "You're a hypocrite and a spy, and you're going to burn in hell, Clyde Beecher!"

She felt the blow then. It sent her reeling sideways. Beecher jerked her up and hit her again, several times, before one of the other men pulled him off. "Put a gag on her and get her in the coach," the man ordered one of the others. He turned to Beecher. "It's about time you got here! We've been here three days already!"

"I couldn't get her alone until today. And I get a turn at her first," Beecher growled. "You boys just go find something to do until I'm through with her!"

"No!" One of them was helping Samantha to her feet. He stuffed a handkerchief into her mouth, then began tying a bandanna around her mouth tightly, drawing back her lips painfully. "The boss didn't say anything about raping her," the man shouted to Beecher. "I'm all for putting an abolitionist in jail, but I'm not going to let you rape a pregnant woman, for God's sake!"

"It's my business,' Beecher roared. "I'm the one who set this up! I'm to have full authority! She's a nigger lover! She doesn't deserve any better!"

The man pulled a pistol and pointed it at Beecher. "It's one thing raping a slave woman," he barked. "But not a pregnant *white* woman, even if she *is* an abolitionist! The boss said that judge in Independence is already wary enough of doing this. She's well known in Lawrence, and this whole thing could backfire, especially if she's raped! It's going to be bad enough that you put bruises on her! She's just supposed to spend some time in prison to be taught a lesson!"

Beecher stepped closer, and the man cocked the pistol. "I've got orders to do you in if you threaten to mess this up, Beecher. You know what will happen to you if you spill the wrong name or do something that will keep the woman from going to jail."

Samantha watched in horror, hardly able to believe what was happening before her eyes. Would these men shoot Clyde Beecher right in front of her? Who were they? Who was the "boss"? Nick West, perhaps? And Blake! Beecher claimed he was dead. Was it true? Blake! No, not Blake!

Her eyes swam with tears, and a piece of the handkerchief began to get caught in her throat as sobs welled up from deep inside so that she thought she might vomit. She wanted to scream, needed to scream. But she could only make muffled little squeals.

"You just go on back to Lawrence," the man with the gun was telling Beecher. "Anybody see you ride out with her?"

"No," Beecher answered, looking frightened now.

"Good. You go back like nothing is wrong. You'd better go see whoever she was staying with, pretend to be checking on her. You show concern just like everybody else when she turns up missing. It will be a cold day in hell before she's found clear over in Independence. Now get going. Everything has worked out the way the boss planned it."

Beecher glowered at the man, shifting his dark eyes to Samantha for a moment, looking her over hungrily. He looked back at the man with the gun. "What's the difference if she's found raped and shot?

387

People will just think it's another bushwhacker attack."

"And right afterward you just happen to show up in Lawrence," the other man sneered. "We'll do this the way the boss said, Beecher. You know he doesn't like to be crossed. If she's found raped and killed, half of Kansas will be scouring around to find out who did it. That could lead people to the wrong places. She's too well known and too well liked. Now get the hell back to Lawrence! You've got a few people to hand over before the boss is through. Then you can skip town before the woman is released. You've got a good six months. Do this right, and you know you'll be paid well like always. Mess it up, and you'll die like any other man who crosses the boss!"

Beecher shifted, brushing at his dark suit jacket. "You just make damn sure she's put in jail for a good six months! I don't need her coming back before I'm finished!"

The other man lowered his gun. "Get going then."

Beecher turned, climbing into the buggy. He looked once more at Samantha. "Enjoy your stay in prison, Miss High and Mighty! More than likely your baby will *die* there! Maybe even *you* will die! Then you can join your loved ones in that heaven you believe in! Either way I will have left Lawrence by then, a rich man, I might add. My work is just about finished here."

He turned the carriage, and Samantha stared after him. Was this all some kind of unholy nightmare? One moment she had been praying peacefully in a church, and now she was bound and gagged and being taken off to prison! Her face felt hot as fire from Beecher's blows, and the realization that Blake had been more than right about the man left her in near shock.

Clyde Beecher! All these months he had been her father's right-hand man! How glad she was that Blake had not allowed him to speak over her father's grave! He had been right all along.

Blake! How could he really be dead? It must be true. Beecher had said it, and so had these men. If it was true, what hope did she have of ever being found and helped? They were taking her to jail, to a place no one would think to look for her! Did they really intend for her to have her baby there?

The man brandishing the gun grasped her arm painfully and led her to the coach, helping her inside. She tripped on the hem of her now-soiled yellow gingham dress and half fell into the coach. The man helped her up and plunked her into a seat.

"Now you just sit there and try to relax," he told her. "I don't want you going into labor on me." He sat down across from her and closed the door, pulling down all the shades so that no one could see inside. After a moment her eyes adjusted, and she could see his face again. The man had kept Beecher from raping her. She didn't know whether to thank him or spit on him.

She felt the coach rock as the other men climbed aboard, and suddenly they were off. To Independence? That was what the men had said. She wondered who had ordered all of this, who owned the coach. It was quite fancy, and at least comfortable. But what difference did it make, considering where she was going? And who would ever find her? With Blake dead . . .

No! She could not believe it! The thought of it overwhelmed her, taking precedence over her current predicament, over the shock of finding out the truth about Clyde Beecher, over the trauma of Beecher's blows and threats. Blake was dead! It didn't matter so much that he could not come and help her. It only mattered that he was gone, that she would never see her precious husband again, never be held in his arms, never lie beside him in the night. The baby inside her would never know his or her daddy.

She felt suddenly dizzy, little realizing how vicious Beecher's blows had been, for she had been too stunned by what was happening around her. One ear began to ring loudly, and the next thing she knew everything was going black. She felt herself slipping off the seat, felt someone grab her.

Samantha awoke to the gentle rocking of the coach. She lay still for a moment, opening her eyes to let them adjust to the dim light provided by a small shaft of sunlight through the edge of one of the curtains. She realized then that her seat had been folded back so that she could lie down. The man who had forced her into the coach sat across from her, dozing lightly.

She raised her head just a little, wincing at the pain the movement brought her. She worked her jaw slightly, realizing her guard had removed her gag. She could tell the left side of her face was swollen. Her left ear pained her and her lower lip stung from a cut. She licked at the cut, tasting old blood.

So, she thought, this was no nightmare. This was real. Beecher had offered her up to the enemy like Judas. She was being taken off to prison for being a traitor, but not to a proper prison in Kansas. She was being taken to Missouri, to a judge who had no doubt been bribed to put her away, probably without even so much as a trial. Most likely, she was to be kept there until she broke, until she swore to never again work for the abolitionist movement. Her baby would

ikely be born there, and probably die there. What
aby could live in prison conditions?

Who was there to find her? Drew would never
now where to search. Only Blake might piece it
ogether, might suspect Clyde Beecher and get the
ruth out of him. But Blake was dead. Dead! It was
till difficult to believe it, and sometimes she even felt
is presence with her. Was it just his spirit? The
ealization of the awful truth brought new tears, and
sob welled up from deep inside, coming out in a
huddering gasp that woke up her guard.

He looked at her, pushing back his hat. "Well,
ou're awake."

She started to move, realizing then that her right
vrist was cuffed to a steel brace at the side of the
oach. She remained lying on her side, watching
im, breathing deeply to regain her control. She told
erself that there would be time later for mourning.
Blake would want her to keep her wits about her, to
lo whatever she could to get out of this, for the baby's
ake. "I need . . . a handkerchief," she told the man.

He untied the bandanna from around his neck.
'Don't have one. You can use this."

He handed it to her. It smelled of his perspiration,
out at the moment she didn't have much choice but to
ise it. She blew her nose with her free hand. "Why are
you doing this?" she asked then, her voice raspy from
er earlier effort to scream through her gag.

"Boss's orders."

"Who's your boss?"

"Sorry. No names."

"It's Nick West, isn't it?"

He just stared at her.

"I see," she said, sighing. "No names—no proof."
She wiped at her eyes, then studied him, a man who
could be handsome if he shaved and cleaned up, a

man she guessed to be about Blake's age. He had blue eyes and sandy hair, and if not for what he was doing now, she would have thought him a perfectly normal, innocent person if she passed him in the street. That was the worst part of this ugly fighting. The nicest man a person might meet could be his worst enemy. How did one know who on earth to trust?

"What about you?" she asked. "We have a long ride ahead of us. Can't you at least tell me your name?"

Ted Wilson studied her, thinking what a pretty wife Blake Hastings had. Again he felt a looming guilt at what he was doing, but he really had no choice, not if he wanted to protect his own skin, and his family. Nick West expected orders to be obeyed. "No, ma'am," he answered. "The less you know, the better. I wouldn't want to have to kill you."

She smiled bitterly. "Well, I have to be able to call you *something*."

"Call me Joe."

She sat up wearily, her hair falling in strands from the neat curls into which she had pinned it earlier that morning. "Well, Joe," she said. "I suppose I should thank you for keeping Clyde Beecher away from me. But then maybe I'd be better off if he'd shot me." She held his eyes, for the first time understanding Blake's deep hatred. "How can you save me that way, and then send me off to prison, threaten to kill me?"

"I just do what I'm told," he answered.

"Like a little puppet," she sneered. "How can you call yourself a man?"

He leaned closer, grasping her wrist. "You'd better shut your trap, or I'll forget what I said about not hurting you." He squeezed her wrist until she grimaced with pain, then let go of her.

Samantha moved farther back on the seat, realizing her safety depended on this man's mood. She reminded herself to think of the baby. A struggle, a wrong blow, getting raped—all could cause her to lose her child. That was one thing she was not going to let happen. The baby was all she had now.

"Is it true, about my husband being dead?"

The man nodded. "It's true."

She swallowed, refusing to let herself break down in front of him. "How? When?"

Wilson turned to pull a shade away, looking outside, suddenly unable to meet her eyes. *I was supposed to shoot him,* he could have answered. *But I didn't have to. He's long dead by now from wounds and exposure and loss of blood.* He finally met her eyes. "Four—five days ago. You don't want to know how. I'm just saying he's dead and out of his misery. I know it for a fact."

She held her chin proudly. "Well, Joe Whoever-you-are, my husband died for a good cause. He lived and died much more proudly than you ever will."

"I told you to watch your mouth."

She grinned wryly, realizing she had hit a nerve. "Such brave men all of you are, hauling a pregnant woman off to prison. Am I such a big threat?"

"Some think you are."

"You mean Nick West?"

Again he just stared at her a moment. "I don't know who you're talking about," he lied. He wondered how she knew so much. West had sent him and the men with him to rendezvous with Beecher, using West's own coach so Samantha Hastings could be taken to Independence in secret. "This has to do with certain people within the Kansas government who intend to put a stop to you abolitionists. You've been told over and over that it's against the law to preach against slavery, but you continue to do it. Now people are going to understand that the law is going to be upheld. We've taught Lawrence a lesson, and now certain people will learn an even harder lesson."

Samantha nodded. "Yes, I suppose so. But that won't stop the movement. It's getting too big now. What you're doing is wrong, and it's useless. You'll find that out in the long run, and you'll regret the things you've done, Joe. I hope you can live with yourself when you're old."

The man folded his arms and leaned back in his seat. "Look, lady, it could have been a lot worse for you."

"Worse than . . ." The lump returned to her throat, the panic to her soul, the pain to her heart. Blake was dead! She had to hang on, keep her head. She couldn't give up! "Worse than losing my parents in a fire—two brave, caring people who never harmed a soul in their lives? Worse than finding out my husband is dead, not even knowing where his body is? Worse than going to prison while I'm carrying a child?"

"Be glad of that." His eyes moved over her as though he could see exactly how she looked naked. "It will keep me and the boys in line. More than that, it's the only reason my boss decided to send you to prison instead of selling you off in Mexico. That was his original plan, but nobody wants a pregnant woman."

Samantha felt the color rising in her cheeks as she realized what he meant by selling her off in Mexico. White slavery, forced prostitution! "My, what a fine, respectable man your boss must be," she mocked. "And brave, no less. I always thought that wars were fought among men, not men against one woman."

He sighed, running a hand through his hair. "I'll say one thing. I can see why certain people would want to shut you up." He reached over and picked up a canteen beside him, removing the cap. "Take a drink of this. We'll be going through a small town soon and you'll have to be gagged again. Now that I've listened to your blabber, I think I'll leave you that way."

She held his eyes boldly as she took the canteen and swallowed some of the water. "Do you have a family, Joe?" she asked, handing back the canteen.

He took it from her and recapped it. "None of your business."

"I think you do. What if this was happening to *your* wife?"

He eyed her narrowly, leaning closer. "Look, be glad I arranged for it to be me inside here with you. Neither one of those other two would be half as nice. Now I'm getting paid good for this, but even if I decided it was wrong, it wouldn't do any good, because I'd have to go through those other men first, and I'd never survive. That would leave you alone with them, and believe me, you'd rather make it to prison safely."

He leaned over to pick up her gag, stuffing it back into her mouth. Samantha felt sick at its smelly dampness. The man retied the bandana, then sat back to watch her. "Don't try anything stupid like trying to reach out a window with that free hand. I'd grab it before you could draw any attention, and you don't want me to get rough with you, not if you want to hang on to that kid. Besides, it might cause one of the others to want to change places with me, and you don't want that, either. We'll be in Independence by tomorrow. We're driving straight through. You'll eat

395

inside the coach."

She just watched him, wondering if he had any compassion whatsoever. What kind of men did things like this? Her father had once said such men were desperate and full of fear—fear of the unknown. They didn't understand what good people the Negroes could be. Most were fighting to keep slavery for economic reasons, putting their precious plantations and free labor above the lives of innocent people. If men like these and like John Brown could become so radical in their beliefs, what lay ahead for the United States? Most of all, what lay ahead for her baby?

If only Blake were alive. Then she would at least have some hope. Even if Drew and others could figure out that she might be in prison, they would never think to look in Missouri. Her eyes teared anew as hopelessness again tried to overwhelm and defeat her. She felt dizzy and sick again, and she moved to lie back down, closing her eyes and thinking of Blake, remembering the good times, the gentle nights, the feel of his strong arms around her. Was this man sure he was dead? Had he actually seen him die?

She moved in and out of sleep due to her weariness and the effect of Clyde Beecher's blows. Day turned to night, and she ate a little, forcing herself for the baby's sake. She had no idea how many hours had passed, or how many more before the coach stoepped and someone opened the door. "We're here," she heard a voice saying.

The man called Joe helped her sit up, but he left the gag on her. He unhooked the handcuff from the steel brace and put it around her free hand so that she was cuffed again. He helped her out of the coach, and she stumbled, finding it hard to get her bearings because of the aftereffects of the swaying coach and her injuries. She realized it was dawn, and that they were in some kind of alley. She thought it must be very early. The town was quiet.

"Wait here," Wilson told the others. He led her through a back door, and she found herself in a small hall that led through a row of cells.

"Whooey! What you got there, mister?" a man called from one of the cells. "You can put her in here with me."

"Shut up," Wilson answered, shoving Samantha toward another door. He opened it, and Samantha blinked at the light of a fully lit oil lamp. "You Sheriff Stevens?" he asked a heavyset man behind a desk.

The man slowly rose, eyeing Samantha. "I am."

"This is Samantha Hastings, an abolitionist from Lawrence. I think a certain man told you to expect her. I'm not supposed to mention his name. You're supposed to get a judge over here. Judge Quill, I think."

The sheriff nodded. "Right." He walked from behind his desk and to the door, calling for someone outside to go and get the judge. Wilson led Samantha to a chair and sat her down, leaning close while the sheriff said something more to his man.

"Look, I'll do this much for you," Wilson told her quietly. "After about two months I'll send an anonymous letter to your people in Lawrence and tell them where you are. After that it's up to them to see if they can get you out. I can't do it any sooner than that or I'll be suspect."

The sheriff came back inside and Wilson untied Samantha's gag. She looked at him, her eyes tired and circled, her lower lip swollen, and the side of her face bruised. Her eyes teared with a silent pleading that he keep his promise. In the next moment the sheriff was standing in front of her. "Looks like somebody got rough with her."

"She'll be all right. Just make sure you get some food to her soon," Joe answered.

"Mmm-hmm." The sheriff rubbed at his whiskers. "She been searched?"

Samantha looked at him in wide-eyed shock and terror. Wilson rose, removing his gun. "Yes," he lied. "And if the boss finds out you did your own searching, you won't be sheriff much longer. In fact, you won't even be alive."

The sheriff looked down at the gun and backed off. Wilson suspected Nick West didn't give a damn how Samantha Hastings was treated, but if he could keep the sheriff away from her with just the threat, he figured it was worth a try. Something about her had got to him, and it angered him. This was the first time he had had second thoughts about this whole mess. It had been bad enough watching her husband whipped nearly to death and then helping load him into the death wagon. Now here was the wife, a beautiful young woman a good seven months pregnant. She was right. This wasn't the way wars were supposed to be fought, but he didn't dare cross Nick West now. The best he could do was inform her family or friends.

One of the prisoners in the other room shouted something to the sheriff. The man lumbered into the cell room and Wilson turned to Samantha. "Who should I contact?"

She swallowed, beginning to shiver with the reality of her situation. "My brother—Drew Walters. You can contact him through Jonas Hanks. I was staying with the Hankses . . . before—"

She stopped talking as soon as the sheriff came back inside. Someone knocked at the door then and came inside. He was a tall, cold-looking man wearing a dark suit and hat. He glanced at Samantha for only a moment, then handed a paper to the sheriff.

"There's the legal papers," he said.

"Thanks, Judge," Sheriff Stevens answered. "That's all I need."

Samantha raised her chin, rising from the chair. "How much did Nick West pay you, Judge Quill?" she asked boldly.

The man turned. "What?"

"You heard me. For all that money, don't I even get a trial? But then, that wouldn't even be necessary, because you have no jurisdiction over me. I'm a citizen of Kansas Territory, not Missouri!"

The man smiled grimly. "Well, now, it doesn't much matter, does it? You don't have anyone left to come for you anyway. When you're released, you can go back to your precious Kansas, and it will still be a slave state. By then I don't think you'll be in too much of a mood to resume your work for abolition."

"Stopping two, three, four, five people—that's not going to stop the whole movement! Don't any of you understand that?"

"We'll stop more than two or three before we're through," the judge answered.

Samantha stiffened, realizing the fighting was not going to end anytime soon, perhaps not for years. "And how long do you intend to keep me here?" she asked.

The judge adjusted his hat. "Six months."

"Six months! I'm going to have a baby in two months!"

"Well, now, that's your problem, isn't it? We have some knowledgeable prostitutes in this town. The sheriff can send for one of them to assist you." He turned toward the door. "Now, I have a card game to get back to. Good evening, all."

"Night, Judge," the sheriff answered with a grin. He approached Samantha then, taking hold of her arm. "Give me the key to the cuffs," he said to Wilson. "I'll take them off her when I get her to her cell and I'll send for some food."

Wilson looked at Sam as he handed out the key, telling her with his eyes that he would do as he had promised. He looked at the sheriff then. "Remember what I said about not touching her. It wouldn't set well with the boss, and you know how he can be."

"I'll remember," Stevens sneered. "Go on with you now before somebody sees that coach behind my jail."

"What about that prisoner in the other room. Will he say anything?"

"I'll tell him she was released. I'm putting her in the cellar. He'll never know she's there, and neither will anybody else who comes in here."

To Samantha's dismay, Wilson put the key in the sheriff's hand, officially turning her over. "You got enough blankets down there for her? The boss doesn't want her to get sick and die. He just wants to teach her a good lesson."

"There's blankets. Now get going."

Wilson hesitated a moment, glancing at Samantha once more and looking for a moment as though he might grab her back. Samantha felt her heart break into smaller pieces when he turned then and left.

"Let's go," the sheriff told her, leading her to a door at the corner of the room. He opened it, and the musty smell of dampness and mold struck Samantha's nostrils. The sheriff kept hold of her arm but walked behind her as she descended narrow wooden steps to a small room that she could feel had a dirt floor. "Hold it right there," the sheriff told her. He lit a lantern that hung on a post at the bottom of the steps, and to her horror, Samantha saw a rat scamper away.

The sheriff led her through a second door into another dark area, where he lit another lamp, then gave her a little shove toward the only cell in the second room, its bars rusty from the dampness. He opened the cell door and led her inside, then removed her handcuffs.

"There's a pot over there for your personal needs," he told her. "Some blankets on that cot, and a wash pan. I'll bring a pitcher of fresh water each morning, for washing and for drinking. You'll eat twice a day, midmorning and late afternoon. No sense trying to scream your way out of here. If anybody could hear you, I'd tell them I've got a madwoman down here. But nobody will hear you. Once I close the door to this room and then the outer room, nobody can hear a thing. This cell is actually under the street, not the jail. No better insulation against sound than good ole dirt, is there? Kind of like being buried alive."

He closed the cell door and locked it. "Have a good night's sleep." He walked out, shutting the door. Sam stared after him, listening to the second door close. Everything was total silence then, except for the occasional tiny squeal of a rat. She thanked God that at least he had left the lantern lit, but then she wondered why she thought she should be thankful for such a minor thing, considering where she was.

She moved to the cot, lifting the blankets to be sure there were no bugs or mice in the covers. She saw nothing, then sat down, looking around the room, its walls and ceiling made of damp masonry, the floor only dirt. Yes, this was very much like being buried alive. She touched her belly, feeling movement. How could she bring an innocent baby into this horror? Would the man called Joe keep his promise to tell someone where she was? He was her only hope.

"Blake," she whimpered. How could he be dead? What was there left without Blake? She could not fight it any longer. The horror of the last frightening hours and of her present predicament was only made more dreadful by the realization that it was true, and she had to face it. Blake was not coming for her—not ever. She lay down on the cot, the gut-wrenching sobs coming then, tears of hopelessness and utter, agonizing loneliness. She curled up, fighting to stop crying, afraid the painful sobbing would make her lose the baby. But she could not stop the tears. She clung to the pillow, imagining it was Blake and that his arms would come around her any moment.

Twenty-One

For over three weeks Blake lay in unbearable agony, wishing many times that the Indians who had rescued him would kill him and end the pain. He was barely cognizant of his surroundings; the first several days of pain and sickness he was only vaguely aware that he lay in a tipi, that an older woman was tending him. She dressed him with a horrid-smelling salve, but Blake gradually accepted the stink when he began to realize how much the salve helped the pain.

The flesh wound at his side seemed to be healing well now, but the whipping and the scarring tissue it had created left his skin tender and tight so that every move was miserable, as though he had been burned. The first several days he had been almost completely delirious and the Indians told him he had come close to death from loss of blood. After that serious infection had set in so that every touch of the salve brought new horror. He had suffered fever and delirium, and again death had hung over him, trying to snatch him away.

Finally hard scabs began to form, but in spite of them, the pain was tremendous. It was as though the whip had gone deep into his muscles. He ached as though he had been beaten with a club. The injury from the blow to his back had also taken a long time to heal. Now the pain had diminished considerably, but a maddening itch covered his entire backside from new skin beginning to grow beneath the scabs.

He had spent most of the past three weeks flat on his belly, and in his more lucid moments he could think of nothing but killing Clyde Beecher and Nick West. Those thoughts were mingled with a desperate need to get to Samantha before she was harmed. Surely Beecher and West wouldn't do something like this to her! It sickened him to be so helpless, and he felt crazy with a desire for vengeance and an ache to be with Samantha. And what about George and poor Jesse? Would West sell them off before he could decide how to help them?

The old woman, who Blake now knew was called Horse Woman, again began applying the smelly salve to his back. Blake could tell it was dark outside, and a small fire glowed softly nearby. He managed to turn his head when a man came inside, Horse Woman's husband, Many Buffalo, a name earned from killing more buffalo than anyone else in his tribe. It was a story Blake had heard many times over, as Many Buffalo seemed to enjoy telling it.

Many Buffalo sat down across the fire from Blake. Blake guessed him to be perhaps fifty. His head was shaved, Pawnee fashion, a patch of graying hair left at the top of his head and greased up into a scalp lock. Blake had grown accustomed to the different smells of Indians—not unpleasant, just different, a mixture of bear grease and buffalo meat, hides and earth and the smoky smell from the fire kept constantly burning at the center of the tipi.

Why they had decided to help him, Blake still was not quite sure. He could only be grateful that they had. Many Buffalo stared at the fire quietly for a moment while Horse Woman continued putting fresh salve on Blake's now-healing wounds.

The old Indian man lit a white man's pipe, and Blake wondered if it had been taken in trade or stolen off some white man's dead body. He knew the Pawnee could be vicious, but now they were close to signing a peace treaty. Many Buffalo and Horse Woman were part of a tribe out hunting buffalo.

Blake had never bothered asking what the smelly salve Horse Woman used on him was made of, or, for that matter, the ingredients of the hot broth he had been fed the first two weeks. He had a feeling he didn't want to know.

"You white men are strange," Many Bufalo spoke up then. "You tell us we must live in peace, that we must not war with other Indians or against the white man; but look what you do to each other. Such forked tongues you speak with."

Blake managed a faint grin. "I suppose we do," he answered. "I thank you, Many Buffalo, for not speaking with a forked tongue when you told me that you would help me. There is really nothing I can do to repay you."

"I thought of leaving you there. It is not wise for Indians to mix in white man's business."

"It won't matter in this case." Blake pushed his hands against the ground, grimacing with pain as he forced himself to his knees. Sweat broke out on his brow. "I've got to start moving around, Many Buffalo. I want to start eating more solid food . . . maybe try to walk tomorrow."

The Indian nodded. "You have vengeance in your heart."

Their eyes held. "Yes, I do," Blake answered. "There are a couple of men who must die for this. And they . . . threatened my wife. I've got to get back to Lawrence as soon as I can ride."

Many Buffalo puffed his pipe. "I will have my son take you to the tracks of the iron horse. It will be the quickest way for you. But you must let yourself heal longer. If you want to help your woman, and if you want to be strong enough to seek your vengeance, you must be fully healed. We will feed you well, build your strength. You are not ready yet, my friend, and to move too soon could mean you will be of no use at all."

Blake shivered with weakness and pain, not even caring that he was naked. It didn't seem to matter to these people, and since they had brought him here, there had been no place on his backside where clothes could be worn for fear of sticking to his skin. They had kept him warm at night by surrounding him with hot rocks and making a little tentlike structure over him with blankets to keep in the heat, but the June days had been hot, and even some of the nights warm enough that most of the time he did not need to be covered.

He lay back down, groaning with the effort and breathing a sigh of relief at being prone again. "I don't know how to thank you, Many Buffalo."

"It is not necessary. I told you I almost left you, but then a hawk flew overhead, and it seemed to be telling me I must help. I was only obeying the hawk's spirit. I think you are a good white man, Blake. The men who did this to you should die, and you have the right to kill them. Only a coward does what was done to you. An enemy should be fought face-to-face, not whipped from behind." The Indian puffed his pipe again, then barked something to Horse Woman, who immediately set an iron frypan over the fire and threw in some buffalo fat. "My woman will make you buffalo meat. She also has some bread and turnips."

Blake raised his head, pulling a pillow made of

rawhide and stuffed with buffalo hair under his head so that it was propped up more. "I would like that, Many Buffalo. This is the first time I have felt true hunger in a long time."

"You have been with us for many sunrises. Soon it will be one full moon since we found you," the Indian answered.

Blake frowned, his heart tightening. One full moon. That was nearly a month! He must have been here a good three weeks. Anything could have happened to Sam by now! "I won't burden you much longer," he told Many Buffalo. "I am determined to get to my wife soon."

Many Buffalo nodded. "Horse Woman will know when the time is right."

Blake felt like weeping. It tore at his guts to be lying here so helpless when Sam might need him. And what must she be thinking by now? That he was dead? Was Drew with her? Was she safe, or had Beecher somehow gotten to her? "I don't have time to wait any longer than it takes me to get on my feet," he told Many Buffalo.

The Indian leaned closer to the fire, pointing his pipe at Blake. "Remember this. Never go after your enemy when you know he is still stronger than you. You must be healed, Blake, or he will find your weakness and defeat you again. Remember, too, that y ou will be a surprise for him. He thinks that you are dead. You must be strong, so that he does not get away from you again, and so that you can taste the vengeance for which you hunger."

Blake stared at the flames. Yes, his greatest hunger was indeed for vengeance, and he did have to be strong enough to taste it. And taste it he would! His hands moved into fists, and he gritted his teeth as he envisioned Clyde Beecher and Nick West burning alive in the flames of the fire.

*   *   *

Samantha scooted back onto the cot as Sheriff Stevens brought her another tray of food. He set it down and opened the cell door, coming closer to cuff her to the frame of the cot as he always did before going back to get the tray. "Can't have you trying something funny while that door is open," he had told her. He set the tray on the bed, then walked over to pick up the pot kept in the corner of the cell, which he emptied only once every two weeks.

"It's about time," she told the man dully as he carried it out. He stopped and glared at her.

"Sure does stink down here."

"Then let me out of here so I can live like a normal human being," she answered. "Either that, or bring a lid for that pot. And I need more paper. I also need to change this dress. I'm filthy, and you never leave me enough water to wash properly."

"All part of being in prison, lady. Maybe you'll think twice about doing anything again to get thrown back in here." The man left, and Samantha stared at the tray. She pulled it closer, lifting the cloth to see one piece of chicken, a few potatoes, a piece of bread and a spoonful of corn. She craved fresh milk, but as always, there was only a cup of lukewarm coffee on the tray.

She picked up the chicken, biting into it listlessly, not really hungry but knowing she should eat. Even though she forced down whatever food was brought to her, she knew she was losing weight in spite of the baby. She worried what the lack of food, let alone its questionable freshness, was going to do to her baby. She thought about the birth now with more and more terror. In roughly five weeks her child would be born right here in this squalid cell, with only some strange prostitute helping her. And what

408

if the baby came at a time when she could not get word to the sheriff? He only checked on her twice a day, and in between he couldn't hear her screams. It was entirely possible she would have the child alone. She didn't know anything about what to do. It seemed almost certain that her baby would die under such conditions.

She wondered why she bothered to eat at all . . . for the tiny hope that she could have the baby and that both of them would live? Yes, that was all that kept her going. The baby was all she had left of Blake, and she would not let Nick West and Clyde Beecher realize total victory by dying or by letting her baby die.

The desire to show her husband's murderers that they had not won at all was the only fire in her soul that kept her going. She was going to live through this, and she was going to fight harder than ever for abolition, continue the efforts of men like her father and Blake and John Hale; and she would tell the whole world about Clyde Beecher and Nick West! The man called Joe had not mentioned West by name, but she knew in her heart he was behind what had happened to her, and to Blake, and she would find a way to prove it!

She managed to swallow some of the potatoes and washed them down with the cooling coffee. She told herself it was ridiculous to think Joe would really contact anyone in Lawrence. The conditions she had endured had destroyed any thoughts of faith in anyone but herself. Even her faith in God was dwindling. How could any God have let Blake be killed? How could any God have caused her to be here in this stinking, dark, damp cell?

She felt dirty and smelly, and her clothes scratched her. She still wore the same dress and underwear as when she arrived here. According to the marks she had been making on the dirt floor under her cot, she had been here nearly three weeks. Since there was no light in the cell, she could only tell the passing of each day by the fact that the sheriff brought her breakfast and supper.

She passed part of her time drawing tic-tac-toe in the dirt floor with a spoon, even writing poems and Bible verses, trying to remember those which had once sustained her faith and courage. She felt guilty at times for her flagging faith, considering her upbringing. Her father would have told her to keep her faith during all trials and tribulations, but now the only thing that helped sustain her sanity was talking to her baby. She would rub her belly and pretend the baby, her little bit of Blake, was in her arms. Each movement reminded her there was life, reminded her she was not alone at all. Blake was with her, in the spirit of his child. Blake. Such a wonderful, vital man he had been. She would never love that way again.

The sheriff returned, this time with a lid on the pot. Samantha smiled to herself. He had probably put it on for his own relief, but at least she had the lid now. To her surprise he had also brought more toiletry paper and a couple of clean towels. "You done with that food yet?" he asked.

"No."

"Well, hurry it up." He put his hands on his hips. "You want a bath, I can bring down a tin tub tomorrow and some extra water."

She watched his eyes, deciding she would rather be crawling with maggots than to undress alone in this cell with the "kind" Sheriff Stevens able to walk in on her whenever he pleased.

"No, thank you," she answered. "The bowl and pitcher are enough. Couldn't you at least bring me a change of clothes?"

He glared at her, obviously upset at her refusal. "No bath—no clean clothes," he answered. "Can't have one without the other." His eyes moved over her, and she knew that to a man like this one her pregnant condition mattered little.

"Then I'll keep what I'm wearing," she answered. She handed him the tray. "Here."

The man snickered, taking the tray and setting it outside the cell. "Suit yourself," he answered.

"Couldn't you bring me a Bible?" she asked then. "And bring the oil lamp inside the cell, too, so I can read?"

He leaned closer to unlock her cuffs, and she could smell his perspiration. "You're asking an awful lot for not giving me anything in return, honey."

"Just don't forget what could happen to you if you lay a hand on me," she warned, holding his eyes boldly.

The man stiffened, reaching over and angrily unlocking the cuffs. "And maybe nobody out there cares anymore," he grumbled. "Maybe I'll even get Judge Quill to add a few more months to your sentence. That should fix you up real good! You'll soon learn you get a lot more from me by being nice than opening that smart mouth of yours!"

The man lumbered out of the cell, slamming the cell door and locking it. He walked out, closing the wooden door of the room. Again came the sound of the second door closing, and again the cell was still as a tomb.

Samantha shivered, her eyes tearing. She never let herself cry in front of the sheriff. She leaned back against the wall, letting the tears flow, rubbing her hands gently over her stomach. "Oh, Blake," she whispered. "If only you hadn't gone." She found herself praying again, in spite of her anger and confusion that God would let this happen. She told

411

herself to remember all her father's sermons, all of God's promises.

She moved to the edge of the cot, then got to her knees, taking the spoon she kept for writing in the dirt and scratching out her favorite verse again. *And all things, whatsoever ye shall ask in prayer, believing, ye shall receive. . . .*

It was nearly the end of June when everyone at the Hanks table looked up at the sound of their front door bursting open. They could barely hear the footsteps of whoever had come into the house, realizing why when he appeared in the dining room. He wore Indian buckskin clothing and moccasins.

Jonas Hanks's eyes widened, and he slowly rose. "Blake!" He looked him over, seeing that Blake was thinner, seeing a hard look in the man's eyes. "My God, man, where have you been!"

"It's a long damn story, Jonas, but as soon as I was well enough I came straight here. I'll explain it all after I know if Sam is all right."

Jonas paled slightly. Mrs. Hanks hung her head, while all the Hanks children gawked at Blake in awe, wondering if he was white or Indian. Blake felt as though someone was squeezing his heart in a vise at the look on Jonas's face. He scanned the table, his eyes falling on a new face, a young man with blue eyes—Sam's eyes.

"You're Drew," he said, more as a statement than a question.

Drew rose, sorrow showing in his eyes. "Yes." His eyes moved over Blake, a handsome man, Drew thought, honed hard, though he looked a little wild. "I'd like to say I'm glad to meet you, and I am, but not under these conditions. We all thought maybe you were dead."

"Where's Sam?" Blake asked.

Drew's eyes teared. "That's what we'd like to know. She disappeared one day . . . almost a month ago. She went to the Presbyterian church to pray, and she never came back." He watched the agony in Blake's eyes, knew instinctively that nothing that had happened had been Blake's fault, except perhaps the fact that he had left in the first place. "We've been searching ever since, Blake," Drew added. "We've sent telegrams and men to just about every town in Kansas, asking about Sam, checking all the jails. She's just not there. We searched for you, too."

Blake's jaws flexed with repressed rage. "How about Nick West's place over in Missouri? Did anybody think to check there?"

Drew nodded. "Several men and I went to Independence to ask about you. Sam told me before she disappeared to see if anyone knew what might have happened to you. We couldn't find anything, though somebody told us a team of John Hale's wagon horses came wandering back into town a couple of days after he was murdered. Did you know about that?"

Blake nodded. "I heard," he almost growled.

"Well, we never found any clue as to your whereabouts. Sam was taken off while I was gone. My first thought was West, so we went right back to his place. The man was real upset that we kept accusing him of evil deeds, but he let us search his place, top to bottom, though he wouldn't let us talk to any of his Negro slaves. We didn't find a thing." Drew swallowed, his own grief still very fresh. He had come here to visit his parents' graves, and now his sister had disappeared, surely in the hands of proslavery men, if she was even still alive.

Blake turned away, his hands in fists. He breathed deeply, visibly shaking with a mixture of sorrow and rage. He finally moved his eyes to Jonas. "Has Clyde Beecher been here?"

"Beecher?" Jonas slowly rose. "Blake, do you still think—"

"I don't *think!* I *know!*" Blake looked at Mrs. Hanks. "I'm sorry to barge in on your family this way, Mrs. Hanks. Could you get the children out of here for a minute? I want to show something to your husband and Drew."

The woman quickly obeyed, whisking the children away. Blake turned then and removed his buckskin shirt, showing the men his back.

"My God," Jonas said, putting a hand to his stomach. Drew closed his eyes and turned away.

Blake put the shirt back on and looked at Jonas. "This is why I couldn't get here any sooner. I came as close to dying as any man can come without looking God in the face! Pawnee Indians helped me, gave me these clothes, a horse, and an old rifle. Nick West put these scars on me, and Clyde Beecher helped him!"

Jonas stared at him in shock. "Beecher!"

"Beecher! And he knows exactly what's happened to Sam because he's the one who arranged for her disappearance. Where is he, Jonas?"

Jonas swallowed, running a hand through his hair. "He's over near the site of Reverend Walters's burned-down church. It's been cleaned up now, and he's holding a rally at the site, trying to raise funds to build a new church."

"Money he plans to leave town with," Blake sneered. "Beecher has no intention of staying in Lawrence now! He's come back just long enough to look innocent and to line his pockets with a little more money. That son of a bitch knows where Sam is, and he's going to tell us!"

Blake turned and stormed out. Jonas looked at Drew, who was still shaken by the sight of Blake's back. "We'd better go along," Jonas told him. "This is going to be bad."

Drew nodded, hurrying around the table and out into the hall to grab his hat. Jonas called out to his wife that he would be back soon, telling her to keep the children inside. Both men hurried after Blake, who had swung himself up on an Indian pony and was riding in the direction of the old church site. Both men began running after him, and other people stared at the man in buckskins riding hard to the west end of town.

"Isn't that Blake Hastings?" one man asked another.

"Sure looked like him. Wonder where in hell he's been? Too bad about poor Samantha."

Both men turned then to see Jonas and Drew running down the street. "Come on," Jonas shouted to them. "It's Beecher! He's a spy for the bushwhackers!"

"A *spy?*" one of them exclaimed. "Clyde Beecher?" Both men followed, shouting the news to others as they ran, gathering a crowd by the time they reached the site of the church, where Blake had already charged right through a gathering of faithful followers and lit into Beecher.

Women were screaming, most of them hurriedly herding their children away from the violence. Men gathered in a circle, some cursing Blake for attacking such a God-fearing man as Beecher, then rooting for Blake as the rumor quickly spread that Clyde Beecher was a bushwhacker spy.

Blake landed blow after blow, his fury knowing no bounds as he pounded the helpless Beecher into a bloody pulp, growling with each blow the same question—"Where's Sam? Where's my wife?"

Beecher's head reeled. Blake Hastings was alive! How in God's name had he survived? He knew

415

instantly what was going to happen the minute he realized the identity of the buckskin-clad man who was riding down on him. He had tried to run, but in an instant Blake Hastings had landed into him. This was no dead man! He tried to fight back, but it had taken only two or three blows before he was hardly aware of his surroundings. Blake was like a roaring bull, charging, gouging, pummeling, until finally several men gathered the courage to dive in and pull Blake off him.

"Blake, you'll kill him!" Drew Walters was shouting. "How are we going to find out about Samantha if he's dead!"

Beecher swallowed blood, rolled to his knees, and grasped his stomach. He could barely see, and his ears rang painfully. Every bone and muscle screamed. He was only vaguely aware of the shouts of the men who had gathered around him, of Drew and Jonas Hanks arguing with a struggling Blake to hold back so they could get the truth out of Beecher. Others were demanding to know what was going on.

"All right, all right!" Blake shouted. The men holding him finally let go of him cautiously. "Clyde Beecher is a traitor!" Blake accused. "He works for Nick West, helped West's men know which homes and businesses to burn the night of the raid on Lawrence!" He pulled off the shirt again and turned for everyone to see his scars. Men gasped and cursed. "Nick West did this to me," he told them. "Clyde Beecher was with him! When West was through with me, Beecher took over. They hauled me off into Indian country and left me for dead!"

Beecher was still on his knees, and Blake threw aside the shirt and knelt to grasp him by the front of his jacket and jerking him close, his teeth gritted in hatred, his eyes blazing. "The man who was supposed to blow my brains out didn't do it!" he

416

snarled. "You didn't count on that, *did* you, Beecher? He probably figured I'd die anyway, but an old Pawnee man found me and helped me. And now here I am!" His lips curled. "Where is she, Beecher? Where's *Samantha!*"

Blood poured from Beecher's nose and mouth, and from several cuts on his face. He panted with a mixture of pain and terror. "You . . . bastard," he choked out.

Blake shook him slightly. "The only thing that keeps me from killing you, Beecher, is needing to know where Samantha is! Tell me, you goddamn son of a bitch, or I'll kill you anyway and get the information out of Nick West!"

Beecher looked around at the crowd, hardly able to see them but realizing he was suddenly a rabbit in a lion's den. He knew instinctively Blake would kill him if he didn't tell, and not one man watching would stop him. "If I tell you, you've got to promise to let me go."

Blake glared at him. "You've got that promise."

Beecher grimaced with pain. "She's in jail . . . in Independence. West paid a judge to draw up papers to put her in jail for . . . six months."

People mumbled among themselves, feeling shock and horror at hearing what had been done to Samantha Hastings.

"You filthy bastard," Blake growled. "She's going to have a baby in another month or so! What jail? Who's the sheriff?"

"Sheriff Stevens . . . big, heavyset man."

The crowd gathered closer, revenge burning in every heart. Clyde Beecher had actually helped mastermind the raid on Lawrence, a trusted man who preached the word of God. It was one thing to be the enemy and show it openly, but to be a hypocrite like Beecher was unforgivable.

"Who took her there? You?" Blake asked.

"No. I just got her out of town. Told her I knew where you were and . . . that you were hurt. Some of West's men took her in West's coach. Lou, Buck . . . and that Ted Wilson."

Lou and Buck. Blake felt like vomiting. They were part of those who had attacked him and taken him to West's farm.

"You said you wouldn't kill me," Beecher reminded him.

"I know what *I* said," Blake sneered. "But I didn't say I wouldn't turn you over to the rest of these men!" He gave the man a hard shove, and a couple of the other men caught him.

"Let's show him what happens to spies and traitors!" one of them yelled.

Shouts went up, along with fists. Quickly the rest of the crowd pushed around Beecher, hauling him away, some shouting, "Get a rope!"—others saying they should tar and feather him. Beecher began screaming for forgiveness and mercy.

"Let him live," some yelled, "but let him suffer! Pour hot tar on him and run him out of town!"

"Strip him down" came other shouts.

Blake just stood watching after them, some of his misery and anger vented in the beating he had given Beecher. He had dearly wanted to kill the man himself, but he decided the rest of these people needed to feel some of their own revenge. Even if Beecher was left alive, he would be wishing he was dead, and he'd never again show his face in Lawrence.

He grasped at his side, still panting, his knuckles bleeding, everything aching. He had not really been ready for this, but his fury had been uncontrollable. Sam! In jail in her condition! What a horror for her. And she must have been told that he was dead.

"Blake, you'd better take a minute to calm down," Drew was telling him. "You don't look too good. We can't help Sam if you go into a relapse. Come on back to the house. We'll talk about what to do next."

"We're going to get Sam, that's what we'll do next," Blake answered angrily, jerking away.

"Damn it, man, I've just met you, but I can see you've got one hell of a temper," Drew answered. "Use your head, Blake! We've got to do this right or we'll *all* end up in jail! We can't just go charging into a proslavery state and demand at gunpoint that Sam be released! We've got to have a *plan*. For God's sake, I want my sister out of there as much as you do!"

Blake just stared at him a minute, realizing what a shock all of this must be to Samantha's brother. He breathed deeply, holding the young man's eyes. "This is one hell of a way to get to know each other, isn't it?"

Drew smiled grimly. "I guess so." He put out his hand. "We'll get her out of there, Blake—both of us. I've been going crazy myself wondering what to do next." Blake grasped his hand. "You showing up is the best thing that has happened in weeks," Drew told him. "I consider it a damn good sign. We'll get her back, Blake. And you know Sam. She's a fighter, stubborn as hell. If they think they can break her in that jail, they've got another think coming."

Blake's eyes misted. "Yeah, I expect so," he answered. He walked over to grasp the reins of his Indian pony, leading it to where his shirt lay in the street and picking it up. He and Drew and Jonas headed back to Jonas's house.

In the distance a mob of unruly, vengeful men hung Clyde Beecher just long enough to let him begin turning blue, enjoying the look of terror in his eyes. They cut him down then and stripped him, relishing his screams as they poured hot tar on him and covered him with chicken feathers. They dragged him to a wagon and threw him into it, several others jumping on as the driver took off, heading east. Once out of town they jerked Beecher off the wagon, stretching him out in the hot sun and laying him across the railroad tracks, tying his wrists and feet.

"Now, traitor," one man who had lost his home and business in the raid sneered, "you'll get your just punishment. The six o'clock train should be along any time now."

They all climbed back into the wagon and drove off, Beecher's screams and pleas for mercy ringing in their ears.

Back at the Hanks household Blake soaked his sore hands in warm water, spilling out the entire story of what had happened to him to Jonas and Drew, beginning to feel the results of his raging attack on Beecher. He was not ready for such violence, but hatred and revenge still burned too hot in his guts to worry about his own health. He thought how Samantha hated violence, wondered what she would think of what he had done and still planned to do. In the distance he heard a train whistle, thinking how nothing in Lawrence had changed much. The six-o'clock train was right on time.

Twenty-Two

Blake studied his swollen knuckles. "We've got to get her out of that jail," he told Drew. He closed his eyes, literally shaking with horror.

"We will," Drew answered him. "But you won't get anywhere charging in there like you did with Clyde Beecher. We're talking Missouri, Blake, a slave state. Apparently Nick West bribed some judge to draw up legal papers. That sheriff isn't going to let her out on your say-so, and if you try getting her out of there with guns, you'll both be hunted. We've got to find a way that's legal and won't draw any suspicion. The same goes for getting your friend George and that women he loves away from Nick West."

Blake looked at him. "I know you and your family don't believe in violence, but there's only one way to deal with Nick West. The man has to die, and *I'm* going to kill him. It's that simple."

Drew could see the burning hatred in Blake's dark eyes. It was obvious that a man wouldn't have much chance against Blake, especially when he was raging mad. He nodded his head. "I understand your need to kill him, but first we have to get George and Jesse away from him and get Sam out of jail. I say we do this calmly, one step at a time, have some kind of plan. Personally, I've got an idea how to get Jesse."

Blake studied the young man's blue eyes. His heart ached with a terrible longing for Samantha. Watching Drew reminded him so much of her. He sighed, standing up and untying a tobacco pouch from the beaded belt of his buckskin leggings. "All right," he said. "Let's hear it." He sat back down, opening the pouch and taking out a cigarette paper, then filling it with the tobacco.

"Nick West doesn't know me," Drew told him. "He might not even know Sam has a brother. At any rate, you said West mentioned he was interested in selling Jesse March. How about if I go in there and buy her, legally. No stealing her away, no risking anyone's life, no worry about the law. She'd be mine, free and clear, and then I'd give her her freedom papers. There wouldn't be a damn thing West could do about it."

Blake licked the cigarette paper and sealed it, then lit it. He smoked quietly for a moment, then nodded. "Damn smart idea. I see why you're studying law." He looked at Drew with a bit of sarcasm on his face. "What the hell would you buy her with? Your smile?"

Drew grinned. "I've got over two thousand dollars left in my education fund. My father inherited some money from his own father, plus I've worked extra jobs myself. It doesn't matter where it came from. It only matters that I had the money wired out here once Sam was missing. I knew I couldn't go back to Massachusetts without her, or at least not until I knew what had happened to her, so I figured I might need the money. I'm not going back to school until this is settled."

Blake frowned. "You'd spend your education money on freeing a Negro woman?"

Drew shrugged. "I have no doubt that's what Father would want me to do if it became necessary. It's just my way of continuing his fight, Blake. It's the least I can do."

Blake sighed deeply, staring at the smoke from his cigarette. "What about school?"

"I have one scholarship left. That's why I haven't had to spend all the money yet. And I can always get some extra work."

"Two thousand dollars is a lot of money."

"Compared to the hell Jesse March is living in, it's nothing. Besides, I'm not going to offer all of it. You said at one time West said he'd had an offer of fifteen hundred for Jesse. Maybe he was lying, I don't know. I'll start out at less than that."

Blake met his eyes and Drew noticed the first trace of a smile he had seen on his brother-in-law's face. "Your whole family sure has guts, I'll say that," Blake told him. "Leave it to a Walters to come up with an idea that doesn't involve violence." He rose. "If you're willing to go that far, it's worth a try. I'd rather get her out of there legally, like you said. I can always find a way to take care of West later." He smoked and paced for a moment, his big frame seeming to fill the Hanks's parlor. Blake and Drew talked alone, behind closed doors, not wanting to get anyone else involved in whatever plan they came up with.

"We'll go even further than that," Blake said. He walked to a piano and set his cigarette in an ash tray, then turned to face Drew. "When you talk to West about Jesse, you tell him you found out about her over a card game in Independence, that a man named Ted Wilson was at your table. When Wilson heard you were looking for a young Negro woman, he mentioned Jesse, you say. That's how you knew about her. If West sells her, you ask him where Ted Wilson lives. The man has a wife and a couple of kids, so he must have a place of his own, even though he works for West at his farm. Tell him you want to find the man and thank him for telling you about Jesse, that you want to pay him a little something, kind of like a finder's fee."

Drew frowned. "Why?"

Blake walked to a window. "Because *I* want to find Ted Wilson. Beecher said Wilson was one of those men who took Sam to that jail. I have a feeling I can convince him to go back there with us and tell the sheriff West gave him instructions to release Samantha to be taken back to West's farm. If it's one of West's own men who goes to get her, the sheriff won't think anything about it. He'll let her out of there."

Drew ran a hand through his hair. "Why would this Wilson help you if he works for West?"

Blake faced him. "Because I saw something in the man's eyes the day I was whipped. He had doubts. I saw him turn away like he couldn't stand to watch. Wilson is the one who was supposed to blow my brains out later, but he just took me out there and dumped me. He might have figured I was going to die anyway, but the point is, he couldn't bring himself to shoot me in cold blood. Once he sees I'm still alive, he might just be scared enough and remorseful enough to do this one thing for me. I don't think he really likes being a part of the things West is doing. Anyway it's always easier to deal with a man who has a wife and kids."

Blake walked back to the piano to take a last drag from his cigarette. "You said we had to try all this legally first. If Wilson can get Sam out of there without a fuss, that will be another barrier crossed. We'd have Sam *and* Jesse. You could take them on to Massachusetts with you, get them the hell out of Missouri and Kansas. Once they're safe, I'll figure out how to take care of West and how to get George back. Maybe Wilson will help us there, too. I have a second set of freedom papers for George if I can get him back into my hands."

Drew sighed, rising himself, shoving his hands into the pants pockets of his tweed suit. Blake thought how articulate and well dressed he was—a young man on the way to becoming a successful lawyer, perhaps someday something really important, maybe even a congressman.

Now it was Drew who paced, stopping after a moment to meet Blake's eyes. "Now you're using your head instead of those fists, but I'm still not sure about Ted Wilson. Won't he be afraid West would find out he's the one who got Sam released? West would be even more furious if Wilson helped George escape."

"Wilson won't have to worry about West. The man won't live long enough to do him any harm. I guarantee it. And if Wilson tells the other men that everything he did was on West's orders, no one is going to think anything of it."

Drew nodded. "I guess we don't have much choice. The only part I don't like is you wanting to kill West. I hope you realize what it will do to Sam to find out you're alive, only to have something happen to you after all."

An evil glint came into Blake's eyes. "Nothing is going to happen to me. *I'll* be the hunter this time, Drew, not the hunted. And I have one big advantage. West doesn't know I'm alive, so he won't be watching for me."

Drew smiled. "Yes, I can see where that would be an advantage." He put out his hand. "We have some packing to do and places to go, brother-in-law."

Blake took his hand, squeezing it firmly. "I'm glad as hell you're here, Drew. If you can get Jesse out of there, George and I will both find a way to repay you for what you've done."

Drew shook his head. "Not necessary. I'm doing it in memory of my parents. That's how they'd want it."

Blake nodded, his eyes tearing slightly. "I expect they would."

Drew walked around Jesse, hoping his nervousness didn't show. Now that he realized the things of which Nick West was capable, he knew that to be found out could mean his life. He felt lucky and secretly overjoyed that West had agreed to see him at all. Apparently the man was ripe for a sell.

He looked Jesse over, appearing to sum her up as though she was a prize cow. "My, my," he said, drawling the words in perfect southern accent. "Mr. Wilson was certainly right about her beauty."

He was glad now a couple of his good friends at school came from Georgia. It was easy to mimic the way they talked. He had told Nick West he was the son of a wealthy plantation owner in Georgia, come to Missouri to meet with a cotton buyer in St. Louis. He had been told there that some farm owners near the Kansas border were selling their slaves because of the violence owning them was creating. He had heard about Jesse March from Ted Wilson, had come across Wilson in a card game in Independence.

"I assure you I don't fear the border violence,"

West told him. "I have plenty of men to guard this place, and I still have all my niggers. The only reason I'm selling Jesse is because she has served her usefulness for me. Frankly, I'm getting tired of her, but I can guarantee that she'll serve you well, in any capacity."

Drew struggled to keep his contempt for the man from showing, forcing the hungry look to remain in his eyes. He secretly thanked God Jesse was still here. He looked at West and grinned. "My father always lets me have the young ones for a while," he drawled. "Says it's good training."

West chuckled. "That it is. But you have to remember that you can't treat most white women the way you treat a nigger. And most of them aren't as willing or passionate. I can have her strip for you if you want to check the merchandise."

Drew looked back at Jesse, who stood staring into nothingness, holding her chin high. "I, uh, I don't think so," he answered, licking his lips. "I prefer to be surprised. In this case, I'm sure it will be a very pleasant surprise." He frowned. "Unless she's scarred. I don't want to have to look at scars when I'm having at it, and neither does my father."

West smiled wryly. "Just a few scars, on her backside and in places you don't usually see them. There are ways of making a woman submit without leaving scars on them, and as you can see, she's too beautiful to ruin her that way. I assure you, she knows her place well. You'll get no trouble from her."

Jesse stood unflinching, feeling sick at the conversation. Her only hope was that this buyer would be kinder to her than Nick West had been, but from the way he talked, he seemed little better. Now she would be used by not just one man, but a father and son.

And this man would take her to Georgia, so far away from George! That was what hurt the most. Once she was sold, she would probably never see George again. He might even die right here on this plantation. She was going to be taken away, without even a chance to say good-bye to him.

The man who had come to look at her, and who called himself James Hills, stopped in front of her, grasping her chin in his hand and studying her face. She caught a strange glint in his eye then, a look that made her think he wanted to laugh. Her eyebrows arched in wonder when he winked at her, his back to West. "I'll give you eight hundred for her," he said then.

West folded his arms. "That's robbery. I can't take less than fifteen hundred."

Drew scowled, turning to look at the man. "Fifteen hundred! I'll remind you, sir, that she is not a virgin. You have used her considerably and you say she carries some scars."

"Not in places easy to see."

Drew walked closer. "Well, Mr. West, you might be surprised at what I explore when I'm with a woman." He grinned, then turned to look Jesse over again. "One thousand . . . cash . . . right here and now, and she's off your hands."

West sighed deeply, rubbing his chin. "Eleven hundred."

"Sold," Drew told him, putting out his hand. "Just show me the ownership papers."

West grinned. "You sure you don't want to strip her down first?"

Drew fished in his pocket, pulling out an impressive wad of bills, his eyes on Jesse. "No. I'll take my time, in private."

Jesse thought it strange that he didn't want to see

428

her naked. For the kind of money he was paying, it would seem he would want to be sure what he was getting. Something was amiss, but she couldn't be quite sure what it was. She decided that perhaps this man was simply a little strange. It gave her the shivers. Maybe he would be worse than Nick, if that was possible. She watched him pay Nick; then he grabbed her wrist.

"My things," she protested.

"You won't need them," Drew told her. "We're going to Independence and buy you all new clothes." He pulled her close. "But first we're getting a hotel room. I know a man there who'll let me take a nigger to my room, for a small fee. I aim to find out soon as I can just what I got for my money." He turned to West, keeping hold of Jesse's arm. "I'd better be pleased, or I might be back," he warned.

"You'll be pleased." West eyed him narrowly. "The deal is done now, Mr. Hills. I don't give refunds." He walked over to a table, taking out some papers and signing them. He turned and handed them to Drew. "I've signed off my ownership of her. These are the papers you'll need."

Drew took them with a strange smile. "Thank you, Mr. West. By the way, I wonder if you might be able to tell me where this Mr. Wilson lives. Apparently he works for you. I'd like to thank him—give him a little money for leading me here. Sort of an agent's fee, you might call it."

West grinned smugly, thinking what a good deal he had just made. "He'll be glad to hear that. You'll find Ted just this side of Independence, a small white house next to a brick school. It's trimmed in green, and there is a big willow tree in his front yard. Ted does odd jobs at the railroad warehouse when he's not working for me. I expect you would find him at home later this evening. I ought to thank him myself. He saved me the trouble of putting Jesse up for auction."

Drew smiled broadly, feeling like dancing. "Well, I thank you for the information. It's been pleasant doing business with you, Mr. West. Perhaps we'll do it again sometime."

"Maybe. Right now I've got no other niggers for sale." He looked at Jesse with the evil, victorious grin she had learned to hate. She knew he meant George, knew he enjoyed taunting her by selling her far away from the man she loved. "Good-bye, Jesse," he said coolly.

So, that was all there was to it. She was like a prize pig he had nurtured and fattened up and now was being handed over for the slaughter. She meant no more to him than that. Now that he had used her shamefully and most likely ruined her chance to ever have children, he was through with her.

Her new owner hastened her outside, telling her to climb up on his horse, a bay-colored horse with black feet. He climbed up behind her, wrapping his arms around her to pick up the reins, then nodded to West and rode off with her.

For nearly a mile they rode at a rapid gait before Jesse's new owner slowed the horse. She noticed someone in the distance, wearing white man's clothes but sitting on an Indian pony. She stiffened.

"Don't worry, Jesse," the man who had just bought her said. "I'm not going to touch you, and neither is he. You're a free woman now."

Jesse frowned, turning to look at him. "What?" She realized he no longer spoke with an accent.

Drew grinned. "I'm Drew Walters—brother-in-law to Blake Hastings. I faked this whole thing to get you out from under Nick West. That's Blake up there

430

waiting for us."

Jesse turned to look. As they came closer, she realized the man riding with her was telling the truth. Blake Hastings! Alive! Her mind whirled with the reality of it, her heart pounding harder. Was it true? She was going to be freed? Did she dare believe it? They came closer, and her eyes teared. He was thinner, but the man on the Indian pony was indeed Blake Hastings. "Blake!" she gasped.

He smiled. "Hello, Jesse." He looked at Drew. "It worked?"

Drew grinned. "Eleven hundred. I didn't even have to spend all my money. And he told me where Ted Wilson lives—about three miles from here." He dismounted, reaching up and taking Jesse off the horse. Blake walked closer and drew Jesse close, hugging her and whirling her around.

"This is almost as good as shoving a knife in Nick West's belly," he shouted, kissing Jesse's hair. He set her on her feet. "Everything is all right, Jesse. This man is my brother-in-law. He's going to take you to New England and give you your freedom papers. West had my wife put in prison, but we're going now to try to get her out, and you'll all go to New England together."

With shaking hands Jesse touched his arms, looking him over. "I . . . I don't understand. Nick . . . had you shot!"

"Ted Wilson was supposed to do it. He chickened out and left me for dead, but I didn't die! Pawnee Indians helped me. And as long as Nick West thinks I'm dead, I don't have to worry about him coming after me. We decided to have Drew buy you legally so you wouldn't have to worry about being hunted, either. Drew can set you free, and Nick West can't do a damn thing about it!"

"I . . . I can't believe this is happening." Jesse swallowed, her eyes tearing more.

Blake saw all the past horrors in those eyes, mingled with a sudden overwhelming relief. She broke into pitiful sobbing, and he pulled her close. "It's all over now, Jesse. As soon as Drew gets you and my wife out of here, I'm going to find a way to get George. I promise you I'll bring him to you."

Her only reaction was to cling to him, weeping pitifully. Blake looked at Drew, who had dismounted. "Your father would be damn proud of you right now, and so will Sam when she finds out." He gently released a still-weeping Jesse. "You get her to that deserted house outside of town and I'll pay a visit to our friend, Mr. Wilson."

Both men were grateful that at least this first part of their plan had worked. Maybe God was with them after all. "I just hope your Mr. Wilson cooperates," Drew told Blake. "I'd like to be there to see the look on his face when he sees you."

The deep joy of vengeance shone brightly in Blake's dark eyes. "Yes, that should be quite a treat." He touched Jesse's shoulder. "Drew is taking you to a deserted farmhouse we found outside of Independence. You'll be safe there. He's got the papers of ownership now, so West can't touch you, Jesse. This will all be over soon."

She grasped his arms, looking up at him. "Do you really think you can get George out?"

"I'm going to try my best." He brushed at her tears. "Before you know it we'll all be together in New England."

She sniffed, reaching up and touching his face. "God bless you, Blake Hastings, and God help you." She turned to Drew. "And you, too, Mr. Walters."

Drew just grinned. "I'm sorry for some of the things I had to say back there, but I had to convince West."

She shook her head. "It wouldn't have mattered what you had to do or say. Just the thought of being out from under Nick West's hold . . ." She shivered, beginning to cry all over again. "It's like a miracle." She looked back at Blake. "I just hope you can get George away."

Blake sighed. "So do I. You just stay with Drew now and do whatever he tells you."

She nodded. "Yes, sir, I will."

Blake grasped her about the waist and put her back on Drew's horse, the Reverend Walters's black-footed bay that had been left behind after the raid on Lawrence. Blake thought again what a handsome couple Jesse and George would make, if he could just get them together. The feel of her slender body made him think of Samantha, how much he missed her, needed her, longed for her. Soon . . . soon she would be in his arms again. He could only pray she was still alive, and that she wasn't sick and hadn't lost the baby. If anything worse had happened to her, he would never forgive himself for leaving her in the first place. He already felt responsible for the horrors she must have suffered, and he vowed to spend the rest of his life making up for it.

He mounted his own horse and looked over at Drew. "One down and two to go," he told his brother-in-law. "Sam is next." He picked up the reins of a pack horse they had purchased in Lawrence to carry what was left of Blake and Samantha's personal belongings.

The two men's eyes held, both of them feeling the same desperateness. "Let's get going then," Drew answered. He kicked his horse into a gentle lope, and Blake followed, leading the pack horse, both men heading for Independence.

Ted Wilson looked across the table at his wife when they heard a knock at their back door. They and their two young children were eating supper in the kitchen. Wilson's wife saw the worried look in her husband's eyes, something that had been there a lot lately. She had suspected for months that he was a part of bushwhacker raids, and she did not like what it was doing to him, in spite of her firm belief that slaves should not be freed. She suspected he was putting the whole family in danger.

"No one ever comes visiting at the back door," she told Ted.

The man slowly rose. "Take the kids into the parlor," he told her, walking to where his gunbelt hung on a hook, glad the back door had no windows so that whoever was out there couldn't see his actions.

"Ted, this has to end," the woman told him, picking up a baby girl from a chair and taking the hand of their six-year-old son.

"Just get out of the kitchen."

The woman quickly left, and Ted cocked his six-gun, standing against the wall near the door. "Who is it?" he called out.

"Buck," Blake lied from outside. "Let me in. We've got a job to do."

Ted thought the voice sounded different, but decided it was just because he was talking through a door. He breathed a little easier and opened the door, then gasped when a big man barged in, holding a rifle barrel to his throat. "Let go of the gun, Wilson!"

434

Blake growled. He kicked the door shut.

Ted stared at him wide-eyed, dropping the six-gun. He swallowed. "Look, Hastings, I . . . I don't know how you survived, but you ought to know it's only because of me. I was supposed to shoot you, remember?"

"I remember, all right!" Blake seethed through gritted teeth. He saw a movement to his right and he swung the rifle, startling the woman and children.

"Ted, what is going on?" the woman demanded to know.

"Get back in the parlor," Ted snapped. "Get the children out of here!"

Blake moved the rifle back to Ted's head and shoved hard, making Ted stumble backward. "What's wrong, Wilson? You afraid I'd bring harm to innocent women and children, like *you've* done?"

The man just stood there, still staring at him as though he was a ghost, sweat breaking out on his brow.

"What does he mean, Ted?" the woman asked. "What have you done?"

"Get *out* of here!" the man repeated.

"No! I want some answers!"

Blake kept his eyes on Wilson, pushing the rifle so that it hurt the man's throat. "Your husband watched me be whipped, and then was supposed to blow my head off!" he sneered. "I suppose I should thank him for not doing the latter, but I won't forget being dumped out on the prairie in a bloody, dying heap! If not for some Pawnee Indians, I would be *dead!* But that's not the *worst* of it, is it, Wilson?" he snarled. "You helped put my pregnant wife in *prison!*" The room hung silent for a moment, until Wilson's son started crying at the sight of a man holding a gun on his father.

"Please . . ." Mrs. Wilson begged Blake. "I don't know who you are, but my children are watching. Please don't kill my husband, or hurt us!"

Blake backed off slightly, still keeping watch on Wilson. "I didn't come here to kill him. I came here to give him a chance to save his life—if he does what I ask him to do." He nudged Wilson in the shoulder with the rifle. "Sit down!" he ordered.

Wilson, visibly shaken, slowly took a chair. Mrs. Wilson told her son to stop crying and asked him to take his little sister into the parlor and play with their toys, ordering them to stay there until she came for them. The children ran off, and their mother approached the table, picking up plates that still held uneaten pork chops and potatoes. She moved them to one end of the table and sat down near her husband.

"Is it true?" she asked the man. "You helped put this man's wife in prison?"

Wilson kept his eyes on Blake. "It's true," he answered. "But I never meant for her to have to stay the whole six months. I was just tomorrow going to send an anonymous telegram to Lawrence to let her brother know where she was."

Blake wanted dearly to pull the trigger. At the moment only the presence of the man's wife and children, and the fact that Ted might be able to help, kept him from doing so. "What good would that have done?" he sneered.

"I'm not sure. At least they would have known where she was. Maybe there was something legal they could do. The orders putting her in there were trumped up by a judge—paid off by Nick West."

"She was *pregnant*," Blake growled. "A good eight months by now, close to nine! How did you think she was going to survive, having a baby in *jail*, her *first*, no less! She could *die*, and so could my baby, if they aren't *already* dead!''

"*Why*, Ted!" The man's wife felt sick at the thought of it. "What else have you done? And why?''

He moved his eyes to his wife. "We needed the money,'' he answered. "Nick West pays well. How do you think I managed to rent such a nice house for you?''

The woman paled. "My God, Ted, I don't want the damn house if it means you have to resort to murder and torturing pregnant women!''

"She wasn't tortured, and I've never actually murdered anyone! Hastings would have been my first! But I didn't *do* it!''

"Just being in jail is torture enough for that poor woman! And you left this man to *die*, Ted! That's as good as trying to kill him!" She looked up at Blake. "Who are you?''

Blake leaned against a cupboard, keeping his eyes on both of them, as he related his whole story.

When he finished, Mrs. Wilson looked pale, and she turned to her husband. "You told me you just did messenger work for Mr. West.''

Wilson kept his eyes on Blake. "What do you want, Hastings? Do you realize that if West finds out you're still alive, I'll be killed?''

Blake grinned a little. "Do you think I care?''

"You should. I saved your life.''

"You didn't save my life. You just chickened out of a dirty job.''

"I also saved your wife from being raped,'' Wilson retorted. He watched Blake stiffen at the word. "Ask her. She'll tell you. Clyde Beecher wanted to rape her. He started beating her, but I stopped him. I told him to get the hell back to Lawrence and we'd take care of her. A couple of the men with me also might have

437

raped her, but I kept them at bay, and I didn't let any of them ride in the coach with us when we brought her here. I also threatened the sheriff. Told him if he touched her he'd answer to West. And I meant my promise to let her brother know where she was."

Blake's jaw flexed with rage at the thought of Beecher hitting Samantha. He would be lucky to find her alive, let alone discover she hadn't lost the baby. "How noble of you," he growled.

Wilson put his elbows on the table, holding his head in his hand for a moment. "Look, Hastings, I had already decided I was through with West. The money seemed good at first. All I had to do was ride on a few raids, burn a few crops and barns. I didn't have to kill anybody." He breathed deeply, leaning back in his chair again, his eyes red and watery when he looked at Blake again. "But once you start working for West, he expects more and more of you. Then you get to where you're afraid to quit him because he's got things on you and he could bring harm to your family. I told him my wife's been ill and that I had to back out for a while. He didn't seem to mind, once I told him I had finished you off. Now my whole family is in danger."

"Oh, Ted, how could you!" his wife groaned. She covered her eyes with her hand.

Blake pulled out a chair and put his foot up on it, resting the rifle across his knee. "I'd make arrangements to get out of Independence if I were you, Wilson. It won't be long before word gets around I'm alive, since everyone in Lawrence knows it. Clyde Beecher is dead. A mob in Lawrence tarred and feathered him and tied him to the train tracks." Susan Wilson shuddered at the remark, spoken matter-of-factly by Blake. "If you stay here in Independence, some of West's men might come gunning for you," Blake continued. "But if you get out of town, and I take care of West, you should be all right. With West out of the way, the rest of his men won't bother hunting you down. It's West who would follow you all the way to California if he had to. But if things go right, I'll have my wife back, *and* George; and you won't have to worry about Nick West any longer."

Wilson and his wife both looked at him in surprise. "What are you talking about?" Wilson asked.

"I'm saying you're going to help me free my wife, Wilson, and then you're going to get my friend George Freedom away from West's farm. I have my own plans for West, and when I'm through, he won't be around to direct any more raids."

Wilson looked at the rifle, back to Blake's eyes. "You're going to kill him?"

"If I can find a way—yes."

Wilson ran a hand through his hair. "Well, you'd better do it soon. He's fixing to go to St. Louis by riverboat. Makes the trip every summer—likes to gamble on the riverboats, looks for new slaves on the market in St. Louis."

Blake put his foot down, all senses alert. "When?"

"In about three days."

"Does he ever check on Samantha?"

"No. He knows Sheriff Stevens will keep her until he's told otherwise."

"Good. Then the first thing you're going to do is go over to that jail—*tonight!* You're going to tell the sheriff that West has ordered him to turn my wife over to your custody and that you're to take her to West's place. The man knows you work for West. He'll do what you ask. You get her out of there and bring her to me. I'm holed up in a deserted house just west of here."

Wilson frowned. "West will hang me by the heels!"

"I told you not to worry about West. Once I have my wife in safe hands, I'll take care of him. I want you to nose around and find out exactly which riverboat West is taking. As soon as he's on his way, you're going to go and get George. I want West gone first, so when he's found dead there will be no suspicion that George might have done it. Tell the others you saw West in town before he left, and before he boarded the riverboat he sent you back to get George—that he's been sold to the same man who purchased Jesse March."

Wilson frowned. "Jesse? West sold her?"

Blake grinned. "He sold her, to my *brother*-in-law. West thought he was a wealthy plantation owner from Georgia. Jesse will be a free woman now. But you aren't going to tell that to anyone else, are you?" He leveled the rifle again. "Do all this my way, and there will be no suspicion against you, or even against George or Jesse. The rest of them think I'm dead, Wilson, at least for now. Like I said, once West is out of the way, none of the others will bother coming for you if you get the hell out of Independence."

"How do I know you'll do it?"

Blake headed toward the door. "All I need is to know which riverboat he's going to board. The man hanged my father, whipped me nearly to death, and incarcerated my wife. That's enough incentive, don't you think? Trouble is, can I trust you to never mention my name?"

Their eyes held. "I'd be pretty stupid to do that. If I name you, I'm the one in trouble, especially if West's men find out you're still alive."

Blake nodded. "Then we have an understanding?"

"You've got to help him, Ted," his wife told him. "It's the least you can do. How could you help torture innocent people?"

He closed his eyes. "It wasn't like that, Jennifer. At least it wasn't supposed to be."

Blake raised his rifle, resting it on his shoulder. "It's hard for a man to remain passive in these times," he told the woman. "I know that from experience. My own wife wanted me to stay that way, but a man can be pushed only so far."

Wilson looked up at him. "It won't end here, you know. Maybe for you and your family, but this whole slavery issue won't end. This is just the beginning. This whole country will be at war before it's over."

Blake nodded. "I suppose it will. And I expect if it comes to that, you'll be fighting for the southern cause, and I'll be fighting to preserve the Union and free the slaves. Maybe we'll meet again . . . on a *battlefield!*"

Their eyes held, neither man wanting it to come to that, yet both knowing they would be in the middle of the fighting if it did. "Maybe we will," Wilson answered. "Kind of a shame, isn't it? Under other circumstances, I expect you and I might have been able to be friends."

Blake opened the back door. "Before this is over, a lot of friendships are going to be ruined, Wilson; even families. Let's go. I want my wife out of that jail tonight."

Wilson sighed, rising. "I'd better put on my gun or it will look suspicious to the sheriff."

Blake eyed him carefully. "Go ahead. Take your horse so it looks like you're ready to ride out to West's place. I'll be waiting in the shadows out back of the

441

jail. In the dark the sheriff won't know me from any of West's men. You keep Sam with you until we're well away. I don't want her yelling out my name in surprise. You ride with me to where I'm holed up with Jesse and my friend. Once you hand Samantha over, you find out about West and come back to report to me. Then we'll see about freeing George. You can make your own plans and excuses for getting out of Independence. You should be all right. You think you can handle all that?"

Wilson looked at his wife again as he buckled his gunbelt. "Please, Ted, do it for me. If there is going to be war, then go and fight your battles if you have to—on the *battlefield*, where wars are *supposed* to be fought, not against innocent people!"

The man put on his hat while Blake emptied the bullets from his six-gun so Ted couldn't use it on him if he decided to change his mind. "Considering the fact that you're alive, I don't really have a whole lot of choice but to do this," Ted told Blake. "I'd have too much explaining to do once it's discovered, especially after West is found dead. I'm doing this mostly for my family." He turned to his wife. "You'd better start packing."

A tear slipped down Jennifer Wilson's cheek as she suddenly realized she hardly knew the man she had married.

Wilson looked back at Blake, taking his empty gun from the man and slipping it into its holster. "I'll say one thing. You wouldn't have had to force me to go and get your wife out. I felt even worse about that than I did over leaving you for dead. The only reason I went along with it was I knew I'd never be able to take the other two men with me; and if I got killed, she'd have been worse off left alone with them. And that's the God's truth. Even if I had been successful,

442

West would have hunted me down, and it still would have been bad for your wife. She was better off taken straight to that jail." He adjusted his hat, suddenly looking sheepish and guilty. "I'll go saddle my horse." He headed out the door.

Blake looked at Wilson's wife. "Please don't hurt him," she asked. "I know how much you must hate him."

"All he has to do is exactly what I told him."

"He will. He's been a tormented man lately, Mr. Hastings. I just didn't understand why. I'm sorry . . . for all the bloodshed and heartache. This isn't the way." She rose. "I hope you realize that your plans for Mr. West . . . they're wrong."

He shook his head. "Not when it comes to Nick West. He's a murderer, plain and simple, and you'd better hope I'm successful, for your husband's sake." He turned to leave then, thinking how ironic it was that Wilson's wife spoke against this violence, very much like Samantha would speak. It seemed it was always the women who had to struggle to keep the peace. He turned from the doorway. "No one really wins in a mess like this," he told the woman. "No one."

Twenty-Three

Blake watched in silent agony when he saw that Ted Wilson had to help Samantha walk when he brought her out the back door of the jail. She had a blanket draped around her shoulders, and in the darkness he couldn't tell for sure how she looked.

"What's West got planned for her?" the sheriff was asking.

"How the hell do I know?" Wilson answered him. "All I know is, he told me to come and get her. You just keep quiet about it, understand? No one is supposed to know West is the one who sent her here."

"He's gonna wait till she has that baby and then sell her to white slavers, that's what," the sheriff answered. "I'd sure like to be there to see it."

"You'll be *dead* if you don't keep your mouth shut," Wilson answered.

The sheriff stood and watched as Wilson helped a very pregnant Samantha climb up on his horse. Blake waited in the shadows. He could hear Samantha begging Wilson not to take her to West. "You promised . . ." Her words were muffled when Wilson put his hand over her mouth.

"Shut up and get up on that horse," he growled,

afraid for the sheriff to hear her mention that he had promised to contact her brother. Samantha strained to mount up. She appeared to be weak and disoriented, and she was heavy with child. It took all the stamina Blake could muster to keep from going to her; but he didn't dare do so yet for fear she would give everything away. Wilson mounted his horse, reaching around her to pick up the reins.

"Please . . . my baby," Samantha said weakly. "Don't ride too fast."

"You don't really think West gives a damn whether or not you lose the kid, do you," Wilson said coldly. He turned when he finally heard the door close. The sheriff had gone back inside. "Goddamn, it's about time," he muttered. "Let's go, Buck," he said a little louder then to Blake.

Blake gave no reply, keeping his hat pulled down over his face. It was obvious Samantha was too consumed with fear for her own well-being to bother looking at him to see who he was. They rode at a gentle lope, heading out of town.

"Why are you doing this?" Samantha asked Wilson. "It won't . . . change anything. And you promised to contact my brother."

"I make a lot of promises I don't keep," Wilson answered. "Just keep your mouth shut until we get out of town."

"You know me better than that," she answered tersely. With that she started to scream. Wilson's hand came around her mouth firmly, and Samantha began scratching. She started to fall from the horse, but Wilson managed to hang on to her while Blake rode up close and managed to stop the horse.

"Jesus Christ, how do you shut her up?" Wilson asked him. "She'll give it all away."

Blake reached over and grabbed her, moving his

own hand around her mouth, noticing a foul smell. He realized she had apparently been kept in horribly unsanitary conditions. "Get hold of her legs. Help me put her on my horse," he told Wilson.

Sam instantly relaxed, realizing the voice was familiar. Was she going mad? Wasn't that Blake's voice?

"Relax, Sam, and keep your mouth shut," he was saying quietly into her ear. "It's me . . . Blake."

"You got her?" Wilson asked.

"Yes. You get back to your wife. Ride out to West's place tomorrow and see what you can find out. You know where I'll be."

She was dreaming. That was it, Samantha was sure. Blake was dead, and this was a dream. Or maybe she had died and was with him now.

"I'm sorry about her condition," Wilson answered. "It was pretty bad down there where he was keeping her. She looks pretty thin and worn. She's still wearing the dress she wore when I brought her in." He turned his horse. "I'll meet you at the cabin tomorrow."

The man rode off, and Blake trotted his horse through the back side of town and into a thick growth of trees. "It's all right, Sam," he said, slowly taking his hand away from her mouth. "Just be still and don't shout my name. I'm taking you to a place where your brother and Jesse March are waiting. Drew is taking both of you to New England right away."

She turned. In the moonlight she could make out his face. It was thinner, but it was Blake's. She touched his chest, his face. "Blake," she whispered.

He put both hands to either side of her face, gently kissing her forehead. "I don't know if you can ever forgive me, Sam. I'll spend the rest of my life trying to make this up to you."

The thrill of the reality of it swept through her. This was Blake, and she was not dreaming! "Blake," she repeated. "They told me . . . you were dead!" She grasped his wrist, and he was horrified at how bony her hand felt, even her face when he touched it. "Blake," she squeaked again. She reached around his neck, breaking into pitiful sobs. "Oh, my God! My God," she wept almost hysterically. "Thank you, thank you, Lord Jesus!"

She clung to him tightly, wanting to be sure he was real. There they were, Blake's strong arms around her! There was the scent of him, the feel of him. She never thought she would feel such warmth and love and protection again. Blake! By some miracle he was alive!

Blake wept his own silent tears at the realization of the pitiful way she had been treated. He thanked God that her belly was still big with their child. She sat sideways in front of him, and he moved one hand down to gently touch her stomach, relieved when he felt a movement.

"You've got to calm down, Sam," he told her gently then. "Someone might hear. We've got to get going."

She continued to cling to him, afraid to let go, loving the smell of him, the feel of his arms around her. "Blake, you're alive," she repeated. "I don't understand. What happened to you! Where have you been? How did you find me?"

"I'll answer all your questions once I get you someplace where we can clean you up and let you rest for a couple of days. He grasped her arms and gently pulled them from around his neck, kissing her cheeks, her eyes, not caring about her condition, only caring that she was alive. "I'm so damn sorry, Sam. This is all my fault."

"No," she answered, wiping at her eyes. "It's war, Blake . . . just like you said. I know you meant to come right back. And you were right . . . about Clyde Beecher." More tears started to flow. "Oh, Blake, he told me you were badly hurt . . . and that he'd take me to you. I believed him. I should have listened to you!"

He raised up slightly in his stirrups, taking a handkerchief from his back pocket and handing it to her. "What's done is done. We've found each other now, and everything is going to be all right. Beecher is dead."

She blew her nose, looking up at him then. "Dead!"

"It's a long story. Let's get you to where we can help you first."

"You said Drew is with you? And Jesse? How, Blake?"

"Don't worry about it right now." He reached around her and picked up the reins. "I'll try to go easy." He headed the horse farther from town. Samantha leaned against his chest, wrapping her warms around him, her mind swirling with questions. But none of them mattered for the moment. Blake was alive! She was free of that horrid, smelly, rat-infested cell! The shock of her sudden release and the discovery her husband was alive suddenly set in; it combined with a weakened state from neglect and not enough food so that she felt light-headed and dizzy.

"Blake," she whimpered, beginning to slip from the horse. He slowed the animal, getting a firm hold on her.

"Hang on, Sam. It's not much farther."

The night seemed like a strange dream to Samantha. She still struggled to believe it was really Blake she saw by the soft light of an oil lamp; that it was really Blake who was giving orders to someone to light a fire and heat water. Was that really Drew's voice saying he'd found an old washtub? She rested in Blake's arms, having no idea where he had brought her, and not caring. She was with him, and that was all that mattered.

"I'll keep watch outside while you and Jesse clean her up" came Drew's voice again.

Someone undressed her. "My God, look at her," Blake swore. "I'd love to get my hands on that sheriff. The son of a bitch!"

"You just concentrate on taking care of your wife for now. You have enough danger ahead without worrying about him," a woman answered.

Danger? What was Blake going to do next? What was going on? Samantha felt herself being lowered into blessedly warm water, breathed deeply of the exotic smell of soap. The warm water relaxed her, and she slipped in and out of a strange state that she was not sure was sleep or unconsciousness, aware of Blake's gentle hands washing her, helped by a lovely Negro woman who carefully washed Sam's hair.

"Thank God I have all her clothes with me," Blake was saying. "For tonight we'll just put a flannel gown on her."

"Yes, sir."

"Will you quit calling me that?" Blake told the woman. "I'm your friend, Jesse, not your master. The same goes for Drew."

Samantha heard a soft laugh. "You have to understand, sir . . . I mean, Blake—it takes some getting used to for someone like me."

Samantha luxuriated in the warm bath, thinking somewhere deep in her mind that this beautiful, kind

450

woman was part of the reason she had gone to jail, the kind of person for whom Blake had risked his life. It had to be the mysterious Jesse. She remembered some of the things she had heard about the woman, remembered that George loved her.

Now Blake and Jesse were drying her off. "I must . . . look terrible," she remembered saying, trying to cover her belly with her arms, realizing Blake had never seen her naked in such a pregnant condition.

"You've never looked more beautiful to me than right now," he was telling her. He wrapped a blanket around her and helped her rinse her mouth with baking soda and gave her a small piece of peppermint candy to suck on. It tasted wonderful, the first real treat she had had since before she was confined.

Blake and Jesse helped her to another room where blankets were spread out over an old mattress and helped her lie back. She felt Blake and Jesse both patting her with powder and rubbing her down with a lovely smelling lotion. She never dreamed it could feel this wonderful to be clean.

"She's so thin," Blake was saying. "I hope her debilitated condition won't affect the baby."

"Babies are pretty strong little things," Jesse assured him. "And that baby is part of the reason she's so thin. He'll take all the nourishment he can from her, leaving her with not much to go on. I imagine the baby is a lot healthier right now than your wife."

Someone slipped a soft flannel gown over her head. Was all this real? Would she wake up in the ugly cell? She wanted to talk more, ask more questions, but this strange, consuming weariness made talking seem like such an effort. Blake helped her sit up while Jesse managed to comb the tangles from her long dark hair. "After what that man did to

451

me, sometimes I wonder if I'll ever be able to give George a child," the woman was saying.

"You can't give up hope yet, Jesse," Blake answered. "Once we get to Massachusetts, Drew can help find you a good doctor. As far as George goes, just being free and being able to be with you is all that will matter to him."

"I just hope that Mr. Wilson can really get him out," Jesse said.

"Blake, I don't understand . . . what happened," Samantha murmured. "What are you going to do?"

"We'll talk in the morning," he told her. "I just want you to sleep now. In the morning Jesse will make you the biggest breakfast you ever ate." He laid her back into soft blankets. "Thanks, Jesse. Do me a favor and take her old clothes outside to the fire and burn them."

"Yes, sir . . . I mean, Blake. You just lie there and keep your arms around your wife for tonight. I expect she needs that more than anything."

Samantha heard a door close, felt Blake settle in beside her. His arms came around her then, and she settled against him. "Just sleep now," he told her.

"Don't let go, Blake," she whispered.

He kissed at her damp hair, nuzzled her neck, gently caressed her full breasts for a moment. He gave no thought to the aching in his body for her. He just wanted to enjoy the feel of her, the strange, secure feeling he got from touching the soft breasts and holding her close. He just wanted to keep reminding himself she was really alive and here in his arms.

"I won't let go," he answered, stroking the damp hair away from her face. "You just sleep now. Sleep all you want."

At first she thought it strange, that she could be so tired after being in a cell with nothing to do for over six weeks, but then she realized that she had lived under constant tension, fear, and frustration. That, and malnutrition, and her pregnancy, added to the shock of what had happened to her this night—all had left her so weak. She fell asleep to the feel of Blake's big, gentle hand still stroking her hair.

Sunshine filtered through a window, and a bird just outside chirped loudly, waking Samantha. At first she wondered at the sound. She lay still, gathering her thoughts, remembering bits and pieces from the night before. Oh, how good the sunshine looked! How sweet the sound of that bird! How fresh the morning summer air smelled!

It was true! She felt clean, could still smell the lilac water Blake had put on her the night before. Blake! She stirred, touching the strong forearm that was still wrapped around her. She turned then. She had to see for herself, see him in the morning light. She felt alarm at how thin his face looked. She wanted to see the rest of him, to know that he was really all right, but he had left his shirt and pants on—probably, she guessed, because he had to be ready in case an enemy came looking for them.

Blake opened his eyes and smiled. "Good morning. How do you feel?"

She touched his face. "I don't even know yet. Oh, Blake, how did all this happen? When Joe told me you were dead—he seemed so sure of it. Knowing Nick West, I believed him."

"Joe?"

"The man who took me out of jail last night."

He kissed her eyes. "His name isn't Joe. It's Ted. Ted Wilson."

She traced her fingers over his lips. "I *knew* Joe

wasn't his real name. He wouldn't tell me his name that day he and his friends brought me to Independence. I *knew* Nick West had to be behind it, but he wouldn't tell me that, either. Blake, what has happened? Where have you been? How did you find me?"

He put a finger to her lips. "First there's us . . . then breakfast . . . then the explanations." So long they had been apart! So joyous were their hearts at finding each other again, at knowing they were both alive! He kissed her gently, sweetly. For several minutes they just touched and kissed and drank in each other's presence, the lovely morning sounds of birds and a rooster crowing somewhere in the distance pure music to Samantha's ears.

Yes, God was good after all! They were free and alive and together, and from now on life was going to be good. She still had the baby, and her precious Blake! She smiled softly, touched his hair. "Blake, you're thinner. What happened to you? You must have been hurt badly for Ted Wilson to be so sure you were dead."

He sighed deeply, kissing her once more before rising. "I think you'd better eat some breakfast before I tell you all of it. I wouldn't want to spoil your appetite."

She frowned, managing to sit up. "Blake, what is it?"

He got up and tucked in his shirt. "I was hauling guns to John Brown, but I never made it. West and his men caught me. I was beaten and shot and taken to West's farm; but that wasn't the worst of it." He took a deep breath, suddenly looking like a sorry little boy, as though he thought she might not want him if she knew.

"West had me whipped," he finally said, aching at

her gasp and her eyes wide with horror. "He and Clyde Beecher did the honors. By the time they were through, I had hardly more than a trickle of life left in me. I was dumped off and left to die by none other than Ted Wilson, who was supposed to finish me off. But he didn't do it. He just left me out on the prairie to bleed to death, or die from flies and infection. Some Pawnee Indians came along and saved my life, but I was a long time recovering."

She just stared at him, letting the horror of it sink in. Her eyes moved over him, and she knew instinctively that at this moment she had to be very strong. Now she knew why he had left on his clothes. She could see by his eyes he was afraid for her to see his back. "Take off your shirt, Blake."

He turned away, picking up his boots. "No."

"Take it off! You're my husband, and I'd love you if you had come back with no arms or no legs. It doesn't matter, Blake. You might as well show me and get it over with."

He stood still, his back to her. He breathed deeply and slowly unbuttoned the shirt, then removed it. Samantha made a pitiful choking sound. Her beautiful Blake! His back was scarred as though he had been terribly burned.

"My God, Blake!" she gasped.

"They go all the way down my backside," he told her, slowly putting the shirt back on. "After West finished with my back, Beecher took over my hips and the back of my legs. West still had Jesse and had captured George—was using him like a common slave. He made Jesse and George both watch my whipping."

Samantha covered her face, breaking into tears. "If only I could have been with you . . . helped you," she wept. "I felt you calling for me. Now I know why."

She felt him beside her then, his arms coming around her. "I feel the same way about you. You were suffering alone."

"But you went through something much worse." She moved her arms around him. "Oh, Blake, my darling Blake. We can only thank God He brought those Indians to help you." She jerked in a sob as she leaned back to study his handsome face, touching it, so glad there were no horrible scars there. He was still her Blake, still strong and virile, still alive. But something remained in his eyes, the same look he had carried before he left Lawrence—a continuing need for revenge. She felt a sudden dread. "It's not over, is it?"

He touched her hair. "No, Sam."

Their eyes held. After what she had seen, and what had been done to her, how could she expect him to feel any other way? "I don't want to lose you again, Blake," she said, new tears coming.

"You won't. But we do have to be apart again, just for a little while. You and Jesse are going to Massachusetts with Drew. I want you the hell out of Missouri *and* Kansas, someplace where I know you'll be safe."

She shook her head. "I . . . don't understand. How did you manage to get Jesse away from Nick West? And what about George?"

Blake rose, walking over to pull on his boots. "I'll tell you everything, from beginning to end, including what I plan to do next. First I want you to eat some breakfast."

She looked around the dusty room, which contained only an old dresser and the mattress on which they had slept. "Where are we?"

"We're just outside of Independence in an abandoned farmhouse. The sooner you and Jesse get out

456

of here, the better, just in case West discovers you've been freed."

She frowned, looking back at him. "Ted Wilson. Why did he help you get me out of there last night?"

Blake strapped on a gun he had purchased along with some clothes in Lawrence before leaving. "More out of a guilty conscience than anything else, I expect, as well as more than a little fear. Now that I'm alive, he'll have some explaining to do if things don't work out the way we've planned it. I'll go get some water so you can wash your face and clean your teeth. We'll talk over breakfast." He tied the strap of his holster around his thigh, then straightened. "I love you, Sam. I'll never let anything like that happen to you again, and the right people are going to pay for this."

She watched him, wanting to protest any thoughts of vengeance, yet knowing it was useless. How could a man not want to avenge such an atrocity, especially a man like Blake? Blake turned and left the room, and a moment later the beautiful Negro woman came in, wearing a pale-pink dress of cotton and lace. Her hair was curled up into a fancy knot on top of her head, a few strands coming loose now, the pretty dress wrinkled from a night's sleep. She carried a pan of water.

"I have some breakfast cooking," she told Samantha, helping her get to her feet. "How are you this morning? Do you need help dressing and washing?"

"No. I think I can do it." Samantha studied the soft-spoken woman. "You're Jesse."

Jesse nodded. "Yes, ma'am."

Samantha smiled through tears. "You're even more beautiful than George described you."

"Thank you, ma'am. You're very lovely yourself.

457

How is that baby doing?"

Samantha touched her stomach. "Fine, so far."

Jesse smiled. "I'm glad you're all right, for your husband's sake. He's a good man, Mrs. Hastings." The woman turned to leave and Samantha called out to her, walking up and touching her arm.

"Please, call me Sam." She smiled. "Thank you so much for helping last night. I'm glad Blake got you away from Nick West." She saw remnants of horror in Jesse's eyes.

"Yes," Jesse answered. "Now if only George can also escape."

"I don't know what they have planned, Jesse, and I wanted to tell Blake to forget it. The last thing I want is for him to put himself in danger again. But I know the feeling now of losing the man you love, of fearing you'll never see him again, never feel his arms around you again. I won't try to stop him. I hope you get George back." She sighed. "I feel . . . almost honored to meet you."

Jesse's eyes widened. *"Honored?* Why would you feel honored to meet a Negro woman?"

Samantha's eyes teared. "Look at what you've suffered. Yet you stand there so beautiful and dignified, still looking so proud. You must be a very strong woman, Jesse."

Jesse smiled softly then. "You have experienced your own suffering. There is no doubt you're a strong woman, too, Mrs. . . . I mean . . . Samantha."

"Sam. Just Sam." She smiled in return, and suddenly both women embraced. Samantha broke into tears, hugging Jesse tightly. This was what it was all for, and it was worth it.

Samantha glanced up at Ted Wilson as he came

inside the abandoned house. Their eyes held for a moment, hers showing a mixture of contempt and a tiny bit of gratitude for what he was doing now; his filled only with remorse. Jesse's eyes widened at the sight of one of West's men, and Samantha heard the woman's breathing quicken. She reached over and grasped Jesse's hand. "It's all right now, Jesse," she told her.

Wilson reddened slightly, looking at Blake. "West is leaving day after tomorrow. He'll be taking the *Missouri Maiden*. It leaves around ten in the morning."

Samantha, Jesse, and Drew all sat on crates, using two more crates for coffee cups and tin plates, which held a little food from breakfast. Samantha wore a blue calico dress designed for pregnant women that Blake had bought for her before leaving Lawrence, knowing that when he found her she would need clothes. The dress was gathered just under the breast to allow fullness for her condition. Her long dark hair was brushed out softly and pulled back at the sides with tortoiseshell combs.

Wilson glanced at her again. He had forgotten how beautiful she was, since the day he had first brought her to Lawrence her face had been dirty and swollen from Beecher's beating, her dress torn and soiled.

"You want some coffee?" Blake asked him.

Wilson looked back at him. "No." He removed his hat and ran a hand through his hair nervously. "I just want to get back to my wife. Soon as this is over, we're heading east. We've got kin in Kentucky. I guess that's where we'll go."

Blake nodded. "By noon today my wife and these other two will also be gone. I'll wait here. As soon as West leaves, you bring George here. Then you can be on your way. I'll never mention where you've gone and you don't know where I've gone. That will be the end of it. I have papers proving George is a free man."

"How can you be sure you can trust him, Blake?" Drew spoke up. "Once we're gone, he could come back here and shoot you down. That would solve his problem of your still being alive."

Blake held Wilson's eyes. "He didn't shoot me when he had a lot easier chance to do it. Why would he do it now, after going this far for us?"

Wilson sighed deeply. "I guess you're just going to have to trust me, aren't you," he said to Blake. "After all, I *did* show up. I could have already left Kansas last night."

"I have a feeling it's your *wife* who made sure you came back," Blake answered. "I'll wager that if you ever want to be welcome in your own house again, you'd better finish this job. Besides, it's a little late for me to be found dead. Between that and my wife being freed, a lot of fingers would point to you, wouldn't they? And I wouldn't be around to get rid of Nick West, so he'd be after you, too. There is too much at stake now for you to turn on me, Wilson."

The man put his hat back on. "There's a lot at stake for *both* of us." He sighed, hooking his thumbs in his gunbelt. "I'll have George Freedom here day after tomorrow, a few hours after West leaves. I still don't understand how you're going to take care of West. He'll be well on his way to St. Louis."

"Don't worry. After seeing the condition my wife was in last night, nothing can keep me from catching up with Nick West."

Wilson looked over at Samantha again. "I know it doesn't mean much to you now, ma'am, but I am sorry. I really did intend to get hold of your brother

460

That thing with you, that's the last job I pulled for West."

Sam just glared at him. "It's too bad you didn't quit a little sooner."

Wilson glanced from her to Jesse and back to Sam. "Be glad I didn't, or someone else would have been ordered to kill your husband and would have *done* it. And you would have suffered something a lot worse than prison if I hadn't been there the day Beecher brought you to us."

Samantha's cheeks reddened slightly. "I thank you for that much, Mr. Wilson. It's such a waste, isn't it—all this violence among supposedly civilized people? I hope men like those you rode with don't harm your own wife," Samantha answered. "I suggest you do like Blake says and leave Missouri as soon as you deliver George."

Wilson looked back at Blake. "He'll be here around noon day after tomorrow."

Blake nodded. "I'll be waiting."

Wilson glanced at Samantha once more. "I really am sorry. It probably doesn't make a whole lot of difference to you, but after leaving your husband to die, I spent a lot of sleepless nights. I figured the only way to make up for it was to do what I could for you. I knew I couldn't stop West, but I could at least protect you somewhat by volunteering to be among those who were to bring you in, so I could make sure the others didn't hurt you."

Samantha thought about how he had held a gun on Beecher to keep him away from her. She realized then that when a man worked for West, he didn't have a lot of options. She rose from the crate and walked over to stand near him. "I was brought up a Christian, Mr. Wilson, taught forgiveness and abstention from violence. Right now I am finding it very hard to fight

461

the same vengeful feelings against Nick West that my husband carries. I've seen Blake's back. I understand violence more clearly than I ever have before. I can only hope God will forgive me for what I feel for that man, and I suppose the only way I can begin to accept such things is to at least forgive you. It's a small start at finding the love I used to carry in my heart for all people. Just don't double cross my husband. I need him to come back to me, the same as your wife needs you."

The man's eyes seemed to tear slightly. He only swallowed, then turned and left. Samantha closed her eyes, hating the anger and vengeance that stormed in her own soul. She turned to Blake, and he pulled her close. "How can I leave you behind, Blake?" she groaned.

"Because it simply has to be done. I can't have the burden of worrying about you. I'll be all right, Sam." He looked over at Drew. "Go ahead and start loading everything onto the packhorse. Leave your horse and mine so there will be an extra horse for George. Let Sam ride on the packhorse into town. Take the next train east. You've got plenty of money."

"What if I run into one of West's men?"

"You've got no problem with Jesse. She's yours, free and clear. You'd better leave Sam off at the edge of town. She should visit a clothing store right away and buy a hooded cape. She can wear it until she's on that train and you're all well on your way. Have her buy a ticket herself and board the train as though she doesn't even know you. She's just a woman taking a trip. If she keeps her face hidden under a hood, no one will recognize her. Besides, there are only three other men besides Wilson who even know who she is, and by now they probably don't even remember. She's the last person they'd expect to see walking free in town. Just keep an eye out for that sheriff. If Sam does run into any trouble, you get right back out here to me."

He pulled back, looking down at Samantha. "Try not to attract attention in town. Just get on that train and get yourself to Massachusetts. If things go right, I'll be there myself in about two weeks. You'll be staying with the family Drew has been living with."

Their eyes held, and Samantha touched his face. "Come to me, Blake."

He grasped her hand, kissing her palm. "Nothing is going to keep us apart this time. I'll be there." He looked over at Jesse. "And George will be with me."

Jesse's eyes teared, and she bowed her head, praying that the white man who called George his friend was right. She had never known white men to be kind, was amazed that men like Drew Walters and Blake Hastings even existed. Her heart quickened at the thought of seeing George again, at the thought of both of them being free to love and share their lives. Could such a thing really happen?

She rose to help Drew begin cleaning up and packing. Within an hour they were ready. Blake hated the thought of Samantha having to make such a long trip right away, but it was vital to get her out of Independence. He helped her up onto the packhorse. "I know you dread this trip, Sam, but we have no choice. You've got to get out of here."

She grasped his hand. "I'll be all right."

Blake looked at Drew. "Let her ride until you reach town, then let her off. Give her a light bag to carry and some money so she looks like she's traveling. After she buys a cape she'll have to walk to the train station on her own, not with you. Keep her in sight at all times. Once you're all on the train and it leaves, wait a couple of hours before moving to sit next to each other. Anybody asks questions about Jesse, she's your slave. You use that southern accent you do so well and make it convincing."

"I know what to do."

Blake looked back at Samantha. "I hope you're up to this. If anything happens to that baby now, after coming this far—"

"I can force myself to do anything if it means we can be together. Once I make it to New England, I'll have plenty of time to recuperate. The minister Drew lives with was a good friend of Father's. They used to live near us in Vermont. They're good people, Blake. They'll help us resettle, and you'll love New England. It's so pretty."

The word sounded good—resettle. Could they have a place of their own again? Live in peace? Somehow she suspected deep inside that this was not the end. Maybe they would even come back to Kansas and continue the battle. But not just yet. First they had to heal, to enjoy their baby. There were a lot of decisions to be made, but first he had to get through the next few days alive.

"So much has changed since that night I came to you," she said wistfully. "so much loss. I wish Mother and Father could have seen New England again."

Blake reached up and touched her face. "We're going to make it, Sam."

"We'd better get started," Drew spoke up then. He handed out a piece of paper to Blake. "Hang onto that. It's the address where you'll find us in Massachusetts."

Samantha leaned down from the horse, meeting Blake's lips lightly. "Good-bye," she said, her voice choking.

"No good-byes. I'll see you in a couple of weeks or less."

She nodded, forcing back the tears. It would only make this all harder for him. Blake took the paper from Drew, meeting Samantha's eyes again as he stepped back. Samantha forced a supportive smile, waving as the horse started away. She thought about the hideous scars on his back. If Nick West could do something like that, what would he do if he found Blake still alive and managed to get the upper hand? Blake's only chance was to get Nick West alone on the riverboat, without the man's thugs around to protect him. That was the plan, but a lot depended on Ted Wilson doing his part and getting George to Blake. Samantha knew Blake would never leave Missouri without the man.

She watched him until the horse moved over a rise and she could no longer see him. Again she had to wonder if after today he would be gone from her life forever.

Twenty-Four

George rode quietly on the horse Ted Wilson had brought for him, his ankles chained under the animal's belly and another chain draped around under the horse's neck so that it was impossible to get away. In spite of the fact that he was being sold, it felt good to be off West's farm for the first time in the many months since he first left Lawrence. His greatest regret was that he had failed at helping Jesse, and he had heard through the secret way West's slaves had of communicating that poor Jesse had been sold off just three days ago.

Everything seemed hopeless now. What did it matter where he was being taken? Those he loved most were gone: Blake dead, Jesse sold away, probably never to be found again even if he could escape. He could only pray her new owner was a kinder man than Nick West, though he could not imagine that West knew anyone who was kind.

George decided the only reason he was himself being sold now was because Jesse was no longer around for West to use to taunt him. He had grown tired of her and had sold her off like a prize mare. Now George would be sold, most likely bringing good money because of his size and strength, maybe even for stud service, like an animal.

"Where are you taking me?" he asked Wilson again.

"I told you I don't know the buyer's name. I'm not supposed to know. I'm just supposed to deliver you."

George felt a rage in his soul, knowing this was the man who had killed Blake. "Tell me, Wilson," he asked. "How does it feel to put a gun to an innocent man's head and blow his brains out? Do you ever dream about it?"

"Shut up, nigger, or it will be *your* brains lying on the road," Wilson answered. He wanted to keep the belligerent look on George's face in case they came across any other men working for West. He couldn't tell George the truth yet. If he looked too happy, it might give things away.

"You'd never shoot me," George retorted. "I'm too valuable. West would slaughter you."

Wilson just continued on in silence, and George started singing an old Negro hymn of hope. It felt good to sing again, something all Negroes were denied on the West plantation.

The men rode for three miles, coming then to an old abandoned farm near a town.

"That Independence?" George asked.

"It is."

"My new master waiting there?"

"He's waiting." They came closer to the abandoned house. Wilson dismounted, taking a key from his pocket and coming around to unlock the cuffs from George's ankles and wrists.

George frowned in puzzlement. "What are you doing?"

"Somebody is waiting for you in that house. Get down off your horse and get over there."

George looked toward the house and back at Wilson. "What is this?" he asked suspiciously as he slowly dismounted. "You supposed to shoot me in the back? Claim I was trying to run?"

"Nope." Wilson picked up the chains and slung them over the saddle of the extra horse. "Nothing like that. My part of this job is done now. Just get over to that house." To George's dismay, Wilson mounted up, picking up the reins to the extra horse. He looked at George. "I love my family more than I hate the idea of abolition, nigger. It's that simple. Tell the man in that house that I said good luck, and that I hope we never meet again." He turned the horses and rode toward town.

George stared after Wilson in disbelief, totally confused. He looked at the house, seeing two horses tied outside. He started walking toward it, hardly able to keep his balance because of his free ankles. He had worn the leg irons for so long that he felt almost top-heavy, as though he could bounce or float across the ground. He watched the house. Was he going to be murdered? Why had Wilson wished whoever was inside good luck?

He had nearly reached the porch when someone stepped out. George stopped cold, staring in disbelief. The man standing there was thinner, but the face had not changed. "Blake?"

"Come on inside" came the familiar voice. "We have a lot to talk about."

George's eyes teared. "What the hell—" He mounted the steps, staring in shock.

"I'm not a ghost," Blake assured him. "Good to see you as two free men again, old friend." He put out his hand, and in utter awe George took it, not believing this was real until he felt Blake's firm grip.

"My God," he muttered. In the next moment the

men embraced, both of them misty-eyed. They hugged for a long, silent moment. "For God's sake, white man, what does it take to kill you?" George teased then, a few tears beginning to trickle down his cheeks.

"A lot more than Nick West's whip," Blake answered, slapping his back. "Come on inside."

George hesitated, glancing in the direction in which Ted Wilson had ridden. "Wilson . . . he's the one who was supposed to kill you!" He looked back at Blake. "He just let me go—took off my chains! Nick West can't possibly know about this."

"He doesn't. It's a long story, George. Come on." He stepped inside, and George blinked, still gazing after Wilson. "He might work for West, but the *Lord* surely put him on West's payroll." He followed Blake, looking him over again. "I guess God is merciful after all," he said, his voice gruff with emotion.

"To those who deserve it, George, only to those who deserve it." Blake put an arm around him, leading him to sit down on a crate. "There's no time to waste, George. We've got a riverboat to catch up with."

Raucous piano music and heavy smoke filled the gambling room of the riverboat, where Nick West sat in a silk suit and ruffled white shirt smoking a thin cigar and playing a game of five-card stud. Gold and diamond rings decorated his well-manicured hands. He enjoyed these gambling trips, taken every summer in the hottest time of the year. It always felt good to get off the farm and let the niggers worry about working in the fields and in the smelly stables. His help was well paid to keep things going and to make sure the slaves stayed in line.

He lost the hand, then dealt another, finding it hard to concentrate. He was hoping he'd find a good replacement for Jesse when he reached St. Louis. He wondered what her new owner thought of her by now, even missed her a little. But as soon as he had a new girl to replace her, she'd be quickly forgotten.

This time he won his hand. He leaned across the table to scoop in the pot, pleased with his evening's winnings. He had been playing for hours and was getting tired. He poured his winnings into a leather pouch and thanked the other players, then rose from the table and walked out onto the lower deck of the riverboat, breathing deeply of the night air.

It was late, and few people wandered the decks this hour. Most were either in their cabins or in the gambling hall, and West enjoyed the quiet. He walked toward the back of the boat, where the stairs to the upper cabins were located. A silent figure followed behind him, his footsteps unheard because of the Indian moccasins he wore. As West approached the back of the riverboat, the noise of the paddlewheel swishing lazily through the water helped even more to drown out any sound behind him.

West hesitated at the stairs, deciding to walk to the deck rail at the back of the boat to watch the water for a moment. It sparkled in the moonlight, foamed white when churned up by the paddlewheel. He felt good, victorious. Blake Hastings was dead, and his wife was rotting away in jail where she and her baby would probably die. Her parents had been silenced. He had gotten a good sum of money for Jesse, and now he could look forward to a new young virgin in his bed. It even looked like it would be a good year for the farm.

Those were his last thoughts. Without warning a tall figure loomed up behind him, and before he realized what was happening, a heavy chain came around his neck from behind and was yanked hard and tight, cutting off his air.

"We meet again" came a familiar voice. "Remember me, Nick? Blake Hastings!"

West tried to dig his fingers under the chain to loosen it, but to no avail. Blake's grip was too strong. West's mind whirled with disbelief. Blake Hastings? How could it be!

Blake dragged the man backward into the shadows. "You had my father hanged, choking off *his* air," Blake growled, "making him die slowly, like you're dying now! Rather fitting, don't you think? Only I'm not using a rope. I'm using a *chain*, like the ones you kept on George all these months! Well, George is *free* now, my friend, and so is Jesse! Yes, *Jesse!* You sold her to my brother-in-law, West. How's *that* for laughs!"

The attack had been so sudden; in seconds West had no strength to fight back and his hands dropped limply at his side. Blake pulled even tighter, feeling sick inside with a mixture of rage and hatred, combined with a distant remorse for what he was doing. The firm belief that the world was better off without this man, and the memory of what West had put himself and Sam and George and Jesse through, were all he needed to keep the chain tight until he felt West's whole body going limp. Still he didn't let go. He felt controlled now by the hatred that ate at his guts. He literally shook with rage, finally managing to let West's body slump to the deck.

Blake leaned over him, his breathing heavy, his chest aching, his eyes stinging with tears. He slowly pulled the chain away and checked for a pulse. There

472

was none. He wiped at his eyes with his shirtsleeves. "It's over now, you bastard," he growled in a whisper. He breathed deeply to regain control of himself, thinking how Sam had not wanted him to do this, but that she had finally realized he had little choice. More innocent people would suffer if he hadn't—Ted Wilson's wife and children for starters. He told himself to think only of them.

He moved away from West's body, noticing a dark object lying on the deck. He picked it up, realizing it was a leather pouch full of money. Robbery seemed a decent enough motive for West's death. By the time his body was found downriver, no one would be able to determine exactly where the riverboat was when West was killed, and if the man's money was missing, it would be figured he was attacked and robbed. Whatever people thought the motive was, Nick West would be dead, and he and George would be safe in New England. No one on the riverboat knew their names or that they had anything against Nick West. George had wanted to help with the killing, his own vengeance great, but Blake didn't want him anywhere near, in case something went wrong. "It would go a lot worse for you than for me," he had told him.

Blake stuffed the money into his pants pockets, then carried the chain and leather pouch to the side of the ship and threw both items overboard. He looked around again, saw no one watching. To his relief the moon moved behind a cloud as he went back for West's body. He picked it up, quickly carrying it to the rail and dumping it overboard. The splash it made into the river was shrouded by the much louder splashing of the paddlewheel. Since it was night, and since the body would float downstream while the boat continued to chug upstream, Blake figured that by the time the body was found it would be many miles from the riverboat. It would take several days for the law to determine where the body might have come from, and by then he and George would be long gone.

The moon came back out from behind the cloud, and Blake checked the area once more, finding nothing. He quickly went below deck, where he and George slept on bedrolls with the lower-paying passengers. Animals, wagons, and an assortment of supplies filled the lower area and helped create enough confusion that one man's movements were little heeded.

Blake bedded down next to George then. The big man lay on his back staring into the dark night. "Is it done?" George asked quietly.

"Done," Blake answered.

"You all right?"

Blake grasped his stomach, turning on his side. It was one thing to kill men who were shooting at him. He had never simply killed outright this way. "No," he answered. "But I will be . . . soon as I'm with Sam again. We'll get off at the next stop and take the next train east. I just want to get the hell out of here."

Blake's voice broke on the words. He knew now Samantha was right. The killing had to stop somewhere.

Mid-July 1856

Samantha heard the commotion downstairs, and her heart quickened. Was that really Blake's voice? She, Drew, and Jesse were staying in the home of a Methodist minister, and for the past two weeks Samantha had spent every day in prayer for her

474

husband's safety and in a new appreciation for freedom and peace and simple comforts like a real bed and home-cooked food. She heard familiar footsteps coming up the stairs then, and she sat up straighter in bed, wondering how she looked.

The door opened, and Blake stopped short, drinking in the beautiful view of his wife and new baby son. "They told me . . . downstairs," he said, closing the door and coming closer. His eyes misted as he leaned over her. "My God, Sam," he said softly. "This is the most beautiful sight I've ever laid eyes on."

She cradled the baby in one arm, reaching out to him. "Oh, Blake, thank God!" she cried. "You're all right? You're not hurt?"

He sat down on the bed carefully, leaning over to take both her and the baby in his arms. "I'm all right." For several minutes they just clung to each other, enjoying the exquisite ecstasy of merely embracing, of knowing it was over now and they were together and safe. Blake pulled back then to study her. "What about you? The woman downstairs . . . Mrs. Dills, is it? She said you had kind of a hard time."

"They say the first one is always harder, and he came a little early." Samantha sniffed and wiped at tears, not sure if she wanted to laugh or cry. "I was hoping he'd wait until you got here. I haven't named him yet. I wanted to wait for you." She kissed the baby's head. "He's beautiful, Blake. Perfect. Thank God my ordeal didn't seem to have any effect on him." She touched his arm. "He's got your physical strength and my stubbornness."

They both laughed, but Blake's eyes were also misty. He watched his wife and son lovingly, unable to get his fill. "I need to hold him," he told her.

Samantha helped him pick up the tiny infant. Blake laid his new son in his lap. "I thought we'd name him Ben, after your father," Samantha told him. "If it's all right with you."

He breathed in a long, deep, shuddering sigh, opening the blanket and studying his son, the perfect shape of the child's feet and hands, the pretty face and dark, fuzzy hair. "Ben is a good choice," he answered. He closed his eyes, bringing the infant up against his chest and nuzzling at his hair. "Thank you, Sam. Thank you for giving me a family."

She watched him a moment. He was a different man from the one she had left back at Independence. A lot of the bitterness seemed to be gone. "Did you bring George?"

He kissed the baby's cheek. "Yes. He's out back with Jesse. They have a lot of catching up to do, a lot of horror to try to overcome." He laid the baby back down beside her, reaching out then to touch her face, her hair. "You're still so thin."

"I'll fatten up quick enough, especially if I stay in this house much longer. Mrs. Dills is a marvelous cook. Drew is going to stay here until the fall semester starts, then go back to school. Now that you're back he'll send a wire to the Hankses to let them know we're all fine."

Their eyes held, and he knew she was full of questions. His eyes teared more and he turned away, running a hand through his hair. "It wasn't like I thought it would be, Sam . . . the feeling of victory," he told her. "We really are at war, you know."

"There is a lot we can do right here, Blake. George and Jesse can talk in churches in the area, tell people what slavery is really like. I've already decided to start up an abolitionist newspaper here as soon as the baby is weaned. As long as most people in the North are

476

wanting to put an end to slavery, we've got to keep the movement alive."

He looked at her, smiling sadly. "You never quit, do you?"

"No. And you aren't going to quit, either."

Blake rose, looking thin and weary. He walked to a window. "George is worried about the slaves back on West's plantation, wonders what will happen to them. They'll most likely be auctioned off by the state. I never heard of West having any close relatives."

"Someday it won't matter, Blake. They're all going to be free. I believe that with all my heart. Now that I've seen so many of God's miracles—you still alive, George and Jesse free, a beautiful, perfect little son lying in my arms—I know He'll see us through all of this and that when it's over, there will be no more slavery."

"I hope you're right." He pulled back the curtains. The window was next to Samantha's bed. "Look out there," he told her. "Can you see them?"

Samantha sat up straighter to look. George and Jesse were sitting on a bench, Jesse's head on George's shoulder. She was obviously crying.

"You should have seen their faces when we first got here," Blake said. "That's what it's all for, Sam, right there. I guess if I had to do it over, I would." He turned to look at her and their eyes held.

"And so would I," she answered. "Come sit on the bed beside me, Blake. You look so tired."

He rubbed at his eyes. "Bone-tired. It's all starting to catch up with me." He walked around the bed, sitting down to take off his boots. He moved up beside her then, nestling into her shoulder.

"God, it feels good to lie next to you," he told her softly.

"My husband in one arm and my son in the other," she answered through tears. "What more could a woman ask for?" She kissed Blake's hair. "I love you. You told my father once that maybe sometimes God uses people like you to mete out His just punishment. I think God understands, Blake."

He moved an arm around her. "It was nothing like I thought it would be. I thought revenge was supposed to taste sweet, but it doesn't. And if this leads to all-out war, I'll probably be back out there, killing men over an idea, a belief, men who are nothing like Nick West, innocent men."

"You have to remember why, Blake. You just answered your own question when you looked at George and Jesse and said that was what it was all for—that you'd do it again. For now we have found some peace. Let's stay here a while and enjoy it. Let's do what we can socially, politically, and pray that war never comes."

She felt the wetness through her gown then, where his face was nestled against her. She felt his shoulders shaking. Her own tears wanted to come at the thought of his own agony. "It's over now, Blake," she told him, caressing his hair. "Things will be good for us here, peaceful. We can love and laugh, and we can be near George and Jesse, have more babies. God has brought us this far. He won't desert us now."

Blake reached over and touched little Ben, and the baby wrapped his tiny hand around one of his father's fingers.

Epilogue

In July of 1856, the House of Representatives voted to admit Kansas as a state with its antislavery constitution, but the Senate rejected admission. Kansas remained in bloody disarray for the next three years, but abolitionists hung on and finally managed to ratify an antislavery constitution in October of 1859. In January of 1861, Kansas was admitted to the Union by the House and Senate as a slave-free state. Four months later, South Carolina forces under General Beauregard fired on Fort Sumter. Congress officially declared the country to be at war; but for many years before that, war had already been raging in the hearts of many men . . . and women.

From the Author

I hope you have enjoyed my story. If you would like to know more about me and other books I have written, please feel free to write me at:

6013 North Coloma Road
Coloma, MI 49038

Be sure to include a legal size, self-addressed, stamped envelope.

Rosanne Bittner